Skeletons In The Cellar
Book & Mug Mysteries, Book 4

Michelle L. Levigne

Mt Zion Ridge Press
Books Off the Beaten Path

www.MtZionRidgePress.com

Mt Zion Ridge Press LLC
295 Gum Springs Rd, NW
Georgetown, TN 37366

https://www.mtzionridgepress.com

ISBN 13: 978-1-962862-98-1

Published in the United States of America
Publication Date: October 15, 2025

Editor-In-Chief: Michelle Levigne
Executive Editor: Tamera Lynn Kraft

Cover art design by Tamera Lynn Kraft
Cover Art Copyright by Mt Zion Ridge Press LLC © 2025

Chapter One

Three years ago
Monday, May 20

"Hey, Kai?" Olivia Tucker stepped into the kitchen of Book & Mug, where Kai Shane had just emerged from fishing yet another fork from the inner workings of the dishwasher.

Why was it always forks? How did they fly out of the flatware tray to mess up the works, anyway? He gave an extra hard twist to the valve to turn the water on.

"Somebody up front to see you," the head barista continued. "She's got a copy of that article about the fuss when you gutted the building."

"Please don't tell me another nutcase from the HIGs is on the attack," Kai groaned, and slammed down the sliding panel for the dishwasher for punctuation. The machine hummed for two seconds, then deepened, and water slammed against the insides of the machine again.

He had come up with the acronym for the radical extremist historical society in Cadburn Township just a year after he and his cousins bought the Aurora Building and renovated it. HIG stood for "history is god," as opposed to their rival reasonable, friendly historical society. He referred to them as the HIFs, "history is fun," with an implied, "come and play with us." If they could, Kai was sure the HIGs would tear out all telephone and electrical connections throughout the township and prohibit anything more advanced than horse-drawn buggies on the streets. They would probably tear out all the modern pavement and return to brick pavers if they could.

When he and his cousins had bought their building three years ago, they had done the preliminary renovations themselves. They had no idea how lucky they were when they hired people for the finishing work who sided with the HIFs. No one tattled to the HIGs until most of the work was done. Then, an official who had been inspecting every step of the renovations went on vacation. His replacement sided with the HIGs, who claimed authority they didn't have. Kai, Troy and Eden had refused to respond to their demands for updates and offended the HIGs by never once asking for input or permission. Once the spy reported to them, the fallout started. Attempts to take the cousins to court for "desecration of a historical landmark" had resulted in the HIGs' officers being ridiculed across multiple media outlets. Their historical society wasn't official and didn't have the approval of the Ohio Historical Society. Their embarrassment hadn't endeared Kai, Eden and Troy to the powers-that-wanted-to-be in Cadburn Township, either.

"She's not with them. At least, not yet." Olivia shrugged. "Phoebe mentioned some history students from Case, running around since March, trying to kiss up to anybody who specializes in Cadburn Civil War history. I've seen her around. You can't miss her. She wears a Rebel gray cap with a Union blue jacket. She might be with that group of film students setting up to film down in the creek." She tipped her head toward the front of the coffee shop. "Asked for you by name."

"Always a sign of trouble." He looked down at his shirt to make sure he hadn't smeared it with something disgusting from the bottom pan of the dishwasher, then nodded for Olivia to go. He would follow in a moment. He grabbed a towel from the rack on the front of the sink and dried his face, then raked his fingers through his damp hair. It was always a sweaty business, dealing with the dishwasher.

Kai considered what waited for him. Olivia didn't think this visitor was with the HIGs. She was a pretty good and quick judge of character. Running a coffee shop and dealing with people desperate for their first jolt of the day necessitated that talent. Too bad she hadn't already been working for him when he and his cousins found those old books hidden in the walls during their renovations. Olivia might have advised him to go in a different direction. He might have turned those books over to Mrs. Tinderbeck as the head librarian, rather than going to the HIFs. Kai had gotten himself on the dirt list with the HIGS because they interpreted his actions as an insult to Roger Cadburn, head trustee and custodian of the Cadburn family legacy.

He came out of the back room and looked around. This was the afternoon lull between the lunch crowd and the after-work crowd. Only one person sat in a booth. A young woman stood at the counter. She wore that gray Rebel slouch cap Olivia had mentioned.

"Hi, I'm Kai Shane, the owner. How can I help you?" he said before his gaze fully landed on her.

He summarized her with a glance. Long, caramel-colored braid studded with some bright, multi-colored plastic hair bobbles. Navy Case Western Reserve University polo shirt. The hat and Union blue jacket, hanging open. Notepad sitting open on the counter. And smiling. Definitely not a HIG. Kai doubted a single one knew how to smile. Not even when they managed to kill some motion for anything that would allow change in the township.

"Hi. Lyndsy Auretta. I emailed you a couple weeks ago, asking about those tunnels you found a few years ago." She mouthed "thanks" as Olivia put a tall paper cup in front of her, whipped cream mounded high, with cinnamon sprinkles on top. Iced cinnamon green tea latte, the special of the day.

"Tunnels?" Kai blanked for a few seconds. Then he laughed, with a vague recollection of the email. "Sorry, but I told you they weren't tunnels. More like someone started to dig a cellar and got discouraged."

"But other people around Cadburn have found the remains of tunnels. This building is old enough, and you're close enough to the creek, chances are good there was at least an effort to build a tunnel as part of the Underground Railroad."

Kai winced. He had been hearing those two words far too often lately. Just four days ago, Myron Ellsworth and Josiah Crandall, two prominent and loud members of the HIGs, had been arguing about the topic in one of the back booths. From the fragments of conversation, Crandall believed he was on the verge of finally proving Cadburn Township's role in the Underground Railroad, using the creek as a highway between towns. Ellsworth's contribution had mostly consisted of "Yeah, you said that before," and "When are you going to get your priorities straight?"

Crandall had been leader of the HIGs but stepped down to have more time for research. Most of them resented him for it, because the new leader, Edna Peabarker-Barnes, was a virago, regularly making decisions without anyone's input. It was their own fault. No one was willing to step into the void he left. They had to let her stay in power because the only community meeting room in the township that hadn't banned them was at the fire station, where her cousin was fire chief. While Chief Barnes was acknowledged as a fearless leader when it came to fighting fires, he lived in terror of Cousin Edna. They could have met at the library, but the HIFs met there, and Mrs. Tinderbeck belonged to the HIFs.

"What exactly do you want?" Kai asked.

Lyndsy looked far too nice and reasonable for him to tell her to go pester someone else. Such as Josiah Crandall, who certainly had to have a good idea of where there *weren't* tunnels to the creek.

"Just a chance to take some pictures, some measurements."

Why not? He couldn't see any harm in it. But that didn't mean he would let her go down there by herself. That was just opening up the Mug for a lawsuit if she fell. Who could he send down with her? One of the girls on the crew was the best choice. After the snide remarks at the last trustee meeting, Kai wouldn't put it past Roger Cadburn to send this total stranger in and stage something that could be blown out of all proportion. Like a sexual harassment suit.

Maybe he should check with Troy to see if their pooled finances could handle the bill for finishing that cellar, turning it into a meeting room, or just use it for more storage.

And wouldn't that irritate the HIGs? Another "drastic, irredeemable change" to the structure of a historic building.

"Let me see if there's anybody who's free to help you," he said, and gestured for her to take a seat.

Phoebe McCoy sailed through the door, early for her shift, and Kai immediately tagged her for the task. Phoebe was Olivia's roommate, an aspiring actress, and starting to get a nice reputation in the theater scene in Northeast Ohio. She belonged to the Spirits of '62, the Civil War reenactors group in Cadburn and currently the only girl. She hadn't let their leader, Steve Edison's perfectionist tendencies drive her away, and proved herself a valuable member by handling gorily realistic makeup for their reenactments. She could also hold her own against some of the wacko customers who sometimes invaded Book & Mug.

~~~~~

More than an hour later, Phoebe came to report on Lyndsy's activities. Kai was surprised the investigation had taken that long. Phoebe verified what Olivia had said.

"She joined the Spirits?" Kai said, as they unloaded a rack of freshly washed glasses.

"Trying to. With that Rebel hat, she takes two steps back for every half-step forward she makes with Steve. After a month, she still hasn't gotten the memo that we're all Union here." She snickered. "Did I tell you about the big ruckus last spring, when we did that reenactment at Frostville Museum? These guys showed up in Rebel uniforms and wanted to play along. Play along?" She paused to bend down with a handful of glasses and put them on a lower shelf. "Steve nearly lost his voice, lecturing them on how their weapons were wrong for the time period, and no real historical reenactor would ever be caught dead in polyester."

"Ouch," Kai muttered. But he had to laugh. "That bad, huh?" He wondered if Steve belonged to the HIGs. Then again, Phoebe wouldn't put up with him if he was. She could handle a lot of things, but any member of that particular historical society who stepped foot into Book & Mug got iced coffee at twenty paces if she was on duty at the counter. He reminded himself to ask her someday just what they had done to make her that coldly furious.

"Sometimes. When he isn't lecturing on accuracy, he's really kind of a nice guy." She snorted. "He'll pitch fits when onlookers show up during our rehearsals and take pictures or video without permission. That's sure to get Lyndsy on his bad side, if she isn't already."

"Why?"

"Video camera. That's what took most of the time downstairs. She got video of everything. Took a couple chunks of rock, some of that really crumbly cement. Even some water samples."
~~~~~

"Water?" Kai straightened up from where he had been leaning against the door frame. "We've got another leak down there?"

"I don't know if it's a leak, but there was some standing water, right in the lowest spot where the last gang of history sleuths stopped digging." She frowned. "They were pretty sure it wasn't Civil War-era construction, weren't they?"

"Yeah, that's what they said. They just laughed when I asked them to put it in writing for me, to show the next people who showed up." Kai started to turn away, his brain spinning through the options of what to do next. "Oh. Thanks for telling me." He sighed and rubbed his temples, sorting through a list of names of who to call to come check out this new problem. "Should have had that hole filled with cement when we first found it," he muttered, as he left the kitchen, heading for the stairs to go up to the office.

First, tell Eden and Troy as co-owners of the building. Then check his list of what services and companies in Cadburn Township wouldn't report the problem to the HIGs.

Tuesday, May 21

The doorbell rang five minutes after Olivia reached her third-floor room, kicked off her shoes, and collapsed on her bed. She held her breath, listening for footsteps on the stairs, praying Phoebe was home. She didn't have rehearsal tonight, did she?

Olivia counted to twenty. No sounds of movement. Groaning, she swung her legs off the bed, sat up, and hurried down the stairs. When she reached the kitchen, a note in bright green marker in Mrs. Tinderbeck's distinctive, loopy handwriting greeted her from the dry erase board next to the refrigerator. What had happened to have their landlady drop in during the day?

> *Sorry, girls! Emergency meeting tonight. Library all booked up. I hope you don't have plans for the living room. Free, Phoebe? Need your input as a Spirit. Bringing dinner, to make up for barging in.*

"Barging in," Olivia said, punctuated with a snort. Mrs. Tinderbeck did a lot of things and made sure that things were done right in Cadburn Township, but no one could ever accuse her of barging in. Especially since this was her house.

If their landlady wanted Phoebe's input, the meeting was probably the historical society. Olivia gnawed on the possibilities, what she had overheard of township gossip, as she hurried to the front door. If she was lucky, the person outside had given up and gone away.

No such luck. Through the multiple facets of the antique leaded glass door, she made out a tall figure in dark blue, topped with a short cap of white hair. A giggle-snort escaped her when she pulled the door open and recognized that girl from the Mug, in Union blue and Rebel gray.

"Lyndsy, right?"

"Uh—yeah. Do I know … oh, right, from the coffee shop." Lyndsy's wary expression warmed into a smile. "Is Mrs. Tinderbeck here?"

"No, sorry. Are you here about the room for rent?"

"Ah … yeah. And to ask some questions. There are so many really cool, historical buildings here, along the creek. What's it like living here?"

"It's good." Olivia wondered what really brought Lyndsy here. She knew the signs of someone changing a plan of approach. Usually, though, it was a customer who had one drink in mind and changed that five times before reaching the counter. "Mrs. T is the greatest landlord."

"When will she be back? Could I look at the room right now? I'm comparing prices, nearness to the bus line, that sort of thing."

"I guess." She checked her watch. 5:15. Mrs. Tinderbeck said she was bringing dinner. The meeting would probably start at 7:30 at the latest, so dinner around 6-ish? She would probably arrive before Lyndsy finished looking over the rooms and heard what was involved. Olivia stepped back. "Come on in."

She reached into her pocket, checking for her cell phone. Just in case something went horribly wrong, and she had to call for help. Just because Cadburn was a peaceful, friendly little town, that didn't mean wackos and utter creeps wouldn't come slithering through to cause trouble. Even someone who came across as a slightly obsessed college history major.

"There are single rooms available on the second and third floors, and a small double room on the first floor. Each floor has a bathroom. The living room is shared by everybody. Right now it's just Phoebe and me. She's the one who took you down to the basement."

"Right! Yeah, I recognized her after I left." Lyndsy shrugged, and her embarrassed grin seemed fairly genuine. "Things were kind of tense the few times I tried to catch up with the reenactor guys. Is this going to make it awkward if I do rent a room?"

"Nah. Phoebe's a sweetheart. Unless you ask her for really messy makeup with no advance warning."

"Makeup?"

"She's a theater major, does the makeup when the guys do mock battles."

"Cool." Lyndsy looked around the living room, with two and three-seater couches, floor pillows, and game boxes stacked on the hearth. The fireplace held an artificial flower arrangement. "This looks like a nice place to relax."

"It's great. Anyway, Phoebe and I pretty much have the same tastes in TV and movies, so we don't argue, but the house rule per Mrs. T is to negotiate for equal time with the TV and keep the volume below chop-and-liquefy." Olivia gestured around the living room that took up the front half of the first floor. She led Lyndsy down a short hallway with a door on either side. "These two rooms are pretty small, but they're furnished and come as a set because they're so small. It's kind of understood that everyone is free to use the bathroom down here. If that's a negative for you, keep that in mind."

She fought a grin, remembering how the last young woman who had come to look at rooms had basically responded to everything with a wrinkled nose and murmurs of disgust. Her final comments as she stomped out the door were along the lines of the cost of disinfectant and the threat to her health if she had to use it four times a day. She refused to share her bathroom with "the great unwashed." Phoebe had mentioned that encounter to one of her friends who did comedy, and the routine that resulted had been hilarious, if slightly disgusting. Well, it was bathroom humor.

From there, Olivia took Lyndsy into the kitchen. The stairs were hidden behind a large door, going down into the cellar and upstairs. Olivia explained the rules for the kitchen. The pots and pans and utensils were for everyone to share. Each renter had two shelves in the cupboard for dry goods, and two milk crates in the double-wide refrigerator for groceries. They would face the wrath of Mrs. Tinderbeck, not the other boarders, if anyone took what didn't belong to them. They were expected to clean up after themselves and not leave any dirty dishes in the sink.

"Too many rules?" she asked, when Lyndsy looked around the kitchen, lips slightly pursed, her gaze distant.

"Not really. Just a lot of common sense. And what my granny called common courtesy. Which, she also said, wasn't very common anymore." She snorted. "Any other rules you think I might not like?"

"Well, Mrs. T does have some strong ideas of what she calls proper decorum for the young ladies under her roof. She doesn't rent to young men, and she expects them to be out of the house by ten on weeknights, and eleven on weekends."

"Wow …" Lyndsy shook her head. "I kind of like that. I mean, think of all the problems girls could avoid if they had somebody laying down rules like that. My roommate is … well, she's a snoop, for one thing, and her new boyfriend is … Inconvenient." She waved her hand, as if pushing the topic away. "Doesn't matter, does it?"

"That's why you're moving out?"

For a moment, Lyndsy gave her a look like she didn't understand what Olivia was talking about. Then her eyes widened and she nodded with a crooked grin.

"Yeah. One way or another, I have to get out of there. You said there were rooms upstairs, too?"

Olivia led her upstairs to the third floor. She showed Lyndsy the door to the narrow stairs up to the attic, then the single room available on that floor. It was almost twice the size of the bedroom downstairs. Phoebe rented two rooms on the second floor, one for her bedroom, the other to work on costumes and makeup and playwriting. Olivia had two rooms on the third floor, using the second room as her office for online classes, mostly in literature and ancient cultures. The available room on the second floor was just as large as on the third floor. They returned to the kitchen, and Olivia offered her a bottle of tea, rationalizing that keeping Lyndsy there until Mrs. Tinderbeck showed up would avoid problems or misunderstandings later. She hoped.

"So…" Lyndsy gestured down the stairs with the unopened bottle. "I'm guessing we can use the attic, but if I took the rooms downstairs, wouldn't it be easier if I put stuff in the cellar?"

"I guess so."

"Could I see it?"

Olivia remembered what Phoebe had said about Lyndsy's visit to the Mug the day before and almost laughed aloud. Was that what her visit was really about? Tricking her way into people's houses to look at their cellars and hunt for signs of Underground Railroad tunnels?

That wasn't going to do Lyndsy any good. Mrs. Tinderbeck's house was on the south side of Cadburn Creek, the high side. There was a good drop of at least twenty feet, most of it sandstone, down to the creek bed. On the north side of the creek, the land was only two or three feet above water level, depending on the rainfall and time of year. A raw stone flood wall had been built maybe fifty years ago to protect the houses on the shallow bend in the creek from flooding. Every few years, someone started griping about how ugly it was, how it wasn't historically accurate, how it ought to be torn down. Usually someone in the HIGs group.

Olivia muffled a snort of laughter at Kai's sense of humor. And maybe irreverence. How did she get so lucky to have a boss like him?

If there were any foundation to the stories of Underground Railroad tunnels up from Cadburn Creek, those tunnels would be on the north side of the creek. Fugitive slaves would have had to climb a sheer rock wall to get to the houses on the south side of the creek at this point.

Olivia was just curious enough she didn't confront Lyndsy with her suspicions. She seemed honestly irritated with her roommate, so who knew? Maybe she would rent after all, even if the search for tunnels was the main reason for coming here.

"Ah … sure," she said, and gestured at the stairs, just as Mrs. Tinderbeck's smiling face appeared in the back door window. "Hold on a second." Olivia hurried to get the door, knowing her landlady's arms would be full.

"Oh, thank you, sweetheart. I hope you're in the mood for pierogis and brats and sauerkraut." Mrs. Tinderbeck handed her one of the plastic bags full of takeout containers before finishing coming up the steps.

"From Frenchy's? Any day." She stepped back and gestured at Lyndsy. "This is Lyndsy. She's interested in a room."

"Thank you. Again." Mrs. Tinderbeck put her suitcase-sized purse down on the counter and turned to Lyndsy. "Hello again! I didn't think I'd run into you so soon." She chuckled. "You did say you'd be back."

"Yeah, but I didn't make the connection that you owned this house when I got the address off the bulletin board at the library." Lyndsy's smile and chuckle both struck Olivia as a little uneasy.

"I told Lyndsy here she needs Steve Edison, if she wants the inside scoop on all the Civil War era history here in Cadburn. I swear, he knows more than both history societies put together." Mrs. Tinderbeck chuckled. "Except maybe Josiah Crandall. Much easier to get along with. So, Olivia already gave you the grand tour? Anything you need to know?"

"She was asking about the cellar," Olivia offered.

"Was she? Well, let me handle that part of the tour, at least." She stepped over to the stairs. "My family has owned this house since the early 1900s, and we've made some changes over the years, but the foundation is original and still solid," she began, as she started down.

Olivia half-listened to the mini lecture as she moved around the kitchen, setting the table for the three of them. She supposed it only made sense for Lyndsy to have stopped at the library at some point in searching the township for Underground Railroad tunnels. Especially since there was no official historical society building or museum for her to turn to for information. Someday, the two groups would have to either stop feuding and learn to work together, or one group would drive the other out so they could devote their time and energy and resources to becoming official. Olivia hoped Mrs. Tinderbeck's group would win.

"Of course, it'll probably take dropping a house on some of the nasties," she muttered. "Starting with that Barnes woman. Maybe take out those Crandall and Ellsworth creeps at the same time, if we're lucky."

"Hey-hey!" Phoebe called, pushing the back door open. "What's Mrs. T doing here?"

Olivia barely finished filling her in before Mrs. Tinderbeck and Lyndsy came upstairs again.

"Small world, huh?" Phoebe said with a chuckle.

"You couldn't have better roommates, if you decide to rent," Mrs.

Tinderbeck said. "I can always depend on them to look after the old family homestead. And let me add, it would be highly convenient for all your historical research to be settled here, rather than having to hike back and forth between the university and here. Especially since you're so interested in the creek ..." She waggled her eyebrows suggestively.

"I really do need to get out of that apartment," Lyndsy said, seeming the slightest bit rushed. "My roommate's new boyfriend ..." She glanced at Phoebe, then bent her head to search her purse.

"Oh!" Phoebe nodded. "That's what you and Mike were arguing about last week. When I got to the meeting late. Your roommate is Macy? He's dating her? Oh, don't worry, I think he's a creep, too. Mrs. T, you have to let her stay here. Mike is the jerk who was threatening to sue you for sexual harassment because you wouldn't rent to him."

"A young man who doesn't know the difference between sexual harassment and discrimination based on gender isn't intelligent enough to rent one of my rooms," Mrs. Tinderbeck said with a sniff and a toss of her head. And the next moment burst out in one of her wonderful, rolling chuckles.

That seemed to clear the atmosphere. Lyndsy left soon after. She said she had a couple other places she was looking at, but she would contact Mrs. Tinderbeck in a few days. She needed to be out of the apartment by the end of the month if she was going to move at all. Olivia didn't think she could break her lease so quickly, but what did she know about apartments and the rules for renters around Case Western Reserve University? Or anywhere else, for that matter. She had been lucky to have Mrs. Tinderbeck's house to land in when her three aunts who had raised her moved to Arizona just before she graduated from Cadburn High.

Olivia and Mrs. Tinderbeck and Phoebe discussed Lyndsy over dinner and agreed that the cellar had been the primary reason for coming to the house. Lyndsy had been studying a Criss-Cross directory and a Red Map book of the township in the library, along with the listing of historic buildings that the HIGs had put together several years ago. She must have seen the neat index card on the community bulletin board in the library, that listed the information for the rooms for rent. It was the only place in town Mrs. Tinderbeck advertised her boarding house. She claimed she used it as a filter, ensuring only literate people applied.

Their conversation turned to the meeting tonight. As Olivia had guessed, it was for the HIFs. A team of film students from Case were working on a historical piece, or so they claimed, that would have Cadburn Creek and Whips Ledges in Medina as stand-in settings for a long-running conflict between settlers and Native Americans. The flood wall along the bend behind Creekbend Court was a visible contradiction to the historical accuracy of the setting. There was no other place where the filmmakers could stage their action without modern buildings getting into the shot. The rock wall on the high side of the creek was perfect for backdrop for the water scenes. They didn't have the budget for CGI and other special effects to remove anachronisms.

Several members of the HIGs had heard the film team's leaders grumbling about the "perfect setting" being ruined by the flood wall. They wanted to take this opportunity to push again to have it removed, because it violated their standards of historical accuracy. The homeowners along that stretch of Creekbend Court were divided on whether it was wise to do so. Yes, that wall was ugly, and encouraged stagnation and algae and caught trash that got swept up in the creek. But this had been an unusually wet spring. What if Cadburn suffered the same flooding that had prompted building the wall fifty years ago?

All Phoebe could offer, from the viewpoint of the reenactors group, was that the higher water this spring meant every time they had rehearsals in the creek, they had to go up onto the bank. The flood wall blocked access to the shallower part of the creek in that spot. The water was too deep further out to wade. But whenever they did come up onto the bank and cross six different property lines, someone was always there to complain. Half the time, Mr. Fendergast shouted at them to get off his property. Or worse, silently waved his rifle at them.

"Or what's even worse than that," she added after several moments, studying the last pierogi on her plate, "he watches *me*, and he calls me his ghost, and begs me to come home."

"Oh, sweetheart," Mrs. Tinderbeck murmured. "Why didn't you say anything sooner?" She reached across the corner of the table to rest her hand on Phoebe's shoulder.

"He's just a crazy old man. What's anybody going to do?"

"Steve did complain to Captain Beakman," Olivia said. "He said they got what they deserved, trespassing on private property."

"The sooner Roger Cadburn gets voted out of office, and his cohorts get the boot, the better for this township." Mrs. Tinderbeck's lips flattened until there was a white line around her generous mouth. "Yes, Andrew Fendergast is a crazy old man, but he's had a lot of hurt, a lot of disappointment in his life. Try to pity him. And for heaven's sake, don't go near his place in your costume after dark."

"Why?" Phoebe wanted to know. "What does he mean, saying I'm his ghost?"

"You never heard of the Cadburn ghost?"

Phoebe hadn't grown up here. She had moved to Cadburn two years ago from St. Louis.

"The Cadburn ghost is supposedly the restless spirit of a Cadburn daughter who ran off to the Civil War, disguised as a boy, and never came home," Mrs. Tinderbeck said. "Andrew's home, much of the property along that part of the creek, was originally Cadburn family property. He's descended from the Cadburns. I suppose the story of Annabelle Cadburn … spoke to his lonely heart." She shrugged, and something sad and thoughtful in her expression stopped Olivia from asking any more questions.

Chapter Two

Wednesday, May 22

"Yeah, high water in the creek this spring. Highest it's been in forty-some years." Evan Orcutt snorted and grinned. "At least, that's what people tell me. Don't get my dad and uncle started by asking them."

"Meaning?" Kai almost didn't slide Evan's usual dark roast with three pumps of dark chocolate syrup across the counter to him. He wasn't going to hand the drink over until the contractor told him his conclusions.

On the other hand, he was grateful that Evan had come out so quickly in response to his call. The Orcutts were a five-generations-established business in Cadburn, known to be honest with their inspections and fair with the prices they charged for repairs.

"It's got nothing at all to do with the water in your place, first of all. This side of the creek is sitting too high to worry about high water levels. Not until the people downstream from you are taking shelter on their roofs. The water you found came from a crack in the water main north of you. We already got things cleaned up in the buildings that back up to yours before you called me." Evan nodded his thanks as Kai slid the cup into his reach.

"You could have said that on the phone and saved yourself a trip."

"I would have come in anyway, just to make sure it really was from the leak, and not something coming from the other side of the street. The last time the creek flooded, a couple tunnels downstream were revealed. The water was higher than normal this spring, so who knows what might have been opened up?"

"So your verdict?"

"You've got nothing to worry about." Evan took a quick sip of his coffee and saluted Kai with the cup. "We're supposed to have a dry summer." He snorted. "Won't stop the worrywarts, yapping about taking down that ugly flood wall, down near the shallows."

Thursday, May 23

"Now what happened?" Phoebe muttered across the counter from Olivia at the end of her shift at the Mug that evening. She gestured with a tip of her head toward the Spirits of '62 spilling through the front door. Followed by Lindsey Auretta in her Union jacket and Rebel hat, with a big Confederate flag patch on the front of her fringed leather purse. Was she really trying to hack off the guys in the entire group with that getup?

Phoebe had only said she didn't mind missing out on rehearsal for Memorial Day weekend reenactments. She didn't explain why. Maybe Lyndsy's presence was part of it. Or maybe Mike's. Olivia remembered Phoebe's instant sympathy for Lyndsy when she made the connection between him and her roommate.

The guys, led by big, husky, stereotyped blond hero Steve Edison, all seemed equally irritated by something.

"Have fun," Olivia said under her breath. Phoebe stuck her tongue out at her and headed over to the seating area behind the bookstore half of the shop, where the Spirits usually sat. And griped.

Then the crowd of twenty reenactors reached the counter. Truman hurried to duck under the drawbridge and joined her to help take their orders. Olivia gave him a smile of thanks.

The group's conversation while they waited to place their orders revealed what irked them tonight. The film students invading Cadburn this spring had gotten in the way of their staging in the township park. Worse than getting in the way, three film students had tried to record what the reenactors were doing, all the while calling out advice on changing their staging to be more dramatic. A verbal fight had ensued.

Of course it did.

Steve and most of his followers cared about accuracy more than drama. The film students disagreed.

"Did you drive those Johnny Rebs out of town?" Olivia asked, as she handed Steve his iced cinnamon Americano, extra whipped cream.

He snorted and his frown relaxed into a partial grin. "They want accuracy? How about some buckshot?" He nodded and snatched up his cup. "Saving my life. Again." He turned away from the counter, going to the right, just as Lyndsy stepped up on his right side and opened her mouth to say something. His grin flattened back into a scowl. He cursed when a few drops slopped out of his tall paper cup.

"I swear, between you and those film creeps, I'm taking out restraining orders!" He yanked the Rebel cap off her head. Her wince and yelp indicated he had taken some hair with it.

Olivia's sympathy died right there. The guy really was a dictator.

"What is your problem?" Lyndsy stepped back, barely missing the toes of Dylan, Phoebe's current hopeful boyfriend.

She was hesitant to make it official because she was afraid he was only interested in her makeup kit. Especially her recipe for fake blood.

"No Rebel troops got this far north." Steve waved the cap in her face.

"You keep asking how come we won't let you participate. This is part of it. And this." He caught hold of the sleeve of her jacket. "Not authentic, either."

"Hey, I got it from Clandestine Costumers. They guarantee—"

"They lie. And they probably charged you three times more than this is worth."

"Well if you had been polite enough to just answer my questions last month, I wouldn't have gone to them, now would I?" She waved the notebook she held in her right hand, nearly slapping his face.

Olivia almost wished she had.

"Hey, Steve, lay off her. She's got a point," Mike said, sidling up to the counter. Lyndsy immediately backed up two steps. "If nobody will answer her questions, how will she know?"

"Why do you keep trailing us like you do?" Steve sagged a little and sounded more tired than hacked off now.

"I want to learn. Besides." She snorted and looked around, and her grin got a little wider. "Some of those old guys living along the creek are talking about the Cadburn Ghost showing up, when they see me running around in my uniform. Especially when you're doing those nighttime maneuvers. It's hilarious, how spooked some of them sound. Especially old Fendergast."

"Be careful," Ramon said. Olivia thought he would be a better match for Phoebe. He was their special effects man, creating realistic explosions and smoke clouds. "That guy isn't all there. He can be your best buddy one day and come after you with a rifle the next."

"Wish his family would lock him up. The guy acts like he owns the whole creek, from one end to another," one of the newer guys said from the back of the group. Since Olivia didn't know him, she thought he was one of the history students from Case who had arrived with Mike.

"But think about all the stories a guy that old could tell, about the history in this town," Lyndsy said.

"What are you really after?" Steve said. "Why do you keep tailing us? You really expect us to take you seriously, dressed like that?"

"I want to learn!" She waved the notebook at the entire group, then turned back to Steve. "Make you a deal? Play nice for a change, and answer some of my questions?"

Steve scowled, his brows lowering. Olivia wondered if all those lines around his mouth and eyes would become permanent. He let out a long, rattling sort of sigh. "What do we get out of it?"

"How about I play double agent?"

"With who?" Mike snorted. "Not that I don't doubt you're good at lying." He smirked at Lyndsy.

She didn't look at him. Her shoulders hunched slightly. Olivia could almost feel the chill radiating from her.

"Those film jerks keep asking all sorts of questions. How about I tell them the exact opposite of what they want to know? Send them on a wild goose chase, get them out of your hair?" she said, her voice a few notes higher than normal.

Olivia and Truman exchanged eye rolls and finished filling the last orders. At least the Spirits bought enough drinks to make up for the noise they made and the tables they took up.

"I don't know if letting you hang with us will do us any good." Steve gestured toward the seating area where Phoebe had pushed the tables together to accommodate their group. He led the migration to the other side of the coffee shop. "What are you looking for?"

"Same thing we both are," Mike said. "Underground Railroad tunnels. Hey, instead of going after the film jerks, go sweettalk old Crandall. Word is, he's close to finding one."

"They've been saying that for years," Steve said. "You'd be better off trying to talk to Fendergast. At least he lives on the creek."

"Now see, that's the kind of information I'm trying to find. Why don't we work together?" Lyndsy said.

"Hey, I've been saying that for months," Mike said. "Why do you want to work with him, but not me? We're in classes together."

"Tell me what really happened to that report I sent to Dr. Onslow, and maybe I'll consider it," she snapped.

"What report?" Mike stiffened and stopped, when the rest of the group kept moving.

"Exactly." She looked back at him, just long enough for Olivia to see the icy fury in her eyes.

Olivia exchanged a shrug with Truman and got to work cleaning up from filling the orders.

"She needs to get in good with old Crandall," someone said, amid the sounds of chairs scraping on the tile floor. "He's been digging for those tunnels for years."

"Yeah, and nearly got shot by Fendergast," someone else said.

"Somebody needs to push that old nutcase over the edge, so they can stop waiting for his relatives to lock him up where he won't cause any more trouble," Myron Ellsworth grumbled as he walked up to the counter.

Olivia pasted on her professional smile and stepped up to wait on him. Truman had dealt with Ellsworth the last time he came into Book & Mug, so that made it her turn now. She was positive the cranky old man never remembered any of the staff from one visit to the next. He launched into describing exactly how he wanted his coffee made. It was the same personal recipe every time he came in. It never seemed to occur to him that he came in often enough that the staff would remember. Olivia preferred hearing his recipe as opposed to the other topic of grumbling when he came in: the "unapproved changes" that the cousins made to the building when they took it over three years ago.

Friday, May 24

Olivia settled down in the living room with her notebook computer and turned on the morning news to keep her company while she checked her email. She had turned in her homework for her summer term class on Thornton Wilder in plenty of time for the professor to read and respond before his day ended yesterday. The university offering this particular online class was in Hawaii.

A loud thumping resounded from the front door just as she raised her bottle of vanilla chai to her lips. Sputtering, she slid her computer off her lap, praying she hadn't spilled on the keyboard. She could not afford to buy another computer just now. Whoever dared to bang so loud, and keep banging, at—she checked her watch—6:37am?—was going to get a piece of her mind. And maybe a good right hook.

She opened the front door to Myron Ellsworth, waving a neon orange sheet of paper in her face. "Just what is the meaning of this?"

"Excuse me?" Olivia had taken lessons from Phoebe on putting ice into her voice.

"You've ignored this notice for five days! Irresponsible! Just left it hanging on your door. People like you shouldn't be allowed to own historic homes." He leaned forward, one foot raised, clearly intending to bull his way into the house.

Olivia gripped the door frame and shifted her stance, so she could raise her right knee in self-defense, if necessary. She made a mental note to remind Phoebe she had to keep the screen door locked.

"Just give me a reason to use my pepper spray." She dug her hand into the empty pocket of her sweatpants.

"Why would—pepper spray is illegal!" he snapped. But he did take four big steps back, so he nearly toppled off the top step of the porch.

"So is breaking into someone's house, shrieking at them for no good reason. First of all, I am not the homeowner. And second of all, that ugly piece of paper has not been here for five days! And third of all, Mrs. Tinderbeck has told you a thousand times—"

"Tinderbeck? Lydia Tinderbeck owns this place?"

Olivia was convinced Ellsworth had progressive brain damage. Whenever the seasons changed, he came around to all the historic homes in Cadburn with his list of approved contractors, if the changing weather caused any damage. He always used an ugly fluorescent shade, and he always had a snit fit when he demanded to talk to the homeowner and she or Phoebe told him to see Mrs. Tinderbeck. As if not living in the house she owned was a personal attack on him.

"There is a serious storm coming, young lady!" He waved the paper at her. "You give this to that floozy, and you tell her she's in serious trouble if there is flood damage to this house and she doesn't follow the official guidelines."

"Hello? We're twenty feet above the creek."

He was going to get pepper in his coffee, the next time he came into Book & Mug. Who was he to call Mrs. Tinderbeck a floozy?

"What does that have to do with it? Some people have no appreciation for the seriousness of the situation!" he announced, waving his hand in the air as if making a grand point. Then he turned, nearly toppling off the top step, and somehow made it to the ground without tripping over himself. Head tilted back, legs stiff, he stomped away.

"We really need to talk Mrs. T into one of those doorbell cameras," Phoebe said, startling a squeak out of Olivia. She draped an arm over her shoulders, and they leaned on each other as they watched Ellsworth stomp away down the sidewalk.

"Wonder when he'll realize he took the paper with him ..."

Sputtering giggles, they stepped back. Phoebe closed the door, and Olivia went to get her phone to send a text to tell Mrs. Tinderbeck what had just happened. She would have to follow it up with more details in an email. Ellsworth was in rare form today.

Lyndsy had come through the front door on Tuesday, so the paper had probably been on the front door two days at the most. Olivia had a good idea of Ellsworth's route when it came to harassing the historic home owners. He would probably get to Creekbend Court some time today.

Phoebe looked up from whipping some eggs for breakfast, when Olivia stepped into the kitchen. "What's so funny?"

"Bet that nutcase hasn't seen old Fendergast's preparations for that deck on the back of his house." Olivia settled at the table and leaned back, waiting, until Phoebe's eyes got wide and her mouth dropped open. Then they both burst out in giggles.

"Oh, and I've got to work today! Can you camp out on the back porch and try to record it? It's gotta be good."

"Record it with what? My phone is three years old. Spy gear, it is not."

"Trent." Phoebe snapped her fingers. "He's got one of those fancy telephoto thingies. He was talking about using it to record us, send it to that competition we want to do in Gettysburg next fall. I'll call him when I get to work, see if he can come over and set it up."

Two hours later, Phoebe called during a lull to report that Trent had to work all day and couldn't get away to set up the camera. In the end, that didn't matter, because the downpour started less than twenty minutes after she left for work and pounded down steadily most of the day. If Ellsworth plastered his instruction sheets on the front doors of the homes on Creekbend Court, he didn't take his usual walking tour around all the properties, to uncover any alterations made to the properties since the last time the self-appointed guardian of historical purity made his inspection. From her cozy sheltered spot on the back porch, Olivia could see piles of lumber and bricks and bags of cement safely tucked under the royal blue tarps that had covered them since Mr. Fendergast had them delivered last week. Nobody was going to be out in this sopping weather to dig foundation holes and pour concrete.

Olivia found it rather relaxing to curl up with a quilt under the cover of the wide back porch of the house with her computer, work on her homework, and drink hot chocolate. She watched the rain turn the world to a hazy gray drizzle while she waited for the fireworks to start. She wasn't really disappointed when nothing happened. It was a pleasant way to spend the day. Although yes, she would have enjoyed seeing Ellsworth stomping around in one of his rages, lose his footing in the mud, and go down with a splash.

Her gaze strayed several times to the rickety old arch of a footbridge that crossed the creek. Mr. Creekbaum on the west side of them said it had been there before his parents built their house. Folks on the street called it the sweetheart bridge. They claimed a courting couple lived on opposite sides of the creek and used it for secret meetings. Olivia wondered how secret those meetings could be, since the bridge was pretty easy to spot even with all the trees shadowing the creek. She shuddered at the idea of trying to cross that bridge now. Most of what remained was a rusty iron frame and sporadic ragged boards. A couple times, she had crept down the bank to the bridge to study it, drawn by the idea of desperate lovers risking a wet landing to be together. The bridge was barely wide enough for one person, with no handrails to hold onto.

Phoebe, of course, thought it entirely romantic, and every once in a while, she pulled out notes for a screenplay she wanted to write about the bridge and the different couples through the generations who used it to meet up. She had actually tried to walk the bridge once. Just once. She barely got a third of the way across. The bridge creaked and swayed so much she turned around and crept back on her hands and knees.

Sometimes, when the wind was especially rough, Olivia thought she heard the bridge creaking. She thought of the Cadburn Ghost now and made a note to herself to mention adding the bridge to Phoebe's plan to write a play about the ghost. Maybe Annabelle Cadburn could haunt the bridge, crossing over and over again, looking for ... what? Her lost gun?

Her regiment? The way home? Her missing sweetheart?

Who built the bridge, and which side of the creek did they live on? The bridge was on the dividing line between Mrs. Tinderbeck's house and Mr. Creekbaum on the high side and landed on the property to the west of the Fendergast house. Supposedly most of the property along the creek on that side belonged to Cadburns, so maybe Annabelle Cadburn had actually walked that bridge? Definitely, she had to remember to mention that idea to Phoebe.

Monday, May 27

Phoebe left a note for Olivia when she got home mid-afternoon on Monday, after opening the Mug for the day.

> *Don't even try to take a nap. They're taking down the wall. Lots of noise. Lots of shouting. Fendergast was out there, shrieking about the Ghost for a little while. Scared off the workers with a gun. Beakman even showed up. It settled down for a while but the noise is starting up. Glad I have auditions tonight!*

For punctuation, an engine revved down in the creek. Olivia doubted that was a boat, though the water was still supposedly running high after all the rain. She put down her purse and stepped out onto the back porch and walked to the railing. From this angle, with all the trees in the way, she couldn't see a lot of detail, but she made out the bright green of one of those all-purpose utility vehicles she kept seeing advertised on TV. It looked like someone was using it to push down part of the flood wall. A few revs and roars later, cheers and a massive splash confirmed that theory. Olivia glanced up at the narrow window in the attic. From that angle she would have a clear view of everything going on down in the creek. The question was why she would want to watch all those people getting muddy and wet.

Faintly, she heard the front doorbell ringing. She stepped back inside and seriously considered ignoring it. Ellsworth had probably come back with a replacement list. She couldn't ignore the front door, though. Her landlady trusted her and Phoebe to watch out for her house and supervise the people temporarily in the other rooms, such as guest speakers at church or the library. She muffed a sigh and went to answer the door.

Somehow, she wasn't surprised to see Lyndsy there.

"Oh, good, I thought I saw you coming home." Lyndsy sort of bounced on her toes for a moment. "Would you mind too much if I watched the wall coming down from here? The film guys said they got all the homeowners to agree, and they need to get it done before that old loony changes his mind." She rolled her eyes.

"Mr. Fendergast?" Olivia stepped back and gestured for Lyndsy to come in.

"What is with him?" She waited for Olivia to close the door and lead the way through the house and out the kitchen door, onto the porch.

"What do you mean?"

"I was down there with the guys, doing some filming, and he came charging out of his house, waving his gun, and then he just shifted gears and tried to grab me. He was wailing about some ghost and begging me to lay down and rest and it was just …" She shuddered.

For a moment, Olivia thought she was afraid. Then Lyndsy's expression hardened, and her eyes narrowed. "And then some good old boy showed up, throwing his weight around and he blamed me for the ruckus! Like a badge makes him better than everybody?"

"Let me guess." Olivia fought a grin. The description of "good old boy" certainly applied. "Captain Beakman?"

"I guess. He told me if I didn't move my butt and keep it out of his sight, he'd arrest me. Said I was endangering the work. Distracting all those he-men tearing down the wall. I wanted to pop Steve, standing there and smirking. The big suck-up is helping that loony haul stones out of the creek, getting a good look at whatever they're going to uncover when they take down that wall. After I did all that research." She stepped up to the porch railing and pounded it twice with her fists.

"Steve?" Olivia asked, sensing that was the safer topic. "Edison? I thought he hated you."

"The guy's a Nazi when it comes to his holy grail of historical accuracy." Lyndsay made air quotes around the last two words. "But like I said, a suck-up when it comes to research. He's trying to land this gig assisting some history writer in Missouri, and the more experience he has under his belt, the better his chances. But if that bozo thinks he can ride on my coattails … he better think again."

Definitely, Olivia wasn't going to ask what she thought would be uncovered when they took down that flood wall.

Lyndsy made a disappointed sound and moved down the porch, leaning over the railing, clearly trying to see through the leaves and branches in the way. She stepped back the other way, until finally she found a spot she liked. She pulled out a small video camera and braced herself with her elbows on the railing and got to work. Olivia watched her for a few moments, then turned to go back inside.

"Sorry," Lyndsy said. "Thanks. This is a big help."

"Sure. Want something to drink?"

"I'm good. Thanks."

Olivia went back inside. She made a mental note to tell Lyndsy about the Cadburn Ghost, what Mrs. Tinderbeck had said about Fendergast, and her warning to Phoebe, not to go down to the creek after dark in her costume. Lyndsy seemed to wear her Union jacket and Rebel hat all the time, probably to irritate Steve. That had probably brought on Fendergast's fit of calling to the ghost.

After less than half an hour, Lyndsy came inside. Olivia had stayed in the kitchen, figuring this was a good time to do some baking and prep for meals for the next week, without being obvious that she was keeping an eye on the visitor.

"How'd it go?" she asked, guessing the answer wasn't good. Lyndsy's drooping shoulders and the pout taking over her mouth probably meant she hadn't gotten what she wanted.

"Too much stuff in the way. I need a higher elevation to get past all those trees, better angle down into the creek. I just hope what I recorded before that nutcase came charging out is enough for the guys from Case. They want to document everything they're doing for their film."

"So that's their equipment?" Olivia didn't know anything about cameras, but she could guess that was pretty expensive equipment for a college student.

"Huh? Oh, this?" Lyndsy hefted the camera, then slid it into her big suede purse. It gaped open, revealing a notebook and water bottle. She shrugged. "I don't suppose there's a way to get onto the roof? Or would that get the neighbors calling for the cops again?" She grinned.

"Don't know about the roof, but there is a little window in the attic that looks down on the creek."

"Yeah? Could I?" She pointed upward.

On the way upstairs and into the attic, Olivia told her about Fendergast and what Mrs. Tinderbeck said about his ghost obsession. The other girl thanked her and promised she would keep the warning in mind. Olivia thought she sounded amused. They had to move crates and old furniture that blocked access to the window, which sat in a little nook formed by the gable on that side of the house. Lyndsy seemed pleased. She shoved over a crate to sit on and wiped the glass clean with her sleeve and made a happy little sound like a purr when she found the latch to push the window open, for a better angle.

"How long can I stay up here?"

"I'm home all night ..."

"Oh, don't worry. The guys should be done before supper. The thing is, that old man wants all those stones on his property. I want to see what he's doing. He was grumbling something about teaching Gibbons a lesson, see if he can climb rocks. What's that about?"

"Gibbons is the neighbor on the right, and he's been fighting with

Fendergast for years about who owns that ridge between their houses."

"Why?"

Olivia had no idea. She had never really thought about it. When she admitted that, Lyndsy laughed.

"From up here, it's pretty crooked. Maybe it starts on the old guy's property, but it ends up on the other guy's. Gotta wonder why they put it there."

"Wasn't it Robert Frost who said good fences make good neighbors?"

"Only if being a good neighbor means staying on your side."

Olivia settled in her office to get work done and listen for Lyndsy coming down the stairs. She was relieved when her estimate of time proved true. The demolition work on the wall finished shortly before dinner, but Lyndsy stayed for another half hour, apparently watching Steve and the demolition crew helping Fendergast move all those huge stones out of the creek and onto the ridge between the two properties.

She heard Lyndsy's footsteps on the creaky attic stairs, and then the opening notes of the Darth Vader march. She muffled a chuckle, guessing it was a ring tone. A moment later Lyndsy said, "Yeah? What happened?"

A muffled chuckle. "So, how nuts?"

A pause. Several creaks, probably meaning Lyndsy continued down the attic stairs.

"Did you get anything good?" A clearly exasperated sigh. "Come on, you were right there, on top of everything. What kind of Indiana Jones are you, if you can't sneak a couple shots every once in a while without—"

The footsteps ended, punctuated with the sigh of the attic door closing. Olivia decided, much as she wanted to eavesdrop, she would be smarter to step out into the hall and let Lyndsy know she was there.

"I'm working entirely on theory, just like you. How about you go—" Lyndsy stopped short, her gaze meeting Olivia's. Then she winked and grinned. "How about you go talk to Crandall, since you're on his good side, and see if he has any information he wouldn't share with me, the newbie who's too young to know anything?"

She nodded, listening, rolling her eyes, ending with, "Okay, meet you at that Chinese place." She lowered her phone and tapped the screen, then stuck her tongue out at it. "Steve is a useless jerk."

"What happened?"

"Oh, the neighbor got home just as everybody was leaving. Blew a gasket. Turns out, nobody got his permission to drive that little tractor thingy down the slope on his property. Then according to Steve, he went soprano when he saw all the stone piled up on the ridge. They all got out of there while the guy was still screaming about siccing the cops on them." She chuckled.

"So what didn't Steve do?"

Lyndsy rolled her eyes again. "What's so hard about keeping your phone ready to snap pictures of anything that looks interesting while they're taking the wall down? You never know what got covered up, what might be revealed. Anyway … what's with that bridge?" She hooked her thumb over her shoulder in the direction of the creek. "How old is it?"

Olivia told her what little she knew about it as she led Lyndsy downstairs and to the front door.

"That's kind of cool. Wonder what great stories are attached to it. Sometimes the smallest, quietest little towns have the greatest stories," Lyndsy commented as she pushed the door open. "Oh, by the way, I called Mrs. Tinderbeck. I'm looking forward to being roommates."

"Oh. Great. Welcome to the house." Olivia held onto what she called her professional smile, reserved for exhausting days with unreasonable customers, until Lyndsy reached the sidewalk. She stayed in the doorway, watching until she saw her step into the street and get into a dark green Mini Cooper.

So, Lyndsy had money. Or else she came from a family with a lot of money. That made sense, if a history student could run around pursuing private research projects and not worry about part-time jobs.

Must be nice.

Chapter Three

Thursday, May 30

That green Mini Cooper, with some paper ream boxes in the back seat, sat in the driveway when Olivia got back from work that evening. The door of the first-floor bedroom stood open when she came in through the kitchen door. She paused, listening for movement. Nothing. She looked through the foot-wide gap between door and frame. Two duffels and a milk crate. No sign of Lyndsy. The office door on the opposite side of the hall was latched. She thought about knocking, then figured if Lyndsy was working on something, she had the door closed for a reason. She backstepped to the kitchen and put a bottle of the new seltzer Eden had recommended into the freezer to chill, then headed upstairs. First a long shower, then that veggie pizza she had been craving for the last two hours.

The attic door hung open when she reached the third floor. She listened for footsteps. For such an old house, it was a little too quiet. Shouldn't there be a few creaks?

"Hello?" Should she go up or wait down here?

"Oh, hey…" Lyndsy's voice filtered down the stairs. "Just a sec."

Footsteps thumped reassuringly on the stairs, and then Lyndsy appeared in the doorway. She offered a crooked grin and an even more crooked shrug.

"Just checking out that view. The moonlight's kind of spooky on the water." She shut the door with a decisive thump.

"Need help hauling stuff in?"

"You don't have to. I saw you at work. You've got to be dead on your feet." She shrugged. "Besides, there's nothing else to bring in. What's in my car goes to my storage locker."

"How many more trips do you have to make?"

"What? From my old place? No more." A sour twist to her mouth and a brief shudder, then she seemed to shake it off. "I travel light."

"Makes sense." Olivia decided to be a good roommate and not pry. At least, not this early in the relationship. "I'm going to get a shower before I make dinner. Want to split a pizza? Warning, though. White pizza, no tomato."

"Allergic?"

"Not most of the time. Sometimes the acid just doesn't sit right."

"White pizza sounds great. Thanks." Lyndsy headed for the stairs. She paused with her foot on the third step down and looked back. "I'm gonna make a pot of tea. Blackberry spice. Want some?"

"Sounds great." Olivia headed for the bathroom. She thought about warning Lyndsy that Phoebe could go into an hour-long discussion-slash-lecture on the tea industry and "Philistines" who didn't deserve the name of tea makers, because of all the fillers they "polluted" their tea with, and then the proper procedure for making tea. And maybe a side trip into how wonderful Cadburn's water was for making tea.

Lyndsy was in her shower when Olivia got down to the kitchen. A pot of tea sat on the counter, with the infuser resting on a saucer, draining. A tempting aroma of blackberries, cinnamon, and something peppery filled the kitchen. Olivia chuckled. The new member of the household didn't need a lecture on what made "proper" tea. She transferred the seltzer from the freezer to the refrigerator, then dug through the drawer that had all the flyers with coupons and deals for the restaurants in town. She had just finished placing the order over the phone when the doorbell rang. Olivia considered ignoring it, just for a moment. Who would stop by this late in the evening?

While she debated pretending to have hearing problems, the doorbell rang a second time. Followed by thumps on the front door. That didn't sound like Ellsworth. He had skinny knuckles so even when he was at his most furious, it was a rapping sound, not a thump. Olivia got up and kept her phone in her hand, in case she needed to call the police. Somebody so insistent this late at night probably wasn't in a good mood. She, on the other hand, felt good, kind of floaty and drowsy, and she wasn't going to let anyone destroy that after the long day she had.

"Hey." Mike, one of the Spirits of '62 guys. A head taller than her, all angles, with a buzz cut and perpetual 5 o'clock shadow. He grinned and reached to pull the screen door open. It didn't move. His grin shifted to a frown. Did he think he could just walk right in without being invited?

Olivia muffled her grin. With Ellsworth on the rampage again, she and Phoebe now locked the screen door, to make it harder for him to leave his lists. And easier for the wind to pick up something taped to the outside door and carry it away before they got home.

"Phoebe's not here," she said. "She's closing tonight."

"Phoebe? Yeah, that's right, she lives here too. What're the odds? Nah, I want talk to Lyndsy." He nodded at the driveway. "That's her car, isn't it?"

"Why?" She considered asking him just how many people he knew who drove a dark green Cooper. Her drowsy feeling was fading.

"Need to talk to her about some research." He pulled on the screen door handle again. Phoebe had mentioned he was working on his master's in history. Were all academics this oblivious? No wonder she thought he was a creep.

"That's the neighbor's driveway, so someone's visiting Mr. Siders." She felt no guilt about lying. Roommates stuck together.

He turned to look at the driveway again. "No, that's her car. I'd know it anywhere. What's she doing here? Is she moving in?"

"You know, if she doesn't tell you what she's doing, then I'm guessing it's none of your business. Besides, aren't you dating her roommate?"

She could see now why Lyndsy got that distasteful look when she mentioned Mike.

"Yeah, she's moving. Of all the—" Mike let out a gusting sigh and leaned against the door. "Look, she got her panties in a knot over Macy poking around in her computer, but that was just a joke, okay? That's what Macy does, she untangles computer programs. She's gotta break every puzzle. No reason to move out." He nearly pressed his nose against the screen. "So why don't you be a pal and go get her, okay? I gotta talk to her about some research we're doing."

"We're not," Lyndsy snapped. Her footsteps were loud, sharp thuds on the hardwood floor underneath the living room carpet as she stepped up next to Olivia. "We're not working together, and we never will. Don't even think about horning in on my project or stealing my research."

"I'm not!" Mike backed up, spreading his hands and widening his eyes in a display of innocence Olivia didn't believe for a second. "All I've been saying is there's more than enough to go around. And hey, we'll get twice as much work done if we team up."

"You burned your bridges. I'm not risking my in with Mr. Crandall for your sake." She turned to Olivia. "Mr. I-know-everything here screwed up royally at the encampment at Frostville two months ago. Got the local expert so ticked at him, it's a miracle he's allowed in town."

"Yeah, shows what you know. That old fart doesn't have any authority around here," Mike growled, nearly pressing his nose against the screen again. "And neither does Steve. Don't hitch your future to his if you know what's good for you."

"Are you threatening her?" Olivia's grip tightened on her phone. Call the police or just record this conversation for evidence later? Was Mike was one of those self-righteous jerks who would react badly, and then claim it was her fault if anyone got hurt?

"Me? Never. We both want the same thing, Lyns, so why not work together? Trying to spare you a lot of grief when good old Steve takes off in a few weeks to work for his bigtime history writer—who he still won't name, shows just how much the guy trusts anybody—and claims all the hard work you're doing, so you're left empty-handed, and maybe even accused of stealing yourself. How's it feel, shoe on the other foot?"

"You're getting kind of loud. The neighbors are going to call the cops if I don't," Olivia said.

"Hey, hey, we're just having a friendly talk. One history geek to another." Again, he put on that innocent mask and spread his hands. A big guy like Mike didn't do "harmless" very convincingly.

"Go home, Mike." Lyndsy just sounded and looked tired now. "I'm not helping you with Crandall, and I'm not sharing anything I've found. Not after you had Macy break into my cloud account. Which I'm not using anymore, by the way. Waste of effort."

"Hey, if she stole anything, she didn't share it with me. But just to prove I'm on your side, and good old Steve is the bad guy here, I'm gonna send you a paper he shot off to the writer guy. Proof he stole all that stuff you were talking about the other day. The codes the Underground Railroad guides used? Remember? He convinced you that you mis-read that journal, that the signs were blurred from water damage? He claimed that as his own work. Yeah, the guy can't be trusted."

Olivia caught the tiny stiffening of Lyndsy's shoulders, the sharp little inhalation, the twitch of her lips that told her something Mike said had hurt. Maybe all of it? She wanted to help. They were officially roommates now, after all.

"If you got into Steve's email, it sounds to me like you can't be trusted either," Olivia said.

"Baby, the history department is a dog-eat-dog kinda place." Mike rested his hands on either side of the screen door. "Come on, Lyndsy, we gotta team up if we're going to survive. You want to beat Steve to the big story, don't you?"

"Yeah," Lyndsy whispered. "But you sure haven't done anything to convince me to trust you."

"Give me a chance. That's all I'm asking." He gestured up at the house. "So ... you're living here now?"

"Until I can move into my new place."

"You know, you don't have to move out. Macy just did it as a joke."

"All my work is here. Why keep commuting back and forth, wasting money and gas?" Lyndsy shrugged.

"Makes sense." He grinned and took a step back. "So, partners?"

"I'll think about it."

That seemed to satisfy him. Olivia wanted to slap that smug little smile off his face. Mike said goodnight and headed down the porch steps. She and Lyndsy watched him go down the flagstone path to the street. They waited until he got in his car, a brown sedan, any other features hard to make out in the shadows between streetlights. Finally, he drove away.

"I gotta find a place to park my car so he doesn't see it in the driveway when he comes back," Lyndsy said. She wrapped her arms tight around herself, staring down the street until the sound of Mike's engine faded.

"There are a couple municipal lots," Olivia offered. "And there's one behind the fire station. One of the girls from my church used it when a guy from school was stalking her."

"Thanks." She reached to shut the door.

"No, wait." Olivia pointed at the headlights coming down the street from the other direction. "Our pizza."

Lyndsy went into her office while Olivia waited for the delivery driver. She was talking to someone, her voice soft and urgent, as Olivia came down the hallway to the kitchen. Phoebe came in through the back door, bubbling over about the director of a summer theater program for elementary age students who stopped in at Book & Mug just before closing. He wanted Phoebe's help. Lyndsy joined them as Olivia pulled out plates.

"Kai is the greatest boss in the world. He said it'd be no problem to rearrange the schedule to let me work mornings with the kids. Even before I thought about asking him." Phoebe closed the refrigerator, pirouetting away with a two-liter of ginger ale, and plunked it down on the table with a giggle.

"So you're gonna do it?" Lyndsy said. "Just like that?"

"It's a great opportunity," Olivia said. "You always have fun working with kids."

"How often does a chance like that come along?" Phoebe added. "I've worked with Monroe before. He's a doll to work with. The kids love him, and he knows he can depend on me, and who knows what doors this could open for me?"

"Wow, that's amazing." Lyndsy shook her head. Her smile was crooked. "Must be nice to have things work out like that."

"Pay it forward. Treat people how you want to be treated." She shrugged. "Help when you can."

"Yeah." She let out a big sigh. "So … you two wouldn't happen to know someone who's really good with computers?"

"You were talking with Steve, weren't you?" Olivia guessed.

"Yeah. I knew Steve sent that information…" She sighed. "But not that he's claiming it as his own. The thing is, Mike got into his email. If Macy is helping him, it won't do Steve any good to just change his passwords. So …" Another shrug. "Do you?"

"Rufus," Phoebe said.

"He's a guy from our church," Olivia explained. "Genius with computers. His sister Devona works for Kai, handling the bookstore. You've probably seen him around. The cute guy in the wheelchair? He's back from college, talking about setting up a computer repair shop."

"You trust him?" Lyndsy said. Both Phoebe and Olivia nodded. "Great. What's his number?"

Friday, May 31

"Is that Devona's brother?" Eden said, then ducked under the drawbridge to get behind the counter. She gestured with a lift of her chin toward the glass block wall that divided the coffee shop from the bookstore.

Olivia bent down to open the under-counter refrigerator and pull out the carafe with the iced matcha latte. She handed it to Eden, who grinned and plunked down her black, oversized mug on the counter to fill it. Olivia and Kai had a bet going on how many times Eden would come down for a fill-up today. So far, she was winning at three, and it was only going on 4:30.

"Yeah, that's Rufus," she said, stepping back to give Eden a clear view of Steve Edison sitting at the table, leaning far over so he could look at the screen of his notebook computer. Rufus tapped rapidly on the keyboard while bright yellow figures scrolled up the black screen.

"What's he doing?"

Eden's eyes narrowed as Olivia explained about Lyndsy's fear that more than Steve's email had been hacked. She went on to explain about Rufus doing all sorts of computer repair work since middle school, majoring in programming and computer science in college. He had put in two years of short-term missionary work between high school and college, helping the global outreach organization his parents worked for.

"Really? Interesting," Eden said, after Olivia added that Rufus was planning to open his own computer repair business. "How good is he?"

"You know when that nasty virus was going around last summer? The one that came attached to fake text messages from banks and insurance companies, and turned into ransomware? Rufus came up with his own vaccine for it, two days after someone tried to zap him, and he sent it to Devona to pass out. Pastor Roy sent it to everybody at our church. Saved a lot of people from getting locked out of their computers."

"You're ... No, you're not joking, are you? He's Galahad?" Eden snorted when Olivia gave her a blank look. "I've got a friend in the Bureau, and somebody sent a pretty little bit of programming to the local office, offering it to anyone who needed help with that bug. He referred to the programmer as Galahad. Interesting."

"That sounds like Rufus."

"Why's he in the chair?"

"Broke his back trying to learn to surf, when his parents were serving in Australia."

"Ouch," Eden whispered. She kept watching Rufus and Steve while she put the carafe back in the refrigerator. Her cell phone chimed and she scowled as she pulled it out. "Great timing, jerkface," she muttered. "Hey, if I don't get back down here before they're finished over there, could you ask Rufus to wait for me? Or better yet, send him upstairs?"

She nodded her thanks when Olivia said yes, picked up her mug, and hurried away. The afternoon lull had set in, so Olivia got busy restocking and hauling dirty dishes to the kitchen and clean mugs and cups and plates back from the kitchen. She checked on Rufus and Steve each time. The fact that Rufus had been working on Steve's computer nearly an hour now meant Lyndsy had been right. There was more than email hacking going on. Mike was definitely a creep. He had looked and sounded kind of proud last night when he mentioned getting into Steve's email. Considering the fuss he had raised when Mrs. Tinderbeck refused to rent a room to him, Olivia had a better picture of what a self-centered snot he was, justifying whatever harm he inflicted on others.

"How long has he been here?" Lyndsy's voice startled Olivia out of her thoughts.

She looked over to the other end of the counter. Lyndsy had paused in putting a mug and plate in the bus pan for dirty dishes. Behind her, Josiah Crandall made his slow, dignified way past the mostly empty tables, heading for the door. His shoulders hunched, his head of thick white hair bent, and his face looked wrinkled in deep thought. He seemed to lean a little more heavily on his glossy black cane than usual.

"Going on about an hour," Olivia said. "Why?"

Lyndsy didn't answer but turned to watch Crandall. She let out a sigh when he stepped through the door and turned left, immediately stepping out of sight, thanks to Devona's newest display of books in the deep picture window on that side of the shop.

"Any progress?" Lyndsy said, turning back and gesturing at Rufus and Steve.

Olivia shrugged. Even if she was close enough to see what was scrolling up the computer screen, she wouldn't understand what was going on. Not unless Rufus narrated what he was doing.

"If they've been working so long, that means Macy helped Mike hack him. I should have left a few of my cameras at her place, get some evidence to use against her," Lyndsy muttered. Then she stopped, glancing at Olivia as if startled to hear herself say that aloud. "I'd better get out before he …" She gestured at Steve and headed for the door, looking back every couple of steps, visibly afraid he would look up and see her.

"Okay, tell me that wasn't weird." Olivia grinned as she remembered more of last night's weird confrontation. "Guess history majors really are kind of cutthroat."

She ducked under the drawbridge and stepped over into the seating area that went around the side of the building, by the doors to the bathrooms and the stairs and the old brass cage elevator. Just like always, Mr. Crandall hadn't bothered picking up his dishes and utensils, just left them on the table for someone else to clean up.

On the other hand, he always left a nice tip. This time, four $1 bills tucked under the plate that had crumbs and a smear of mustard. Olivia stacked everything, turned to carry it to the counter, and the toe of her boot caught on something. She bent down and saw what looked like a piece of cloth partially under the support of the pedestal leg of the two-seater table where Crandall had been sitting.

Old cloth. With embroidery on it. A square of yellowed cloth that felt like cotton, maybe muslin. If Crandall had dropped it, maybe it was old enough to mean something to him? Part of his ongoing research?

Considering how Lyndsy had relaxed a little once Crandall left the Mug, maybe she was afraid Steve would see him? Maybe she had been meeting with Crandall? Maybe Lyndsy dropped the piece of cloth?

The more important question, Olivia decided right then, was how much trouble she would get in if she gave the cloth to Crandall if Lyndsy dropped it, or she gave the cloth to Lyndsy if Crandall had dropped it.

She was still pondering the options when movement from the corner of her eye caught her attention. She looked over at the table to see Steve standing up and reaching to shake Rufus's hand. He picked up his closed computer, slid it into his case, and slung the strap over his shoulder. On his way to the door, he detoured over to the counter.

"Thanks. Really appreciate the help." His smile looked tired, and was the nicest expression Olivia had ever seen him wear.

"Glad to help." She bit back a few comments on what a skunk Mike was. Why did Steve let him hang around with the Spirits of '62? She watched him leave, and turned her head just in time to see Rufus aim his wheelchair at the bookstore side of the shop. "Hey, Rufus?"

He popped a wheelie and spun around, to glide over to the counter.

"Hey, thanks for sending him over. Word of mouth is the best advertising," Rufus said. "What's up?"

"Eden wants to see you. Kai's cousin. She's got an office upstairs," Olivia added, although she was pretty sure Rufus knew that from Devona.

"What'd I do?" He grinned and gave a good hard shove on his wheels to glide past the counter.

He didn't come down for more than an hour, grinning and nearly glowing when he did. Eden had hired him to assist her with computer work related to her business, Finders Inc. He would be working with her on an as-needed basis, until they figured out if they worked well together, if they "clicked and synched," in Rufus's words. Meanwhile, he would keep working on setting up his computer repair business.

Kai offered Rufus an extra-large iced whipped mocha, the special of the day, to celebrate. They were still talking about several possible locations for Rufus's shop, or whether he should just work out of his home, when Mrs. Tinderbeck came in at the end of her workday. Olivia knew then what to do about that piece of cloth she had found.

She waited until Rufus and Kai had both left, before pulling it out and walking over to Mrs. Tinderbeck's booth.

"Where did you get—no, that can't be what I think it is," Mrs. Tinderbeck said. She gingerly smoothed out the wrinkled square of cloth, and Olivia had the awful feeling that wadding it up in her pocket had been the wrong thing to do.

"What is it?" she asked.

"It looks like a quilt square." The elderly woman smoothed out one particularly wrinkled corner and with the tip of her finger delicately traced the lines of embroidery that filled it in big, thick, almost plush stitches.

"Old?"

"I don't know. If it is the real thing, it should be preserved between glass, sealed to protect it from the air and light." She gestured at the markings. "These are codes for conductors on the Underground Railroad, indicating that a nearby building was a safe haven for runaway slaves to hide. They put the marks up in charcoal on whitewashed fences, or carved them into the clay on a riverbank, or even carved them into trees. After the war, women made quilts to memorialize that effort and honor the people who risked their lives to help." She glanced up at Olivia. "Where did you get it?"

Olivia slid onto the bench facing her landlady. "I cleared off the table after Mr. Crandall left, and this was on the floor, under the leg. I almost threw it out."

"I can't imagine Josiah Crandall dropping something so precious and valuable and not realizing it."

"Then Lyndsy dropped it."

"Lyndsy? Auretta?" Mrs. Tinderbeck nodded, lips pressed tightly together for a few moments. "I had a feeling that girl was up to much more than just harassing those reenactor boys. I'm tempted to teach her a lesson and hold onto this until she gets frantic. The problem is, I'm just curious enough about where she found this, I'd rather confront her."

"Better you than me," Olivia said. That got a chuckle from her landlady.

~~~~~
~~~~~

Mrs. Tinderbeck did confront Lyndsy, who was waiting in the kitchen when Olivia got home from work that evening.

"I can't begin to tell you how grateful I am," Lyndsy said. She sat in the corner at the kitchen table. "That quilt square is one of my best clues, and I would be better off dead if I had lost it."

"Clues to what?" Olivia said.

"Railroad tunnels. Underground Railroad," she corrected. "I have six quilt squares. One has the outline of Ohio, with the area along the lake darkened by something. I only have this summer to prove my theory. If I lost any of those quilt squares ..." She shuddered, with a crooked grin. Something dark in her eyes made a lie of her attempted humor. "So anyway ... thanks. I don't understand why you're so nice, when you don't even know me."

"Hey, Mrs. T asks us to look out for each other," Olivia muttered.

An hour later, as she tried to relax and let sleep come, she mentally kicked herself. She should have said something like, "It's what Jesus would want me to do." That would have been the perfect opportunity to urge Lyndsy to come to church with her.

Olivia had the awful feeling that Lyndsy really needed some spiritual teaching and repair work.

Chapter Four

Sunday, June 2

Olivia took a double dose of Nyquil when she got home from work Saturday night, to fight off the sniffles and aches that she feared was a cold starting up. She woke at 7:20 and debated going downstairs for peppermint tea to ease her chest and sinuses, but that felt like too much work. She fell asleep again before she could build up enough willpower to stumble to the shower and see if that would help clear her head.

She woke again around 10:30, to find a note from Phoebe on her bedside table, peppermint tea in a sealed travel mug, and an onion bagel dripping in butter and honey in an old cottage cheese tub. The note scolded her for a lazy heathen, signed with a P full of curlicues and a snaggle-tooth smiley face. Underneath that, she was ordered to feel better.

Olivia did feel better by the time she ate half the bagel and drank all the tea. She wanted more tea, so she exchanged her pajamas for gym shorts and a T-shirt and toddled down the stairs. A sound like hammering caught her attention as she stepped into the kitchen. The back door was open, and she stepped out onto the porch. A bright flash of green caught her attention. She rubbed the sleep crud out of her eyes and blinked until her eyes focused and found Lyndsy. Her new roommate was on her hands and knees three feet onto the sweetheart bridge, hanging over the side, attaching something to one of the rotted wooden planks.

Knowing better than to speak and startle Lyndsy, and maybe send her tumbling down into the rocky creek bed, Olivia leaned on the porch railing and watched. Whatever she was doing, it seemed to take a lot of time. Once she stopped hammering, Lyndsy kept leaning over, reaching under the bridge, fiddling with something. Olivia debated going back into the house to make more tea or keeping watch. Just in case Lyndsy got in trouble. If she fell, someone would have to call the EMTs.

Getting bored with waiting, she looked around and found an open backpack and a tool kit sitting on the ground, safely far enough back from where the steep slope down to the bridge began. Several packages wrapped in what looked like bubble wrap filled the backpack. More strips of bubble wrap stuck out from under the backpack. Probably from whatever Lyndsy was attaching underneath the bridge.

"Oh. Hey. What are you doing home?" Lyndsy said, startling Olivia.

That ominous creaking of the bridge had probably been Lyndsy moving back to solid ground.

"Sick." She shrugged. "What are you doing?"

Lyndsy grinned, then looked around and pressed a finger to her lips. "Can you keep a secret?" She stepped over to her backpack and picked up one of the bundles of bubble wrap. "Installing video cameras. There's something going on at night down in the creek. Those two slimebags aren't going to get the march on me. Not when they've been trying to ride on all my hard work."

Olivia assumed "those two slimebags" meant Mike and Steve. She was just curious enough, she stepped down from the porch when Lyndsy beckoned, and followed her to the right, to where a tree leaned out, its tangled roots digging in among the sandstone and packed dirt at the edge of the sheer drop. Maybe she still had too much Nyquil in her system, because she didn't protest when Lyndsy asked her to hold the toolbox, while she herself climbed out onto that tree to install another camera.

"You know ... you've got an awful lot of nice stuff for someone who's just a history major."

Definitely, she still had too much cold medicine in her system. She shouldn't have taken several different brands, so close together.

"Sshh." Lyndsy peered back at her from under the arm holding tight to the tree branch over her head. "That's my secret power. I've got a grant, giving me a lot of gear, paying my way. But I have to produce by the end of the summer, or ..." She made a throat-cutting gesture, chuckled, and turned back to work on the camera.

Olivia couldn't wrap her brain around how video cameras would help Lyndsy with research into Underground Railroad and Civil War-era history. It wasn't like the cameras could see through time, to catch what people did more than a century ago.

Yeah, definitely, too much cold medicine.

"The thing is, the water level is going down, and somebody is changing how the land looks down there. Maybe destroying the clues I'm looking for. Stuff was revealed when they took that flood wall down. Somebody is trying to hide stuff, but I can't prove it unless I catch them and ..." She shrugged. "Everything looks different at night. Shadows aren't there, or they're at a different angle. I've gotta protect myself, and maybe catch something that's revealed by the moonlight, and by how the angle of the sun changes the way things look during the day. I certainly can't sit up here, trying to see through the leaves, for a couple days straight," Lyndsy continued. "I've got this theory ... and I can't depend on anybody but myself."

She moved back down the tree trunk a few feet. For a few moments she just lay there, as if exhausted. Or maybe afraid that one wrong move would tip her over the side. When she held out the screwdriver behind herself, Olivia reached to take it.

"Thanks." Lyndsy crawled backward down the trunk.

"Are you done?"

"What I can do up here, yeah. Gotta get down there and put in a few cameras on the other side of the creek."

"How?"

"Oh, I've made friends with some of the people on that street. They'll help me out." She chuckled. "If only to totally hack off those old nasties in the historical society."

Monday, June 3

"You know, sometimes I feel sorry for that crazy old man down there," Phoebe said, coming into the living room.

"Why? Who?" Olivia frowned at the TV remote. Either the batteries needed replacing, or it was so old the contacts were worn. She had to press a button at least three times to change the channel, or in this case, take the DVR'd movie off pause.

"Old Mr. Fendergast. You can't hear him? He's having one of his fits, calling for the Ghost to come home." Phoebe set down the fresh bowl of popcorn on the coffee table and dropped onto the sofa.

"You know there's something wrong with the world when I actually agree with Ellsworth," Olivia muttered. She let out a sigh as the movie started forward again, at the point in *Coco* where Hector helped disguise Miguel so he looked like another walking skeleton.

"Agree about what?" Phoebe scooped up a handful of popcorn.

"Someone needs to convince his relatives to lock him up so he doesn't hurt anybody when he has one of his fits."

"You actually heard him say that?"

"Y'know, I think I heard some other people say that. Why?"

"Well, Mrs. T said Ellsworth is always trying to suck up to Mr. Fendergast, so he'll leave his house to his historical society when he dies. If his family takes over and puts him in assisted living or something, then Ellsworth doesn't get the house."

"Then I wouldn't put it past the creep to try to drive Fendergast into a heart attack."

In the movie, Miguel had argued with Hector and run away when Olivia heard the back door creak open, and whispering, laughing voices. A man and a woman. She almost reached for the remote to pause the movie. Phoebe had fallen asleep. She put the DVD on pause. She would need to rewind anyway, back to the place where her roommate had dropped off. Olivia turned to look down the hall to the kitchen. The voices stayed soft. Curiosity had her getting up, to creep to the end of the hallway to the kitchen.

Steve and Lyndsy huddled together, looking at a tablet he held. Light and color splashed on their faces. Olivia heard Fendergast calling, faintly, "Ghost! Come back, Ghost! You gotta rest. Please?"

The two muffled more laughter behind their hands. Olivia stepped back before they looked up and caught her watching them.

They were both in costume. Olivia had the awful feeling they had been down at the creek, running around in the mist and shadows, teasing that poor old man. That was what Phoebe had heard a little while ago.

Steve and Lyndsy were lucky Fendergast hadn't come out waving his rifle around. One of these days, he was going to have it loaded. They wouldn't be laughing then, would they?

Should she tell someone? Who?

She went back to the living room and gnawed on the question of what to do and who in authority she should tell, until Phoebe woke up. It wasn't long, maybe fifteen minutes. Then they spent at least ten minutes rewinding the movie, trying to decide where Phoebe had fallen asleep, before Lyndsy joined them. She had changed into lounging pants and a long-sleeve T-shirt, and she had taken her hair out of her multi-colored hair bobbles. Steve had obviously gone home. Unless he was hiding in Lyndsy's bedroom, waiting for her roommates to go to bed?

Olivia didn't feel quite as sorry for Lyndsy as she had for the last few days. She decided not to confront her about what she and Steve had been doing. Instead, Olivia decided to go to Lt. Sunderson and tell her what she suspected. Sunderson was one of the officers in the Cadburn Police department who managed to work around Chief Beakman and Trustee Cadburn to make sure things were done right, without slamming up against all the stupid political maneuvering in the township. Besides, Sunderson went to Cadburn Bible Chapel, so Olivia knew she could trust the woman. The township would be a lot better off if Sunderson was captain instead of Beakman.

Sunday, June 9

Olivia and Phoebe both had the day off that Sunday. The weather was supposed to be gorgeous all day, which was a nice change after all the rain that had taken up a lot of May. The Singles group agreed to have a picnic at the park after church, and the roommates decided to walk to church and walk home. After the picnic, they went east from the park, cutting through the meandering residential area that followed the bend of the creek, and crossed at Bridge Street, so named for the footbridge that had been built by the original settlers. Then they came west again down Creekside.

The brown sedan sat on their side of the street with its back to them. It was the only car on the street for six houses in either direction, so it caught Olivia's attention right away. A chill went down her back at the realization that she had seen that car multiple times over the last two weeks. No, more accurately, since Lyndsy moved in.

Usually, the car was on the other side of the street, further down toward Apple. Always facing their house.

Watching for Lyndsy?

"So what do you think?" Phoebe said. "Liv?" She rested a hand on Olivia's shoulder. "What's—"

"Let's keep walking." She forced a smile and tried not to speed up.

Olivia hadn't seen enough of it on the night Lyndsy moved in, but she was sure that was Mike's car.

Except that wasn't Mike sitting in the passenger seat, with what looked like a computer resting on the dashboard. That was a woman, or at least someone with a pale face and long, medium brown hair. Olivia couldn't look very long. She didn't want to get caught studying the stranger. Although, from that glimpse she had, the woman was focused on her computer.

Why sit in her car to work on her computer when there were several coffee shops with Wi-Fi, and the library had opened after lunch?

Olivia's neck actually ached from the effort not to look at their house as they walked past it. Not to look for Lyndsy, maybe sitting on the front porch, or at least visible in the front windows.

Now she really wished she had asked a second time, inviting Lyndsy to come to church with them. She had a sudden image of their roommate trapped in the house, afraid to come out. If she saw the car before she stepped outside. But if that was Mike's car, who was that woman sitting in it? And where was Mike? Was he prowling around the house, trying to sneak up on Lyndsy?

Maybe he was walking around, trying to find her, since her green Cooper hadn't been in the driveway since the morning after she moved in.

"Are you going to tell me what's up?" Phoebe whispered, when they had gone down Creekside far enough it shifted from residential to shops.

"I feel like I'm in a bad spy novel," Olivia admitted. "Sorry." She tried to remember what Phoebe had been talking about before that brown car snagged her attention. Actually, she wouldn't do too badly as a spy, because she had made out the license plate and make of the car. That was enough to report to the police. If they would do anything about it.

Telling Phoebe what she had seen and listing the other times she had seen that car didn't take very long. They reached the Apple Street bridge, crossed to Center, and turned east to walk to the police station. Phoebe was silent, frowning. Despite being a drama major, she wasn't excitable, going off on tangents over good news or bad news or frightening situations. Like now. Because yes, if Olivia was right, this wasn't just frightening, but possibly dangerous. What if Mike was stalking Lyndsy? And being helped by that woman in the car?

This couldn't all be just rivalry for some historical discovery, could it?

Maybe that woman was the ex-roommate, Macy. It made sense, if she and Mike were a pair, and Macy had helped Mike steal some breakthrough information or clues or whatever from Lyndsy's computer.

Olivia made a mental note to have a talk with Mrs. Tinderbeck and clarify just how big the discovery of an Underground Railroad tunnel in Cadburn Township would be. Would something like that put the township on the map, in a historical sense? Maybe validate the historical societies? Maybe give one historical group precedence over the other? She snorted at the idea of the HIG group finally being slapped back, and the HIF group, as Kai called them, taking power and authority. They at least wouldn't run around scolding people for making improvements to their homes and accusing them of "destroying the history of our township."

Then Olivia thought of something that drove that humorous image from her mind. If Captain Beakman was on duty today, she would be wasting her time to ask for help. Everybody in the township knew he looked the other way when people harassed anyone on Roger Cadburn's dirt list. Beakman would recognize her and Phoebe as Mug employees. If he didn't immediately brush off their request as a waste of time, he would throw out the report as soon as they left the building.

"Then we pray really hard," Phoebe said, when Olivia spoke her thoughts. "We've got maybe fifty feet," she added, gesturing down the street to the police station. She caught hold of Olivia's hand and whispered, "Please, Lord, make this the Beak's day off. Have somebody really smart and reasonable on duty, and have them believe us? Please? If Lyndsy's in trouble, we need to help her."

Lt. Sunderson crossed the street, carrying a Sugarbush Bakery bag and a tray of coffee cups, just before the girls reached the door of the station. Olivia hurried to get ahead of her and open the door. The woman officer thanked them and led the way into the lobby. Her smile faded slightly as she took a second look at them.

"Something wrong?" she asked. "Take this?" She held out the tray. Olivia took it, and Sunderson unlocked the door that led back into the station and gestured them through. She took them to one of the interview rooms, then promised to be back in a minute. She returned with a legal pad, after apparently distributing the bakery and coffee.

Relating what she had seen, her suspicions, the conflict between Mike and Lyndsy and what little their new roommate had mentioned about her former roommate didn't take Olivia much time. Sunderson's face didn't give away anything of what she thought. But she nodded, and took lots of notes, and went over everything once, to make sure she got it all down correctly. Olivia always thought that when the police on TV went over someone's story three or four or five times, that meant they didn't believe a word the witness said.

"Okay, you are right to be concerned, but at the same time, nothing has happened to make this a priority to investigate. I'm sorry. And yeah, how many times have we heard about the authorities saying this, and then the low-priority harassment case turns into something serious?" Sunderson met Olivia and Phoebe's gazes. "I will start a low-level search for information, at least identify the car's owner. I'll have to be discrete, work slowly, because ..."

"Because the rumors are true, and reports get tossed out, and good cops get penalized for doing their job because certain people don't like the ones who are asking for help?" Phoebe whispered.

"I'm not verifying or denying anything. But I'll help you girls the best I can. I can promise that I'll ask the guys I trust to keep an eye out for that car. That should help."

"Thanks." Olivia told herself that sort of dropping sensation was the feeling of a weight falling off her shoulders and not a sense of doom. "I've got the awful feeling Lyndsy is in bigger trouble than she's letting on."

"If she's involved in any of those complaints of ruckus, down in the creek, yeah, she's definitely in trouble. Fendergast is going to remember to load his rifle one of these days, and he was a crack shot when he was younger. Back before he fell off the bridge and landed on his head."

Olivia shivered and wondered if that was what made the old man so touchy. Maybe that was why Mrs. Tinderbeck urged them to feel sorry for him and not judge him too harshly when he went off on his tangents.

Tuesday, June 11

Mrs. Tinderbeck stopped by the house Tuesday night after she closed up the library. Phoebe had suggested they tell her about their worries for Lyndsy. Naturally, since Mrs. Tinderbeck had come by to check on her newest tenant, Lyndsy wasn't there. The three settled in the kitchen to drink tea and nibble on the raisin-filled cookies Mrs. Tinderbeck had brought and pray. Olivia tried not to wriggle too much when their landlady suggested they pray. She hadn't thought about praying for Lyndsy. Yes, she was concerned enough to ask Lt. Sunderson to investigate, but Phoebe had been the one to get Mrs. Tinderbeck involved. A glance at Phoebe, looking a little uneasy, nearly startled a bubble of laughter out of Olivia. Phoebe hadn't thought about praying, either.

They held hands and Mrs. Tinderbeck led off the prayers, which suited Olivia just fine. Until their landlady said amen, and silence seemed to ring through the kitchen. Olivia took a deep breath and silently asked God to give her the words.

Mr. Fendergast's voice rang through the evening quiet, echoing off the sandstone face of the creek bank. The three let go of each other's hands and opened their eyes. Mrs. Tinderbeck got to the kitchen door first, moving much faster than Olivia thought she could.

"What has set that old fool off now?" she muttered and leaned on the porch railing.

"No! You can't have her! She's mine. Ghost!" The angry rattle in his voice changed to a wail that made something ache in Olivia's chest. "Ghost, come back! You're safe here. Come back!"

"Somebody needs to do something about him," Phoebe said. "Mr. Gibbons was in the Mug the other day, and he's gone from furious over all those stones he dumped on the ridge to scared stiff. And Captain Beakman won't do anything. He just laughs."

"Yes, he would. That skunk, Roger, has tried to intimidate Andrew's few remaining relatives into having him declared a danger to himself, commit him, and hand that property back to the Cadburns." Mrs. Tinderbeck shook her head. She flinched as the sounds of deep sobbing filtered up through the darkness and leaves and moonlight. "Andrew! Andrew Fendergast, you listen to me. Just calm down and go home. Everything will be all right in the morning. Do you hear me? Calm down—"

A gunshot splintered the held-breath quiet of the night. Phoebe leaped on Mrs. Tinderbeck and hauled her down to the porch deck. Olivia couldn't move. She couldn't breathe. She held perfectly still, waiting for another gunshot, positive she was in the rifle sights. If she didn't move, he wouldn't see her, would he?

No, that was only supposed to work with big dinosaurs, and that hadn't worked very well in *Jurassic Park*, had it?

"Help me," Phoebe said. She struggled to her feet, an arm around Mrs. Tinderbeck, trying to haul her upright.

Stupid, stupid, stupid, Olivia scolded herself and bent down to help.

Mrs. Tinderbeck wasn't shaking, but she let both girls support her through the door and back to her seat at the kitchen table.

"Well, that was a bit of unexpected excitement, wasn't it?" She smiled and wiped a few drops of sweat off her forehead with her napkin. Phoebe only put out napkins when Mrs. Tinderbeck visited. That was fortunate. Olivia couldn't imagine Mrs. Tinderbeck using her sleeve to wipe her face.

"Are you all right?" Phoebe wrapped her hands around the teapot. "Still hot enough. Or would you rather I made some chamomile?"

"I don't need soothing. What I need is that time machine those boys were talking about in the teen book chat this afternoon." Mrs. Tinderbeck managed a slightly shaky chuckle. "I would give anything to go back in time and slap some sense into Andrew's parents. It's their fault he is the way he is."

"Lt. Sunderson said he fell off the bridge and landed on his head," Phoebe said.

Mrs. Tinderbeck snorted. "Exactly. He had a fight with his parents, and the numbskull knew that bridge wasn't safe, but he went storming across it, just to get away from them as fast as he could. And yes, he fell. The water was very low that summer." She sighed. "He hasn't been right since." Another sigh. "The night was misty, and he thought he saw Annabelle Cadburn's ghost. He's been obsessed with her ever since."

As if in punctuation, a siren wailed on the other side of the creek. Olivia imagined one of Fendergast's neighbors had called the police. She was surprised anyone came out. Maybe that gunshot made a difference.

"That's why you told me to stay away when I was in uniform for Spirits rehearsals," Phoebe said.

Mrs. Tinderbeck nodded and squeezed Phoebe's hand. Laughing voices filtered through the quiet. Olivia heard footsteps on the wooden steps of the front porch. The front door was open, the screen door locked. Olivia braced to get up, as soon as the doorbell rang. Who could be out there, this late in the evening?

"No, don't," Lyndsy said. "We can't go tracking mud on the carpet. Come around the back."

A few more sputters of laughter traced the path of several people coming down the driveway. Whoever she was with was male. Olivia held her breath as heavy footsteps came up the back porch steps. Who was Lyndsy with, and where had they been and why was she worried about mud on the carpet?

"Mud?" Olivia whispered and looked at Mrs. Tinderbeck. "Like maybe they were down in the creek?"

Mrs. Tinderbeck's mouth flattened in that disappointed look that could make snotty high school boys tremble with guilt.

"Sshh," Lyndsy said as her silhouette appeared against the screen of the back door. "I don't know who's visiting, but maybe you should stay out here. I'll bring you some flip-flips to wear to go home."

"I gotta change my clothes," the man said as Lyndsy pulled the door open. "If Mike sees me in costume, this late at night—"

They both stopped short, just inside the spill of light from the kitchen. Lyndsy and Steve Edison. Both were in costume, wet up to their knees.

"Was that you two down in the creek, tormenting that silly old fool?" Mrs. Tinderbeck said.

"Not on purpose," Steve said. "We were playing with Lyndsy's camera, testing out the night vision setting and ..." He shrugged and offered an innocent look that didn't fool Olivia for a moment.

"In uniform?" Phoebe said.

"I'm working on a presentation," Lyndsy said. "For my grant funding. We figured, see how well the uniforms come across."

"I just need to get out of my wet clothes," Steve added. "Is that okay? I'll leave right away."

"You had better hide that incriminating evidence before the police show up," Mrs. Tinderbeck said, her tone cool.

"Police?" He flinched when another siren joined the first. "Why would they come here? Nobody saw us."

"You hope," Phoebe said.

"If anybody recognized Mrs. T's voice," Olivia added, "it won't take long for them to figure out where she was and come here."

"That was you?" Lyndsy inhaled sharply. "Are you all right? He didn't—he didn't shoot you, did he?"

"He may have shot *at* me, but no, thank you, he didn't hit me. Or anything else, as far as I can tell." Mrs. Tinderbeck's voice warmed a little.

Olivia lost a little of her irritation with Lyndsy. She did look worried about Mrs. Tinderbeck, and that made all the difference.

The three of them were quiet, waiting, while Lyndsy retrieved Steve's backpack of clothes from her office and he ducked into the bathroom to change. When he emerged in record time, he looked rather silly, and slightly uncomfortable, in her neon pink flip-flops that were clearly several sizes too small for his big feet. He said a quiet good night to the four of them and ducked out the back door.

"I'm sorry," Lyndsy said. "Really. We didn't plan on any of that happening." She obeyed Mrs. Tinderbeck's gesture to join them at the table. "We were wading in the shallows, and I swear, somebody was following us. Steve got ticked with me when I said we should come back some other time. We must have gotten louder than I thought, because the next thing I knew, that old man came out yelling and waving his rifle around." She paused, frowning, her eyes narrowing. "Now that I come to think of it, I thought I heard some pounding. Like ... I don't know, somebody knocking on wood."

"Or a door?" Olivia said. "Probably Mike. I wouldn't be surprised if he's been following you around. He probably knocked on Fendergast's door to get him to come out and see you."

"How do you know?"

"I saw his car, the day you moved in. And I've seen it parked on our street a few times. But the last time, there was a girl in it, working on a computer, and Phoebe agrees with me, she was watching our house. Maybe waiting for you to come out."

"What kind of car?"

Olivia described it. Before she had finished, Lyndsy shuddered, her mouth flattening and twisting a little, like she wanted to spit.

"That's not Mike's car, that's Macy's. Yeah, she's been playing her poor pitiful me card, claiming I totally misunderstood, she's sorry, please come home. Stalking me is right up her alley." She rested her elbows on the table and hid her face in her hands. "If Mike wasn't trying so hard to team up with me, I'd swear they're both trying to drive me away." She lowered her hands, looking slightly ashamed. "And I shouldn't be dumping any of this on you." A tiny, raw sort of chuckle escaped her. "I don't even know why I'm telling you any of this."

"Because you know we care, dear, no matter how short a time we've known you." Mrs. Tinderbeck reached over to rest her hand on Lyndsy's. "Something tells me you've been alone for a very long time. You need some place safe, and you need friends."

"Yeah, well ..." Lyndsy blinked rapidly a few times. Olivia wasn't sure, but maybe she fought back some tears. "Sorry, but I'm just not used to people being nice just to ... I don't know, to be nice. Without getting something out of it."

"You haven't been hanging around with the right kind of people," Phoebe offered.

"You got that right." Another raw chuckle escaped her. "Why are you so nice?"

"Because that's how our Savior wants us to live." Mrs. Tinderbeck squeezed her hand and released her. "And we've laid far too much on your mind and heart for one night. Think about what we've said, and the situation you're in, and when you want to talk, come to me, call me, any time of the day or night. Stop by the library. What's the use of having an office with a nice thick door if I can't have private conversations?" She chuckled as she got to her feet. "I know my girls will listen, and they'll be praying for you."

"Wow ... that's ... Um, thanks." Lyndsy raked her fingers through her hair. "I'm just ..."

"Feeling awkward? It's okay to go hide," Phoebe said.

"Girls, walk me out to my car," Mrs. Tinderbeck said. She patted Lyndsy's cheek, then scooped up her purse and turned to the door.

The three of them were silent as they stepped onto the porch. They walked down the driveway to Mrs. Tinderbeck's car, parked on the street. The evening felt heavy with questions and ideas.

"I want you to bring her to church on Sunday if you have to tie her up and throw her in the trunk of your car," Mrs. Tinderbeck said.

"Yes, Ma'am," Phoebe said, and saluted her. That got a chuckle from their landlady. She hugged them both and got into her car, and they waited on the sidewalk until she drove down the street and around the bend and out of sight.

Chapter Five

Wednesday, June 12

Olivia didn't have to open that morning, so she slept in until the decadent hour of 8:15, then crept down to the kitchen so she wouldn't disturb Lyndsy. She had just pulled milk out of her crate in the refrigerator and added it and eggs and oatmeal to her shopping list when Lyndsy snarled several unintelligible words. They were muffled by her anger and the office door, but Olivia knew they had to be curses.

She had thought a long time about Lyndsy and her situation before she fell asleep last night. Maybe it was her resolution to be nicer and her sense of guilt that drove her, or maybe it was Mrs. Tinderbeck's expectations, or maybe she was just being a better Christian. She went down the short hall and knocked on Lyndsy's door.

"It's Olivia. Are you okay?"

Lyndsy opened the door and stepped back, clearly inviting her in. She pointed to her open computer sitting on her desk. The screen showed a dark scene, with a streak of what had to be moonlight. Olivia got closer, and her eyes adjusted, and she realized that was moonlight on water.

"You were right." Lyndsy's voice cracked. She settled in front of the computer and tapped several keys, and the view changed. It looked like a film negative. More taps, and the image enlarged and shifted to focus on the upper right corner. A man-shape crept up to a blur of light. Olivia flinched when the muted sound of knocking came from the computer.

Again, it struck her how odd that Lyndsy had such high-tech, expensive gear to use. Just how much money did she get from that grant to fund her research?

"That slimebag Mike sent the old fart after us. Bet he'll use that to get inside his house." She slammed her hand flat on the desk, making the laptop computer jolt a little. "Mike and Steve have both been trying to kiss up to the old man, but they keep messing up. It's like a big game to them, to see who can get inside, into the cellar, first. Mike's been trying to sabotage things between me and Mr. Crandall, too. Next thing you know, he'll be taking my grant money. It's just not fair!"

"You need to turn this in to the police," Olivia offered. "Mike tried to get you into trouble. All the neighbors will testify that Fendergast was shooting his rifle, too. Heck, the police even came out, finally."

"Can't." She shook her head, blinking back what were clearly more tears. "I've tried showing the cops some other video I got of Mike and Steve fighting. Mike threatening to break his neck, calling him a wannabe, telling him to get out of the way, he's just playing games, he's not serious about history and ..." She scrubbed her eyes with her fists. "Captain Beakman got in my face the second time I took a flash drive with video to the station. He told me he'd throw me in jail if I bothered his department anymore. I believe him."

"Yeah, he's the kind of jerk who'd do it, too. I don't suppose you have a lawyer handy?" Olivia offered a smile to show she was joking. It felt flat. Lyndsy didn't even try to smile.

"What am I going to do?"

"You've got friends here, remember? We'll stand with you. We'll figure something out. And ... okay, this is going to sound kind of wimpy, but Mrs. T gave us orders to bring you to church with us on Sunday."

"Religion is a crutch," Lyndsy whispered. Her mouth twisted up on one side, and Olivia hoped she meant it as a joke.

"Yeah, but when you've got a broken leg, a crutch kind of comes in handy."

"I guess." Lyndsy reached for her purse and pulled out her cell phone. "More important, I gotta warn Steve. Mike is a really sore loser. Steve told me that Rufus guy installed some software on his computer, and it's detected a few attempts to break in again. Mike's gotta be steamed, you know?"

Olivia stayed as Lyndsy made the call since she didn't give any indication she wanted to be alone. She had to leave a message since Steve didn't answer his phone. Olivia tried to pray, but her mind kept swirling through the possibilities, all of them nasty and frightening as Lyndsy told Steve what she saw on her recordings from the night before.

Then she had an idea. She called the police station and asked to speak to Lt. Sunderson. The front desk officer informed her Sunderson was on temporary leave. Could he help?

The stiffness in his voice gave Olivia several ideas. First was that Sunderson wasn't "on leave," but on suspension. She had finally crossed the line with Beakman. Olivia hoped her request for information on that brown car, Macy's car, hadn't been the tipping point. Maybe because she, head barista for Book & Mug, wanted help.

She thanked the officer and declined to leave her information. He probably had caller identification anyway, so if he really wanted to know who was calling for Sunderson, he could find out without any trouble. Maybe his stiffness came from Captain Beakman being in the room.

"Okay, God, now what?" she murmured, after hanging up.

"What's wrong?" Lyndsy said.

Olivia got her next idea even as she explained that Sunderson wasn't available. She took a few deep breaths and called the church. Patty Hill answered. She knew Sunderson's home number off the top of her head, and didn't hesitate to give it, once Olivia explained.

"Who was that?" Lyndsy asked, when Olivia got off the phone.

"Patty. Pastor Roy's sister. She's the church secretary, and a ton of other things."

"The people at your church just ... do things like that?" Lyndsy looked thoughtful, and maybe a little stunned.

Olivia got that stomach-twisting sense of guilt. She really had been judging Lyndsy lately, which wasn't fair, because it certainly seemed like she didn't have anybody she could trust or depend on for help.

"Yeah, we're family, if you really think about it."

Lyndsy snorted. "Don't talk to me about family." Then she brushed away the subject. "So, are you going to call her?"

Olivia did, and put the call on speaker so Lyndsy could join the conversation if necessary. She started by apologizing for causing trouble, and Sunderson laughed.

"It wasn't your request. That ruckus down in the creek last night. Beakman suspended the officer who responded to the gunshot report and managed to get Old Fendergast's gun away from him. Then he suspended the officer who protested the order to give it back to him. Then I got suspended for pointing out that both officers were following proper procedure."

"I'm sorry."

"Don't worry about it. He can't keep getting away with kissing up to certain people and their agendas. There are only so many times he can brush this off with the officers' union, and I've got it on good authority he passed that number quite a while ago."

Olivia still didn't think that was quite fair. She told Sunderson that Lyndsy had identified the car as Macy's, and what had been recorded on the cameras. That Mike had in effect incited the ruckus last night.

"Problem," Sunderson said, after a long pause that had Olivia wondering if the connection had broken. "Does your friend have permission from the property owners to install those cameras? She's basically invading the privacy of anyone living along the creek."

Lyndsy rolled her eyes and settled back in her desk chair. Clearly, she didn't want to speak up.

"Not all of them," Olivia said. She remembered what Lyndsy had said about several houses along the creek. "Although I'm sure Mrs. T will give permission for the cameras on her property."

"Tell her to take down those other cameras before someone finds them and raises a ruckus with Beakman. But for heaven's sake, don't do it at night. Fendergast has his gun back."

Olivia promised to tell Lyndsy to be careful. Sunderson said she would ask some of the officers she could trust to keep an eye out for Mike and the car and be ready for any trouble down by the creek.

That was all they could do for now. Olivia had to make her very late breakfast and get ready to go to work. She left Lyndsy working at her computer, and said a prayer that her roommate wouldn't take any foolish risks today.

~~~~~

"Hey, Eden?" Rufus wheeled halfway out of the brass cage elevator opening into the office on the second floor. "Can I ask a big favor?"

"Depends on how big." She leaned back in her old wooden swivel chair and stretched her arms over her head. Then she saw the solemn expression on his square-cut face. "What's wrong?"

She had already liked everything she heard about Rufus Lucciarola before she even met him. Someone like Devona, who handled the bookstore side of Book & Mug, had to have a good brother. Kai spoke well of him, and the long talk they had had the other day confirmed an idea she had been playing with for a few months now.

She had so much work to do that dealt with computers and computer security, and while she had a wide range of contacts, people she could call on to help when she was in over her head, her investigations business had grown to the point where she needed to have someone on staff, the same person she could turn to and know he was available. Rufus was already proving to be that person she had envisioned. Besides, she just flat out liked him, without considering his incredible skills and instincts when it came to computers.

"I'm meeting someone whose computers got encrypted. I'm guessing ransomware, but nobody has contacted her yet with any demands. Could I work on them up here?"

"Absolutely. You know where the inputs are, and all the spare cables and connections." She gestured at an open stretch in the horseshoe-shaped workstation she and her cousins shared. "Make yourself comfortable."

"Thanks. I really appreciate it." He flashed her a smile and backed into the elevator. The door closed with a squeal and a clang, and the elevator descended with a groan a few seconds later.

Eden was on the phone for the next hour with a constant stream of calls, either reporting to clients or asking questions for new investigations. She was aware of Rufus and the young woman who came upstairs with him, carrying several computer cases. One time, Eden turned around to get a new bottle of seltzer from the mini-fridge, and she took the time to count the cases. Five computers, all open, all showing the same long column of error messages.
~~~~~

That made her smile. The last time she had dealt with a client whose computer had been encrypted and held for ransom, the hackers had indulged in splashing a large bloody skull and crossbones on the screen. That was how she and two hacker friends had tracked them down. They decoded the artwork, found the source and artist, uncovered a watermark that recorded when it had been purchased, and identified the hackers. Whoever had gotten into this girl's computers at least had the sense not to be flashy.

Why five computers? What was she doing with five computers, that all of them had been encrypted?

Eden went upstairs to see if Troy was home from his business trip to Columbus yet and warn him about the stranger in the office. He had a tendency to peel out of his business suits and run around in socks and briefs after a really long day, and not even realize he was doing it. She was used to it, he was family, and she had strong enough instincts to help her ignore him when he was being sloppy. This girl Rufus was helping didn't deserve the shock. She had enough to deal with, trying to get access to her computers again.

Troy was back, but all she found was his suit coat and shoes flung on his kitchen table. Chances were good he was either in the greenhouse on the roof, or he was downstairs getting Kai to whip up something extremely rich to ease away the day's stress. Eden mentally tossed a coin and headed down to Book & Mug.

She was right. She found Troy leaning against the back wall behind the counter while Kai and Olivia and Truman dealt with a sudden influx of after-dinner customers. Whatever Kai had made for him, it filled an oversized glass root beer mug, big enough to hold half a gallon. The contents were bright green with stripes of red and orange and brown swirled through it. Troy took a long swallow and watched through half-lidded eyes as Eden ducked under the drawbridge to join him.

"Is this a celebration drink or a drown-your-sorrows drink?" she asked, pitching her voice low and watching Kai and the others juggle all those orders. She shook her head, always amazed at the skill and patience those three showed. How did they keep everything straight? Especially when some of those customers didn't want to wait their turn and shouted their orders like they were in a New York delicatessen during rush hour.

"This is progress on our personal hunt, but no idea where these new leads will take us." He offered the other side of the enormous, frosty glass mug for her to sip. Eden shook her head. "My new botanist friend says he's seen images of plants that certainly look like the ones from our mystery seeds. The problem is that they're from fragile historic documents, and anybody trying to access them without explaining what they want ... well, that might generate too much interest from the wrong people."

"And that's good how?"

"He hates bureaucracy, he's been scorched by Mulcahy-Dresden Pharma, and once he learned that we weren't their best friends, he practically begged me for the chance to beat them to the answer. And yes, before you raise the paranoia flag, I'm going to do a deep dive investigation into him, to make sure he isn't another double agent like the last guy who stole from us."

Her lips twitched into a brief smile. Eden wasn't proud of herself when she had to play nasty tricks, but that time, the guy had it coming.

Someday, they would find out what plants grew from the seeds hidden in their Venetian glass heart lockets, where those seeds came from, where the three cousins came from, why they had been separated from their families and dropped into the system with new identities and purged records, and who had done it to them.

"Kai's already called Seaver's to order dinner," Troy added as the tidal surge of customers showed signs of slowing down.

"Bless him. I am not up cooking."

Troy snorted. "He forgot it was my turn to cook tonight."

That got a chuckle from her. "When is the order coming? Rufus is upstairs working with a client. I don't want to disturb them."

"Weather's nice, we could eat on the roof."

"Sounds great." She pushed off from the wall, in preparation for heading upstairs, when Kai finished with his last customer and stepped back from the counter. "Hey, do you know who's upstairs with Rufus?"

Kai gave her an odd look. She laughed, knowing he was going to ask why she hadn't found out.

"I was on the phone when they got up there and they've been so busy, and I've been busy and ..." Eden spread her hands, as if that was explanation enough.

"Remember that girl who came in a few weeks ago, asking about the tunnel in the basement?" Kai hooked his thumb over his shoulder at Olivia, who was loading up a bus pan to take to the kitchen. "Lyndsy something. They're roommates now at Mrs. T's, and she sent her to Rufus."

That made sense. Olivia was that kind of helpful person. Although Eden wasn't sure how the history researcher girl found her way to Mrs. Tinderbeck's house. Did she really need to know?

Kai agreed they would eat dinner on the roof. He would send up the food in the dumb waiter when it was delivered. Eden headed upstairs. She stepped into the office just as the elevator door clanged and creaked open. A glance to the conference table where the computers had been sitting open showed three still processing through whatever Rufus had done to, as he termed it, "vaccinate" them. Lyndsy had two computer cases hanging from her shoulder as she stepped into the elevator.

"Check with me at lunchtime tomorrow," Rufus said. "I can't promise, but they should be all cleared up by then."

"You are saving my life. Are you sure I can't pay you more?" Lyndsy said.

"Hey, it was fun. I like a challenge." He made a show of cracking his knuckles, making Eden flinch. Lyndsy laughed, and the elevator door creak-groaned closed.

"There's challenge, and then there's challenge," Eden said. "Why are these taking longer than the two you sent home with her? Or are those hopeless and she's going to junk them?" She had run into several instances of that being necessary.

"The encryption program passed from one computer to another. She's got them linked in some kind of new network formation I've never seen before. That's why I'm not charging her as much as she thinks I should," he added as he wheeled back across the office to the conference table. "Can't wait to take it apart and figure out how it works. Anyway, the network kind of slowed the program digging in roots, so the two I cleared were the most recently infected. These others have been locked down longer. If I can crack the coding ... well, it's not like I'd steal someone else's coding, but I could sure learn a lot and adapt it for my own use. And maybe report this to the proper authorities who can stop the scumbuzzards from doing it to someone else," he added, his voice taking on a rasp as a frown creased his forehead.

"Where have you been all my life?" Eden murmured. Rufus grinned and got to work, and she laughed as a flush crept up his neck to his cheeks and then his forehead. Guys who blushed were few and far between, and adorable, in her estimation.

Friday, June 14

Lyndsy stopped at the Mug to get her last computer from Rufus that afternoon. She waited for Olivia to finish her shift, and they walked home together.

"So have you been able to take down those cameras, like Sunderson suggested?" Olivia asked. Other than seeing Lyndsy come in on Wednesday to meet with Rufus, they hadn't met up to talk. Lyndsy never seemed to be at home.

"Too scared to go back there," Lyndsy said, punctuated with a shrug. "Besides, I've been too busy pumping that Crandall guy for information. He really does know his stuff." A snicker escaped her.

"What did you do?" Olivia didn't know whether to be amused or worried for her.

"I keep waiting for Steve to pounce on me and demand I share what I've been learning. Huh." She shook her head. "I just realized. I haven't seen him since that night we nearly got caught. He's probably nursing a grudge."

"Or a cold. He did get pretty wet."

"Yeah, we did." Another snicker.

"So, I've been meaning to ask you, why so many computers?"

"Storage. After Macy hacked into my cloud account, I didn't dare keep anything there, and all that video takes up a lot of room. I have two cameras go to each computer, and that means I spend a lot of time watching and deleting the stuff that doesn't do me any good."

"Sounds like a headache."

"Yeah. My computers were still recording while I couldn't get into them, so I am way behind. Now that I've gotten everything I can from Crandall, I plan to spend the whole weekend just catching up."

Her phone pinged, and Lyndsy flinched. Olivia watched her as she pulled her phone from her pocket and tapped it. Whatever she saw on the screen made her shoulders visibly relax.

"Good news?" Olivia asked.

"Huh? Oh. No. Just a stupid ad. Why?"

"You seemed kind of glad to see it."

"Not glad." Lyndsy scowled at some distant point and shook her head. "Relieved. Or maybe I'm stupid to be relieved. I don't know. Rufus seems to think whatever encrypted my computers was ransomware, but nobody has contacted me to demand a ransom. So what were they after?"

"Maybe they're letting you stew for a few more days until you're desperate," Olivia offered.

"Hmm. Maybe."

When they got back to the house, Lyndsy didn't seem in any hurry to get to work catching up on ridding out her video recordings. She settled in the living room with Olivia for a *Despicable Me* marathon. They hadn't planned on watching all three movies. Olivia intended to watch the first before heading upstairs to get some work done on her paper for her summer online class. Halfway through the first movie, they decided to order Chinese, and they weren't done eating it by the time the movie ended, so they started the second movie. Then they watched the third movie. And by then Phoebe had come home, exhausted from working summer theater camp in the morning and a full shift into the evening. She fell asleep during the last twenty minutes and needed help sleepwalking up to her room. Lyndsy helped Olivia get her upstairs.

55

Chapter Six

Saturday, June 15

When Olivia got home from work that afternoon, Lyndsy was parked on the back porch in one of the dark green Adirondak chairs, a computer on her lap, studying the screen. She barely glanced away from her work when Olivia climbed the porch steps and greeted her on the way to the kitchen door.

"How's it going?"

"The creeps aren't as smart as they think they are. My computers kept recording everything the cameras caught. I was positive they were trying to erase something. All they managed to do was futz up the date and time coding, and sometimes there's some static messing with the image, but most of that is in the daytime. I don't know what they wanted."

"Still no ransom call?" Olivia asked.

"Nothing makes sense." She turned her head, looking out into the trees that blocked the view of the creek and the opposite bank.

"Has Steve called you back? Phoebe said he missed the last rehearsal. They were supposed to work on their routine for the 4th of July demonstration at Hale Farm."

"Well, looks like he's ghosting everybody then, not just me." Lyndsy shook her head. "I keep waiting to see him on one of my cameras, sneaking around and getting into … Doesn't matter. Nobody is gonna steal my discovery. I just have to find a way to get around that crazy old man."

"Lyndsy, you know what Mrs. Tinderbeck said."

"Oh, don't worry." She flashed a grin at Olivia. "Nothing in the world could convince me to go down there at night. Getting shot at once is more than enough."

Sunday, June 16

Lyndsy came to church with Olivia and Phoebe. The three of them met up with Mrs. Tinderbeck before the service. Their landlady made a point of introducing Lyndsy to all her friends, which felt like nearly the entire congregation. Olivia tried to pay attention to the sermon but couldn't help glancing over at Lyndsy every few minutes, trying to judge her reaction to the sermon. Pastor Roy always had a good message, with something that seemed applicable to her life the past week. Olivia hoped that something he said struck a chord in Lyndsy today. She really couldn't tell from those few glances what the other girl was thinking.

Mrs. Tinderbeck invited them to have lunch with her and a handful of ladies from church who were also in her historical group. Olivia wasn't surprised when Lyndsy declined.

"Well, maybe it is best to go slowly," Mrs. Tinderbeck said, watching Lyndsy walk across the parking lot. "I just can't help feeling that girl needs a big change in her life, before it's too late."

Phoebe had to decline lunch, too. Simon had called a meeting of the Spirits. They had been invited to do some demonstrations at several local historical society meetings and needed to compare schedules and decide which ones they could do.

Olivia decided to stop by Frenchy's and pick up something for lunch. Phoebe and Lyndsy would have had something to contribute to the lunch meeting with Mrs. Tinderbeck and her friends, but she would have just felt awkward, even though she did know and like all the ladies.

The brown sedan was sitting in front of the house when Olivia came around the last bend in the street. No one was sitting in it. She fought down a surge of panic. Who could she call if Lyndsy needed help?

Then she saw Lyndsy sitting on the front porch. The woman sitting with her had been in the brown car, working on her computer.

Olivia walked slowly, trying to pray, trying to listen to the conversation. Their voices didn't sound angry or raised louder than normal. Was that good or bad?

"I'm just trying to say I'm sorry, okay? They found the back door I made into your network, and they used it, thinking they were hurting me." Macy sounded tired, and a little irritated. "I'm asking because this will help you. At least get back at the creeps. I know you couldn't care less, but these guys scare me, okay?"

"What do they want you for, if they can do everything they did to me?" Lyndsy said.

Olivia stopped a good dozen steps away and stepped backward onto the neighbor's lawn, so she was partially shielded by the bushes on either side of the front steps.

"They're good at breaking things, but I'm good at building things. They want me to work for them, and I'm scared to, okay? You've got the connections. Just put in a good word for me. Ask them to help me out. Is that too much to ask?"

"Just how am I supposed to contact Al and his friends when my computer is still locked up?" Lyndsy snapped.

"So you haven't untangled all that?"

"No. And I'm even more hacked off at you than I was before."

"I didn't do it!" Macy insisted.

"Yeah, but you just said that it's basically your fault. They hit me when they thought they were hacking you."

"Look, Lyns, you just aren't listening."

Olivia shivered, hearing something in Macy's voice she didn't like. She wasn't going to let this go any further. Lyndsy needed her help.

She stepped back onto the sidewalk and made sure her sandals slapped a few times on the cement. In a few steps, she was close enough to clearly see them, and they could see her.

"Hey, Lyndsy, have you had lunch yet?" Olivia raised the takeout bag from Frenchy's. "I brought enough for both of us." She met Macy's eyes. "Oh, hi, didn't see you there."

She knew she wasn't as good an actress as Phoebe, but she hoped she could fool Macy. The problem was that untrustworthy people were the most cynical, and the hardest to fool.

Macy sneered as she got to her feet and came down the porch steps. "I gotta be somewhere. Think about what I said, okay, Lyns?"

"Sure." Lyndsy stood up, her arms wrapped around her middle, and watched as Macy crossed the tree lawn to her car.

"What was that about?" Olivia asked, pitching her voice soft, once Macy was in her car. The engine turned over with a rattle and roar, and she fully expected to see a black cloud of exhaust pour out of the tailpipe. That was just her impression of Macy.

"She's insisting she had nothing to do with my computers getting encrypted."

"You believe her?"

"The things she's gotten into? Yeah, it makes perfect sense that somebody nasty is out to get her, and I'm just collateral damage." Lyndsy waited until Macy had driven away, then turned and went into the house.

Olivia followed her. Lyndsy went into her office and shut the door. She came out again, wearing her Union jacket and Rebel cap as Olivia was getting a bottle of tea from the refrigerator.

"Are you okay?"

"Yeah. I just need to think through some things." Lyndsy went out the back door. Her boots thudded softly on the porch steps.

~~~~~

Phoebe returned from the Spirits meeting to report that Steve had left town. He had emailed Simon as his second-in-command, handing everything over to him, then left brief voicemail messages with two other members of the group. Both of them were still irritated when they reported that Steve had been laughing, gloating. He had not only gotten an internship he had been working for, which no one had known about,
~~~~~

but his boss needed him to start work right away. He was following up an important story that would take them to Canada for at least two months.

"Well, Lyndsy knew about the internship," Olivia offered. "So I guess that makes his story true. Kind of rude, but ..."

"Yeah, it fits with how Steve does things." Phoebe slouched on the couch where she had settled when she delivered her news. "The guys were kind of upset when I told them that. About Lyndsy knowing. Steve trusted her with something he wouldn't tell the rest of them. A few of them tried to call him, but his voicemail is turned off."

"That's kind of rude."

"Yeah, well, like I said. Typical Steve. A use 'em and lose 'em kind of guy."

Olivia wondered how Lyndsy would react when they told her. Maybe they shouldn't tell her? But that would be cruel, leaving her wondering. Then she thought of something.

"Was Mike there?"

"Yeah. He seemed kind of surprised, then he said he had noticed Steve's car was never in the parking lot the last few days. I didn't know they were in the same complex." Phoebe shook her head. "What's really sad is nobody is going to miss him. I mean, yeah, he was a good leader, good with the details, but he just wasn't that good with people."

That, Olivia decided, was a sad sort of epitaph for someone who had just walked out of their lives without a backward glance.

Monday, June 17

"Hey, Olivia?" Rufus wheeled up to the counter, grabbed the edge, and pulled himself upright so he could see over the top. "When Lyndsy gets here, send her up to the office, would you?"

"Sure. What's up?"

He shrugged, which was a little bit impressive, since he was holding himself up with his arms. Rufus dropped back down in his chair and wheeled around through the seating area.

Olivia worked on cleaning up behind the counter, since she had a lull. She kept watch for Lyndsy, and almost didn't recognize her. She wasn't wearing her Union jacket and had her hair tucked up in a Cavaliers baseball cap, instead of the Rebel cap. Their gazes met. Olivia pointed upward with her thumb, then gestured around the corner to the elevator. Lyndsy managed a crooked smile and scurried around the corner.

Olivia remembered the conversation she had overheard. Considering the things she had heard about Lyndsy's former roommate, she could believe Macy would get in trouble with really nasty people. The kind of people who wouldn't care about collateral damage.

She thought about calling Phoebe, but she was probably already asleep. This new schedule, working with the children in the morning and putting in a full shift at the Mug in the afternoon, was draining her. Today was her first day off from the Mug and she needed to collapse.

The only other person who knew what Lyndsy was going through and cared was Mrs. Tinderbeck. Olivia calculated the traffic visible in the growing dusk outside. Chances were good that the moment she got on the phone with her landlady, a dozen customers would bomb through the door. Better to text her and fill in the details later.

~~~~~

"Hey, Eden?" Rufus tipped back his wheelchair and pivoted around to face her. "Could you take a look at this?"

"Sure. What's up?" Eden put her game on pause and set her tablet down on the desk. She had promised herself half an hour of her favorite three-dimensional sorting game as a reward for untangling her client's file in half the time she had calculated. Once she had figured out the pattern that he apparently unconsciously followed when he made multiple copies of his files, she was able to sort things out. More coherent labels helped greatly.

"You trust me, right?" Rufus said, as she scooted her rolling chair over to join them. He and Lyndsy had been talking and looking at some sort of video for the last twenty minutes. "Trust Eden. She knows the right people to help you."

Eden caught her breath. She barely knew Rufus, he barely knew her. How could he have that much faith in her so soon?

"What's the problem?"

"Just watch this." Rufus tapped the dark screen.

He tapped a few more commands and the image lightened. Likely filmed at night. Two people stepped into view, harshly lit, until Rufus adjusted the image. Eden guessed they had stepped into moonlight.

One she recognized immediately and glanced at Lyndsy to be sure. It was her, but … something just felt wrong about the image. Then she recognized that blond guy who led the reenactors group. They walked up to a long spill of light on the ground. No that wasn't the ground. The light rippled. That was water.

Lyndsy pulled a gun out of her pocket. Steve stumbled away, backward, holding out his hands. His mouth moved, but no sound accompanied the images. Eden imagined he was begging Lyndsy not to shoot him. He stumbled over something and fell. Lyndsy waved the gun. Her mouth moved, but again, something felt wrong about the image. Eden wished this hadn't been filmed at night. Then again, it probably wouldn't have happened in daylight.
~~~~~

Steve got to his feet, hunched over. He threw something at Lyndsy. She ducked, but it hit her face. She stumbled backward. Steve fled.

The camera angle changed. Another camera. Who was filming this? The new angle showed Steve running along the bank of the creek. Something stuck up from the ground, arched, skeletal, with wide gaps between what looked like railroad tracks in midair. Steve ran to it. He jumped up, catching a bar over his head, and pulled himself up. The entire framework shook. Steve scrambled across, bent over to hold on with his hands, keeping his center of gravity low. Eden gripped the arms of her chair, expecting Steve to fall off the shaking framework any moment. Or for it to fall apart underneath him.

Lyndsy stumbled up to the frame. She grabbed it and shook it.

Eden turned to look at the Lyndsy next to her. She watched herself on the computer screen, shaking her head. She looked sick. And scared.

Steve fell. The camera angle changed again. The new angle showed Steve falling what had to be at least twenty feet, headfirst, into the creek. He flailed but couldn't seem to get up. Lyndsy waded out into water over her ankles. She hauled back and punched Steve in the face, then threw herself on him and held him down. He thrashed, churning up water that looked white in the moonlight.

The thrashing died far too quickly.

"That's not me," Lyndsy whispered, as the video ended.

"Who recorded all this?" Eden said.

"My—" Her voice cracked. "My cameras. I've got ten, spread out along the creek, all focused on four houses. I know it looks like me, but I didn't do that. Please, can't you prove someone played with the files, they stole the files and they… I don't know … they put my face, my body in there on top of whoever really did it? I mean, I don't own a gun. I don't even know how to shoot one."

Eden's experience was that when someone was desperate enough, afraid enough, angry enough, they could figure out how to shoot a gun quite easily and quickly.

"I guess the first question is to find the guy you supposedly killed."

"He left town. I went to his apartment and the manager was pissed. He just took off, left an email, his place emptied out with no warning. Nobody can get hold of him. Nobody knows where he went! Why would someone fake his death and make it look like I did it?"

"Is this guy tech savvy enough to do that? Does he have a grudge against you, maybe?"

"No. At least I don't think so. But what if—" Lyndsy choked and flicked her fingers at the blank computer screen.

"What if somebody really did kill him, and put this together to frame you?" Eden nodded. "I know a few people. It's going to take a lot of time to tweak all the layers apart. You sure these came from your cameras?" Lyndsy nodded. "The first step is to find the originals. When we have those, we can prove they were altered. Do you still have them?"

"I think so." Lyndsy swallowed hard and took a few deep breaths and her faint shivering stopped. "Somebody hacked into my computer network and blocked me. Rufus unlocked everything for me. I've been playing catchup the last few days, going through all my files. There were so many recordings, they kept uploading to my computers through a temporary cloud file I set up, even though I was locked out."

"The question is if these people who locked you out were able to destroy the original recordings. We'll need access. Everything you haven't looked at yet. Did you delete anything?"

"Hours of files, but I can retrieve them, if you need them."

"Yeah, I think we will," Rufus said, exchanging a grim smile with Eden. "You think we can do this?"

"We won't know until we try. Yeah. It'll take some time, but if there's any evidence to be found, we'll find it."

"Who sent this to you?" Rufus said.

"I don't know, but they said I have to turn you over to them," Lyndsy said. She hunched her shoulders when he frowned, shaking his head as if he didn't understand. "They said I have to turn over the guy who broke their lock. So, they know you broke the encryption. I'm guessing you made them kind of mad."

"Okay, this is a whole new level of serious," Eden said. "I think we need to bring in—"

"No!" Lyndsy flinched when her voice seemed to ring off the ceiling. "No police. I can't—I can't afford to have anyone investigating me. I'm hiding. I'm in trouble. I'm sorry. Just please, no cops?"

"What else do they want?" Eden said, pitching her voice soft and soothing as best she could. She had never thought of herself as a comforting or soothing person, and a flicker of some irritation made that hard to fake right now.

"They said they'd contact me again. They already said I have to turn over Rufus, and I'd better not help Macy." She choked on what sounded like an attempt at laughing. "I guess she wasn't lying after all when she said some pretty nasty types were after her. They said they'd kill me if I helped Macy. I don't know what they'll ask for next."

"What will they do if you don't give them what they want?" Rufus said.

"Probably turn this video over to the cops. Maybe bring the dead body out from wherever they hid it," Eden said. Whatever Lyndsy was hiding, the sudden pallor in her face was genuine.

Kai stepped into the office, having come up the stairs. He looked around, raking the fingers of one hand through his hair.

"Hey, Lyndsy? Olivia asked me to come here and warn you not to leave for a while. That guy, Mike is downstairs, looking for you. He says there are some people looking for you and he sounds pretty worried, but Olivia doesn't trust him. Are you in trouble?"

"Yeah," Rufus said. "She's in big trouble.

~~~~~

"Why do I keep feeling like I'm in a bad spy movie?" Olivia muttered. She leaned out from the recessed doorway of the building across Apple from Book & Mug, watching the traffic heading north. Where was Mrs. Tinderbeck?

"I'm sorry," Lyndsy whispered. "All you've done is be a whole lot nicer than I deserve—"

"Hey, I always wanted to be a secret agent." She stepped back and wrapped an arm around the other girl's shoulders. "It's going to be okay, I promise."

The timing had been perfect. Mrs. Tinderbeck had called in response to the text Olivia had sent her more than an hour before. She had come up with the plan. Kai would distract Mike, keeping him on the bookstore side of the Mug while the girls came down the stairs and out the side door onto Apple to wait for Mrs. Tinderbeck to come in her car, to take Lyndsy to a safe place. She hadn't said where, and Olivia suspected the delay in their landlady showing up was because Mrs. Tinderbeck hadn't found someone willing to provide that safe place yet.

"Please, Lord," Olivia whispered, and flinched when she realized she was praying aloud.

How come the only time she thought about praying, other than morning devotions, was when she had a big problem? Okay, maybe it was a step up in her spiritual growth that she was praying for someone else, but seriously, didn't God get sick and tired of people who only thought about Him when they were desperate?

"You really believe all that stuff, don't you?" Lyndsy said.

She leaned back against the wall of the doorway. Fortunately, this was an office building side entrance, with no display windows around them to reveal them to anyone watching. And more important, the building had closed down for the night. No chance of anyone coming out the door. They could stay here all night if necessary, though Olivia certainly didn't want to.

"Yeah, I do. I don't always live that way. I mean, I'm not a thief or murderer or cheat on my taxes or anything like that, but I lie and I'm lazy and I get mad, and I know I have a huge problem with being self-righteous, and I'm sorry for getting kind of judgmental about you."

Olivia was glad for the shadows surrounding them, because her face
~~~~~

was hot and probably bright red. She had heard people talk about their faces being so red they glowed in the dark, but she hoped that wasn't true. They certainly didn't need that right now.

"That's okay. I mean … you're still helping me, even though you probably think I'm a scheming little twit who deserves all the trouble she's getting into. This Jesus stuff is real for you, and it… I don't know … it makes you different."

"Yeah, it does. At least, I hope so."

"My grandmother was like you, and like Mrs. T. She believed all that stuff. She dragged us to Sunday school and all that when we were little." A choked little laugh escaped Lyndsy. "Wish I'd listened."

"It's not too late."

"Yeah, well, if Jesus gets me out of this mess, I'd be pretty stupid not to sign up. Y'know?"

Olivia opened her mouth, intending to tell her, "You'd be pretty stupid not to sign up *before* He gets you out of this mess, because why should He if you're not signed up?" She stopped herself, feeling a little sick, hating the sound of her own voice in her head. It wasn't a nice voice.

Sorry, God. Help me be nicer?

A shiny, powder blue Cavalier pulled around the corner, turning right from Center onto Apple. It stopped with the front wheel pulled up onto the curb, even with the doorway. The interior light flicked on and Mrs. Tinderbeck nodded to them. Olivia gave Lyndsy a shove, just in case she was too scared to move. She leaped ahead of her and opened the back door, and guided Lyndsy in getting in and lying down.

"You be careful yourself," Mrs. Tinderbeck said, as Olivia stepped back and gripped the door to close it. "Proud of you, sweetheart."

Olivia nodded and grinned. She stepped back into the doorway and waited until the car had vanished down Apple, then looked around. She doubted she would see if anyone was watching, but she had to at least try. Then again, the longer she lingered out here, the better the chances someone who was watching could sneak up on her.

That got her moving probably a little faster than she should have, if she wanted to avoid attention. She hurried back across the street and up the sidewalk to the front door, and back inside where there were lights and people and safety in numbers.

Rufus waited until Book & Mug had closed up for the night and drove her home. He told her what had been on the flash drive Lyndsy brought him, and what he and Eden were doing to take it apart, peel away the layers, and prove that Lyndsy wasn't the one who had been fighting with Steve. Then chased him onto the unsteady sweetheart bridge and drowned him when he was stunned from landing on his head.

"That doesn't make any sense," she said, just as Rufus's van pulled into the driveway of her house. "Phoebe said Steve told everyone he was leaving. Why would he come back to the creek? When did he come back?"

"Lyndsy said the videos should have date stamps, but whoever put that video together erased them. He was in that Civil War uniform he was always running around in. That doesn't make any sense either. I mean, yeah, the reenactors are kind of cool, but that guy took it to the extreme."

"They were tormenting old Mr. Fendergast. Running around in their uniforms in the mist at night. You haven't heard about all the ruckus with him chasing the Cadburn Ghost?" Olivia shivered. "We're just across the creek from his house, and in the warm weather, sound travels across the water and … it's just plain creepy."

"The guy was a jerk, but nobody deserves to die that way," Rufus muttered. "Let's hope the walls I put up in Lyndsy's network kept whoever's blackmailing her from erasing the original video."

"Yeah." She shivered again. Suddenly, the walk from Rufus's van to the back door seemed a mile long, and too full of shadows to feel safe. She couldn't sit here forever.

Her cell phone rattled off the teletype sound, meaning she got a text, making her jump. She let out a nervous chuckle and pulled the phone from her pocket.

Patty Hill had texted her. Lyndsy was staying with her and Pastor Roy. Could she get Lyndsy's car from the municipal lot in the morning, and bring Lyndsy's computers and a change of clothes?

That cold feeling faded instantly. Between Pastor Roy and Patty, Lyndsy was in good hands. Maybe she would even "sign up" as she had put it. There was no guarantee that getting her soul taken care of would fix her other problems, but at least she would have the best person possible to rely on through the whole mess.

Chapter Seven

Tuesday, June 18

The spare keys for Lyndsy's car weren't where the text message said they would be. Olivia fought down mixed panic and resentment. She only had so much time to get to the municipal lot, drive to Pastor Roy's house, deliver the car and computers, and walk back to the Mug to start her morning shift. Tearing Lyndsy's office apart wouldn't help.

"Duh, duh, duh," she muttered, and stepped back, took a deep breath, and tried to do as she had resolved last night. Pray more. Start with prayer, instead of diving in and then panicking.

Maybe the praying did the trick, or maybe just calming down and ignoring the ticking clock in her head allowed her to see the keys, on the other side of the desk drawer.

Her next source of irritation was the weight of the four computers in their bags hanging from her shoulders. Then the realization, after she had crossed the bridge and turned down Center, that if anyone was looking for Lyndsy, they might see a girl walking down the street with four computer cases, and decide she was helping Lyndsy.

"Okay, Lord, I would really appreciate some help. This is one of those Brother Andrew moments, when I really need you to make seeing eyes blind." Olivia looked around, positive there were people on the sidewalks who heard her talking to herself.

No, the day was still early enough, none of the businesses had opened and people weren't on their way to work or shopping.

Next problem: Lyndsy's green Cooper wasn't in the odd little corner of the municipal lot behind the fire station, where some overgrown bushes hid it nicely. Olivia had helped her find that spot, so she knew it had to be there. If Lyndsy had moved her car, wouldn't she have said so?

All she could do was ask and stop wasting time. Olivia let the computer cases slide to the ground and pulled out her phone.

Me, Olivia. Did you move your car?

Lyndsy responded almost immediately: *No. Why?*

Not where we put it.

No response. Olivia counted to ten. Then to twenty. What was Lyndsy doing?

Mrs. Hill says there's no time limit on parking, Lyndsy finally texted back. *What happened?*

Stolen? Olivia looked around. *I'll ask if anybody at the station here saw anything. Report it to the police?*

No.

Long pause.

Forget about it.

Olivia's phone rang. Pastor Roy. He was coming to pick her up. He agreed with Lyndsy that it wasn't safe for her to ask any questions about the car. Whoever took it could be waiting to see what reaction they got.

"Yeah, like that doesn't make me want to go hide?" Olivia muttered, after she agreed to wait for her pastor at the picnic tables in the shadow of the fire station.

She didn't have to wait so long that she started to jump at every odd sound that could be footsteps. But she was getting close. Pastor Roy pulled up onto the grass next to the picnic table used by the firemen and leaned across the seat to open the passenger door.

He dropped her off at Book & Mug and headed home with the computers. Like Mrs. Tinderbeck, he told Olivia he was proud of her and asked her to pray hard for Lyndsy.

"The soil is ready for seeds to be planted. Pray God makes her receptive before it's too late."

Olivia had time before her shift started to go upstairs and tell Eden what had happened. Then she called Lt. Sunderson. Just because she couldn't go to the police, that didn't mean she couldn't tell someone who could do something to start the search. After all, if Sunderson was on suspension, she wasn't officially a police officer right now, was she?

Eden laughed at that reasoning, and said she would get to work searching for any cameras that might show activity in that municipal lot. She warned Olivia that very few people knew about that lot, tucked behind the fire station. If no one really used it, she doubted the trustees would have approved money to install a camera there.

Less than an hour later, Eden came downstairs to let Olivia know it was just as she suspected: no security cameras in that part of town.

Wednesday, June 19

"Liv? We've got a problem," Phoebe said.

"Where are you?" Olivia's first thought was that Phoebe's car had broken down on her way back from a meeting for the summer theater program. She looked across the seating area of the Mug to the big picture windows facing Center. Beyond the streetlights, it was dark out. Almost closing time. What was Phoebe's route from the school?

"I'm home. It's Lyndsy. She was heading out just as I got in. I couldn't stop her. She said she knew where Steve was, and she had to get him."

"What was she doing back at the house?" Her phone beeped with call waiting.

"How should I know? She was in that stupid costume of hers and she had this look on her face, like she was scared and furious and …" Phoebe let out a long sigh. "I don't know!"

"Hold on, Miss Patty is calling me." Olivia groaned. "I bet she just got back from church and found out Lyndsy is gone. I'll call you back."

She hung up before Phoebe could answer.

The situation was just as she had thought. Patty got back from Wednesday night choir practice to find Lyndsy gone. She had taken all her computers. She left a note thanking Patty and Pastor Roy for all their help and asking them to pray, because she had to help Steve. She was afraid she was the only one who could. Olivia passed on what Phoebe had told her. Patty said she would call Pastor Roy, who was still at church with a deacons meeting. Maybe they should organize some of the church men to look for her?

Phoebe didn't answer when Olivia called her back. No response to her text, either. Olivia told Kai, who had been leaning against the counter, listening to her side of the conversation with a growing frown. He told her to run upstairs to tell Eden and offered to drive her home to check on Phoebe.

Olivia called her again on her way back down in the elevator. Still no response. No response to her text.

Kai was behind the counter, making a drink for Lisa Pascal when Olivia returned. Lisa had a tote bulging with files resting on the counter and was regaling Kai with what appeared to be a humorous story of some ruckus downtown at the Justice Center. She always had some bizarre story or something new and strange that she witnessed in her job as personal assistant to Bill Worter, head of the legal firm of Worter, Worter & McIntosh. One thing Olivia admired about Lisa was that she could tell those stories without giving away details that could get her sued for invasion of privacy, or just plain humiliating the idiot who made such a mess of his life. Currently, Bill was assisting in prosecuting a serial identity thief. The thief was so inept, so sloppy, and had such a slippery grasp on reality, the case should have been a slam dunk. He kept coming up with new excuses for why he claimed to be multiple different people at the same time. He also changed his lawyers as many times as he changed personalities.

"Hey, hon," Lisa said, when Olivia ducked under the drawbridge and joined Kai behind the counter. "You look like you've had a rough day. Is this big bully beating up on you?" She gestured at Kai with a jerk of her chin and winked at Olivia.

"Still no luck?" Kai said.

Olivia opened her mouth to say no, and her phone rang.

Phoebe.

"Hey." Phoebe's voice wobbled. "Um, I'm at the police station. This is my one phone call. I guess I'm under arrest as accessory to murder or something like that. Help?"

Olivia had no idea how she was so clear-headed, but she switched her phone to speaker and asked Phoebe to repeat herself for Kai and Lisa. Fortunately, Phoebe knew how to tell a story, and both Kai and Lisa knew how to let people finish their stories, instead of interrupting and dragging things out twice as long as necessary. Lisa also turned on the voice recorder on her own phone.

When Phoebe finished, Lisa snapped, "This is finally going to get Beakman tossed out on his arrogant face. I've lost count of how many procedures he and Carruthers violated just in the last hour. Starting with letting their prisoner use her own phone!" Then she got on the phone with Bill Worter, who was on his way home. He promised to head to the police station.

The whole sequence of events made Olivia shake her head as she mentally replayed them. Phoebe was just about to lock up the house and head out to try to catch up with Lyndsy, when Officer Carruthers banged on the front door. He wanted Lyndsy. He had a warrant for her arrest for the murder of Steve Edison. Phoebe pointed down the street—in the opposite direction she had seen Lyndsy go, she had proudly assured her listeners—and told him to head in that direction, maybe he could catch up with her.

Carruthers called her a lying little slut who was protecting a murderer, and if she didn't let him into the house to search for Lyndsy, he'd break the door down and arrest her for aiding and abetting. Phoebe admitted she had had a very long, stressful day with a handful of children who had been eating too much sugar. She sassed back at Carruthers and told him he really should stop learning police procedures from TV. She had taken a screenwriting class that focused on translating suspense and true crime novels to the screen and knew for a fact that screenwriters changed details for the sake of drama.

When she demanded to see his search warrant before she would open the door, Carruthers broke the screen, just punched his fist right through it, unlocked the door, yanked it open, and came after Phoebe. She was so busy dialing 911, she didn't watch where she was going and tripped over the hassock on her way through the living room. Carruthers dragged her to her feet and out of the house to his patrol car. He laughed at her when she asked him to at least let her lock up the house. Could Olivia take care of that? And tell Mrs. Tinderbeck about the screen door?

"I'm guessing the blackmailers sent that video to Beakman when they couldn't catch up with Lyndsy," Kai said.

"What blackmailers and what video?" Lisa said. "Hold on a second." She tapped her phone, turning on the voice recorder again. "I don't want to have to repeat this for Bill, either."

There was a delay while they went upstairs to get the story from Eden and Rufus. Then Troy and Kai took Olivia home and documented the hole in the screen door. They couldn't do anything about repairing it until tomorrow when Lowe's or Menards opened up. They also insisted on searching the house, just to make sure no one had been attracted by the ruckus and took advantage. Mrs. Tinderbeck met them there.

While they were doing that, Eden said she would check for businesses or houses nearby with cameras, to catch Caruthers breaking the screen door. Common sense said he would deny doing any such thing.

Troy, Kai, Olivia and Mrs. Tinderbeck settled down in the kitchen to discuss the disparate pieces of the story. Olivia made a big pot of matcha latte and pulled out the package of stroopwaffels she had picked up on a whim. Kai and Troy had never eaten such things before, and their reaction to the cookie confection provided a light moment. It didn't last long enough.

Lyndsy's office door was open, and Olivia verified all four of her computers were there. Why had she come back to the house, when she was safe at Patty and Pastor Roy's house?

At nearly 11, Lisa stopped by the house, as promised. She had gone up to the police station to meet Bill and help Phoebe, with the intent of getting her out and bringing her home. The booking had processed faster than anyone expected. Phoebe had been officially charged. She would spend the night in jail, because there was no judge available to agree to bail. They had to wait until morning, when Phoebe would stand before one of the judges who handled Cadburn Township's cases. Bill promised he would start pulling strings and calling in favors, to make sure Phoebe stood before a judge who was not only reasonable, but despised Captain Beakman.

"Yes, Beakman got the video framing Lyndsy for Steve Edison's murder," Lisa said, after she had been served a mug of matcha. The stroopwaffels were already gone. She took a deep breath, then a long drink of matcha. "Anyway, Bill is about as excited as I've ever seen him, and I've been working for him going on fifteen years now. This is finally our chance to get rid of Beakman. This is the capper for all the complaints and investigations, the trigger for the avalanche that will finally sweep him away. If we're lucky, and the evidence holds up, we can blunt Lord Roger's power, so he can't put someone just as bad in his place."

"That's all fine and good, and the answer to years of prayers," Mrs. Tinderbeck said, "but what about Phoebe? She has to spend the night in jail."

"Don't worry. Brenda is on duty. She'll make sure Phoebe is comfortable and keep Beakman's yes-men from harassing her." Lisa nodded for punctuation. "She'll be fine."

"So that just leaves us with the question of where did Lyndsy go and what did she find out?" Olivia said.

"I admire her for wanting to help Steve, but she should have asked for help," Mrs. Tinderbeck said.

"From what you've told me about her," Lisa said, "it sounds like she wasn't used to getting help from anyone. If you feel like you're on your own, you can't trust anyone, that's a hard habit, a hard mindset to break."

Olivia didn't even try to go to bed after the others left. It wasn't that she felt uncomfortable or unsafe. Troy and Kai had made sure the house was locked up tight and had searched it. Troy had even gone up to the attic, because he made a remark about all the boxes and old furniture stored up there, and how much room there was. Olivia just didn't want to go to bed and miss Lyndsy coming back to the house.

She settled in the living room for a *How to Train Your Dragon* marathon and didn't start feeling sleepy until the big fight scene with the dragon hunters who controlled the Light Fury.

Lyndsy never came back to the house. She never answered the calls from Olivia and Mrs. Tinderbeck and Patty.

Thursday, June 20

Still no calls from Lyndsy that morning. Olivia was grateful that Kai had told her to take the day off, to be ready to go with Bill Worter when he went to court to get the charges against Phoebe dropped.

She missed the moment when Bill and the lawyer for Cadburn Township stepped up to the bench to present their arguments to the judge. Olivia's phone rang and she stepped out of the courtroom before she even looked at caller I.D.

Mrs. Tinderbeck called to report that she had asked if anyone had seen Lyndsy. No one had, but the town was abuzz over the knock-down, drag-out fight in the township park the night before between Myron Ellsworth and Josiah Crandall. Crandall was in the hospital, under observation, after Ellsworth had clobbered him across the back of the head with a tire iron. Ellsworth had gone into his martyr act, insisting he was suffering for preserving the history and integrity of Cadburn Township. Edna Peabarker-Barnes had already called an emergency meeting of her historical society and had drummed Crandall out of the society, vilifying him for attacking Ellsworth. Neither man wanted to talk about the incident.

Other than that ruckus, and the rumors that Captain Beakman's head was already on the chopping block, everything was quiet.

Olivia stepped back into the courtroom to see Phoebe hugging Bill. The township's lawyer wore a relieved grin as he walked over, holding out his hand to shake hers.

"Thanks, God," Olivia whispered. "Now, if You could just get Lyndsy back safe and sound, everything will be perfect."

Saturday, June 22

"Hey, Olivia." Mike spoke in a lowered voice and leaned halfway across the counter.

The lunchtime rush had slowed down, so there were no customers for the moment. Olivia paused in picking up the bus pan full of dirty mugs and plates and utensils to haul back to the kitchen.

"Something I can help you with?" She wanted to tell him to go away.

"Did Lyndsy call you yet?" He offered a crooked smile and couldn't meet her gaze. Did he feel embarrassed or scared? Olivia told herself she should ask Phoebe for some pointers in reading people.

"No. Why?"

Why was he concerned? Phoebe had called the Spirits of '62, to ask for their help in tracking down Lyndsy. Mike had to know she was missing, so why was he asking if Olivia had heard from her?

"She said she would. I only have a couple hours free between my jobs." He drummed on the edge of the counter.

"What do you mean, she said she would?" Olivia put down the bus pan and stepped back over to face him. "Have you heard from her?"

"Yeah. She's been hiding out with Macy. Those creeps came after her and …" Mike raked one hand through his hair. "It's bad, but not as bad as it could have been."

"Uh, considering she's wanted by the police for Steve Edison's murder," Olivia snapped back, barely remembering in time to keep her voice down, "yeah, it's about as bad as it can get."

"What? Who said Steve was murdered?" His voice cracked. He leaned closer and lowered his voice more. "She didn't say anything about that. She said she was being blackmailed, but not … oh, man, no wonder she's getting out of here."

"What do you mean, getting out of here?" She hated this feeling of being two steps behind and totally clueless.

"Lyndsy was supposed to call you, to let me get her stuff. She's running home to hide. Scared, y'know?"

"Uh, yeah, I can understand that."

"If she hasn't called you yet ..." Mike shook his head, looking around like he was afraid someone could overhear them. "Maybe I should get back to Macy's and make sure they're okay."

Olivia's phone rang, startling her. Then again, everything lately startled her. She pulled it out of her pocket and caught her breath when she saw the caller I.D. She turned it around so Mike could see and he grinned, letting out a long, gusting sigh.

Lyndsy.

"Hey, where are you? Are you okay?" Olivia demanded.

"No, I'm not okay. This is just too much. I'm running home. Can you give my stuff to Mike? He should be stopping by when he gets off work." Lyndsy's voice crackled and the phone signal wavered a few times, like there was some kind of interference. She let out a laugh that struck Olivia as too high-pitched. Then again, after all the scares Lyndsy had had, who would expect her to sound normal?

"He's here right now," Olivia said.

"Can you take him back to the house and give him my stuff?"

"I'm on duty. I don't get off until four."

"Aw, come on! Please? I want out of here as fast as I can."

Olivia had never thought Lyndsy would be a whiner. Maybe stress brought out people's true natures?

"Phoebe is home. I guess she can let Mike in. You know, they arrested her when they couldn't find you."

"What? Why would—why arrest me?"

"The blackmailers turned the video over to the cops."

Olivia flinched as Lyndsy ripped out a half-dozen curses. That cold feeling settled heavy in her stomach. What was going on here? Lyndsy had never talked like that before. She could almost make herself believe that was someone else on the phone, pretending to be Lyndsy.

"That's it. I'm out of here. Nobody is arresting me for something I didn't do. Please, can you call Phoebe and tell her to give my stuff to Mike? Please? Be a pal?"

"Yeah, sure. I'll call her right now."

"Thanks! You're the best."

"Okay. Hey, Lyndsy, take care? Call when you get home? Let me know you got there okay?"

"Sure. You bet."

"Hey, where is--?" Olivia sighed and turned the phone to look at the screen. Lyndsy had hung up.

"So ... is everything okay?" Mike asked.

"Yeah. Fine. Go on over to the house. I'll call Phoebe to let you in."
She waited until Mike was out the door before she did so, though. Then
she hauled the bus pan into the kitchen. Truman returned from cleaning
up after a big lunch group in the back area behind the bookstore, with
another loaded bus pan. When he returned from taking it into the kitchen
and loading the dishwasher, Olivia told him she was taking a break.

She went upstairs and told Eden and Rufus everything that had
happened.

"She didn't say anything about sending her the video, when we get
it peeled?" Rufus said.

"If they're going to charge her with murder, running across state lines
will only make things worse," Eden added. "Give me her number. Maybe
she doesn't understand how serious this is."

"Any progress on seeing what really happened?" Olivia asked, while
Eden made the call.

"Whoever put it together, they're good. They erased a lot of layers of
data that most people don't even know about. There's enough in the way
of glitches, really tiny ones, to prove that the video was tampered with,"
Rufus said, then paused, listening to Eden speak. In just a few seconds, it
was clear she was leaving a voicemail for Lyndsy. "But nothing clear
enough to identify who really was fighting with that guy. I'm not a lawyer,
but until there's a dead body, anybody can argue that he recovered and
got out of the creek and ran for it."

Olivia had thought of that. She added a few more grudges to the list
against Steve Edison. Why did he have to be such a jerk and cut all ties
when he took his new job? The only person who seemed to know that he
was leaving was Lyndsy. Did she know where he was going, and who he
would be working for? They would have to ask her, when she returned
their calls.

~~~~~

Lyndsy never called in to report she had gotten home. She never
returned any of the calls from Mrs. Tinderbeck, Eden, or Bill Worter. Mike
dropped out of the Spirits of '62, after a nasty argument almost splintered
them over a brief battle for the leadership role. Phoebe sadly admitted that
despite his arrogance and perfectionism, Steve at least knew how to lead
and get people to work together.

Olivia and Eden found three of the ten cameras Lyndsy said she had
installed. They put them in storage, to wait until she came back or
contacted them to have them sent to her. Eden agreed that it was strange
that Mike didn't know about Lyndsy's cameras, and didn't ask for them
or look for them. Then again, maybe that proved she didn't trust Mike
enough to trust him with her cameras. The memory in them held two
days' worth of recordings and had rewritten four times since the night
~~~~~

Lyndsy vanished. Even the night Andrew Fendergast had his final breakdown and ran through the creek, shooting his rifle in the air and screaming that his Ghost had come home, was lost. That was all for the best. His relatives didn't need any more evidence to help them have him committed and treated.

Josiah Crandall changed, visibly, once he was released from the hospital. Olivia was used to seeing him strolling around Cadburn looking dapper and neat, if slightly old-fashioned. His hair had always been neatly styled, under a jaunty hat. Sometimes, depending on the weather, Crandall had a cane in one hand. She had always suspected he didn't carry it to help him keep his balance, but to have it handy to whack someone who disagreed with him about Cadburn history and politics.

Now, the Josiah Crandall who sat for hours in Book & Mug, staring into space, looked a good ten years older than he had just two weeks before. His hair was mussed, he had no hat, his sweater hung crooked, and his collar was mashed down on one side. He smiled more, even if it was somewhat sadly, when he ordered his usual pot of tea and chocolate-dipped shortbread cookies. Olivia felt sorry for him even though she was sure that being kicked out of the HIGs was the best thing that could have happened to him.

By the end of the summer, he had swallowed his pride and joined Mrs. Tinderbeck's historical society. Olivia never heard him talking about his passion, proving that the Underground Railroad had operated in Cadburn Township. He listened, in direct proportion to how he used to always lead discussions.

When she commented on the change in him to Mrs. Tinderbeck, her landlady gave her a wistful smile and remarked that some wounds took far longer to heal. Olivia thought about that injury from the tire iron. Could something like that change a personality that drastically?

By October, Josiah Crandall had joined Cadburn Bible Chapel. At Thanksgiving, he took the plunge, literally, getting baptized and joining the church. By the following summer, he stunned the entire township when he revealed a talent for sleight of hand and making balloon animals for Vacation Bible School. Soon, all the children were calling him Uncle Josiah.

Andrew Fendergast's family put his house up for sale, which infuriated Roger Cadburn and Myron Ellsworth. They got into a screaming contest at the next trustee meeting, both insisting that the property should be turned over to them. Ellsworth insisted that Fendergast had promised to put the Cadburn Township Historical Society in his will, to give the property to them. Roger retorted that Fendergast wasn't dead. There was no Cadburn Township Historical Society, and as long as he was head trustee, there never would be. He insisted the house should be turned over to him, as the head of the Cadburn family, as the property had been Cadburn property from the founding of the township.

Fendergast's few remaining relatives ignored Roger and sold the property to a woman named Wilkinson. Ellsworth and Roger mended their friendship over their mutual loathing for her. All the neighbors on Creekbend Court rallied to welcome her and help her stand firm against the expected harassment.

Chapter Eight

The Present
Sunday, October 16

Sometimes heavy rain drove customers into Book & Mug. Sometimes it kept them home, and the coffee shop bookstore was quiet as a tomb. Today was one of the latter days. Olivia leaned her elbows on the counter, studying the gray sheets sleeting down past the big picture windows across the front of the shop. Maybe the difference had to do with when the rain started. Early enough in the morning, only the church-going people stirred from their houses on a Sunday. Late enough in the morning, people were already out and about, running errands, and they needed shelter.

The ventilation system shut off with a muffled thud, just as Bee Wilkinson, at a two-seater table next to the glass block wall of the bookstore side, let out a yelp.

"No, weren't you listening to me?" She looked around, probably startled by how loud her voice seemed now. Her gaze met Olivia's and she rolled her eyes. "I'm coming. Just get them to hold off until I get there, okay?" She got up from the table and snagged her purse from the opposite chair. "I'll email my flight details as soon as I get them." She sighed, closed her eyes, and shook her head. "It's my turn to take care of things. Get over it!" She flinched as her voice rang off the ceiling.

Olivia looked around. Kai and Troy were in the back, trying to figure out why the furnace was making so much noise. Devona was bent over a box of books with earbuds in place, probably listening to an audiobook. The only other customer in the last hour had darted down the sidewalk to his car during a brief lull in the downpour. She had been considering stepping over to catch up with Bee while it was still quiet.

A chuckle escaped Bee. "Yeah, I love you, too. Give the folks a long, hard hug for me. And don't tell them I'm coming until you're leaving for the airport, okay? They'll fret the whole time I'm in the air." She clenched the cell phone between chin and shoulder, managed to sling her coat around her shoulders without dropping it, and mumbled goodbyes to whoever was on the other end. Most likely her twin sister, Delaney.

Sighing, she lifted her head, let the phone drop into her hand, and scooped up her mug to bring to the dish pan at the end of the counter.

"What's wrong with your folks?" Olivia asked.

"Granny Em is sinking, but not nearly as fast as they imagine. They abandoned their tour of the 'great American west,'" she said, making air quotes, "because they're convinced it's all too much for Del to handle. I think them being there is what's too much for her to handle. They're freaking out. Granny was doing fine, nice and calm, obeying the doctors, until Mom and Dad descended on them and started demanding all sorts of tests and…" She set the mug into the bus pan and raked her fingers through her hair. It was still damp from when she came into the Book & Mug nearly two hours ago during the heaviest part of the afternoon's downpour. "I need to go play referee. The thing is …" She glanced out at the gray weather. "I've got somebody coming by Tuesday to check out the roof, and the guy doing the yearly check on the furnace, and if I cancel, at least one of them won't be able to reschedule until the middle of the winter, and a fat lot of good that'll do me then, right?"

"Right."

"What's that grin for?"

"I was starting to think how nice it was that I don't own my place, but when you think about it, Mrs. T kind of treats me and Phoebe like her managers. We had our pre-winter furnace check last week."

"Don't brag." Bee wrinkled up her nose at Olivia and started backing away. "I have to get home and find some plane tickets. I sure hope all those discount sites are telling the truth, and you can get something at the last minute without selling your soul." She reached backward blindly for the door, then a thoughtful look softened the worry lines around her mouth and eyes. "Hey, you and Phoebe are roommates. So it's not like your house would be empty … Would you mind house-sitting? I can give the contractors a call and maybe they'd be flexible enough to work around your schedule, instead of me having to cancel and totally reschedule. Would you mind?"

"Sure. No problem." Olivia squelched a chuckle at the thought that Pastor Roy's sermon this morning must have hit home harder than she thought. He had talked about the Good Samaritan and being ready to go the extra mile, and how ironic it was that people were willing to make sacrifices for strangers but not stop to help their neighbor whose lawn was overgrown or whose puppy was running away.

Bee was her friend, after all. And anyway, she loved the historic old house on the creek that Bee had bought three years ago, just after Old Man Fendergast blew his last circuit. Staying there would be no hardship at all.

She remembered the most important reason to help after Bee hugged her and hurried out the door, muttering about the cost of plane tickets. Phoebe had just gotten cast as Katarina in the local community theater production of *Taming of the Shrew*. She would be snarling and spewing Elizabethan taunts for the next three weeks. If Olivia could escape that without paying a hotel bill, she was all for it.

Monday, October 17

Olivia had the afternoon shift at Book & Mug, which worked out perfectly to stop by Bee's house in the morning and do a walk-through. Bee was so organized, Olivia didn't take long to go through the safety checks, the security alarm system, and a long list of phone numbers and emails and names of who to contact for what emergency, and who to ignore if they called or stopped by and claimed Bee had ordered something or wanted to come take a tour of the house.

"Seriously? People think the house is open for tours?" Olivia blurted, as Bee led her back from the butler's pantry where the controls for the alarm system were neatly tucked away.

"Not tourist tours. Inspection tours. There's been a fight for years about designating this house as a historic site or a heritage site or something like that. That's probably what drove the previous owner off the deep end. The worst one is that nasty little weasel, Ellsworth. Every couple months, he insists the house was promised to his historical society. Like he expects me to just hand him the keys? His loyal followers are almost as bad. They keep trying to dictate what color I paint the walls or what flowers I'm going to put in the garden."

Bee sighed and sank down onto the cushioned bench that filled the curve of the kitchen bay window looking out over the slope down to Cadburn Creek. The waters still churned like lumpy chocolate milk after yesterday's day-long downpour.

Olivia remembered the uproar over that bay window. That was Bee's introduction to the ongoing feud between the two historical societies in Cadburn Township. Less than a month after she bought the house with her inheritance from her Grandpa Ben, a tree had come down in a storm. It had broken the bay window, and the contractor Bee hired to make the repairs was a supporter of the HIGs, as Kai had nicknamed them. He reported the window to Edna Peabarker-Barnes, the head of the society at that time. Edna was enraged over Bee having the "audacity" and the "gall" to make changes to a historical building without her permission. Her campaign to vilify Bee and force her to restore the back of the house to its "historical splendor" resulted in her letters to the editor being banned from four community papers.

The HIFs had come to Bee's rescue. Half an hour in the township records room unearthed the building department's permit to change the entire back side of the house, dated two years before, while Fendergast owned it. Despite that, Edna made a point of confronting Bee in public, at the top of her lungs, calling her a filthy, arrogant liar. She insisted "dear, supportive Andrew would never have done anything to that lovely monument to the history of Cadburn without consulting us." She also threatened to sue the local papers that printed a copy of the permit, insisting they were "perpetuating" a fraud. When a high school teacher corrected her, that the word she wanted was "perpetrating," not "perpetuating," Edna whacked him with her umbrella. The next day, Edna attacked Bee's car with her cane, right in front of the newly installed Captain Sunderson. Edna's family forced her to move to Arizona. Myron Ellsworth took up the reins of the HIGs.

"That reminds me," Bee said, after she and Olivia had laughed over their memories of the whole ridiculous episode. She got up and went over to the little desk tucked into a nook between the kitchen and TV room. "If something happens and you need to make any repairs, heaven forbid, there are about a dozen people you are not, on pain of death, to call for help." She pulled open a drawer and rummaged through papers. "I must have thrown out the last—hah! Here it is." She pulled a neon orange sheet of paper from the bottom of the drawer and offered it to Olivia with a flourish.

"That's Ellsworth's list from last spring," Olivia said. "You actually hold onto that Nazi's orders?"

"It helps me keep track of who is never to step foot on this property, no matter how many discounts they offer, how many specials they promise to give. Anyone he approves is a spy for the enemy."

"Then why are you grinning like that?" Olivia had to ask.

"We have a betting pool on what horrendous color he'll use next."

"Who is 'we'?"

"Oh, everyone on this street, and a handful of people on Shallows Drive whose property slopes down to the creek. They had to band together to protect themselves when there was some flooding four or five years ago, to fight the insurance people. When I bought the place, I was invited to join. Kind of like an HOA, but we don't have dues or officers. We just share information and gripe a lot at picnics. Remind me to invite you to the next one. It's like a block party, going from one lawn to another, down along the creek."

"Sounds like fun. Does it make up for the hassle?"

Bee thought for a moment, then shrugged. She handed the list to Olivia, then reached out and hugged her. "Thanks. You can't imagine how much I appreciate this."

"Hey, what are friends for? Besides, Phoebe is starting to work on her lines for her next performance, so who knows? I might have been begging you to let me stay here with you!"

Tuesday, October 18

Olivia moved in that morning, timing her arrival and the unloading of her car so the neighbors on either side and across the street got a good look at her. Bee said she had told most of her neighbors that she was going out of town and Olivia would be house-sitting. The last thing Olivia needed was for someone to call the police and report she had broken into Bee's house.

A light misting of rain started up between her first trip, carrying a suitcase and her computer, and her second trip with groceries. Only the special things she couldn't live without, and which she knew weren't in the house already. Bee had told her to feel free to use everything and anything in the refrigerator, freezer and pantry. Especially since she couldn't be sure when she would be home. It could be two weeks, it could be a month. It all depended on how long it took for Granny Em to either stabilize or finally let go. Olivia didn't know whether she should envy Bee's legal research job she could do over the Internet, or feel sorry for her. She never really got a vacation, and she had to pay for her own health and life insurance.

The rain started to clear up by the time she came out for two bags of books. Olivia was taking two online classes in literature. Some of her classmates, whom she only knew through the social page for the university and their online classes, complained about the cost of the books they had to buy. None of them minded the reading. They wouldn't be literature majors if they didn't like reading, after all. Olivia smiled at the weight of her books and again blessed Devona, who knew where to hunt to find all the books she needed for her studies at sometimes only a tenth of their like-new price. And she said a prayer of thanks for Kai, for being a boss who loved books and offered to have Devona find those books for her, before Olivia could even think to ask.

She got settled in the guest room, then took a walk-through of the house to make sure everything was locked up tight and no leaks had developed in the ceiling or walls since Bee walked out the door. Then she spent a good ten minutes watching the creek from the bay window. She couldn't tell if the water was any higher, though it certainly looked rougher, thanks to the brief but heavy downpour. She mentally marked the dark gray pillar of stones at the edge of the creek, the last remnants of the flood wall. How many years had it been since the big fuss over taking down that wall? That pillar would be her measuring rod for conditions in the creek. Maybe she would talk to some of the neighbors too, if it kept raining, and get advice from them. Certainly, making the first move to contact them would make them feel more comfortable about her living in

Bee's house. At least, that was the theory.

"Sounds like good sense to me," Eden said a couple hours later.

Eden and Rufus had declared a break from their internet research for a new client and came down to taste test Kai's latest decadent frozen coffee experiment. Olivia had asked Rufus to check his weather app, which tied into more satellites and weather websites and organizations than she could access with the app on her phone. Traffic inside the coffee shop had been slow, perhaps because people were taking advantage of the break in the weather and were getting things done before another drencher struck. This allowed for large blocks of uninterrupted conversation. They chatted for a while about just how reliable even the best satellite tracking programs were, and whether forecasting the weather could be considered a science or something that stopped just short of magic.

Kai got a call from a supplier with truck problems, unable to restock some items in time, so he had to run out to the nearest wholesale club to get supplies to fill in. That interruption shifted the conversation to the condition of Cadburn Creek, the chances of flooding, and Olivia house-sitting. She shared her thoughts about making things secure with the neighbors, and ensuring they knew what was going on at Bee's house.

"Then again," Eden continued, "I've read too many serial killer books where the nicest, most outgoing guy ends up being the psycho. There's a reason modern society is so isolated and does most of its socializing on the Internet instead of face-to-face."

"Grump," Rufus muttered, then winked at Olivia.

"Please don't bring up murders while I'm still getting settled in," Olivia said, holding up her hands. "I've never stayed overnight at Bee's place, so I have no idea what sounds are normal at night. Plus, I still have memories of all the creepy sounds that came across the creek when Old Man Fendergast lived there."

"Oops, sorry." Eden didn't look half as repentant as Olivia thought she should.

"I wouldn't worry too much," Rufus said, and grabbed his wheels to tip back and pivot, clearly aiming to head back to the elevator and upstairs. "We're averaging about one murder a month, and we've had this month's murder. You're safe until November."

"Not comforting at all." Olivia balled up a wet napkin and flung it at him, hitting him in the middle of his forehead.

"Ugh." Eden scooped up their used mugs and slid them down the counter to the bus pan. "I really am sorry, Olivia. Didn't think about that."

"Why should you? This place has been nice and quiet and almost Mayberry for so long. Well, not long enough, in my opinion. I mean, we did have that big mess with Captain Beakman, and all the ugliness with the county over those hunters who claimed they weren't on private property when they shot those horses they thought were deer. Never saw people get so political when they realized that the county has authority over things like hunting and zoning, and we don't have any say. That settled down quickly enough."

"Especially when they realized they couldn't budge certain trustees?" Eden sighed and rubbed her eyes with the heels of her hands. "Why do I have the feeling that all the political rumblings over the upcoming special election aren't going to settle down for a long while?"

"How long have you lived in Cadburn?" She grinned, and Eden nodded, waved farewell, and followed Rufus back up to the office.

Thursday, October 20

A heavy downpour overnight gave way to a surprisingly bright morning. Olivia wondered if she slept as well as she did because the drumming of the rain on the windows muffled all the other unfamiliar sounds in Bee's house. She walked out to the edge of the creek with her bagel and stood a good ten feet back from the water's edge, watching it churn and race past. The creek had always fascinated her when she lived on the other side, twenty feet higher. Being so close to the water was mesmerizing. The idea of sitting for a while and just watching it appealed to her. She had plenty of time until she had to head in to work. Why not pull out a chair from that little storage shed tucked against the back of the house, and sit here on the flagstone pavers leading down to the creek? She would let the sights and sounds of rushing water and sunshine through the fall leaves soothe her, in preparation for what would probably be a busy day at the coffee shop.

She turned around to go to the storage shed. A splotch of white on the right hand door caught her attention.

"What in the …" A snort escaped her as she got close enough to read the familiar, steeply slanted handwriting on the note attached to the shed door with what had to be packaging tape. The two-inch-wide strips covered most of the note, making it mostly waterproof.

Bee had given her specific instructions for what to do when this happened. Olivia pulled her phone out of her pocket and took a picture of the note. She emailed it to Bee, with the caption, "Right on time. You are a prophet." Then she headed into the house to get the list of instructions.

"Ellsworth is an idiot, signing his name," she muttered. "How many times does he have to be cited for trespassing before he stops?"

Every few months, Myron Ellsworth took tours of all the historical properties in the township and wrote up citations no one took seriously. He demanded the owners return their properties to historical conditions.

When this happened, Bee's neighbors had a tradition now of getting together, either for a picnic or in the party room at Frenchy's, depending on the weather. They wrote letters to the zoning board, the building department, and the local newspapers, pointing out, yet again, his historical society had no authority to impose any standards on the property owners in Cadburn Township.

They then filed another complaint of trespassing against Myron Ellsworth. Amos Green was the current secretary for the neighborhood group, and had multiple versions of the complaint, ready to mail. All they had to do was fill in the date, the URL to the YouTube page with security camera footage of the trespassing, and have all the members sign beside their printed names. Those complaints were then added to a growing file in Captain Sunderson's office. Copies were sent to Worter, Worter & McIntosh, who agreed to represent the homeowners, *pro bono*. They also went to Ellsworth's longsuffering lawyer, who was unlucky enough to be a relative and guilt-tripped into representing him.

Olivia wondered just how much more cranky he would be when he came into Book & Mug this week. Roger Cadburn wasn't around to support him against the ire of the other trustees and the homeowners.

A text popped up on her phone. Bee reminded her to send a copy of the note to Brenda Dodge at the Cadburn Police Department. She did that next.

> *Hey, Brenda —*
> *I'm housesitting for Deborah Wilkinson on Creekbend. She's out of town on family business for a few weeks. Attached is the latest threat note from Myron Ellsworth, taped to her storage shed. Let me know if you need the original. Bring you your usual frappe when I come in?*
> *Olivia Tucker*

Her phone rang just before she tapped the button to send the email. Olivia winced when she saw Truman's name. Kelli had been sniffling yesterday, and she just didn't look good when she left the Mug to head out for her college classes. She claimed it was just allergies, the surge of mold in the air after all the rain, but Olivia had heard her talking with some friends the day before about letting her boyfriend and his "idiotic but totally awesome" buddies talk her into taking a rubber raft down the west branch of Rocky River while the water was high. They had overturned four times, getting totally soaked, then it had rained for the last half hour of the river trip. They were all muddy and chilled. There was no telling what sort of filth was in the water from storm sewers and runoff from lawns full of chemicals as people winterized their yards. The girl probably had a bad cold. Was there such a thing as a good cold?

"Hey, Truman. Kelli out?"

Fifteen minutes later, Olivia was heading down the street, to clock in two hours early. She could almost wish the rain from last night had continued into the morning, just to slow down the traffic that Truman cheerfully informed her was "getting kind of crazy."

Naturally, the "crazy" rush slowed within half an hour of Olivia arriving. There were still dishes to put through the dishwasher and stations to refill and more than the usual amount of spillage and dirty floors to mop up. The sidewalks from the municipal parking lot to Book & Mug had been mostly dry, so where had all the mud come from?

"College kids doing botany surveys, down along the creek," Kai said, when Olivia came into the back room to dump the mop bucket and voiced her thoughts. "Here, let me get that. Thanks for coming in on short notice." He hurried over to take the bucket from her before she could lift it out of the frame of the three-wheel trolly it rode in. "I hear Phoebe got the starring role in *Shrew*." He grinned. "My condolences. Eden says you can camp with her when it gets too Shakespearian for you."

"Thanks." She watched him dump the dirty water out. It looked like particularly poisonous chocolate milk, with far too much debris in it. "But I'm good. Bee Wilkinson is out of town and I'm housesitting. You should see the latest renovations. Her reading room is to die for."

"In what way?" He grinned and dropped the bucket back into the trolley. "Like, is there a hidden passageway with a body hiding in it?"

"Oh, don't even get me started ..." Olivia shivered, not entirely in jest. She remembered what Eden had said the other day, and Rufus's attempt at dark humor, talking about one murder every month. "No, it's really great. One huge cushion to lie down and read all day, right next to the window, with a gorgeous view of the creek. At least, it'd be gorgeous if I wasn't worried about flooding. I can't remember the water getting this high in years."

When they came out of the back room, Kai called out to several regulars, asking about the worst flooding in their memories. Several people brought up stories from their grandparents' days. Olivia found some amusement in Doug Parker's observation that incredible stories were always more incredible, and disasters were always bigger in their grandparents' days. They chatted around the order counter for nearly an hour. Naturally, when the talk turned really interesting, bringing up stories from the flood of '46, the Grannies and Geezers bowling league poured into the shop. Olivia still found it amusing to see that name embroidered on their neon pink and blue bowling shirts.

She nearly messed up three different orders from trying to listen to the argument over some tunnels that had been revealed when Cadburn Creek overflowed that year. People living along the south bank, further east down the creek from Bee's house, had water suddenly pouring into their cellars.

In one house, the force of the water pushed open a panel that had been covered by boards and then bricks. When the water went down, the repairmen found a tunnel leading from a cave around the bend in the creek where the landscape dropped again. The bricks on the inside of the house were dated to the 1920s, but the bricks on the other side of the wood panel were tentatively dated to the late 1800s. They had disintegrated with age and theorized regular flooding that got into the tunnel. Impressions in the bricks might have identified who made them, but they were too eroded. Local historians speculated that the tunnels proved the stories of Cadburn Township being a station on the Underground Railroad. Evidence of recent repairs, meaning around the turn of the last century, contradicted what they considered evidence. Further investigation never occurred, to settle the question.

Olivia shivered a little and tried to tune out the brief detour into discussing Josiah Crandall's former obsession with finding Underground Railroad tunnels. He had dropped all his research after that trouble three years ago between Mike Kioto, Steve Edison, and Lindsey Auretta. While some results had been good, including Crandall quitting the HIGs and becoming Uncle Josiah and Captain Beakman getting booted from the Cadburn Police, there were still emotional scars. What really happened to Steve Edison? There was no body. Had Lyndsy really been involved, and where had she gone when she ran away?

Olivia was grateful when a clump of customers came in and serving them gave her a chance to break free of those memories.

Discussion of the tunnels and flood damage and the history of Cadburn Township continued, even when the original participants moved on, to errands or jobs. Saundra Bailey came in at lunch, just in time to get drawn into a friendly argument over which houses in Cadburn were old enough to have been Underground Railroad station houses. She made the mistake of expressing interest. Before Olivia could warn her, Saundra volunteered to do some research into the construction permits and archives of the township that were stored in the library.

Chapter Nine

Friday, October 21

Saundra knew Mrs. Tinderbeck had a passion for Cadburn Township history, but she didn't know about all the ins and outs and feuds until she went to her supervisor for guidance on her research. Part of the reason for the TPC closet, accessible only by permission of Mrs. Tinderbeck—TPC standing for Tinderbeck Private Collection—was because of the depredations and utter thoughtlessness of some self-proclaimed historical experts in the township. Some were obsessed to the point of vandalism, to keep historical records out of the hands of their rivals.

Saundra had learned in the discussion at Book & Mug that Josiah Crandall, a member of their church, had once been diligently researching rumors of Underground Railroad tunnels out to the creek. Mrs. Tinderbeck asked her not to involve him. Several unpleasant incidents a few years ago had resulted in him giving up his research. But she could ask Crandall about anything else having to do with Cadburn Township history, and he would be delighted to help her.

Mrs. Tinderbeck suggested Saundra talk to Phoebe McCoy, to introduce her to the Spirits of '62, a local reenactors group that focused on the Civil War. Most were history students, though none were as devoted to all things Civil War in Cadburn Township history as they had been several years ago.

"You should have been here when the Spirits nearly burst into flames," Mrs. Tinderbeck said, as she and Saundra talked over their first cups of coffee of the day in the library kitchen, while everything was still quiet. "Their leader at that time, Steve Edison, was a stickler for the details. He gave Josiah Crandall a run for his money over who had a bigger pole up his backside. And right out the top of their pointed little heads," she added on a whisper.

Saundra nearly giggled coffee out her nose.

"Rather, the man Josiah used to be." Mrs. Tinderbeck's sparkle of mischief faded. "He's … softened, a great deal since then. There's a sorrow he can't seem to give up to God. But what was I about to say? Oh, yes, stickler for accuracy. A group of students from Case wanted to join them in an upcoming reenactment of some historic battle down in Kentucky, I believe." She paused, frowning, and narrowed her eyes. As if she was either reading the story or seeing the event playing out. "Well, they couldn't just come in blue jeans and sweatshirts and hiking boots, they had to have costumes. They showed up for a meeting right here in the library with costumes they got from the theater department at Tri-C. Not authentic enough for Mr. Edison. He lectured them up and down the walls until I had to step out and ask him to lower his volume. This one's shirt was the wrong style and era, that one's belt was synthetic, on and on.

"Well, Lyndsy had had enough by then." Mrs. Tinderbeck paused and shook her head. "Funny, how I remember her name, but not the rest of them. Well, she was the only girl among those students, and she rented rooms from me for a very short time. In the same house where Olivia and Phoebe live, actually. Lyndsy got in his face and let him know in so many words that the entire reason they were putting up with him and his anal-retentive pinheads—don't you love how she summed him up?—was because they *wanted* to get all those details right. If they already knew those details, they wouldn't ask him, would they? Now, was he going to support the pursuit of historical accuracy, or be a bureaucrat?" She ended with a chuckle and picked up her coffee cup to sip.

"So what happened? Did he let them participate?"

"Well ... yes and no. This is all hearsay from that point, but Steve gave them the names of several people who could make accurate costumes for them in a hurry. The word is he sabotaged Lyndsy by giving her the name of a costumer he had banned the year before. She used synthetic material, instead of sticking to historically accurate, all-natural materials. Polyester is so much lighter and more comfortable for maneuvers in the summer heat than wool, after all. When the students showed up for the reenactment at 4am, because the historic battle started at sunrise, Steve put them through a thorough inspection. When he got to Lyndsy, he proclaimed her disqualified *before* he found the label the costumer had put in the collar. They got into an argument that ended with him banning her from all activities with the Spirits. She essentially thumbed her nose at him and trailed along behind the action, watching everything, taking notes, taking pictures.

"Then to rub Steve's nose in it, she got an A for her extra credit project with all the material she gathered that day. Well, the group was excited to hear that they had featured prominently in her work. They wanted to see the video she made, and she told them no, sorry, they shouldn't fraternize with the enemy." Mrs. Tinderbeck snickered and raised her cup in the air for a salute to the clever student. Then her gaze turned distant. "Then there was that ugly mess... Huh, why didn't I think of that before?"

"What?"

"Lyndsy was searching for station houses here in Cadburn. I know she and Steve and, yes, that's right, that unpleasant Mike somebody were all trying to cozy up to Josiah to get access to his research and his support. I suggest you try to contact her, maybe even Mike. See what they might have found out. Start with Olivia and Phoebe. They tried to be her friends, and Phoebe knew Mike when he participated in the Spirits."

Then Mrs. Tinderbeck gave her the names of several members of the HIF group who specialized in Civil War era history in Cadburn. She recommended Saundra check with the registrar at Case Western Reserve, where Lyndsy had been a student, to see if they would give her any contact information, any idea where the young woman had gone when she left Cadburn so abruptly. She feared that Lyndsy hadn't kept in contact with Olivia and Phoebe. She had been concerned about her former tenant, and the two roommates would have told her if they had any news.

Saturday, October 22

Saundra had that Saturday off work. She planned on a leisurely morning, doing some web surfing and trying to track down Lyndsy and Steve. Sometimes studying two sides of an argument revealed information neither side knew they had. Just before noon, she would head over to the soon-to-open Brighten Your Corner candle shop to check on Cilla and Melba Tweed. The last few days had been so stressful for the two elderly cousins.

The registrar at Case had already responded that they could not release information on former students, other than to confirm they had been students. Phyllis Galloway, a member of Mrs. Tinderbeck's historical society, emailed her. They were meeting at the library that morning. If Saundra wasn't working today, she could stop by after the meeting to pick up the information she had dug out so far. If Saundra couldn't meet her, she would look for her at church.

When Saundra got to the library, Phyllis was waiting by the front door, chatting with several departing members. She gave her a heavy-duty cotton grocery bag full of old books and topographical maps and scrapbooks full of newspaper and magazine articles. Saundra swore the bag was larger and heavier than the ones she received from the warring factions of the Welcome Wagon when she arrived in Cadburn. Phyllis apologized for not weeding out the useful information, but she had to leave immediately. Her niece, Sheri, was in labor. Phyllis needed to dash home and pack and get on the highway. Saundra thanked her, wished her safe travels, when a dark green VW bug careened into the parking lot.

"Oh, good, you're still here!" a creaky tenor voice called, nearly drowned out by the squealing of tires.

"Amos Green," Phyllis said, grinning at the driver. "I mentioned what you were researching and asked the group to be ready to offer help while I'm out of town with Sheri."

"Thanks." Saundra wondered if Phyllis had really done her a favor, as the VW squealed up to park across the back of her car.

The elderly man who hopped out made her think "gnome" immediately. His shiny bald head and protruding ears were just made to be capped by a tall, cone-shaped hat. He chuckled and waved a small, glossy scrapbook with Teenage Mutant Ninja Turtles on the cover.

"I knew this would come in handy someday." He executed some sort of skipping dance step before bowing grandly and holding the scrapbook out to Phyllis. Then two seconds later, shifted and held it out to Saundra. "To be honest, I started gathering the articles to wave in that old blowhard's face, but then it got to be just plain fun for the story itself. Here." He straightened, and before Saundra could reach for the scrapbook, flipped it open toward the back, to several neatly taped, yellowed clippings.

The picture that came with the newspaper article caught Saundra's attention. The photos were black-and-white, but the costumes worn by the couple in the photo certainly looked like Civil War blue Union uniforms. The young man glared at the camera and his mouth was open. Saundra could almost hear him yelling, telling the photographer to go away. The young woman, on the other hand, grinned like she was having a good time causing trouble. She had her hands on her hips and her head tipped to the right, letting a long, complicated braid fall down, revealing a number of small balls decorating it. Some glossy-looking patches on them hinted they were either plastic or glass.

"That certainly isn't historically accurate. The hair bobbles," she added, before either Phyllis or Amos could ask.

"They weren't. Served that young snot right, flinging his rules in his face. If he wouldn't let her come play, why did she have to play by his rules? Am I right?" Amos chuckled. He tipped the scrapbook up, so the folded piece of the article fell down, revealing the headline.

"Cadburn Ghost?" Saundra barely noticed the shiver that ran through her.

"Oh, that's right." Phyllis chuckled now. "Why didn't I connect the names before? You were asking about Lyndsy Auretta? That's her." She wiggled her fingers at the girl in the photo. "She took to hanging around the perimeter whenever the Spirits went on their maneuvers in the Metroparks and along the creek, always in uniform, to irritate that Edison boy. People got spooked when they saw her late in the evening, coming up the bank or crossing a meadow with the mist starting to rise. Started some folks talking about the ghost of the Cadburn girl who went to war and never came home. Then poor old Andrew Fendergast went off on one of his tangents. He was never quite right after he fell off the sweetheart bridge over the creek, always obsessing about bringing Annabelle Cadburn home to rest. I remember now. Lyndsy was cozying up with Josiah Crandall. Both of them were obsessed with finding those Underground Railroad tunnels, from what I heard. He was easier to get along with, having someone look up to him and believe his stories. When he wasn't arguing fit to spit tacks with that idiot, Myron Ellsworth. Oh, he hated Lyndsy. Claimed she had no respect for her betters."

Amos chuckled. No, it was more like a cackle. Full of mischief that made him seem twenty years younger. "I coulda kissed that gal, the way she knew just how to push his buttons. She got permission from most of the folks living along the creek to search the banks for clues. I remember how she was always wearing that Rebel cap, just to hassle that Edison boy. She always stopped to talk, if I was in my back yard working. Smart girl. She didn't deserve whatever happened to make her up and vanish like she did."

His phone rang and he startled, nearly dropping the scrapbook. He handed it to Saundra and pulled out a cell phone in a violent purple case. Phyllis hurried to explain that Amos had kept a scrapbook of all the newspaper stories and police reports that related to the "red flag of the day" issues, starting when Josiah Crandall was head of the HIGs, then when Edna Peabarker-Barnes took over, and now with Myron Ellsworth in charge. Every published trustee meeting report, where he demanded something and got put in his place. Every story in the newspaper that proved him wrong, or when some action he demanded for historical preservation reasons was defeated, and every story that contradicted what he insisted was historically accurate.

Saundra knew Josiah Crandall from church. He was always surrounded by children, calling out to "Uncle Josiah" to tell him something, or show him something, or demand a treat from him. She had seen Crandall in action, and estimated he kept at least a pound of wrapped candy on hand at all times, always showering it on the children. She wondered what he had been like when he belonged to the HIGs, who certainly sounded nasty and self-righteous, and what had brought about the change.

"Sorry, sorry, I've got to run. My turn to get the barbecue for the meeting. Myron's at it again, inspecting and trespassing." Amos chuckled. "We've got bets going that this time, he gets slapped with a couple restraining orders. But anyway, will that help?"

"Oh, it should help enormously, thank you," Saundra hurried to say.

He chuckled and dove back into his VW, which he had left running the entire time. Phyllis asked her to keep in mind that most of the time, both historical societies were nice, friendly, considerate people. Most of the time. She asked Saundra to take the stories in the scrapbook with a grain of salt.

"Although, when Myron is involved … better make it a tablespoon of salt," she added with a chuckle, and finally unlocked her car door.

Saundra thanked her again and slid the scrapbook into the cotton bag as Phyllis pulled out of the parking lot. She and Amos had so much energy, they made Saundra feel tired, and they both had to be older than her Aunt Cleo.

Her phone rang as she turned to walk the three spaces over to her car. The Pink Panther theme meant it was Nick West calling. She had changed that to his ring tone just a few days ago, more to make Kai laugh than to irritate Nick. For once. While she considered Nick something of a big brother, he tended toward an irritating, know-it-all kind of big brother. It didn't help when he swooped in to rescue her or her friends, with connections or information they couldn't get any other way, and then gloated a little bit. She really did like him, but sometimes she just wanted to slap that smug smile off his stereotypical Mafioso handsome face.

She considered for two seconds letting him go to voicemail. Then she thought about how he had gotten involved in protecting the Tweeds. How quickly he reacted to the alarm he put in their shop, when a trap he and Agent Malcolm of the ATF had set for Ernie Benders' former associates had sprung. There were still unanswered questions surrounding Cilla's irritating, domineering cousin, Charlotte, and just who had been trying to break into their duplex to get at the labyrinth chest. Saundra hurried to unlock her car and unload her arms.

"Please tell me you have good news," she said, as the hastily dropped bag tipped sideways in the back seat.

"Well, it looks like Miss Cilla has a beau. You tell me if that's good news." Laughter threatened in his voice.

"Nick—"

"The skunk got greedy and careless. He's been caught and hauled away."

"Thank you." She let out a long sigh and remembered just in time who Melba had named as a suspect.

Saundra didn't need to ask Nick who had been behind all the trouble her elderly friends had been facing. She ached for them. How much did it hurt, to have proof that a relative, someone who had been at least pretending to look after them, was to blame?

"How are they doing?"

"Well, looks like a celebration party is coming together. Go over there and check for yourself. And give them my regrets and apologies. It was a little close for a minute. Miss Melba is one tough cookie. Nerves of steel."

"Do I even want to know what happened?" She smiled, despite her weary sigh, and slammed the back door of her car for punctuation.

"Have them tell you. I have to oversee processing the skunk. Make sure all the charges get filed and he can't reach his lawyer until it's too late to do anything this weekend."

Saundra chuckled, and was still smiling as she pulled out of the parking lot and headed for Brighten Your Corner.

Even the black clouds that rolled across the sky after lunch, and the downpour that pounded down loud and heavy, couldn't dampen the spirits of everyone who had come to celebrate the opening of the candle shop and the solving of several mysteries.

As the celebration wound down, Cilla mentioned seeing Saundra and Mrs. Tinderbeck deep in conversation the other day at the library, and wanted to know, "What had Lydia frowning like that?" When Saundra told them about the research she was doing, just for fun, that started a chain of reminiscences, different viewpoints of the fuss generated by the reenactors and history students, the dismantling of the flood wall in the creek, and Myron Ellsworth attacking Josiah Crandall. Eden added to Saundra's interest in the events of that summer when she related how she had been asked to take apart a video being used to blackmail Lyndsy Auretta, and how the college student had fled town before the work was finished. Eden and Rufus hadn't been able to identify who had actually been in the video with Steve Edison, but they were certain that Lindsey hadn't been the one attacking him. For all they knew, Steve was playing a nasty trick on her. According to some accounts, she accused him of stealing some of her research.

"If you do track down Lyndsy, let her know I want to talk to her, would you?" Eden said.

Saundra promised, but had her doubts that she would have any success. If Eden, a trained investigator, hadn't been able to track down Lyndsy, what chances did she have, after the trail had gone cold?

That was proven when she checked her email that evening. Phoebe had sent out a general email to the Spirits of '62, asking them to contact Saundra. Several had responded with memories and ideas, but no usable information. One of them, Buck Wilcox, added that he had posted the request for information on several historical bulletin boards he belonged to. He apologized, but he had never talked with Lyndsy the entire time she hung around the Spirits of '62, so he had no insights to pass along.

Sunday, October 23

Olivia got drenched walking back to the house after work Saturday night and silently cursed the weather app in her phone that had promised dry skies until Monday. Otherwise, she would have driven to work. She woke up Sunday morning stiff and stuffy, with her head pounding. The gloom and steady drumming of a major downpour didn't help. She pulled the covers over her head and rolled over, intending to try again in fifteen minutes. Her head pounded too much to let her find a comfortable position.

After a good ten minutes searching Bee's bathroom for something to help, she stumbled into the kitchen and found an economy-size bottle of ibuprofen next to the coffeemaker. Olivia managed a smile at the irony. The water-blurred landscape on the other side of the bay window, obscuring the creek, convinced her today was a day to stay home. God would certainly understand better than some people at church.

She downed three pills with a glass of chocolate milk and staggered back to bed. Her phone, still sitting on the nightstand, pinged with a reminder that Phoebe was picking her up for church, as it was her turn to drive this week. Olivia snatched up her phone, dropped it, and twisted a muscle stretching under the bed to retrieve it. She texted her roommate not to come by to pick her up for church. Then she held her breath, waiting for a response or the doorbell ringing. With the rain pounding down, she certainly wouldn't hear Phoebe's car pulling into the driveway.

Phoebe texted back half an hour later to say she had just rolled out of bed, after a rehearsal that turned into a brainstorming session for the all-female Shakespearean troupe she and her friends kept threatening to form. She didn't get home until 3am. She wasn't going to church either.

A few texts later, Olivia somehow found herself responsible for making lunch for the two of them. Phoebe wanted to see the renovations Bee had made since the 4th of July picnic. Olivia slid out of bed and stumbled to the bathroom for a long, hot shower, hoping that would steam some of the congestion out of her head and chest.

Her stomach woke up by the time she was done and demanded a more substantial breakfast than pills and milk. Olivia found several packets of instant oatmeal, added a handful of dried cranberries, brown sugar and water, then popped it in the microwave.

A flicker of movement brought her attention back to the bay window. The rain had slowed down considerably since she had last looked outside. She could see the creek. The water level had risen. That made sense, considering how hard the rain had been pounding yesterday.

More movement brought her closer to the window, just as the microwave pinged. Someone was walking around, poking a stick into the tangle of brambles that partially hid a big pile of bricks and raw stone, sitting in front of a taller pile that ran along the lot line on the east side. Bee said the smaller pile had once been a fireplace, but the previous owner had demolished it and never rebuilt it. She had plans to clear it out, once she finished her interior renovations. Plus, there was the entertainment value of Ellsworth complaining about the "unsightly mess and desecration of a historic landmark" every few months.

Olivia knelt on the window seat and watched the figure, dressed in dark clothes, with a dark ball cap, continue poking around the pile. What was that guy doing back there? Especially on a Sunday morning? Why examine the pile of bricks and stone in the rain? Was that Ellsworth or one of his lackies, looking for evidence for a new complaint campaign?

She checked herself. She wore her blue camouflage print thermal underwear. It could pass for workout clothes. She hoped. At least she was decently covered. She stepped over to the back door, opened it, and grinned when the squeak of the hinges made the trespasser straighten up and stumble away from the rock pile.

"Excuse me? Can I help you with something? You're on private property," she added, and pointed at one of the signs nailed to four trees, evenly spaced, right at the water line.

According to Bee's neighbors, there was always someone every year who believed the creek gave them the right to wander wherever they chose. Even up onto people's patios. The family two doors down on the west had been setting up for a party last summer, and some hikers helped themselves from coolers full of sodas before the homeowner came out and chased them away.

The dark figure hunched over and darted around the end of the ridge of brambles and stone. Olivia stood in the doorway for several minutes, fully expecting him to come back. When the wind picked up and the damp chilled her, she backed into the kitchen and closed the door. She kept watch from the bay window as she stirred up her oatmeal and ate it. The dark figure didn't come back. Then again, he might be sitting under cover of all those brambles, hopefully lying in mud, watching her from cover. She shivered once and wished she hadn't thought of that.

When Phoebe came over, Olivia was still stewing over the brief invasion and had worked herself from fear to irritation. She wanted to do something to frighten away whoever that was. Obviously, the *private property* and *no trespassing* signs Bee already had up weren't working.

"Easy," Phoebe said, as they unpacked the groceries she had picked up on the way over.

Olivia didn't mind being the one to do the cooking when Phoebe did the shopping. She had an instinct for specials and sale prices on good things to eat. It was a miracle they both weren't fifty or sixty pounds overweight, considering all the experimental cooking they did together.

"How easy?" Olivia grinned at the sight of the chocolate peanut butter spread, sitting next to the brownie mix. Phoebe insisted chocolate was a better cure for colds than zinc or herbal teas.

"Franco works at a security business. He handed out a bunch of stickers last night, warning the house or the car or whatever either has an alarm on it or a GPS tracker or a video camera on the premises. He says a lot of his friends don't bother actually getting the equipment. They just put the stickers on their windows and doors and their cars and whatever, and the creeps leave them alone. Put the fear of God in this guy if he comes back, by making him think there's a camera catching every move he makes."

"I don't think a bunch of stickers will do any good if he looks around and can't see a camera."

Phoebe's triumphant, mischievous smile faded. She pouted for a few seconds, then shrugged and finished showing the fruits of her rapid-fire shopping trip. She didn't drop the subject but waited to resume it once their quiche and corn muffins were in the oven.

"Fake cameras. Or just some old ones that don't work anymore. Hang them up. With some wires going back to the house," she hurried to add, stopping Olivia from voicing that objection too.

Olivia had the answer to the next problem: where to find fake cameras, to frighten off the trespasser.

A call to Book & Mug resulted in Rufus and Eden coming over, accompanied by Saundra, with equipment he had slapped together from broken components. Rufus refused to let go of anything that might come in handy. He was always experimenting, trying to build a better security system. Right now, he had four cases, with identifying stickers carefully removed and new ones created on the computer, for nonexistent equipment brands. They were full of blinking lights and a simple, battery-powered mechanism that turned the fake cameras on a pivot at uneven intervals, to simulate activity.

"Gotta hope whoever is sneaking around is the paranoid kind, and he freaks out when he tries to yank the power cords and the cameras don't die." Rufus snickered as he finished assembling the parts that he and Eden had spilled out on the kitchen table.

By this time, Bee had responded to an email Olivia sent her, explaining the trespasser that morning and Phoebe's solution. She texted with a thumbs up emoji and half a dozen varieties of smiley-faces. Then she sent a short email, expressing her thanks and giving her official approval for hanging the fake security cameras in the trees.

Rufus stayed in the house with Olivia. His wheelchair couldn't handle the sopping, muddy back yard, and her cold had settled into a drippy nose and raspy voice. Phoebe, Eden, and Saundra all insisted she shouldn't step outside. She and Rufus watched from the bay window while Phoebe hauled around the ladder taken from the shed behind the house, Saundra carried the plastic milk crate with the fake cameras and wires, and Eden climbed up and fastened them to the trees. The chore took surprisingly little time. Olivia hoped the trespasser was somewhere watching and frustrated to see the security measures being taken.

Or maybe she shouldn't hope that? There were far too many nasty, self-righteous wackos in the world. Some might just take the sight of security cameras as a challenge to trespass further or consider this a violation of their right to go where they pleased. She had read too many diatribes on social media from people who thought privacy was an outmoded, elitist, racist concept, and the only people who insisted on privacy were people who intended harm to everyone around them. Olivia always found it ironic that the people who preached such things wouldn't use their real names.

When the three came in, muddy up to their ankles and fleeing a renewed downpour, Phoebe declared Saundra had given her the best idea for her playwriting class. She toed off her boots, then dashed out of the kitchen in her bare feet.

"Where's she going?" Rufus asked.

"Probably to get her laptop. After a detour to borrow some clothes," Olivia said. "Are you two okay? I swear Bee has five robes hanging on the back of the bathroom door, so you could borrow one while you're drying off. I've got a pot of hot chocolate going, and cookies in the oven."

"Oh, I know. Those smell incredible." Saundra dropped down into a chair and inhaled deeply. "Why don't you bake for the Mug? You'd give Sugarbush a run for their money."

"Ah, no, I wouldn't. That's their recipe for their garbage pail cookies," Olivia said, and stepped over to the oven to open the door just as the timer on the oven flashed down to zero.

"Garbage pail?" She wrinkled up her nose.

"Well, some troublemaker insisted that the kitchen sink cookies Aldi sells is a trademark name. Calling them monster cookies does not even come close." Eden finished peeling off her socks, which had gotten just as soaked as her sneakers. She spread them across the hot air vent in the floor, on the other side of the bath towels Olivia had put next to the door to take their wet shoes.

"Robes? Dry clothes?" Olivia set the two cookie sheets on the stovetop and picked up the ladle to fill the double-size red mugs that went with the red, enameled pot labeled the "hot chocolate cauldron."

Saundra and Eden both assured her they were fine. They used the extra towels to rub the wet out of their hair and insisted that hot chocolate and cookies were more than enough to warm them up again. By that time, Phoebe had returned, wearing the hot pink sweatpants and matching, oversized jersey she had given Olivia for Christmas two years ago. She had a notebook instead of her computer.

They nibbled and sipped. Phoebe scrambled to get down all the ideas that had come to her while they were hanging the fake security cameras. Saundra repeated what the three of them had been discussing out in the rain. She had been telling them about all her research on the Spirits of '62, their activities, and the clashes between the two rival historical societies.

Olivia and Phoebe shared what they could remember of Lyndsy, the few things she had revealed about her family and background, and especially the conflict between her and her former roommate Macy. Olivia wondered again why Lyndsy would turn to Macy and Mike when she was scared enough to leave town. What hadn't she told her new friends?

Talk turned to Phoebe's idea of a play about the Cadburn Ghost, triggered by memories of Lyndsy skulking on the sidelines in her uniform. That led to stories of several encounters people had had, including Phoebe, with Andrew Fendergast, the former owner of this very house, when he was having one of his fits and ran around wailing for Annabelle Cadburn to come home.

Somewhere in the discussion, Phoebe suggested Saundra talk to Patty Hill and Pastor Roy, since Lyndsy had taken shelter with them when things got really tense. Phoebe wanted copies of everything Phyllis had given Saundra, to help with her script idea. By the time Eden, Saundra and Rufus left, Phoebe had retreated with her notebook to the front porch, where she said the renewed drumming of the rain helped her focus. She scribbled away, barely lifting her head to say goodbye.

Olivia left her alone for the rest of the day, only stepping out to wrap a blanket around her or bring her more hot chocolate. When Phoebe packed up to go home, she admitted she couldn't decide if she would make the play an actual ghost story, or a murder mystery where a serial killer dressed people in Civil War costumes, or maybe a psychotic believed he was in love with the missing Cadburn soldier girl and wanted to raise her from the dead.

Olivia was about to suggest Phoebe write all three scripts. Then she thought better of that. The ideas hit too close to real events. Maybe they even mocked Fendergast's pain and delusions. Mrs. Tinderbeck had asked her and Phoebe to pity and pray for him, after all.

She told Phoebe so. Her roommate agreed and had a thoughtful dimness in her eyes as she got in her car and drove away into the sopping, blustery night.

Chapter Ten

Monday, October 24

On her lunch break, Saundra found two responses to the request posted on the history bulletin boards. Achmed Wilson and Mike Kioto. Both were history students, former members of the Spirits of '62.

They sent photos, including a color version of the photo Amos had given Saundra. Achmed sent a copy of the short video Lyndsy had put together, using the Spirits' war games in Cadburn Creek to illustrate some theories she had about several minor battles in the Civil War. He also included another short video, a rough draft Lyndsey had shared with him, with some ideas about proving and disproving all the stories she had been gathering up about Underground Railroad activities in Cadburn.

Mike and Achmed confirmed what Mrs. Tinderbeck had said. Lyndsy and Steve had both left town in a hurry, under strained circumstances, and cut off everyone. They confirmed the story they had been told: Steve went to work for some history writer and never looked back. No one was really surprised at the suddenness, because it fit his "use 'em and lose 'em" personality. Achmed suspected a partnership, if not a weird kind of romance going on between Lyndsy and Steve.

Mike confirmed what Phoebe had related about Lyndsy packing up and leaving town. He had come to clear out her two rented rooms in Mrs. Tinderbeck's house and later came back and took down some of the cameras she had hung around the creek. He said he had asked Macy if Lyndsy kept in contact with her, but she hadn't responded yet. He and Macy broke up the winter after Lyndsy left town. He provided her email and the last phone number he had for her, but couldn't confirm if she was still living in the Cleveland area.

Saundra used the color copier to enlarge the photos of Lyndsy and Steve, to get more details. She was intrigued to find another picture of Lyndsy and Steve together in modern clothes, leaning in close to each other and laughing. The notation in Achmed's email said this was a history department party. He had taken the photo when they weren't looking, because it was so completely unlike them. Usually they sniped at each other. He had wanted to ask if there was something going on between them but never got the chance. He admitted there were many questions he had wanted to ask Lyndsy, and he regretted never getting to know her better.

Saundra printed out copies of everything to give Phoebe for her scripts. During a break, while Twila was busy and unable to eavesdrop, she reported on what she had found to Mrs. Tinderbeck, knowing the woman was still concerned about Lyndsy after three years. That was just the way she was.

Tuesday, October 25

A remark in the library's kitchen just before the doors opened for the day, about the chances of the creek flooding, started a steady stream of reminiscences passed on by parents and grandparents. Saundra's ears perked up whenever someone mentioned rumors of Underground Railroad tunnels. Unfortunately, most of the stories ended up with flooded cellars, but no tunnels leading from the creek. Several mothers, overhearing the chatter while bringing their preschoolers in for story time, added stories of their own. A handful of stories were repeated during the day, as the rain continued to drum down, then let up, allowing a glimpse of sunshine for half an hour, before the sky clouded over again, and more rain fell.

Saundra heard Josiah Crandall's name mentioned several times, and a book he had been writing about the Underground Railroad activities in Cadburn Township. He had raised the ire of several people with his declarations that he was "this close" to a breakthrough that would shut the mouths of his detractors and naysayers once and for all. He had been seen walking the banks of Cadburn Creek in all weathers, looking for clues. His temper and tales of the fights he got into with some people sounded nothing like the old gentleman she had come to know, always surrounded by children at church. What had changed him?

Saundra went to Mrs. Tinderbeck, to see if she knew the story. She could depend on her supervisor to tell the unpleasant details with a large dose of sympathy and gentle humor. Josiah Crandall's transformation, of course, started with his research project.

"The foundational problem with the claims that our town was part of the Underground Railroad is that there is no proof," Mrs. Tinderbeck said, as she and Saundra chatted in the kitchen at the end of the day.

Tonight was Saundra's turn to clean up the kitchen and prepare the coffeemaker for the next day. Mrs. Tinderbeck surprised her by appearing in the kitchen doorway. She had thought her supervisor had gone home already, but she had only gone out to fetch her dinner from Frenchy's. She planned to stay late to do some research of her own. Saundra started the conversation by relating the stories she had heard during the day. She asked about Josiah Crandall and the change in him. Then her supervisor had made her astonishing statement.

"No proof?" Saundra tossed the sponge into the now-clean sink and settled down at the table across from Mrs. Tinderbeck. "You mean, everything is just stories, no documentation?"

"Oh, there are mentions of Cadburn in various records, especially the documentation of slave hunters, where they looked, what resistance they faced from residents. There are a few names that keep coming up in their lists of the most likely suspects to be hiding escaped slaves, just because those people were most adamant about their opposition to slavery."

"That doesn't make sense. If I was hiding slaves, I wouldn't draw attention to myself by getting in the face of the slave hunters." Saundra grinned as a new thought occurred to her. "On the other hand, I'd expect most people to think that way, so maybe I'd be that noisy, to make people think I couldn't possibly be involved."

"No, I think you'd be careful." The elderly woman chuckled. "Kai and Troy, on the other hand, would most likely follow that tactic. However, suspicion of being involved in the Underground Railroad is not proof of such activity. There have been unpleasant incidents over the years, where members of both historical societies violated the rights of property owners. Especially the homes along the creek. They'd wait until the owners were gone for the day, then come up along the creek and start digging. I remember one incident. Allen Kenward was new to the department at the time and had to answer a terrified call from a woman who came home and went down to her cellar to put away canning supplies, and found her cellar door had been taken entirely off the hinges. While she was on the phone with him, the culprits came back. Allen had to take one of them to the hospital, after she broke several of her brand new Mason jars over his head." Mischief glittered in the woman's eyes.

"That's not the whole story, is it?"

"Oh, not by a mile." She levered herself out of her chair and beckoned for Saundra to follow as she headed back to her office. "It turns out those two nincompoops justified their clumsy breaking-and-entering on a sketch taken from the diary of a Civil War veteran. It was quite blurred and damaged by water. A flood in his great-granddaughter's cellar unearthed the diary. Those two decided it was a map to a tunnel and indicated that house. If they had just done a little more research, they would have learned the house wasn't even built until 1922."

Saundra laughed. She couldn't help it. She did manage not to say the thought that popped into her mind: many people in Cadburn Township were "characters," as her Aunt Cleo would say, with a strong tendency to get themselves involved in outrageous messes.

"Wouldn't it be something, though?" Mrs. Tinderbeck mused, as she settled down at her desk and reached to awaken her computer. "The water level is certainly higher than it has ever been at this time of year. Wouldn't it be something if a little ...hmm... judicious flooding took place, and uncovered the opening of a tunnel?"

Saundra leaned against the door frame. "What do you think Mr. Crandall would do if that happened? The tunnels were his pet project."

"Obsession, you mean." Her gaze went distant. "Poor Josiah."

"What changed him?"

She shook her head. "I'm not at liberty to share someone's sorrows, but ... well, maybe this is something your friend Nick could help with. He does seem to have connections everywhere, and all of them quite useful."

"That's a nice way of putting it."

Saundra wondered if she could go more than a week, two at the most, without Nick West showing up in her thoughts, or her Aunt Cleo mentioning him, or getting an email or phone call from him. Or worse, having him involved in some problem. He had been part of her life for as long as she could remember, a shadowy figure, emerging to provide answers or defend her from bullies and stalkers with incredible timing. Perhaps suspicious timing. He had proved handy to have around since she moved to Cadburn Township, pulling hard-to-find strings to resolve problems.

Where would she and her friends be right now, if Nick hadn't found out vital information when Jacob Styles was harassing her and fell off the roof of the Mug building, or Conrad Price's identical triplet brothers stole his identity and life, or the Tweed cousins nearly had their new business stolen by nasty relatives? Someday, Saundra would uncover the secrets in his past that gave him all those convenient connections. Just not right now. She mentally shook her head and turned her thoughts back to what Mrs. Tinderbeck was saying. If her boss mentioned needing Nick's help, then it was important.

"Josiah was hurt, emotionally, by that whole mess surrounding Lyndsy Auretta and Steve Edison. They were vying for his patronage, I supposed you could say. He played with them, supporting one, then the other, making promises and taking advantage of new research they brought him. Then suddenly everything just ..." Mrs. Tinderbeck shrugged. "Blew up, I suppose. They vanished, and the guilt he feels, the sense that he could have stopped a tragedy of some kind from happening, made him renounce his life's passion. To make matters worse ... well, Josiah admitted just once that someone knew a secret about him, and they were using it to blackmail him."

"I find it hard to believe he was ever the kind of man to have that kind of dangerous secret," Saundra said.

"So do I, but Josiah refuses to share that pain with me, or anyone else.

Perhaps he thinks he deserves this burden. If your Nick could help him find the blackmailer, or even prove him innocent, that would do him a world of good." Mrs. Tinderbeck shrugged, raising her hands palms up in a gesture of helplessness. "The difficult part will be getting Josiah to talk about it."

"I'll ask Nick."

"I'd appreciate that, dear."

~~~~~

Saundra took some time considering just how she would ask Nick for his assistance. The sadly amusing truth was that she resented having to ask him for anything, because his big brother attitude seemed to come out at those times. On the other hand, she did like Josiah Crandall. He reminded her somewhat of her father, with a sad sort of eagerness to bring delight to others. She wondered now, after what Mrs. Tinderbeck said, if Crandall weren't trying to buy forgiveness for that awful secret.

She considered her words all the way home, while she made dinner and half-listened to the news on TV. She prayed over the request, and her concern for Crandall, and finally picked up her phone. A chuckle that was half relief slipped out when she got Nick's voicemail.

"Hi, it's Saundra. I know I'm going to regret this, but I need a favor. It's for a friend at church. A lovely old man who's a favorite with the children. A few years ago, he got into some kind of trouble, and someone is blackmailing him for it. Could you work your magic and get him to trust you, and try to do something? In your spare time, of course. You enjoy swooping out of the shadows and slapping the bad guys around, so, I guess I'm doing you a favor, too. And yes, I know I owe you one for this. And yes, I know you'll make me pay, so …"

She was about to say something lame and end the message, when she thought of something. She ran for the church directory that Patty had given her when she first moved to Cadburn.

"Maybe you can start digging through some back doors, before you talk to him. Maybe you don't need to talk to him at all, but …" She flipped through the directory and mentally crossed her fingers that Crandall wasn't one of those members of the older generation who refused to use email. She thought a silent prayer of thanks when she found his email after his phone. She read it off to Nick, as well as Crandall's phone number, thanked him for the help she knew he was going to give a nice old man, and offered to do some shopping for his half-furnished townhouse that he had bought in Cadburn.

Only after she ended the call did it occur to her to remind him, yet again, not to break into Charli Hall's townhouse, which was in the same complex. Or if he had to break in, he had to promise to only study the Venetian glass heart locket that belonged to Charli's grandmother and not
~~~~~

take it. Her grandmother needed to take it with her as a good luck charm when she went on her trip to Europe. Even if the locket was a vital piece of whatever puzzle or treasure hunt Nick and her Aunt Cleo were involved in, that didn't give him the right to make a sweet, somewhat quirky old lady panic.

On the other hand, reminding Nick not to do something would just spur him to do it. Most of the time she loved knowing he was looking out for her. The rest of the time, she wanted to slap him until he straightened out his know-it-all attitude.

Wednesday, October 26

Olivia opened Book & Mug that morning. Kai was out running down an order of spices and flavoring syrups that inexplicably got delivered to a matching address on the East Side. She was in charge, so that made her responsible to unjam the dishwasher. That resulted in getting thoroughly soaked when one of the water jets that had been knocked crooked suddenly started shooting hot water. She had forgotten to turn off the water before she got to work. Once the dishwasher was humming along properly again, she left everything in Truman's hands and ran back to the house to get some dry clothes.

A brown hatchback was turning around in the cul de sac two doors to the west of Bee's house when Olivia pulled into the driveway. A neon yellow sheet of paper hung on the front door, inside the screen. It shouldn't have been there, because Bee specifically asked her to keep the screen door locked, to frustrate the people who tried to leave things she didn't want to see. All the flyers and pamphlets people and organizations couldn't legally put into the mailbox because of postal regulations.

She got close enough to the screen door to see it ajar maybe half an inch. Not good. Tires crunched on the gravel of the driveway behind her, and she saw the brown hatchback skid into the driveway.

"Where have you been?" the driver demanded, his voice screeching and cracking. He slammed his door open and leaped out. There he was in all his self-righteous misery: skinny and balding, in a faded gray trench coat and the worst case of middle-age acne Olivia had ever seen.

Myron Ellsworth.

He had no business demanding to know where she was.

"I don't think that's any of—"

"I have been banging on your door for nearly half an hour. Why didn't you answer?" He stomped up until he was just a few steps away from her. Close enough she could smell the onion bagel he had eaten some time that morning.

"Uh, hello?" She gestured at her car. "I just got here, so how do you expect me to answer the door when I'm not here?"

He opened his mouth, and from the way his lips curled back, he was going to blast her. Then her words must have gotten through his self-righteous ire, and he stopped himself.

"That is the list of all the approved contractors you're permitted to contact, if there's any damage from flooding." He pointed at the yellow sheet on the door. "You have no excuse for calling the wrong people if something happens with all this rain we've been having."

"Approved?" Olivia muffled a snort and a grin. Then she bit her lip against more laughter when she realized something.

Ellsworth didn't recognize her from all their run-ins at the house on the other side of the creek. More important, he didn't realize she wasn't the homeowner. He had to know Bee lived here, just because of all the clashes they had had since she bought the house.

"Who do you think I am?"

He pulled out the clipboard he had kept tucked inside his trench coat and consulted it. Was his memory that bad, that he needed a reminder? Or was he just trying to look official and important?

"You are—" he began.

"No, I'm not. Bee is out of town and I'm housesitting for her."

"This is the home of Deborah Wilkinson," he snapped, and she swore he spat a little.

"Bee is her nickname. Deborah means bee. As in honeybee?" she added, when he just blinked and looked confused for a moment.

"Be that as it may." He pointed at the yellow paper. "Familiarize yourself with the list of approved—"

"Excuse me, but I have to change my clothes and get back to work." Then she paused, because she didn't want to open the garage door while he was there. She had a vision of Ellsworth letting himself into the house and starting an inspection that Bee had been denying him for three years.

He stomped up to the front door and reached for the handle. "You will follow the regulations laid out—"

"Take your hand off that door right now. You shouldn't have been able to open it because it's kept locked. So that means you broke it."

"No, I didn't." His voice cracked in what she hoped was panic. He moved back three steps, his nose twitching like a rat.

"Yes, you did, and I have proof. Security cameras." She pointed at nonexistent cameras under the eaves. Olivia had learned that trick from Kai, to put down troublemakers at Book & Mug. "Bee will send the images to the police department and send you a bill for damaging the screen door when she gets home." She took a step back and crossed her arms, and wondered if this giddy, snarky feeling was what Kai felt when he dealt with idiot customers.

Ellsworth stumbled forward, bending down and turning his head, clearly looking for the cameras. He went pale, then flushed a dark enough red it almost covered up his acne. "You have to get permission to attach anything to the exterior of a historical building," he squealed.

"Take it up with Bee when she gets back. But don't come back here and try to take those cameras down. Doing that will send an alarm and pictures straight to the police department." She nodded at the screen door. "You're already up for a lawsuit for damaging that door. It's original to the house, meaning it's an antique, and quite valuable," she lied. "You'll be hearing from Bee's lawyer in the morning."

"It's not broken!" His voice screeched and snapped.

Olivia tipped her head to the right and widened her smile, and tried to imagine what Kai would do if he was here. Ellsworth snorted and inhaled loudly, exhaled loudly, looked around, looked back at the door, turned his head, clearly looking for those security cameras, looked back at her, inhaled loudly again, exhaled loudly.

"Fine. Here." He reached into his pocket, pulled out his wallet and took out a twenty.

Olivia gave him as incredulous a look as she could manage. It was hard when she wanted to burst out laughing. He snarled under his breath and pulled out another twenty, then a third, then a fifty. She took the money and barely managed to keep her hand from shaking with the laughter that threatened to choke her.

Snarling, muffling more curses, he stomped back to his car. He gunned the engine and kicked up gravel as he pulled out of the driveway. Olivia felt his gaze on her as she reached in her purse and pulled out the garage door opener and pressed the button. He finally drove away after she was in the garage and pushed the button to close the door.

Nope, home ownership was not worth the hassles.

On the other hand, she had $110 now to play with. Actually, $55. She had to split it with Bee, who would use it to repair the door.

After she changed into dry clothes, she opened the front door and took down the list of contractors. She compared it with the one Bee had left for her. Nothing had changed.

"Well, you were right," Olivia muttered, as she pulled out her phone to send a quick email to Bee, telling her what had happened.

Chapter Eleven

Thursday, October 27

Olivia didn't turn on the lights in the kitchen when she came in from work that night. The play of moonlight on the water always fascinated and calmed her. Tonight, she needed that break to slow down her mind before trying to sleep. She sat in the window seat for a good half hour, letting the movement soothe her. She considered making a snack, something that wouldn't keep her awake too long, once she climbed into bed. Movement on the riverbank, by the ridge of stone and brambles, caught her attention. She held her breath and stood up and got as close to the glass as she could without fogging it with her breath.

A dark figure moved along the riverbank, heading west. It glided along, seeming to float. Olivia shivered a little, remembering some of the Cadburn Ghost stories Saundra had shared with her when she stopped in for a coffee special on her way to work. She got up on her knees on the window seat to get a higher view, looking for the figure's feet. She thought for a moment it wasn't walking on the riverbank but was standing in a boat floating along on the high water. But no, the figure was moving upstream, against the current, not riding it.

Was it a person? Maybe it was an animal? A deer would have a longer profile. That had to be a person.

The figure stopped and bent. Definitely a person. It dropped down, so she thought maybe it was getting into the water. Or checking something on the bank of the creek. Then the figure stood up again. Did it have something in its hands? Too bad the moonlight penetrating the trees came from behind, making it nothing but a black shadow. No light touched it from in front, to reveal features.

Then again, after hearing all those ghost stories at the Mug over the last couple of days, did she want to see its features?

Olivia refused to be frightened. Whoever was out there — and it had to be a "whoever" rather than a "whatever" — had no business being there. What if it was the same person sneaking around the property on Sunday? Too bad she didn't have a real video camera focused on the creek, as threatened by the signs.

The figure glided back behind the pile of stones and brambles and vanished. She hurried off the window seat and carefully opened the back door, so it didn't squeak, and stepped out onto the deck, trying to get a view of the bank past the ridge.

Nothing moved other than some mist seeping across the landscape. Perfect for a horror movie. She thought for maybe ten seconds about taking the big nightstick flashlight Bee kept next to the back door and going out there, to look for footprints. No, that was just asking for trouble.

Dumb. She shook her head, laughing quietly at herself. *That's what the girls with a bra size bigger than their IQs do in slasher movies.*

She stepped back into the house and just as carefully closed the door. She checked that both locks were engaged.

After that, she had lost her appetite. Here in the dark kitchen, no one would have a clue anyone had been there to see that figure go past. If she turned on a light, even if just the refrigerator light, she would give away her presence. If someone was out there, watching.

What exactly was she afraid of? Psychotic historic preservation fanatics attacking her, in fear she would use the wrong contractor?

Olivia looked across the back yard one more time, just in case, then turned and left the kitchen. She made a mental note to give Bee some nice, thick curtains for the bay window for Christmas. She knew all those houses on the other side of the creek had a clear view down on the houses on this side of the creek, once all the leaves had fallen. Why had she never thought there was something creepy about that until now?

Friday, October 28

The fall street festival started early Friday afternoon, before school let out for the weekend. Plenty of time for parents and grandparents to explore before the kids of Cadburn came spilling through, taking advantage of all the fun odds and ends different booths offered to add to their Halloween costumes, and all the bakery and candy treats. The township provided heavy canvas canopies that stretched across the street from the second story of buildings, providing plenty of coverage when the inevitable rain spattered the festivities. Common sense said to provide a roof for an outdoor festival after September rolled in. Common sense did rule — most of the time — in Cadburn Township.

The air was damp enough and chilly enough, Book & Mug's hot drinks did even better business than expected. Olivia was glad Kai chose to pass up having a booth this year. She wasn't out in the damp and chill, and she didn't have to worry about calculating when to send runners to get supplies to replenish whatever they were running out of in the booth. Instead, a table sat outside Book & Mug's door, with two gas-powered heaters creating a bubble of warmth that attracted customers to stop.

Traffic was just as thick outside as inside.

Olivia had the duty of keeping the two ten-gallon spigot dispensers filled with orange-dyed white hot chocolate. She kept the table holding the dispensers stocked with freshly filled scarecrow-face paper cups Kai had hunted down for the occasion. Each cup came with two pieces of candy for the children who were warming up for Trick-or-Treat by going from booth to booth and business to business during the festival.

When the festival officially ended at 10pm, she was grateful. And even more grateful to be worn out so much, she didn't think when she got back to the house. She washed her face, slid into her thermal underwear pajamas, and fell into bed. No pause to stare out the back window and look for that mysterious figure in the night.

Saturday, October 29

The street festivals always started bright and early, but today, thanks to the weather, started not-so-bright and felt far too early at 9am.

The clouds rolled in around 10:30, bringing deep shadows. Soon the festival committee was scrambling to rig some portable lighting to brighten things under the canvas. Olivia thought it felt rather cozy when the rain started falling in misty spurts soon after.

When the wind picked up and the rain thickened, the people with booths next to the gaps in the canvas hurried to move their wares. It didn't matter what side of the festival they were on, they got wet. Within twenty minutes, they were soaked. The only dry spot was down the center of the street, which was left open for festival attendees to walk and see everything.

Then the wind really picked up and the canvas rippled in a regular rhythm that Olivia feared would have made her seasick if she was on Lake Erie in a boat. She wondered how long the canvas would stay anchored. More important, how long would the people stay in their booths? How many people would come out in this weather?

By noon, the festival committee had checked the Weather Channel and the local TV stations' weather forecasts online, and declared the festival canceled. Olivia could have told them that more than twenty minutes earlier, just watching the rapidly dwindling foot traffic through the festival. Even Book & Mug's business was affected. People wanted to get in their cars and get home before the wind got any fiercer and the rain got so cold and hard and heavy that they couldn't see to drive. With the wind blowing in all directions at unpredictable intervals, the awnings along the front of the coffee shop offered no protection.

With the nearly empty coffee shop and bookstore, Kai had more people on hand than he needed. Olivia was ready to volunteer to go home when he asked her if she would mind. She was wet from hauling all the supplies and the tables into the shop when the storm hit. Olivia came close to hugging him. She had had a couple of bosses in the past who would have found work for her to do, most likely cleaning chores that usually got neglected throughout the year. And scolded her for doing it in wet clothes. Kai was a gem. He and Saundra were so good together. Olivia had been glad when the cousins took Saundra under their wing from the day she came to Cadburn, and now even more glad when she saw the growing relationship between her and Kai.

Home by 12:45, she shucked her wet clothes in the mudroom, wrapped in a blanket she had left in the dryer, then hurried to her bedroom to get into dry clothes. She indulged in a bowl of clam chowder and got a pot of dragon tea steeping, then spent the first hour of unexpected freedom checking out Bee's collection of cookbooks. Olivia had to laugh, because some of them were in foreign languages. She wasn't aware that her friend spoke any foreign languages. Maybe Bee used a translation program on her phone, but still, wouldn't the differences between metric and the measuring system used in the US cause her problems? This was something new she was learning about her friend. Olivia anticipated some interesting conversations when Bee came home.

As if thinking of her sent up a signal, Olivia's phone pinged with a text from Bee, checking in. She had been watching the Weather Channel, saw a huge cloud of black weather hanging over northeast Ohio, and wondered how the festival was surviving. Olivia responded with all sorts of emojis: clouds, lightning bolts, horrified faces, raindrops, umbrellas.

Bee called then, and they chatted for nearly half an hour. Bee's grandmother was in better shape than her parents. Her sister, Delany, was nearly weeping with gratitude for Bee's support.

"It looks like I'm going to be here for at least two more weeks," Bee said, after Olivia expressed condolences. "Please use up whatever is in the fridge, okay? Have a dinner party. Help yourself to anything in the pantry. You are doing me such a huge favor."

Olivia mentioned the second sighting of the shadowy figure and how spooked she was when it seemed to just glide along. She knew for a fact, having walked down on the edge of the creek, the terrain was too uneven to allow for gliding.

"Well, there's always talk of the Cadburn Ghost coming back." Bee made "oohing" noises, probably her version of a ghost's cry.

"Funny you should mention her. You did mean the Cadburn daughter, right, and not some other ghost story?" When Bee said yes, Olivia went on to tell her what Saundra had found out, and then her own memories of Lyndsy and Steve and that night they stirred up Fendergast to wail about the ghost. "Something just occurred to me." She let out a breathy laugh. "Ghosts are supposed to haunt where they died, right? So why do people think Annabelle Cadburn is haunting the township if she didn't make it home from the war?"

"Don't ask me. I don't believe in ghosts. Go ask Amos. Have you met him yet?"

"I got invited to the gripe meeting at his house, but I had to work."

"Well, go meet him. He has great stories. He believes she lived in his house for a couple months, before she ran off. If anybody is going to get haunted, it should be him. Of course, one story is that she was engaged, against her will, and she ran to avoid the wedding. She met up with her true sweetheart and they headed west. Amos has made it his life mission to track down all the Cadburn family legends, true and false. He says there are a couple houses on the other side of the river where the secret boyfriend might have lived. Supposedly that old wreck of a bridge was built back before the Civil War, and Annabelle would cross the creek to meet him, or he would cross to her."

"Wow, how do you know all this? I've lived here all my life!"

Bee chuckled. "A lot of what I just told you is kind of a closely held secret of Amos's. He's found all sorts of journals and such hidden in his house. Including love letters to Annabelle. He's a real sweetheart. I've spent a lot of really fun evenings, sitting on the deck at his place, listening to him talk for hours. You need to go talk to him."

"I need to hook him up with Saundra."

"Tell her I want to know about that girl—Lyndsy, you said?—who hacked off Steve Edison. I found some old journals the owner of my place kept. He was furious with the Edison kid. He was digging around in the creek during a really dry spell, finding all sorts of stuff. Broken pottery, utensils, buttons, things like that. Fendergast mostly ignored him, until Edison started digging around that big ridge of stones that wanders across the property line. The old guy blew some circuits. His handwriting even changed. It was kind of creepy, reading it. I gave all those journals I found to Amos. He'll probably show them to you, if you're interested."

"Maybe. More likely I'll tell Saundra. If she keeps digging."

They chatted for a few more minutes, then Olivia heard voices calling on Bee's side of the phone. She repeated her instructions to use whatever Olivia wanted from the pantry and freezer, and to introduce Amos to Saundra.

Olivia laughed after she hung up and slumped over the table with the cookbooks spread out. Talking with Bee could be exhausting.

A snap-bang-rumble of thunder made the antique plates rattle faintly on their thin shelf circling the room near the ceiling. Olivia stepped over to the bay window and looked out. If anything, she thought the rain might be letting up. It was still coming down in sheets, but those sheets weren't thick enough to hide the creek and a good dozen feet of the end of the yard. She turned around and saw the cookbooks, and the strips of paper marking recipes she wanted to try.

"Why not?"

Most important step: find out if her guests could come. She started by inviting Saundra, who would get off work at the library at 4pm.

"If the power doesn't die before that," Saundra said. "Our lights have been flickering a few times an hour since the storm rolled in this morning. We even had the whole place go completely dark around one-ish and had to reboot all—" She let out a yelp.

"What? Are you okay?"

"Blackout again." Saundra chuckled. "You know, it gets a little spooky in here, when it's just us bookworms. Mrs. T decided to cancel all the afternoon storytimes, to spare all those kids having to wade through the parking lot. The message went out on the community bulletin board and the library's website just in time, because we haven't had a single kid come through the door, and no complaints from busy parents."

"Is Mrs. T working today?"

"Not officially. She decided to get some personal research done. Of course, then the computers decided not to cooperate." Another sighing chuckle escaped Saundra.

"I'm going invite her, too. Oh, and Bee said I should introduce you to her neighbor, Amos Green."

"I met him a few days ago. He gave me a scrapbook with some really interesting newspaper articles. Let me walk over to her office."

There was a pause while Saundra crossed the library. Olivia caught distant, muffled voices, and a few words that made her think the power was coming back on and people were checking their equipment. Mrs. Tinderbeck laughed and accepted the invitation and said her timing was good. She was about ready to call it a day and go home since she kept losing the internet research she was doing.

When Saundra took back her phone, she asked if she could bring anything to help with the dinner.

"Since I'm not sure what I'm making yet, I have no idea. Just bring lots of questions for Amos, I guess."

As soon as she hung up with Saundra, Olivia called Eden and extended the invitation to all three cousins. Eden called out to Troy, who was in the office the three shared, and he accepted the invitation. Eden promised Kai would be there, if she had to shut down the coffee shop and drag him out the door.

Olivia laughed as she hung up with Eden, then saw the time. How long were some of those recipes going to take? She needed to check what

Bee had in the refrigerator and freezer, then decide on the recipes.

"Stupid, stupid," she muttered, standing in front of the refrigerator that was so jammed full, she felt as if she couldn't see anything. Olivia dashed into Bee's office, for her list of contacts in her various groups. A neatly typed list titled "Neighbors and Fellow Targets" hung on a tackboard next to her computer. Amos Green's email and phone were at the top of the list.

"Well, hello, and nice to finally put a voice to the face," Amos said, when Olivia had introduced herself. He had a rumbly sort of laugh and agreed quickly when she explained why she called, and who was coming to the dinner party. "Deborah is the loveliest girl. I thanked God when she bought that beautiful old house. Andrew was a hermit. Which was a blessing when his mind started going. The only time I knew he was still alive and kicking was when he had another shouting match with Edna's gang of bullies. I swear, he made changes to his house just to aggravate her." Amos thanked her and promised to be there at 6 o'clock sharp, with lots of photos and copies of journals and other "fascinating tidbits" as he called them.

<div align="center">~~~~~</div>

With a little less than an hour until her guests would start arriving, Olivia dashed to the bathroom for a quick shower. The sky had darkened considerably by the time she came out, and she thought the rain pounded louder. It was hard to tell through the groaning of the wind. What if the rain was so bad, her guests decided not to come? What if the rain was so loud, she couldn't hear when they knocked?

Olivia checked the food in the oven and the three Crock Pots. Bee had five, all of different sizes. Very handy. She glanced out the bay window. A flash of lightning seemed to bounce off not just the creek, but parts of the back yard. She grabbed the big nightstick flashlight, went to the back door, and stepped out onto the deck. A shudder went through her when she saw all the splotches of standing water across the entire backyard, up to the bottom step of the stairs to the deck. Judging by what she could see in the flashlight beam, the creek hadn't overflowed the banks yet.

Yet.

What would she do if it did? What could she do? She went into the office to check the list of Bee's approved contractors. She highlighted the names of two contractors specifically for dealing with flooding. Olivia caught movement out of the corner of her eye. She stepped up to the curtains of the window that opened onto the front of the house. A short figure with a huge, neon green umbrella trudged down the sidewalk and then up the driveway, bent over with a big, lumpy-looking sack over his shoulder. That had to be Amos, because she couldn't imagine anyone else on the street making the effort to come out to see her in this weather. She put down Bee's list and hurried out of the office, to the front door. She flung it open just as Amos was raising his hand to grasp the knocker. His gnome-like features wrinkled in a delighted smile.

"Miss Olivia. So that's who you are. You're probably too busy to notice, but my gaming club meets on Tuesday nights at the Mug."

Olivia laughed and stepped back, gesturing for him to step inside before the next gust of wind knocked them both off their feet. Now she recognized Amos. She knew that grin of his and his cheerful voice, even without the peaked Robin Hood-style hat he always wore. Everybody in the gaming club wore some piece of costume. Miriam, the current president, said the practice had started as a measure to weed out the ones who got "squirmy" about admitting they played role-playing games, especially in public. The club took up all four of the tables in the section of the coffee shop that curved around behind the bookstore. When Olivia worked Tuesday nights, she always enjoyed hearing their laughter and outbursts of fun arguments. Especially when the rules forced them to argue in Lord of the Rings-style dialog.

Saundra and Mrs. Tinderbeck came together, pulling into the driveway just as Olivia was pushing the front door closed against an extra-strong gust of wind. Maybe the rain was dying down, but the wind seemed to be making up for it. Amos dropped his backpack on the tiled area by the door and hurried out to meet them with his umbrella. His gait was quick and had a sort of hopping action that fit perfectly with his gnome-like appearance. He and Mrs. Tinderbeck were chatting and laughing as they came to the front door, holding the umbrella tilted down slightly in front of them to shield against the wind. Saundra followed, carrying a large canvas tote bag, and struggling to keep a grip on her umbrella with the other hand. Once they got up onto the front porch, the wind seemed to double in fierceness. Olivia hurried them inside.

"Sounds like tornado season is settling in early," Amos offered, when the wind howled and shrieked against the door as Olivia shoved it closed.

"Don't take this the wrong way, Amos," Mrs. Tinderbeck said, "but I hope your forecasting skills are failing you."

"I hope so too!"

Saundra hurried to take charge of both umbrellas, folding them up and leaning them against the closet door so they dripped onto the mat. Amos helped Mrs. Tinderbeck out of her coat, with a quiet gallantry that put a funny twitch in Olivia's heart. Bee had mentioned several times how much she adored her elderly neighbor, and now Olivia understood why. She wondered if there was something sweet between him and Mrs. Tinderbeck, or if he was simply an old-fashioned kind of gentleman. They certainly chattered and chuckled together like they were good friends. Saundra helped her hang their coats on the hooks in the mudroom.

The four migrated to the kitchen, where Amos and Mrs. Tinderbeck both exclaimed over the aromas. Olivia was relieved that someone else thought the experimental dishes smelled as good as they did to her. She couldn't quite trust her own judgment, thanks to her anxiety over this dinner party being a success. Yes, she and Phoebe had invited people over for dinners before, but they were usually a potluck of some kind, and informal at best. She would have felt better if Phoebe could come, but she had rehearsal tonight. This was an actual dinner party. And included her boss. Yes, she got along great with Kai and his cousins, but there were the constraints of being in the workplace and in public to smooth things over. How would the three cousins be when they relaxed?

Saundra vanished for a few minutes while Olivia was pulling out the cookbooks to show the recipes to Mrs. Tinderbeck. Amos stood at the bay window, chuckling and relating how every time Fendergast got upset with Ellsworth and his cronies, he changed something on his property.

Saundra led Kai, Eden and Troy into the kitchen, which startled Olivia, because she hadn't heard the doorbell. Troy immediately latched onto Amos, recognizing him from the RPG group. He wanted to know how someone joined, and what exactly they did when they had such intense discussions. They certainly sounded like they were having fun.

The dinner conversation turned to stories of the Cadburn Ghost that always started up with the fall weather. They got into a lively discussion of whether ghosts followed the so-called rules of ghosts and hauntings. Troy started a rabbit trail discussion for a short time, on all the rules made up by Hollywood, that had nothing to do with folklore. Such as for vampires and werewolves and other monsters and denizens of ancient tales. Amos laughed at them all and admitted that he hoped his research would reveal that Annabelle Cadburn had indeed run off with her true love, rather than risking her life in the war. The problem was discovering the name of her sweetheart. Chances were good he was one of the stereotyped poor-but-noble youths who seemed to populate local history. Chances were also good he was one of the nearly forty young men who never came back from the war. Hopefully, not because he died, but because he and Annabelle headed West.

Silence circled the table for several moments, with everyone's expressions thoughtful. Olivia wondered if this was the place where she, as hostess, was supposed to step in and change the path of the conversation. She couldn't think of a thing to say. Except maybe ask if they were ready for dessert.

How did hostesses survive all this tension? Still, she had been having a good time. Up until now.

And the silence stretched on.

Amos slapped his hands on the table on either side of his plate.

Which had been scraped clean, Olivia was pleased to note.

"This is the best time I've had in quite a while. Lydia here can tell you that I don't usually discuss my passion. Most of my associates already know everything I've told you, and I don't want to drive them away." He nodded to Mrs. Tinderbeck.

A muffled thud made everyone jump. The lights died. The wind moaned past the windows, louder, now that the furnace had stopped rumbling softly and blowing. Outside, the streetlights on their tall poles were dark.

Then a humming sort of buzz kicked in, and a moment later the kitchen light came back on. The bulbs in the nest of flower-shaped antique glass cups in the chandelier over the table slowly glowed into life. The furnace rumbled again. The street stayed dark.

"I guess Bee forgot to tell me about the emergency generator," Olivia said with a chuckle.

"It might be wise to turn off all the lights you can," Amos said. "I have a generator myself, and the less strain you put on yours, the longer it will last."

"Makes sense," Troy said. "Need help?"

"I should probably turn off the dishwasher." Olivia got up from the table. "And check Bee's office. And I think I had my computer charging." She headed into the kitchen.

"It's amazing how much we depend on electricity for our everyday life, and never think about it," Mrs. Tinderbeck said.

Olivia ran down the hall, after turning off the dishwasher and the range light, and checked the refrigerator. It was running. She wondered how many appliances and other pieces of equipment were left running that didn't need power right that moment. She unplugged her computer and stepped into each room as she came back down the hall, looking for anything plugged in. The clocks in the guest bedroom and Bee's bedroom were flashing. She unplugged them, even though they probably didn't use much electricity in the course of a day. Every little bit added up, she supposed.

A soft beeping started up as she reached the end of the hall where it met the living room and foyer. Olivia paused, trying to locate the source. She hoped that wasn't an alarm, but just a notification that some equipment was coming back to life.

"What's that sound?" Eden said, as Olivia stepped into the dining room.

"Sounds like it's coming from the basement," Troy said. "Do you have a basement?"

"Yeah. More like an old-fashioned cellar ..." Olivia caught her breath, trying to remember what Bee had said about the cellar, because of the predicted storms. "Oh … heck. The sump pump!"

She hit the corner of the dining room table with her hip as she ran, into the kitchen, yanked open the door to the basement, and took three steps down the stairs. She nearly knocked herself off her feet as she turned around to leap back up and hit the light switch. Kai and Troy were right behind her, and they almost collided with her. She fully expected the light not to come on, because if there wasn't electricity to the sump pump, then why would there be light in the basement?

The light came on, but it was weak, half-strength at best.

"Ah, I think there's water," Troy said, catching her shoulder just before Olivia took the last step and put her foot down.

Half the basement was definitely an old-fashioned cellar. The portion directly under the original house had a flagstone floor and raw stone walls, covered with sheets of thick plastic, held in place with two-by-fours, placed maybe a foot apart. To the right, under the kitchen wing, the floor was poured concrete, with cinderblock walls. Bee had lined the three walls with metal shelving. Everything in the basement sat on those shelves, with the bottom shelf a good foot above the floor.

A floor that glistened darkly in the weak light.

To the left, an alcove jutted out underneath the bedroom side of the house. Nothing had been done with it, other than what looked like more plastic sheeting. No shelves, nothing stored there, most likely because the stairs blocked access to the alcove.

The beeping sump pump sat under the stairs.

Olivia decided the water didn't look that deep, maybe just enough to cover the flagstones. She put one foot down. No ripples in the water. That had to be good, right?

Or maybe not so good. As she turned to walk along the stairs, to the sump pump, ripples appeared. The floor seemed to slope downward a little. So after the fourth step, the water was coming up over the high rubber sides of her sneakers that looked like Keds from the sixties.

"That's not good," Troy said from behind her.

"Oh, don't. You're getting your feet wet," Olivia protested.

"Too late now." He grinned and shrugged. Kai, however, stayed on the bottom step and just shook his head.

"There's a re-set button on the front," Amos called from the top of the stairs. "I bought mine after Bee praised hers so much. It's green. It should be right under the flashing yellow light." He paused. "The light is yellow, isn't it?"

"What if it's a different color?" Troy stepped around Olivia to get a better look at the dark, lumpy shape of the sump pump. He lifted what turned out to be some empty black garbage bags, to reveal a flashing yellow light.

"Oh, red means a repair bill."

Troy pushed the button underneath the flashing light. The light flashed faster, then died. Olivia held her breath, waiting for a red light to appear. A humming began, and a few seconds of silent waiting later, the beeping of the alarm stopped.

"Thanks!" Olivia called up the stairs.

The light at the bottom of the stairs brightened, when she fully expected it to go dark from the extra drain on the generator with the awakening of the sump pump. By the time she and Troy got back to the bottom of the stairs, two more light bulbs came on. They revealed no water on the concrete floor, and dry flagstones along most of the walls in the original cellar portion. Except where the floor dipped under the stairs.

"That's where the water came in," Troy offered. He ducked his head into the alcove, leaning over the railing of the stairs on that side. "Got a flashlight?"

Olivia went up to the kitchen to fetch the flashlight from beside the back door and brought it down to him. The old plastic sheeting made details hard to see, but she agreed with him that water seemed to still be coming in there. A visible ripple in the muddy water confirmed that a few moments later.

They trudged upstairs. Olivia left the basement door open so she could hear if the sump pump went out again. Then she insisted on giving Troy slippers and putting his wet shoes on the hot air vent, to try to dry them out for the rest of the evening. She excused herself and went into the office to make a call to Bee, praying the entire time she would have to leave a message.

God heard her prayer. She left a simple message, assuring Bee that everything was working fine now, the generator kicked in perfectly, and she would start calling contractors in the morning. Someone had to be available, even if tomorrow was Sunday. There was nothing she could do tonight about the problem, other than to make sure the sump pump kept working.

Olivia reminded herself that the whole situation could have been a lot worse. That didn't quite ease the feeling that she had failed in her housesitting obligation.

Her worries interfered with the fun of the long, sometimes silly, sometimes fascinating discussion of everything Saundra had learned about Lyndsy Auretta, Steve Edison, Cadburn Ghost stories, and rumors of Underground Railroad tunnels. Eden insisted on doing some digging, pull some official and not-quite-official strings, to locate Lyndsy and where she called home now. She admitted she felt a little guilty, letting everything drop when Lyndsy fled town three years ago.

"You have to wonder if she found out something dangerous, and she's been lying low," Troy said. "Either the trouble this other girl brought on her, or something she found out digging around in Cadburn history. But if she made that big breakthrough, why hasn't anyone followed up on it?"

"We all know there are quite a few history fanatics in this township," Mrs. Tinderbeck said. "We've all witnessed quite vicious arguments over minor details and conflicting interpretations. Imagine their fury if a mere student made a breakthrough they had been working for. Maybe she ran for her academic life. It has happened before, and it will happen again."

"What did she find?" Amos mused. "A genuine Underground Railroad tunnel, after all these years?" He snorted, and a mischievous grin lit his gnomelike face. "Back in the day, that would have knocked Josiah Crandall on his uppity backside."

"Amos," Mrs. Tinderbeck said, her voice softly reproving.

"I know, I know." He winked at Olivia. "I admit, I had a great deal of fun, back in the day, puncturing his theories, getting him hot and bothered, taking him down a few pegs. He's a good man now, and a lot of that is to your credit. You're a good influence, Lydia."

"He got right with God. That's the good influence." She glanced at Saundra, and Olivia thought she caught some kind of silent conversation between the two of them. Saundra nodded. That seemed to satisfy the older woman.

In the momentary quiet, the wind growled and thudded against the windows. Everyone held still, and Olivia wished she could rid her mind of the image of Dorothy's house falling through the air. She thought of all that churning water in the creek, and the water seeping into the basement.

Please, Lord, protect—

A loud snap penetrated the growling moan of the wind. Everyone jumped. Then a muted crash seemed to send a reverberation through the house.

"That sounded way too close," Troy said. "Lots of old trees here along the creek." He looked around the table, then got up and headed into the kitchen.

Olivia followed and joined him at the bay window. The trees all around them swayed and seemed to churn against the darkness. It seemed especially thick without the streetlights on the street behind them and the street on the other side of the creek. She stood there until the chill seeping through the glass soaked into her, and her eyes ached from the strain, but Olivia couldn't see where any trees had fallen. She hoped that was a good sign.

"Too bad the lightning stopped a while ago," Troy said. That startled a chuckle out of her. "Easier to see what's what. Of course, then we'd probably have a horror movie soundtrack start playing in between the flashes ..."

"Stop right there!" Eden called from the dining room. "Olivia, you have my permission to slap him."

That got laughter from everyone.

~~~~~

Half an hour after everyone had gone home, Olivia settled into bed, slightly achy from all the work she had put in, but feeling rather smug about how well her first official dinner party had gone. Despite the water seeping into the basement. She had taken one last look before going to her bedroom, and as far as she could tell, the sump pump was doing its job. The floor where it dipped down looked damp, rather than wet.

She pulled out her phone to send an email to Bee. Texts were for emergencies, not reports that all was as well as could be expected. Her phone rang just as she hit "send," with a sigh of relief. Phoebe was calling.

"Hey, are you okay? Are the lights back on your side of the street?" she asked.

"Yeah." Phoebe made a little hiccupping sound.

"What's wrong?"

"You know that old pine on the left side of the house, how every time we have a really bad snowstorm you're afraid the roots are going to come up out of the ground and it'll go sliding down into the creek?"

"Yeah." Olivia held her breath. Was that the crashing sound they heard?

"Well, it didn't. It kind of tipped into the house. Don't worry," Phoebe hurried on. "I called Mrs. T and then I called Arnie to have him come look, and he shut off the power and he's got tarps spread in the attic where it kind of cracked the roof, but the rest of the house is okay."

"Are you okay?" Olivia demanded. "Were you there when it happened?" She couldn't get a mental picture of how much of the house would have been hit when that old pine's roots gave way and it fell. Her brain just refused to cooperate.

"No. I mean — no, I wasn't here, but yeah, I'm okay. I just thought you should know."

"You want to come here to stay?"

"Could I?"

"Don't make me come get you."
~~~~~

Chapter Twelve

Sunday, October 30

Olivia and Phoebe went to their house to see it in the light of day before they went to church. Phoebe laughed at herself, because the pine tree had done very little damage. Two branches had punctured the attic roof, but that was all. Arnie, Mrs. Tinderbeck's general handyman, had come over as soon as Phoebe called him. He sawed off the branches and tacked up plastic tarps inside the attic to ward off the last of the rain from the storm. The house was secure and structurally undamaged, and he had promised Phoebe and Mrs. Tinderbeck before he left that he would come back Sunday afternoon and get to work on repairs.

Mrs. Tinderbeck was watching for them to arrive for the service. She hugged Phoebe before asking if she was all right, then thanked her again for taking care of things so quickly.

"You know, this might be good timing. While Arnie is up there, checking things out, maybe now is the time to see if that renovation is even do-able," she said, as the three of them headed into the sanctuary. "I've been considering turning the attic into an apartment, for visiting missionaries and guest speakers and such. What do you think?"

Phoebe and Olivia both agreed it was a good idea. They had supported her every time she had talked about the idea, so why change their minds now?

~~~~~

Olivia started making calls as soon as she got back to Bee's house after church. By the time she had to put in her afternoon shift at Book & Mug, she knew she should have taken on that task last night. Everyone on Bee's list of trusted contractors and repair people was already busy. Either houses had been hit with toppled trees, or they were dealing with the flooding on both sides of the creek, heading east. Amos saw her as she was leaving to go to work and didn't look surprised when she admitted she had had no success lining up someone to look at the flooding. He promised he would send over his contractor, Drake Abbott, as soon as the man was done dealing with the flooding in his cellar. The sump pump hadn't gone out on him when the electricity died on the street, but the force of water coming in had damaged several bore holes put in back in the late 1800s for drainage. Over the years, the owners had made
~~~~~

improvements, such as installing first screens, to keep animals and insects from getting into the cellar, then one-way traps, to stop water from backing up. The traps had broken from the pressure of the water coming from the creek and the bore holes had been washed out. Drake anticipated at least three days to dig down and replace the bore holes with PVC pipe.

Amos reported that his house was the starting point for the flood damage. The cul de sac was the high point of the street, then it inclined down to the creek level before making a short turn north and climbing upward again to meet Overlook. All the houses that had suffered damage were heading east along the creek. Water had gone up over the banks on nearly a dozen houses, going west, but the upward slope of the landscape at that point kept the water from reaching the houses.

Olivia thanked him and placed a call to Bee to report on what had been done, and hadn't been done, and how long the different contractors estimated she would have to wait until they could come look at that wall behind the stairs. On a positive note, though, the standing water in the back yard had already gone down and the skies were clearing.

She parked in the municipal lot and was about to get out of her car to make the dash up Apple to Book & Mug when her phone rang. Phoebe.

"What's wrong?" she demanded, instead of saying hello.

"Not exactly wrong," Phoebe said, with a forced little chuckle. "More like weird. Arnie's here, and he was moving things around, to have room to work. And yeah, he was going to inspect everything to give Mrs. T that estimate and … well, the attic window was blocked."

"How? With what?"

"Somebody moved a bunch of crates and boxes and that really old piece of furniture Mrs. T said was called a secretary. Remember that? And they created a wall. You didn't do that, did you?"

"No."

Olivia tried to recall the people who had rented rooms over the last few years who would have had the nerve to rearrange the attic. She couldn't recall anyone who had stored anything in the attic. Most people who rented rooms from Mrs. Tinderbeck had been short-term, like college students staying for just a semester. There had been more than a dozen people in the years since she had moved into the house who had fallen on hard times and needed a place to get back on their feet. Mrs. Tinderbeck invited them to stay, for free, as part of her ministry. No one she could think of had had enough possessions to put in the attic. Anyone who had more belongings than could fit in their rooms had stored them in the basement.

"Everything in that attic should be Mrs. T's," she said.

"Yeah, well, the cameras and the computer and a bunch of notebooks Arnie found aren't hers."

"Cameras?" Olivia immediately flashed to a memory of Lyndsy being especially interested in that view from the attic window. Then installing that video camera under the sweetheart bridge. "Have you touched anything? Moved anything?"

"I've watched dang too many detective shows to make a mistake like that." Phoebe sighed. "Everything is covered with dust. It's been up here a long time."

"Three years, I'm guessing." Olivia reached for the latch on her car door, then paused, considering. Would Kai be irritated, or totally understanding, if she called off for the afternoon? The weather could keep people away, or it could drive everyone indoors, seeking hot drinks and books, meaning the Mug would be hopping.

"Why three years?"

"Lyndsy. I'm betting that's Lyndsy's stuff."

"But Mike took everything. Why would he leave her stuff in the attic? Even if he forgot, she would have just asked him to come back."

"Unless maybe she didn't tell him about the computer and camera in the attic." Olivia shivered. She needed to get moving, to fight off that creeping sensation of somebody watching her.

"Why wouldn't she?"

"I don't know!" She opened the door and scrambled out of the car. "I'm going in and getting Eden and coming back to the house. Will we be in Arnie's way if we're up there for a while?"

Olivia locked the car door and started jogging up the sidewalk while she waited for Phoebe and Arnie to confer. She liked Arnie, and most of the time his careful, calculating approach to everything was a comfort, but not now. What was so hard about knowing if he could work around them? Phoebe came back when Olivia had reached the alley behind Book & Mug. She stopped, huffing slightly.

"Arnie says he's got everything he needs. He's going to do what patching he can from the inside and then call his cousin who does roofs. He has to wait until the rain stops. Why wouldn't Lyndsy tell Mike she put this stuff up here when she sent him to get her stuff?"

"I don't know. It makes no sense. Let's see what Eden says."

"My first reaction?" Eden said less than fifteen minutes later. "My suspicious mind says maybe Lyndsy didn't ask Mike to get her stuff."

"But we got a phone call from her." Olivia wrapped her arms around herself, chilled despite the cozy warmth of the second-floor office. She found some comfort in how Eden bent down to put on her shoes, then stood up and reached for the bag she took with her to meet clients. Meaning she was going to help.

"Yeah, and there have been computer programs out there for years, getting more sophisticated all the time, that can synthesize people's voices so it takes an even more sophisticated program to detect what's been done." Eden reached for her jacket. "Is the house wheelchair accessible?"

"Huh? Uh …" Olivia choked on a bit of laughter. She had never really thought about it. "Yeah, there's a ramp on the back porch. Rufus?"

"He had his hands on all Lyndsy's computers when he was locking out that hacker. He'll get through the improved security on her system a lot faster than I could, because he built it."

~~~~~

Rufus arrived and settled in the kitchen with Phoebe while Olivia and Eden were still upstairs examining the nook Lyndsy had made to hide her computer and cameras. Eden put on medical gloves before she touched anything, which gave Olivia another shiver. She guessed that the equipment had been left running until they ran out of power. Some of the cables running from the cameras and computers and a portable hard drive went to a series of batteries linked together underneath the cabinet that Lyndsy had borrowed from all the furniture stored in the attic. None of them had leaked. Wiping off the dust coating them, Eden read the information on the capacity and estimated that everything could have run, capturing whatever happened in the creek below, for at least two days before running out of power.

She took pictures with her phone of how everything was set up, and all the phases of dismantling the setup, and dictated verbal notes on what she found, the condition of the equipment, and her theories for how everything operated. All the equipment was dead. If she couldn't charge the batteries, she would have to replace them or jury-rig something before she and Rufus could get into the files.

Halfway through the whole process, Ted Shrieve joined them in the attic. Eden had called the police station to report what had been found, because Lyndsy Auretta, the theorized owner of the equipment in the attic, had been a suspect in the disappearance, if not the murder, of Steve Edison. Ted had a video camera and recorded what Eden was doing, asking her questions, theorizing with her. If Olivia remembered correctly, he had been one of the officers who had protested Phoebe's arrest and had been suspended for a few days, until Captain Beakman's long-awaited fall finally began.

Olivia put on a spare pair of Eden's medical gloves and looked through the notebooks found in the bottom of the little cabinet. She hadn't seen Lyndsy's handwriting, and doubted she would have recognized it from three years before, but there had to be something in the notebooks that would identify who left them there.

One notebook was crammed with scraps of paper scribbled with cryptic notes, what looked like diagrams of floor plans, or crude maps, and what Olivia guessed were symbols used by the Underground
~~~~~

Railroad, to mark safe hiding places and routes, and warn when some place had become dangerous. One of the few conversations she had with Lyndsy, after she found that quilt square, had been about those symbols and the codes contained in them. Lyndsy had come alive when she talked about her passion, her eyes bright, her shoulders relaxed instead of hunched as if always on the alert.

A rectangle of plastic fell out of one notebook when she picked it up. Ted bent to get it and stepped into the light from one of the bare bulbs illuminating the attic. He grunted and studied it front and back.

"Driver's license," he said. "Is this Lyndsy?" He held it out to Eden and Olivia to look at. "Because if it is, that girl had a lot more going on than just hacking off a bunch of people."

"Yeah, that's ..." Eden glanced at Olivia, one eyebrow cocked.

"That's Lyndsy, but she wasn't Lyndsy, was she?" Olivia murmured.

The driver's license had Lyndsy's face, her cocky smile, but the name on the license was for Linda-Sue O'Hara of Oklahoma.

"She did say she was hiding from someone before she got hooked up with Macy and got tangled up in her mess," Eden offered. "Maybe she changed her identity in self-defense."

Olivia suspected Eden didn't quite believe that theory. Well, they had identified the notebook as Lyndsy's, at least. She kept going through the other notebooks.

The fourth she looked through was full of URLs, one to a page, followed by a series of email addresses, what were probably screen names, and passwords. All but the last pair of screen names and passwords on each page were struck out with two lines through them.

"I'm guessing, from things Lyndsy said about her hacker roommate, she had a regular habit of updating her access on every website she used," Eden said.

"Kind of paranoid, if you ask me," Ted offered.

"Which supports my theory that she didn't tell Mike about her little hidey-hole up here, because she didn't want him getting his hands on this information. Or she never sent him here to get her stuff in the first place."

"And it kind of explains why she never let us know when she got home like she promised," Olivia said. "Because she didn't promise. That was someone pretending to be her. So what happened to her?"

"Let's hope we find those answers when we get into her computer."

Underneath the notebooks was a battered old cigar box, containing a few old photos that had faded and gone brittle. Eden handled them carefully. She got Ted's agreement that she would study the photos to try to identify people and places, to get more information on Lyndsy's background and hopefully track her down.

Under those photos was a key, attached to a plastic tag for a self-storage facility. Both Eden and Ted seemed to go on the alert when Olivia told them what Lyndsy had said, about traveling light, but keeping her important research in a storage locker.

"The thing is …" Ted turned the tag and key over in his hands a few times while he thought. "Well, if the key is here, then chances are good she didn't empty out her storage space."

"Or she had two keys, and Mike emptied it for her," Eden pointed out.

"True. But I'm starting to lean toward that space being declared abandoned when payments stopped, and everything being either trashed or auctioned off."

"All we can do is contact them and hope they have detailed records." Eden held out her hand, and Ted gave the key to her. "I don't know what to hope for. Emptied, or abandoned?"

Olivia silently prayed that the locker had been emptied, because that meant Lyndsy really did voluntarily leave Cadburn. An abandoned and auctioned storage space implied something grim had happened to her and added to the mystery.

Finally, they had examined and recorded everything they could and hauled all the equipment downstairs. Phoebe had set up a workspace for Rufus, spreading a plastic picnic tablecloth on the kitchen table to keep everything clean. He got to work, searching through a crate of equipment he had brought with him to find charging cords that would fit. They left him grumbling about how computer manufacturers didn't have the sense to stick with one model and make things interchangeable, and went into the living room. Ted asked them about Lyndsy, everything they could remember. It was probably useless to search the rooms she had used three years ago, since several people had used them since. Mike had been thorough when he hauled away Lyndsy's belongings, even moving furniture away from the walls. Fortunately, both rooms currently had no renters. Ted searched, recorded, and spent more than an hour learning everything he could about the young woman who had called herself Lyndsy Auretta.

Chapter Thirteen

Monday, October 31

Saundra met Patty Hill and Charli Hall for breakfast at Morning Folks, before going to work. Somehow, Patty had talked her into being in charge of the gift-wrapping booth Cadburn Bible Chapel ran every year at the holiday kickoff street festival. Saundra was still trying to figure out how she had agreed to take that responsibility when Patty announced that it only made sense for Charli to be on her team. Then, before Saundra could start to protest, she promised she would be working with them, she just couldn't be in charge this year. And wouldn't it be a nice way for Saundra to really get to know everybody in town just a little better, outside of the library?

Well, that did make sense. And being treated to breakfast helped ease the feeling of having been shanghaied.

The three had a pleasant breakfast, and Charli took plenty of notes. Saundra had the task of researching the best place to get inexpensive, good quality wrapping paper, and Patty would handle decorating the booth. All three of them needed to be involved in recruiting people to man the booth, including a team who would keep the workers stocked with plenty of hot chocolate and thermal hand warmers. They were going to be outdoors in November, after all.

When they were getting up to leave, Saundra checked her watch, pleased to see she had plenty of time to stop at Book & Mug and see how Olivia was doing. She mentioned the dinner party and flooding at Deborah Wilkinson's house, and Amos's prediction that other houses along the creek would be dealing with similar problems. Especially since the power outage might have interfered with their sump pumps or other protections.

"So that's what had Olivia so glum yesterday," Charli said. "I heard her talking to someone about how many houses got flooded."

"Everybody's saying the water hasn't been so high in the creek in years," Patty said as the three headed down the street. "We've gotten a good dozen calls for the prayer chain, just dealing with the storm damage from Saturday. The force of the water eroded the levee Meg Hempstead's father built for them about ten years ago, and it just blasted through their backyard. Then with all that wind, that big old rotten maple got knocked over right into the sliding door. Here." She gestured at her car, parked along the sidewalk. "I want to check in with her. She's probably panicking, since she's responsible for Bee's house." The three climbed into Patty's car and she started the engine and headed down the street before continuing. "Meg said people on either side of them are dealing with a lot of water and tree damage themselves. They all have their favorite people to call for help, but I imagine Olivia wouldn't know who to call."

Patty pursed her lips and seemed to be deep in thought as she drove down Apple and parked four slots down from the front door of Book and Mug. The three of them went inside. Kelli was at the counter. No sign of Olivia. Saundra wondered if she had misunderstood, and Olivia wasn't working this morning.

"Is Olivia in?" Patty asked.

Kelli hooked her thumb around the corner, into the bookstore area. Saundra stepped back, so Charli wasn't blocking her view, and caught sight of Olivia leaning against the glass block wall that divided bookstore from coffee shop. She shook her head, and held a phone handset out from her ear, far enough to see daylight. Saundra had the feeling that if the furnace wasn't rumbling, along with the music spilling through the speakers overhead, she might have heard the very loud voice that prompted her friend to hold the phone so far away. Instead of angry, she looked tired.

"For the tenth time, no. I don't care what he told you," she hurried on. "First of all, I am at work, and I am not leaving to drive over and let you in. And second of all, I am certainly not going to leave you alone in the house when I head back to work." Her voice slowly increased in volume and tension.

The background music paused as one song ended, and now Saundra heard the angry, baritone voice.

"You can send me as many bills as you want, I am not paying them because I did not ask you to come to the house and I most certainly did not stand you up!" Olivia straightened up and headed back across the coffee shop to the counter. "Send the bill to whoever told you to stop by the house." She paused, pulling the phone even further away from her ear. "Your first mistake was calling on a phone with caller I.D. Because as soon as I hang up on you, I'm calling the police and filing a—"

Olivia held the phone out at arm's length, scowling at it. Then she sighed and slumped and shuffled to the counter. She put the phone down on a landline set on the end of the counter. Saundra assumed that line belonged to Book & Mug, which made the situation surrounding the call even more irritating.

"That sounded interesting," Charli said. "Mind if I use it in a book someday?"

"Let me guess." Saundra stepped up to Olivia and put an arm around her shoulders and led her over to the nearest unoccupied table. Fortunately, the morning rush had ended and they were in what Kai called the first lull of the morning. "Someone who thinks they have authority called one of the contractors on Bee's do-not-call list and told him to go over to the house, and when you didn't answer the door, he complained and called you here, and, did I hear right? He's going to bill you for his time wasted?"

"Got it in one." Olivia sighed and rested her head in her hands, with her elbows on the table.

"Wow, you should take up writing," Charli murmured. She sputtered a chuckle when Saundra stuck her tongue out at her.

Saundra realized Patty was on the phone, talking quietly but urgently with someone.

"Take it from someone who has helped investigate too many stupid domestic arguments and business dispute cases." Charli settled down at the table across from Olivia. "You need to file that complaint with the police. I don't care if it was an empty threat. Document this creepazoid who sent the guy to you. Start a trail of evidence or at least suspicions."

"According to Amos, there've already been enough complaints filed against him, nobody will doubt me," Olivia said.

"Olivia?" Patty stepped up to the table and held out her cell phone. "This is Greg Horvath, he's the son of Pastor Horvath at Westside Chapel, in Medina. He can help you. He's even free to head over to the house around noon, if you can meet him then." A sigh and a smile escaped her when Olivia just stared at her for a good ten-count, her mouth slowly falling open. "Take the call. He's waiting."

Olivia hesitated, nearly fumbling the phone when she took it.

"Uh, hi?" she said.

"You're amazing," Saundra whispered, as she and Charli and Patty moved away from the table, to give Olivia some privacy.

"It's nice being an answer to prayer once in a while," Patty said with a shrug.

~~~~~

Olivia left the coffee shop just before 11am, to meet Greg. Eden came downstairs at 12:15, to find out how the meeting went, and to take a break from the research project she was working on for a repeat client. Yesterday, Rufus had brought Lyndsy's equipment back to the office, still looking for the right power cords to charge the batteries. He had chosen to give all her equipment a thorough cleaning before charging. Three years of dust, heat, humidity and idleness could cause more problems than the worst hacker.

The self-storage facility manager was more cooperative than Eden
~~~~~

had hoped, once she explained finding the key and tag and gave a brief description of the circumstances. He apologized for not being the manager at the time Lyndsy had used the facility, and then dug into the records, which were all computerized. In ten minutes, he was able to tell Eden that the contents of the storage locker had been declared abandoned four months after Lyndsy allegedly left Cadburn.

Most of the contents were banker's boxes full of papers and photographs and maps. Those had been thrown out. Three boxes were full of books. The records didn't state what kind of books they were. Eden bet they were research books, likely on the Underground Railroad and Ohio history. Those had gone in an auction a month later. The credit card paying for the storage locker and the contract belonged to Linda Sue O'Hara. The credit card company had stopped payments on the account, and after the phone number on record turned out to be disconnected, and the certified letter sent to the address on the contract had been returned, the locker had been emptied out.

Just before Kai had come upstairs to tell them about Olivia's nasty phone call and Patty's help in finding a contractor, Rufus turned on the computer. He immediately discovered that Lyndsy—hopefully Lyndsy, and not another hacker—had installed multiple firewalls and safeguards in the computer after he had undone all that encryption. The same for the portable hard drive that they both assumed had been storing all the video from the cameras. When Eden headed downstairs to see if Olivia had come back from meeting the contractor, Rufus was talking to himself, alternating between frustration and admiration for the programming genius.

Eden alternated between amusement and disgust when she thought about that phone call Olivia had taken. The top suspect for who had sent the worker from Sharris and Hoomer Construction to harass Olivia was Myron Ellsworth. The really irritating part was that he knew where Olivia worked and gave the Book & Mug phone number to the man when she wasn't at the house. Kai insisted on filing charges, first to protect a valuable employee, and second to add to the pending avalanche of complaints and restraining orders ready to crush Ellsworth.

The lunch rush started just as Olivia came back from her meeting. She hurried to clock back in and get to work.

"How'd it go?" Eden asked, pausing at the counter.

Olivia looked up, grinned, and turned away to snatch up plates to fill with slices of the four-foot-long deli sandwich provided by Deli-licious. That was enough answer to satisfy Eden. She could wait for details after the rush was over.

~~~~~

Saundra had her umbrella ready when she stepped out of the library
~~~~~

to go to a late lunch. She almost didn't believe it when she saw a few streaks of washed-out blue peeking through the gray clouds overhead. She tucked her umbrella under her arm, positive if she fastened it closed or put it in its sleeve before crossing the parking lot, a downpour would catch her before she got her car door open.

A horn bleeped, startling her as she stepped off the sidewalk. She caught herself and looked to her left. Of course, who else? Nick drove up in his sleek black sports car, with the window rolling down.

"Took you long enough," he said, without his usual cocky, teasing grin. He looked even more like a stereotyped Mafioso enforcer when he was somber. "We've got a lunch date with Roy."

"What happened?" She didn't even consider refusing but pulled the passenger door open and tossed her umbrella into his back seat before sitting down.

"Cleo is fine. This has to do with that favor you asked me." He waited until she buckled in, then headed out of the parking lot. "How well do you know this Crandall?"

"He comes into the library once a week to have lunch with Mrs. T, and I see him in church a lot, but we really haven't talked much. The children all love him, so that should be a good enough character witness." She took a deep breath, hating the feeling of impending doom pressing on her shoulders. "Why?"

"Well, he is being blackmailed."

"I knew that. Mrs. Tinderbeck said so."

"Roy thinks highly of him, by the way."

Saundra braced for bad news, maybe implicating Pastor Roy in something.

"He doesn't do a lot online, otherwise. Most of his time is spent taking classes from a couple seminaries and doing historical research. He isn't on any social media. So the few personal emails he gets kind of stand out." Nick stopped at a stop sign before turning down the street for Cadburn Bible Chapel and glanced over at her. "He has a separate bank account for online transactions, which is smart. But he only sends his money electronically to one place."

"The blackmailer?" She caught her breath. Did she dare hope the whole puzzle could be solved that easily and quickly?

"This is where it gets tricky." A grin caught one side of his mouth. "And interesting. And I'm thinking we need to get Roy involved, just in case my next steps stir up some nasty reactions."

"Nasty … how?"

Nick shook his head and said nothing more. He pulled into the parking lot behind the church, got out of the car, and led the way to the back door in silence. Patty was standing at the office window where it looked out onto the parking lot. She raised an eyebrow at them when they came in, but said nothing, just tipped her head toward the open door of Pastor Roy's office.

"If I had thought to come to you three years ago," Pastor Roy said, as Nick and Saundra settled into chairs facing his desk, "we could have settled this problem immediately."

"Why didn't you?" Nick said.

Roy sighed. "Josiah asked me not to get involved. When the blackmail first started, he turned to some students whom he thought were involved. They got hurt. The blackmailer has threatened people close to him. What is a little frightening is that over the years, as Josiah's life has changed, the blackmailer keeps track of the people who matter to him. A harmless comment every month or so, with chilling implications. His friendship with Lydia. Making balloon animals for the children at church. Friends in the historical society. He prefers to keep paying the money and living a quiet life." Another sigh and he frowned at a spot on his desk blotter. "When I've pressed him, he simply says he must pay for his sins, even though he knows he's forgiven. Have you identified the blackmailer?"

"Not yet. Whoever it is, they're good." Nick settled back in his chair, slouching a little. "They've got some boobytraps set up, probably a warning system. I'll have to move slow and careful, or some of those threats might prove real. I backtracked his email, his financial activities. Something very interesting happened four months ago." He glanced at Saundra, then Roy. "The blackmailer changed the link to the site where he sends the payments. The last address, when I checked it, has completely shut down. And what was really interesting, he got a nasty email from a Myron Ellsworth, chewing him out over the change." That one-sided grin caught up his mouth when Roy sat up a little straighter. "You know the guy?"

"Oh, yes." Roy shook his head. "He's head of the historical society — Cadburn has two — the society that throws around a great deal of authority it doesn't possess. I get lectures that question my salvation every time we make some change to our building without asking for his permission and blessing."

"Why would he blame Mr. Crandall for the change?" Saundra asked. She caught her breath when the answer came instantly. "He's being blackmailed too? But … oh, he thinks Mr. Crandall is the blackmailer?"

Nick smirked and tapped his nose. "I did some digging into this guy. Doesn't know the first thing about internet security. I could get into most of his online accounts and really mess him up without breaking a sweat. Considering the tone of the emails he's sending to everybody and his lawyer … the guy deserves a whole lot worse."

"But you won't," Roy said, and leaned back in his chair with a weary smile. "Knowing you, you're gathering up all the evidence you can, just in case."

"Oh, yeah. What's funny is that there was a whole firestorm of emails between Crandall and Ellsworth three years ago, about this time. This guy really needs some lessons in clearing out his caches, deleting emails and covering his tracks."

"Nick ..." Saundra said. Sometimes, he seemed to enjoy drawing out the drama too much. "I'm on my lunch break. Please get to the juicy details?"

That got chuckles from both men.

"I don't have the time to read every single email." Nick dug in his pocket and brought out a flash drive, which he tossed to Roy. "Someone needs to, because those two were going back and forth, blaming each other for something, then turned on each other, about the time those payments started. Something happened four months ago, to make this guy decide Crandall has been working with the blackmailer all along."

"But we won't know until we read every email and figure out what they were talking about." Roy nodded and closed his hand around the flash drive. "What do you want me to do? You're getting me involved for a reason, I'm guessing."

"You need to bring Crandall in from the cold. Get him ready for a nuclear blast, if I make a mistake and trigger a reaction from the blackmailer. He's being watched. A total stranger approaching him will just send up a flare. Saundra, I need you to talk with Mrs. Tinderbeck, find out what happened three years ago. Something big enough for someone to blackmail over. We need to get at this from both sides, squeeze the life out of it before someone gets hurt again."

"I might have some ideas," Saundra said. "Or at least a starting point."

She spent the rest of her lunch hour relating what they had discussed at Olivia's dinner party. Saundra had no idea what the clashes between the Spirits of '62 and the history students had to do with the blackmail, unless Lyndsy found something that painted Josiah Crandall in a bad light. Maybe that was why he gave up his research. Yet how did that crime against historical research include Myron Ellsworth?

~~~~~

"Excuse me?" A tall, thin, shaggy-haired man wearing a faded purple Wizards World t-shirt leaned on the corner of the ordering counter.

"Can I help you?" Kai made a bet with himself that this newcomer would go for the Mo Klah listed on the chalkboard for today's specials. He literally had "geek" written all over him.

"Is Rufus around?"
~~~~~

"Ah … yeah." He stepped over to the shop's phone to call upstairs. "Can I tell him who's here?"

"No. On pain of death and insanity, do not ask that question!" Rufus zipped around the corner, nearly tipping onto one wheel, and skidded on the freshly mopped tiles, where a customer had dropped a tray with four pumpkin lattes less than twenty minutes ago.

Laughing, he and Wizards World bumped fists and hugged and thumped each other on the back. Rufus pivoted around, yanking on his friend's arm to make him face Kai and the order counter again.

"Kai, meet Gunky."

"Excuse me?" He blinked, not sure he heard right.

"So help me, man, if you're gonna start that up again, I'm jumping back in the car and heading back to Iowa!" Gunky—and Kai had the feeling that wasn't his name—made a gun cocking motion at Rufus with thumb and forefinger.

"Nah. They'll stop you at the border." Rufus laughed, making a waving motion like he was wiping out the last few seconds. "Seriously, though, this is J.R., my buddy from college, partner in cyber crime. If things work out, he'll be moving to the area."

"All depends on what we see. I like the town so far."

"How long can you stay?"

"How long can you put up with me in the same house?"

They laughed and bumped fists again. Rufus reached back behind himself and yanked a coat out of the backpack hanging off his chair. He glanced across the coffee shop at the bookstore side of the building, like he always did when he came downstairs during the day. Kai thought that habit had started when Raymond Fontaine had been harassing his sister, Devona, back in September.

"Hey, Vo, look who's here!" he called, and bundled up his coat on his lap before giving his wheelchair a hard push.

Devona had brought another box of books out from the back, to work on inspecting and sorting at the bookstore counter. She looked up and smiled as J.R. followed Rufus over. The three of them talked for a minute or two, then the two young men headed out the front door.

"What's up with Rufus?" Kai asked when Devona brought her mug over to refill from the hot water tap.

"Oh, they're looking at a couple of storefronts for rent. Their programming business has gotten big enough, they need a separate address and phone. Too many people calling them both, all hours of the day and night. J.R. is going to set up the custom designed computer business they've been talking about since college."

"What's with Gunky?" he had to know. Devona laughed as she dunked her tea infuser in the hot water.

"It's from a Bill Cosby routine. J.R.'s last name is Barnes. Junior Barnes picked on Cosby, and when he got really mad he called him a gunky." She shrugged. "Old joke."

Kai laughed with her, and made a note to look up the album it came from. He liked Rufus's sense of humor, so chances were good the routine would be funny.

Rufus and J.R. were back in less than an hour. Rufus headed upstairs, and J.R. settled in a booth to work on a computer and snack and drink through the remainder of the afternoon. Whenever Kai looked up to check on him, he noticed Rufus's college buddy seemed to spend more time watching Devona than whatever was on his computer screen.

~~~~~

Four o'clock, and Olivia thought this had been the longest day of her life. It made entirely no sense at all, until she thought about going back to the house and finding out what Greg had to say. She was still amazed that she was willing to leave him alone in Bee's house, but something about him told her he was trustworthy. She had had to learn to size up people quickly, dealing with the public. Besides, Patty Hill trusted and recommended him.

Olivia had prayed for help with the flooding problem this morning, and she had felt a little odd doing so. She usually didn't pray about big, right-this-moment things. Her prayers were more along the lines of asking for God's peace and being a good witness and living a life that would make people want to know what she knew. Besides, most of the time she just wasn't good with the snappy comebacks and wise, thoughtful responses. She could snark with the best when she was really hacked off, but knowing what to say and saying the right thing when it came to spiritual matters? Nuh uh, she was a total dud.

Still, knowing that her prayer from this morning had been answered in just a few hours made her feel a little dizzy.

And it didn't hurt that Greg was just rough-cut hunkalicious. God did a good job when He made him.

Olivia thought about maybe swinging by Celestial Dragon to pick up something for dinner and hoping he was still working, and he'd be hungry when she got there. Or would it seem more casual, less calculated, if she offered him leftovers from Saturday's dinner party? Then she might impress him a little with her culinary …

"Oh…heck," she breathed, when she realized she was daydreaming about a guy. A hunky, kind, smart guy who put her at ease from the moment she saw him waiting in the driveway. "I am in so much trouble," she whispered, and hoped no one was close enough to hear her.

A buzzing made her jump. She yanked her phone out of her pocket before she realized it was ringing, on vibrate all day per Book & Mug
~~~~~

policy. She didn't recognize the number, although it was a 330 area code, which was Medina and Akron.

"Hi, Greg?" Her face heated as soon as the words left her lips. If it wasn't him, she was going to feel like a total moron.

"Yeah, hi, Olivia. Look … I ran into something. Well, the short version is, when I got all that plastic off, I found a wooden panel in the wall, painted and textured to look like the packed dirt and stone in that part of the cellar. That's where the water came in. There's a tunnel, and…" He sighed. "Can you leave right now? You need to be here."

"Uh, sure." Her shift wasn't over for another hour, since she had taken time off at lunch, but Olivia felt sure the coffee shop traffic would stay sparse. This kind of overcast, chilly weather prompted people to head straight home. "I can probably get there in fifteen minutes."

"Good. I'll be waiting."

The lights in town were all green, and Olivia got there in thirteen minutes. Greg stood out front, talking with Ted Shrieve, both of them leaning against the trunk of a Cadburn patrol car. Two more patrol cars sat on the street, but there were no officers inside. The lights on top of the patrol cars slowly rotated, dull gleams of red and blue reflecting off the water in the street and in yards.

Why was there a police car in Bee's driveway?

"What happened?" She headed for the open garage door.

"No, wait." Ted reached out like he would stop her, then let his hand fall to his side. "We can't go in there. Not until the coroner shows up and the crime scene people are done." He shrugged. "Might be a few days."

"Coroner?" Olivia shook her head. "What happened?"

She choked on a sudden vision of Ellsworth breaking into the house to drive Greg away because he wasn't on the approved list. But that would mean Greg had fought back hard enough to hurt him.

That made no sense at all.

"Sorry, Olivia," Ted said, "but there's a skeleton in your basement."

"It's not mine. The basement," she blurted. "I'm just housesitting."

"Yeah?" He glanced at the house. "You're going to need to call the owner. Who is it?"

"Bee Wilkinson, from church."

Ted was on the phone with Bee when the coroner's van showed up. Olivia had called her, then Greg took over and told her what he had done and found, and Ted finished up. He offered Olivia a thin smile and told Bee he had to go now, they were going to remove the skeleton, and he would copy her on all the reports, as soon as they knew anything.

The arrival of the county coroner's van was like a signal. Or maybe the time of day had something to do with it. Olivia had a hard time keeping impressions straight as she fought for calm and tried not to guess what was going to happen next. She knew from overhearing Charli Hall talking about writing, crime scene investigations did not proceed as portrayed on TV and in the movies. Suddenly, everybody on the street seemed to be outside, watching the three officers or whoever they were in their plastic-covered clothes, carrying a folding stretcher through the front door of Bee's house.

"Can I be any help?" Amos said.

He strolled up the driveway, looking so casual, so kind. Olivia wished he was her grandfather, to cuddle her and promise everything was all right, it was just a bad dream, did she want some ice cream?

She introduced him to Greg. Amos knew Ted Shrieve. She hurried to assure them both he was a good friend of Bee's, then blurted, "Amos, Greg found a panel in the basement, and there was a skeleton in a tunnel."

"Really?" His eyes lit up and his mouth started to stretch into a grin, then he visibly fought to tamp down his excitement. "What kind of skeleton?"

"What do you mean, what kind?" Ted said. "I'm not a doctor, I can't tell you male from female or how long the guy's been dead, if it is a guy, or what killed him. There's just a skeleton, lying on a pile of rubble inside a hole dug in the bedrock, and some rocks on top of the skeleton, like things have been falling down on him, and ..." He shrugged.

"Were there any artifacts on the skeleton? Shreds of clothing? A watch? Jewelry? Hair?" Amos shook his head. "Ted ... how long have you lived in Cadburn? Forget that, I know your family. You have to have heard the arguments over the years, the stories, the theories, about Underground Railroad tunnels along the creek. Determining the era of the skeleton could go a long way toward verifying or proving those stories false."

"It was completely bare, what I could see," Greg said. "There were pieces of rock around it, and dust covering it, but I didn't see any jewelry. Is that good?"

"Well, considering how quickly natural fibers deteriorate, and the decomposition rate of flesh—but you have to take into account the conditions where the skeleton was found. Things like average heat and humidity, if insects could get to the body to help with decay..." Amos chuckled and shrugged. "I can only speculate based on what I've seen on *CSI* and *NCIS*. But a naked skeleton would be a very good start toward being very old. No synthetic materials to resist decay."

Olivia stopped herself before pointing out that someone could have put a naked dead body in the tunnel under the house, to make it harder to identify the victim. It had to be a murder victim, didn't it? Why would someone bury someone there if they didn't die under suspicious circumstances?

She couldn't stay in the house until the scene had been thoroughly searched and documented. The head of the crime scene team speculated that they could let her come back tomorrow, as long as they were able to block all access to the scene. Everything would depend on what the preliminary report from the coroner uncovered.

Greg went home, negating Olivia's hope to impress him with her cooking. Ted came into the house with her while she packed up her clothes and toiletries and computer. She cleaned out the refrigerator, reasoning she could at least take the leftovers back to Phoebe. Movement caught her attention, and she stepped to the bay window to see some people in uniforms standing around the ridge covered with bricks and stones and brambles. She had a feeling like several large chunks of a puzzle had fallen into place in front of her.

"Is that where the tunnel opens out, or the creek tried to come in or something?" She pointed at the uniforms.

"It's just a guess right now. There's another wall, with cracks at the bottom where the water came through," Ted said.

She shuddered.

"You okay?"

"I've seen someone sneaking around back there, poking around the pile. Twice. Ted, what if … what if that skeleton isn't a hundred years old? What if somebody hid the body there and they've been trying to get back in to move it?" A groan escaped her. "That sounded a whole lot more intelligent and scary when it was just in my head."

"Anything is possible right now. But you know, considering everything that's been found today? I'm gonna have to report those sightings, even if they don't end up being connected." He gestured at the table and pulled his phone out of his pocket. He set it up for voice recording as they sat down facing each other.

They were done quickly enough, considering how little there was to tell him. Olivia purposely sat with her back to the window so she wouldn't be distracted, trying to watch the people poking around the rock pile that most likely hid the opening of a tunnel. She had to add this to the long email for Bee, so her friend had everything in writing.

Finally, she went through the house, turning off everything she could find, closing doors, tossing a few things back into the freezer that she had put out to defrost, pulling curtains closed, anything to seal up the house and protect Bee's property and privacy. She handed the keys over to Ted, and he promised he would drop by Book & Mug to give them back to her when she could return.

Olivia's mind raced on the drive home. Phoebe wasn't home, so she could delay explaining what had happened for a few more hours. Was tonight a rehearsal night? She had things to do, and more thinking to do.

Before she wrote to Bee, she called Charli Hall. Fortunately, she was in the church directory. Olivia knew she wrote thrillers, so Charli had the right connections to find out accurate information for her books. Those connections would come in very handy now.

The way Olivia saw it, Bee had the right to know everything that was done to her house and what was found. As the owner of the property where that skeleton was found, she had the right to know everything learned about the victim. Olivia figured Charli would know the right people to talk to, to ensure that. Then she would write that email to Bee. And maybe by then the feeling of everything being slightly off balance would have faded, and her head would stop trying to spin.

"So, do you know who I can talk to, for Bee, to make sure she's not locked out?" Olivia said, finishing her explanation.

"Well, I think your friend needs to talk directly with the right kind of lawyer for this kind of situation," Charli began. "I do have a friend in the county coroner's office, but while she's incredible in helping me put together a crime, she's not the kind of person who will just ignore the rules. This is real, not a hypothetical situation for a book."

"Oh, okay. Do you happen to know the right kind of lawyer?" Olivia was glad she was sitting down. The sudden drop from hope to impending disappointment made her feel drained.

"No, but I know a guy who does. I'm gonna call Carson Fletcher. He's a PI. I'll give you his phone number, and I'll call him while you update Bee. Have her call him. He can start lining up the legal people to make sure the lines of communication are open."

"Thanks. You have no idea how much this means to me. You and your writing friends are getting free drinks for a month on me."

"You don't have to do that," Charli said, with a soft chuckle. "You're afraid someone will try to put the blame for the death on Bee?"

"Pretty much."

"Not going to happen. Not with Carson on the job, and all the strings he can pull. And how about we call the prayer chain at church and get them pounding on the gates of heaven for some protection?"

Olivia choked up as she thanked Charli for her help and advice. She laughed at herself that she hadn't thought to stop and pray since this morning, when all she had to worry about was flooding in Bee's basement. She took the phone number and Carson's website, so Bee could look him up before making the call. Then she wrote the email.

After she closed her notebook computer, she put her head down on the kitchen table and cried. She wished Phoebe didn't have a rehearsal tonight, because she didn't want to be alone with all sorts of strange thoughts and speculations swirling through her mind.

The doorbell rang, while she was trying to decide if she should go to the bathroom to wash her face or just curl up and try to fall asleep until

Phoebe got home. Olivia mopped her eyes with the sleeve of her sweatshirt and went to the front door

"You okay?" Kai asked, once she got the door open wide enough to see him with Saundra.

Was it silly for her to think that maybe God was still giving her some extra care, and He had nudged them to come over and check on her? Olivia pushed that speculation aside and welcomed them in and rubbed more tears from her eyes.

Later, Eden called to let her know Rufus had gotten into Lyndsy's computer. It and the hard drive were jammed full of PDFs, photos, copies of documents, and hundreds of hours of video. She and Rufus had other jobs to work on, and deadlines to meet for several clients, but they would try to put in a couple hours every day to go through the videos.

"Just have to warn you, it could take us weeks to go through those files," Eden said. "Just be patient. I want answers ... well, I was going to say I want them as much as you do, but I have the feeling this is kind of personal for you."

Chapter Fourteen

Tuesday, November 1

Carson Fletcher was waiting when Kai opened the doors of Book & Mug the next morning. He apologized for taking up Olivia's time, when he knew she had duties first thing in the morning, but he just had a couple questions to ask, rather than calling Bee, three time zones away. Would Kai mind if they talked while Olivia worked?

Kai tried to be amused, but having the private investigator involved suddenly made the whole skeleton-in-the-cellar situation a bit grim. He gestured for Carson to come in and called for Olivia to come out from the back, where she had gone to fetch another rack of mugs to bring up front.

"We're good," he told her. "You can go up and use the office if you need some privacy," he added, sliding his hand into his pocket for the stairwell key.

"No, this should only take a minute or two at the most," Carson said.

Olivia gave Kai an "are you sure?" look, and he nodded, then turned to move behind the counter as the first customers hurried through the door. She led the PI around to the seating area tucked behind the bookstore. Kai reached under the counter to turn on the music, and raised the volume two notches, just in case. While Carson didn't think they needed privacy, there was always the chance of curious ears overhearing something and warping it all out of context.

Kai finished the fifth coffee order of the day, a jumbo Americano with a box of almond shortbread cookies, when Carson headed for the door. Olivia hurried to get behind the counter and gave him a grateful smile. Six more people spilled through the doors Carson had just opened, and Kai didn't get a chance to ask how she was doing until the first lull hit about 9:30. Olivia hauled the second bus pan of mugs and spoons back to the kitchen. Kai checked supplies and replenished the syrups and sugar sprinkles. From the clatter and rattle coming through the atmosphere music, she was filling the dishwasher trays. One thing he appreciated about Olivia was her sense of rhythm in the shop, the lulls and how long they would last. If she felt it was safe to spend time doing the dishes, then he could relax for a few minutes, because the lull would last.

Right on time, Olivia came up front with the first rack of steaming fresh, clean mugs at the same time the door opened again. She called out a greeting to the trio coming in, while Kai went to the supply room to get stacks of all four sizes of paper cups and plastic lids. He had made Olivia head barista after three months because she helped Book & Mug glide along like a well-oiled machine. He listened to her chatter with the trio, college students who went to her church, while he filled the dispensers for the paper cups. Paige Owens and her cousin visiting from Nebraska came in as the students were heading for the door, supplied with coffee to get them through their first class of the day. Paige waved and headed for the bookstore, with her cousin in tow. Kai couldn't see anyone else approaching the doors of the shop.

"So, how's it going? Any action from Carson?" he asked, pitching his voice low.

Olivia flinched as she picked up the sponge to wipe down the counter, but she gave him a brave smile. "His lawyer friend is already filing requests for disclosure or whatever. Bee does have rights as the property owner. And Charli called on my way in to say she left a message with her friend in the coroner's office, asking for any information she could give her."

"Like what?" He crossed his arms and leaned on the damp, clean counter.

"Whatever she thinks won't violate privacy or ethics rules. Like, she can say if there are obvious signs of damage to the bones, but she can't mention anything that's still only theory, like say the guy had some disease. She can say if there was a bullet hole, or signs that bones were broken in the past, but can't say if the body was male or female, and speculations on race or age. Charli said it helps that both her friend and the head of the whole department are big fans and they've worked with her before, so they know she'll be discrete. There's a chance they might tell her things they normally wouldn't reveal until the official autopsy report comes out."

"Big fans, huh?" He offered a grin. "Do you have any idea of Charli's writing name? Saundra knows, but she's not telling."

"We should all have a friend as reliable as Saundra." Olivia gestured at the door with a jerk of her chin.

Kai turned to see the next customers come in. He nodded to her, judged the numbers with a glance, and ducked under the drawbridge at the end of the counter to head upstairs and report to Eden. She had promised she would do all she could to wriggle information loose that someone might try to keep away from Carson and his legal friend. Olivia was part of the Book & Mug family, and Bee Wilkinson was a friend.

~~~~~

Eden came downstairs with a notebook, to sit at the counter and do some brainstorming with Olivia when the coffee shop traffic slowed down
~~~~~

enough to let her talk. She stepped behind the counter to fill her jumbo insulated mug with boiling water from the hot tap for tea. Kelli smiled and reached around her to pick up the shop phone, which was flashing. She chirped her greeting as she reached with her other hand for the order pad. Her smile flattened into distaste.

"I'll have to check if she's working today. Just hold on a moment." She tapped the hold button on the console for the phone and put the wireless handset down on its backside. "Liv, call for you. The guy sounds like a total grump. Want me to tell him you're not here?"

"Thanks, but..." Olivia handed a tray of sealed cups to Melba Tweed, and a bag of cookies to Cilla, and kept her smile on her face as the elderly cousins thanked her and hurried out of the shop.

Eden watched the Tweeds go and shuddered a little, remembering how close they had come to losing their dream of a candle shop. Between Ernie Benders' criminal connections punishing him for messing up, and their lunatic and criminal relatives trying to steal from them, Brighten Your Corner almost didn't open. At all. Forget about on time.

"For all I know, he's across the street, and he can tell if you cover for me," Olivia said. "Don't want to get the grump on your case, too." She held up her hand, and Kelli slid the phone down the length of the counter to her. "Want to bet it's Ellsworth?" she murmured, meeting Eden's gaze.

She tapped the button to take the call off hold and greeted the caller. Her eyes rolled ceilingward and she nodded and held the phone out from her head a good six inches. Eden heard the strident voice but couldn't make out the words. Not without getting close enough Olivia would know she was listening in.

"Whoa, whoa, stop right there. Nobody asked you to send somebody to the house. So don't you go throwing around false accusations and calling us liars."

Olivia met Eden's gaze and crossed her eyes.

"Oh, really? *I'm* in trouble for letting people get to work repairing the flood damage on the exterior property? You better fire the nasty little spies reporting to you, because they have no idea what they're—"

Another spurt of strident, strained words.

"Well, you just remember that there's a pending restraining order against you to keep you off Bee's property and not allow you within 100 yards." She mouthed "no" and shook her head to Eden, who muffled laughter behind her hand. "Do your spying from across the creek, but don't you dare step foot on her property. And take a good look at the jackets those construction workers are wearing." Pause. "What do they say?" Olivia snorted. "Crime scene investigation, in case you're not familiar with what those initials stand for."

More angry words, but dropping in volume and pitch.

"No, you do not have any right to know what's going on. Go ask your powerful friends about the body that was found in Bee's basement. Or maybe you don't have to ask. Maybe you put it there?"

More shrieks. Olivia winced and turned her head to look at the phone. "The scuzzbucket called me a liar and hung up on me."

"What is going on?" Kelli demanded.

"Oh...heck." Olivia looked around, her cheeks flushing hot pink. She had managed to keep her voice down, for the most part. The customers sitting in the booths weren't looking at the counter. Nobody seemed to be listening. Eden felt grateful for atmosphere music and a loud furnace ventilation system.

More customers walked in, and the house phone rang again. Olivia winced, then took a deep breath, and reached to answer, politely and cheerfully, as if she hadn't just had an unpleasant conversation.

The call wasn't Ellsworth coming back for round two, but a phone order. Eden finished filling her triple-size travel mug, dug in her jeans pocket for her bags of tea, dropped the bags into the hot water, sealed the mug, and got out of Kelli and Olivia's way as they handled their orders.

She settled into the corner booth instead of at the counter and watched the two baristas work, and she thought. Long and hard. Until she came to a decision and a task that required her computer. An email, to go onto the record. Kai was coming down the stairs as she headed up them, and she stopped him on the landing to brief him on what just happened.

"I'm filing a complaint against Ellsworth as a property owner. You need to file one as Olivia's employer. Have her file one as well. How soon until that egotistical jerk settles so firmly into his delusion that he can justify using violence to enforce his demands?"

"You got it." Kai took two more steps down. "I hate to say this, but the spook has been useful, cutting through the red tape."

"Don't say it." Eden forced a smile. "I already thought of it. I hope I still have that business card with his number. Otherwise, I have to call Saundra to get it. The fewer witnesses ..." She shrugged and continued up the stairs.

Kai chuckled and headed down again. "Better you than me."

Far too quickly, Eden had her complaint letter written and sent to Captain Sunderson. Then she dug in the catchall box on her desk. Nick West's business card sat right on top. She turned it over in her fingers five times before she tapped the number into her phone. She refused to put it in the phone's memory, just yet. She hoped she wouldn't have to call on him for any more favors in the future. For Olivia, she would put herself in his debt. If he was going to be a pain about it ... she would just have to sic Saundra on him, to make him behave.

That thought amused her enough to cut some of her tension. Getting his outgoing message brightened her spirits more.

"This is Eden Cole, of Finders, Inc. I need to ask a favor." She refused to remind him of his recent involvement with the threats to Melba and Cilla Tweed, or that Saundra was a good friend. "One of Kai's employees is housesitting, and the flooding in Cadburn this weekend uncovered a skeleton in the cellar. Could you pull some strings, tell us what the officials know already and aren't releasing?" She gave the address, the homeowner's name, the time of the report, and the responding officers.

Then she thanked him for any help he could give, hung up, and fought the urge to put her cell phone on vibrate and walk away. That would be childish. But there was just something about Nick West, that look in his eyes sometimes, that tone in his voice. It said he knew an important secret, something having to do with her and her cousins, and he was going to make them beg before he'd tell it.

~~~~~

"Hey, can you help a guy?"

That shy, apologetic smile did not belong on the square-cut face sitting on top of a linebacker build. Maybe the stack of books in his arms explained a little bit as the customer shuffled up to the counter where Kai and Truman were going over the menu for Celestial Dragon. The guy had been creeping up and down the short aisles in the bookstore for the last two hours. Kai had a bet on with himself that he had pulled every book off the shelf and read the back cover or the first couple of pages of each one.

"Sure, what do you need?" Kai said.

"This is part of a set." The customer tugged a thick book covered in faded navy blue cloth from the bottom of his stack. "I have number one. Do you have volumes three, five, and six?"

"Not sure." Kai held out his hand and the customer handed the book over. He had to open to the title page to know what the book was, because the ink on the spine and cover had faded enough to be illegible.

The set covered world history, culture, and literature. Kai remembered it because the books had caught his eye at the estate sale he had attended last week. He also remembered it because the library had been a mess, with no order whatsoever. Devona, who had gone to the sale with him to evaluate any books he found, had remarked that it looked like a scene from an old mystery novel, where someone ransacked the library of an old estate, looking for clues in a treasure hunt.

"I think we have the complete set," he said, and the customer's face lit up. "The problem is, we don't have all the books out on the shelves yet. My assistant is going through about a dozen crates, evaluating and repairing and cataloging. When she comes in, I can ask her to call you back and give you an idea how long that will take."
~~~~~

"Thank you. That'd be great. You have no idea how grateful I am."

"No problem."

"When will she be in?"

"She's got the afternoon shift, so around lunchtime."

Kai dug out a business card and underlined the shop number to hand to the customer, then took his name and phone. A tidal wave of customers came in then, and he and Truman got busy filling orders. Phoebe came in halfway through that, and relieved some of the pressure. When they had a break more than an hour later, and Truman ran out to get their lunch from Celestial Dragon, he found the customer sitting in a booth, watching the bookstore counter, where a little chalkboard sign asked people to take their book purchases up to the coffee shop counter.

"Must be nice, having nowhere to go," he muttered, and reached for the sponge to wipe down the counter.

"What?" Phoebe glanced over to the booth when Kai explained about the customer waiting for Devona. "I know him."

"From where?" He stepped over to the box holding pens and business cards and message pads, and dug out the card with the customer's information. Doug Jones.

"He's the new guy at the fire station. Chief Holcomb brought him in last week so we could meet him. The new guy has to pick up orders."

"Oh, right."

Jones was still sitting there, watching the bookstore, when Devona came in. She had a milk crate full of books that she had taken home to repair. Kai hurried around the counter to meet her and help her, but Jones beat him to it. A big, dopey grin covered his face as he approached her and offered to carry the crate. She thanked him, and he watched her with a dazed, starry-eyed gaze.

Well, that was a natural reaction. Devona was a pretty girl with books, and Jones was definitely a bookworm. He was also a firefighter, so on first glance, he seemed the right kind of guy to fall for Devona. She needed a big, strong, hero-type guy, after the rough couple months she had gone through. Kai laughed at himself, knowing he was definitely getting tired, when he thought of keeping a running tally of how many people met at Book & Mug and ended up together.

~~~~~

Just before Olivia headed home, she ran upstairs to the office to report important news. And not the special election results. Everyone knew Sarah Fontaine would be elected, the moment she announced she would run for the open trustee position. Roger Cadburn's supporters only grumbled for a few days about Sarah taking unfair advantage of the sympathy vote, after the murder of her grandson, Conrad Price, but the few who made that complaint faced instant censure from nearly everyone
~~~~~

in the township.

The skeleton in Bee's cellar was a recent death, a modern male, with three implants in his upper jaw and a pin in his right ankle. His right knee had been replaced. Charli had gotten the serial number of the artificial knee joint from her friend in the coroner's office and was pulling all sorts of strings to identify the make and model, and the name of the patient.

Eden only allowed herself to gloat for a few moments, when Olivia called right after *Jeopardy* finished, to report that the patient had been identified. Charli's searching skills had beaten Nick West with all his connections that could normally cut through all the red tape like a hot wire through plastic sheeting.

The implications chilled her. The skeleton was Steve Edison. He hadn't gone to intern for a historical writer. He hadn't been playing a nasty trick on Lyndsy with that video that tried to frame her. He had been murdered in that video, and the murderer had access to the Fendergast house to hide the body. The murderer couldn't be Fendergast, just from the struggle that took place in the creek, but had he helped hide the body?

Had Lyndsy fled in fear for her life because she knew who did kill Steve?

Eden called Saundra, because she was part of the investigation, and not entirely to gloat over Nick losing the unofficial race.

"Thanks," Saundra said. "That just raises a whole bunch of new questions, doesn't it?"

"You don't sound surprised." Eden leaned back in her swivel chair and put one foot, then the other up on her desk. "Why do I have the feeling West gave you that information, and he's butting in?"

"I wouldn't say butting in." Saundra laughed softly, and a man's voice rumbled in the background. "I asked him for some help, trying to track down Lyndsy. Something just didn't feel right about her story, even before you and Olivia found that computer. Phoebe told me Steve called some of the Spirits of '62 and emailed others, saying good-bye, good riddance. Did he come back to meet his murderer? We won't know the timing until the skeleton has been examined more, and they'll need to investigate that tunnel more and ..." She sighed. "This is why I try not to watch all those crime scene investigation shows."

"Yeah, addicting, aren't they?" Eden managed a raspy chuckle. "What's really sad is how those shows mess up trial lawyers, because everybody expects the evidence to be revealed in no time at all, no questions, no doubts, flashing neon sign pointing out guilt."

"Nothing is ever easy, is it? You know ... I was actually bracing to find out that was Lyndsy's body hidden in the tunnel, and we'd be looking for Steve as the prime murder suspect."

"Hmm, yeah, that does make more sense," she admitted. "What time did the spook show up and give you the news?"

Another chuckle from Saundra. "About ten minutes ago. We were debating if we should go see Olivia, or just call her, when you called."

"Good, then Charli beat him out." This time, Eden heard Nick laugh. Maybe he wasn't such a pain in the neck after all. Even if he was a know-it-all.

Thursday, November 3

Thursday afternoon, Olivia got the call that she could come back to Bee's house. Captain Sunderson came by personally to bring the keys back and gave her a condensed version of the report that would be sent to Bee, through Worter, Worter & McIntosh. The lawyer Carson Fletcher recommended was working with the local law firm, to ensure Bee's rights were being guarded from all angles.

Captain Sunderson clearly wasn't willing to go into details in that aspect of the case, but she expressed her appreciation when Olivia offered to send her all the information Saundra and Phoebe had compiled about the members of the Spirits of '62, and the timeline when Steve allegedly left town. So far, four members of the Spirits had come into the station for interviews. After three years, their stories were sketchy. That was as far as the police captain would go.

The scene had been contaminated by damp and mold, a few collapses of dirt and rock, and possibly previous flooding. Captain Sunderson had talked with Greg Horvath already, putting some conditions and restrictions on him as he got back to work on the source of the flooding. She had emailed Bee to warn her that whenever Greg found something questionable, he would have to stop what he was doing until the police could investigate.

Steve Edison was presumed to have been in a costume when he was killed, per the video used to blackmail Lyndsy, because the skeleton was essentially naked. Meaning all natural fibers had totally decayed. Other than the medical hardware and the artificial knee joint that had led to his identification, the only materials found with his skeleton were a medical ID bracelet, warning that he was allergic to penicillin and walnuts, and remnants of his leather boots, which decayed at a slower rate than the wool and cotton that would have made up his clothes.

"From the testimony so far, the man was a stickler for historical accuracy," Sunderson said. "But it does raise some questions, if he was in uniform, and his killer just didn't take his clothes. But then why put his boots back on his feet? Why was he in uniform when he wasn't rehearsing? What?" she said, when Olivia caught her breath at a sudden memory. "You know something?"

"Yeah, but ..." She closed her eyes, trying to remember clearly. She had an image in her head of Steve and Lyndsy, laughing. That was it. "He was up to something with Lyndsy. Basically driving Mr. Fendergast crazy. They came in one night right after he had one of his fits. They were both in costume and laughing. Maybe Steve was down there by himself, and someone got mad at what he was doing to that old man?"

"That ... makes sense," Sunderson said after a short pause that seemed to hum in the silence. She gestured for Olivia to wait, pulled a notebook out of her pocket, and started taking notes.

"Nobody ever mentioned finding his car, abandoned, so did the killer take his keys?" Olivia said.

"Have you considered going into police work?" Captain Sunderson offered a crooked smile.

"Ah, no thanks. I kind of enjoy the crime-solving shows on TV, but I never figure out who did it." That reminded her of Amos's remark about learning about forensics and crime scene investigation from TV shows. She asked if she could keep him updated on all this, since he was Bee's neighbor and friend. Then the moment she asked, she regretted asking. What if Captain Sunderson said no? Maybe it wasn't exactly ethical, but if she wasn't told not to, then she couldn't really get in trouble for telling him, could she? Well, that flimsy get-out-of-trouble card had just been lost.

"Considering the ties with the reenactors and historical groups for this investigation ..." The captain frowned thoughtfully a few moments. "I've consulted with Amos in the past. Building practices in different eras are his specialty. We were able to prove a house was broken into, creating access that the thief used multiple times, because repairs were made with materials that didn't match the rest of the wall in the cellar. It was interesting." She jotted something more in the notebook. "Sure, keep him updated, in case we need to talk to him, but ask him to keep it quiet."

Olivia promised.

"So Lyndsy and Steve didn't run off together," Amos said, when Olivia called him. "I thought I saw a spark between them. When he came down off his high horse and she wasn't having such fun irking him. My niece has told me about far too many unbelievable romance novels that start out with two idiots fighting like cats and dogs. Then again, I'm a fan of genuine romance," he confessed with a chuckle.

"Like Annabelle Cadburn running off with her mystery sweetheart?" Olivia offered.

"I hope so. And lived a long, peaceful, honorable life with the man she loved."

Something wistful in the tone of his voice as it faded away gave Olivia a shiver. Then he laughed at himself.

He asked if he could come over once she got home from work, to see the tunnel. Olivia said yes. Then when the coffee shop had quieted down for the afternoon lull, she invited Kai and asked him if the rest of the dinner party wanted to come see. They had been there when the flooding was discovered, after all.

~~~~~

Greg joined the group at Bee's house that night. He had as much right to be updated on what had been discovered as anyone else.

As a result of what Troy called Dinner Party, Part Two, Eden and Amos agreed to come spend the day on Friday, to document everything Greg did, everything he found, whether it was historical or just evidence of flawed construction techniques. Amos looked so quietly excited about the prospect as they laid out their plans, Olivia thought the elderly man might start glowing in a few more minutes.

She called Bee and put her phone on speaker, so they could confer. Bee loved the idea and granted Greg leeway to make decisions on the spot when it came to solving the flooding problem and fixing any damage he might discover along the way. Amos was granted verbal power of attorney, to oversee protecting anything of historical importance, if it came up during the investigation.

They all trooped downstairs to look at the opening in the cellar. All the plastic and two-by-fours Greg had removed from the wall were neatly bundled up and piled up on the cement floor under the addition to the house. The niche where Steve's body had been was sealed off with more sheets of thick plastic, held in place with a frame of two-by-twos nailed right into the rock, to prevent contamination from further work to deal with the flooding. Just to make sure there was no misunderstanding, strips of crime scene tape went from one side of the sealed area to the other.

Not long after everyone went home, Olivia wished she hadn't come back. She couldn't sleep. The day's events kept playing through her mind. The things the group had discussed that evening kept generating new ideas and questions. She sat in the window seat, looking out over the creek, and that long ridge covered with stones and brambles on the east of the property. It made too much sense that there was a tunnel somewhere under all that, leading from the creek to Bee's cellar.

She watched the mist drifting across the water, and wished the cameras that Rufus had cobbled together weren't useless. She wished the crime scene team had posted someone out there in the dark to keep watch. Just the thought of some creep finding that tunnel and somehow getting into Bee's house in the middle of the night made her shiver. The chill radiating off the glass seemed to double.

"That does it. I either get a blanket, or I get out of here and go to bed," she muttered.
~~~~~

She didn't do either and knew she was being ridiculous. She heated some chai and settled in the window seat again and continued watching the creek as she sipped. Her imagination had gone into overdrive. As long as she kept watch, nothing would happen.

The moment that thought crossed her mind, Olivia flinched and held her breath, the mug against her lips. A dark shape emerged from the mist from her right, heading straight for the ridge and piles of stone and brambles. Her heart pounded louder, until she released that breath. An uneasy chuckle escaped her.

"You are not getting away with this again," she muttered, and glanced around the kitchen. Where did she leave her purse?

It sat on the counter, two steps away. She snatched it up and pulled out her phone. She had the police station on speed dial now, as Chief Sunderson had advised her to do, until this whole mess was cleaned up.

"Frank Novallis is on your street," the dispatcher, Brenda, said the moment the connection opened. "What's happened?"

Olivia breathed a silent prayer of thanks that she had reported the dark figure walking along the creek, when the team interviewed her. All she had to say was, "That intruder is back, poking around the ridge."

Brenda asked her to keep watch and stay on the line and patched Frank into the call. Carl Young was on the street on the other side of the creek. Brenda patched him in, and he responded that he was coming down the slope, about four houses down from Mrs. Tinderbeck's house, where it wasn't a nearly vertical drop down to the creek. Frank said he was coming from the east, on the far side of the ridge. Olivia saw movement and nearly gasped aloud when she saw a streak of light.

"He's got a flashlight. I think," she said, speaking nearly in a whisper. "It looks like he's right on the edge of the bank."

"I see him," Carl said. "Can you get around all that, Frank, if I turn the light on him and he goes back up the creek?"

"No problem," Frank said.

Olivia held her breath again and strained her eyes, although she couldn't see anything except a strong beam of light that put the hunched shape into silhouette. It stood up and ran, heading back the way he came.

And fell, sprawling headfirst on the bank of the creek.

She heard men's voices calling but couldn't make out the words through the sudden thudding of her heart. Carl kept his flashlight beam focused on the figure, as Frank appeared from over the ridge and leaped down, seeming to hold the intruder flat with his own flashlight beam.

"You okay, Olivia?" Brenda said.

"Yeah." Her voice cracked. "I think they got him."

She knew she wouldn't be able to sleep if she didn't get some answers, even if it was just to see the face of whoever had been sneaking around Bee's property. Olivia waited, watching, as Frank restrained the intruder, hauled him to his feet, and started him marching up the west side of the house, to get to the street. She nearly hung up on Brenda, in her hurry to get to the front door and turn on the porch light. Olivia thanked her and promised her a cinnamon hot chocolate when she came into Book & Mug. Brenda laughed, told her to get a good night's sleep, and hung up.

A gasp escaped Olivia when Frank and his prisoner stepped into the light spilling out from the porch. Both men turned to look at her. She knew she had been foolish, coming outside, letting the intruder see her, but she had needed this.

"You know this guy?" Frank said.

"Oh. Hey," Mike Kioto said, and seemed to shrink in on himself. "This is your place?"

"Yeah." Olivia shivered. "He used to be with the Spirits." She fought a surge of nausea. Did Mike know they had found Steve? "What are you doing here?" she blurted. "Was that you last week, sneaking around? What do you want?"

"Hey, sorry ..." Mike shrugged. "That girl from the library, asking all those questions. Got me remembering."

"That really doesn't explain anything," Carl said. "Into the car."

"What were you doing down there?" Olivia demanded.

Another shrug from Mike. She was getting tired of that, because he just couldn't pull off the innocent act. "I remembered what Lyndsy was working on, and I thought, what if, y'know? Wouldn't it be cool if I found what she was looking for? So I dug out all those notes she made and put things together and ... I remembered the old guy who lived here, waving his gun around when we were practicing, and I figured it'd be safer if I came at night. Y'know?"

"Did you really give Lyndsy all her stuff when you cleared out her rooms?"

"What?" Mike's mouth fell open and his face crinkled up like he couldn't make sense of her question.

"Did Lyndsy really ask you to move all her stuff?"

"Yeah. What's this all about? Look, she was scared stiff and I was ready to dump Macy anyway, because honestly? That chick was psycho, she just hid it really well. Get myself free of them both. Y'know? So I figure, a big favor for Lyndsy, make up for giving her such a hard time, help her out. Then I'm done with both of them." He nodded for punctuation. "Why? What's going on?"

"I don't think you should tell him anything more," Frank said. "You gonna be okay, Olivia?"

She nodded and gestured for them to take Mike away. She went around the house, checking all the locks on the doors and windows. Then she jammed a kitchen chair under the doorknob of the door to the basement before she went to bed.

~~~~~

Captain Sunderson was kind enough to copy Olivia on the interrogation. Mike stuck to his story, and didn't add anything to what they knew. They couldn't hold him on any charges other than trespassing. They couldn't even charge him with interfering with a police investigation, because the crime scene people hadn't strung their ubiquitous yellow tape around the ridge. Fortunately for Olivia's peace of mind, they hadn't found the opening into the tunnel yet.

She wished they hadn't let Mike go, though. She had the awful feeling they had missed something important. Some tiny detail that would come back to bite them.
~~~~~

Chapter Fifteen

Friday, November 4

Eden arrived at the house within half an hour of when Olivia had to leave for work. She brought a video camera. Amos arrived moments later, hauling a stadium chair and notebook and camera. Olivia offered them breakfast, and they all laughed when Amos admitted he had been too excited to eat. Greg arrived while she was ransacking the refrigerator. He brought a set of work lights, to illuminate the tunnel.

Water sat in the dips in the uneven stone floor, when Greg pulled back the plywood panel. He didn't seem surprised. He grinned when Olivia let out a cry of dismay.

"That's actually helpful. It's kind of hard to track down a leak if there's no water to mark a trail. Didn't you hear it rain early this morning?" he asked.

"No."

"Well, that shows how good the insulation is in this house, and the seals on the windows. It wasn't a heavy rain, but steady. Watching the weather is kind of vital, considering how it affects my work." He hooked his thumb at the standing water. "That's a big help. And it's a good thing the owner gave me freedom to do what needs doing."

Greg made three trips, bringing in crates of equipment he might need as he dug for the path of the water that got into the house. There would have been more trips, if Eden and Amos hadn't offered to help. Olivia had to leave while he was filling their arms. She laughed at herself as she drove off, because she wanted to stay and watch. Even if nothing really happened. With Amos around, full of stories about Cadburn's history and the ridiculous escapades of characters and scoundrels and politicians, none of them would be bored.

~~~~~

Half an hour into boring at the base of the wall blocking the tunnel, things got messy.

Eden was grateful she had added surgical masks to the kit she kept in her car for on-site investigations. Most of her work occurred via the Internet or making phone calls, but she had learned early on to be prepared for messy situations, and for leads and clues showing up at the most unexpected times. Greg stopped boring when the first cloud of dust
~~~~~

soared upward from the thick spiral of coated steel he was operating manually with a crank. He apologized, but he only had a breather mask for himself. Eden ran up to her car for her kit, and masks for her and Amos.

"Sorry. Should have thought ahead." Greg shrugged, looking a little sheepish.

Eden thought he might have started blushing, but his cheeks were already a little red from effort, so she couldn't be sure. He was kind of cute, in a serious, musclebound way. She hoped the interest she thought she saw when he watched Olivia wasn't her imagination. Olivia deserved a nice guy in her life.

Greg moved the thick pad he was kneeling on after finishing the third bore hole. He arched his back, knelt, picked up the awl, and was about to put it to the wall when a crack visibly crept up the wall from the last hole he had drilled. Eden held out a hand to stop him. He froze. She picked up her video camera and turned it on. It flashed warning that she had already used up fifty percent of the storage capacity in the memory chip. Eden repressed a sigh. She had chosen to use chips to save what she recorded, rather than uploading to the cloud, because the wireless signal was spotty down here in the cellar.

The crack's rise up the wall spread out. She followed the slow progress, zooming in with the telephoto lens.

"The others are starting too." Amos's voice was rich with excitement.

"Can you get it on my cell phone?" she asked.

"I'll use mine." He settled on the floor next to her. "I just love all these newfangled gadgets, don't you?"

Eden decided she seriously adored Amos. She hoped that if she and Kai and Troy ever discovered their identities and found their families, she would have a grandfather just like him.

A crackling sound grew louder, turning into a hiss. Through the camera lens, Eden watched the crack turn into a spiderweb, reaching out, connecting with others.

"Step back." Greg grabbed hold of Eden's shoulder.

Before she could resist or protest, a section of wall a good three feet wide and reaching up to the low roof of the tunnel peeled off and disintegrated in a cloud of dust that smelled of mold and damp and something bitter-rotten, maybe chemical. She choked despite the surgical mask over her mouth and nose. Eden closed her eyes and stepped back, and hoped she managed to keep the video camera aimed at the wall.

"Aw, now that's not fair!" Greg laughed. He coughed, let out a groan, and laughed again.

"What?" She dared to open her eyes and regretted it. They stung from all the gray dust still in the air. There was no telling what was in that stuff. Hopefully it was just stone or dirt, not mold and bacteria and worm carcasses and other junk.

"Here." He caught hold of her hand and put one of the flimsy, crinkly plastic water bottles in it. "Amos, how you doing?"

"It pays to have bottle bottom glasses. Kept most of the junk out," the elderly man said.

Eden started to turn away, but the camera was still running. "A little help? I don't want to miss whatever is happening."

"It's mostly a white cloud, and the wall behind what fell is just a few shades of darker gray," Greg said. "Here." He took the bottle from her. She heard the crack as he broke the seal on the cap. "Can you bend your head?"

She did so, and he spattered water in her eyes, then wiped them with another of the masks from her kit. Eden hoped she was keeping the camera still focused. When she blinked the dust and streaks of mud out of her eyes, she found it pointed slightly downward. But, like Greg had said, the white cloud blocked the view, so she hadn't missed much.

"You think the rest will come down like the first layer?" she said.

"If it does … I'm going to need my shop vac on standby."

Greg certainly was prepared. Or rather, mostly prepared. Eden liked it that he could laugh at himself when the lengths of extension cord he had brought didn't quite let him bring the shop vac into the tunnel. There was only one electrical outlet in Bee's basement, and it was in the new section with the concrete floor. She turned out to be one of those disgustingly organized people who had all sorts of necessary items in neatly labeled boxes. The only problem was that the box holding five extension cords had ordinary, household use extension cords. Greg needed a heavy duty, industrial strength cord with a third, round grounding prong.

Amos was sure Bruce Schultz, on the far side of the cul de sac, a home improvement guru, would have a dozen of the right kind of extension cords. He was also retired and had announced at the picnic on Sunday afternoon, where the street's residents gathered forces to resist Ellsworth's latest campaign, that he was spending this week enclosing his screened-in porch with plastic to winterize it. He would be home.

"He's fast for such a little old guy," Greg murmured, less than twenty minutes later, when the tromping of feet coming down the stairs announced Amos had returned, with company.

The search for the extension cord and Amos's round trip allowed most of the white cloud from the collapse of the wall façade to settle. Eden had checked the recording and found that she had turned the camera away several times while she was blinded, but she had caught the most important part of the crackling and collapse. She took the opportunity to insert another memory chip into the camera. Instinct said this could take a while, and it was going to get even more interesting.

"Hey," Bruce greeted them, as Amos led him through the opening in the wall.

This was going to get crowded pretty soon. Eden studied the off-white wall with grayish streaks in it and speculated on how quickly that would crackle and collapse once Greg started boring at the base of it. How many layers of this stuff were there?

She got out of the way while Bruce and Amos hooked up the extension cords and brought the shop vac in. Greg got to work sucking up the debris. Bruce and Amos put on heavy work gloves he provided, to pick up the larger chunks.

Greg tapped the newly revealed section of wall. "Some composite. Probably fell apart like that because whoever put it up didn't give it time to cure before putting up the next layer or sealing it. Which means a lot of this is modern construction, not Underground Railroad era. Sorry, Amos."

"Right now, I'm too excited to care," Amos said with a chuckle. "Figuring out who put up the wall and why is much more interesting. Especially if it has to do with that poor boy being buried here. Did they say yet what killed him?" he asked, turning to Eden.

"Too much damage to too many bones. It doesn't get resolved as fast in real life as it does on TV," she said, and grinned, remembering some of the comments Carson had made about problems with juries, in murder cases. Too many were contaminated with what was called the "CSI Effect." They expected easy and swift identification, when the current technology took weeks to yield results.

Greg thumped a fist on the newly revealed section of wall. A muffled thud followed. Everyone froze, and Eden was sure they were all holding their breaths.

"Did you hear that?" Amos whispered.

"Like it's hollow on the other side?" Eden said.

"That's a good sign." Greg grinned. "It could have been that muffled sound you get when you bang on something that's filled with water."

Amos chuckled. Bruce looked a little confused. Eden moved up, tightening the focus of the camera while Amos explained what had been happening. Clearly, he hadn't told his neighbor the whole story. How much more was there to tell? Everybody on the street had to know about a skeleton being found here, even if the identity of the body was still supposed to be kept quiet. Eden could only imagine how the news would spread if people like Carruthers were still on the police force, jumping to conclusions and implicating their preferred guilty party, despite what the evidence indicated.

That got her thinking, while Greg speculated on the different materials that had come into favor and fallen out of favor when it came to repairs and construction and renovations. She waited until Greg paused to set aside several chunks of the fallen wall for testing, putting the pieces in some zipper bags and marking them with a grease pencil. That distracted her for a few seconds, so she didn't ask the question she intended.

"Looks like you're prepared to preserve samples," she said, gesturing at the bags Greg put outside of the hidden room.

"Sometimes I have to help the property owners file claims and complaints against whoever did the previous work, if it fails spectacularly. I suspect in this case, someone didn't follow instructions. Curing time, especially in damp conditions with little ventilation, could take a lot longer than under normal conditions." He shook his head.

"So, is it possible to test those pieces and identify when they were manufactured, maybe get an idea of when this work was done?" she said.

"Expensive tests, if we want them done fast and accurately."

"Is it possible, if it was a newer innovation, to track down where it was sold, and to who in the area?" She grinned, hearing Carson grumble about "CSI Effect" in her head. Maybe she had been ruined a little bit by TV crime-solving techniques.

"Won't know until we try." Greg turned back to the wall, studied it a few moments, then glanced at the three standing behind him in what had become a crowded space. "Well, I guess the question is if we proceed slowly and try not to make a mess or just break through and get the suspense over with."

"Depends on what's on the other side," Bruce offered. "If there's water or other crud brought in by the creek, might get messy."

"Yeah." He frowned at the wall.

"Start at the top and work your way down," Amos said, sounding a little too cheerful. Maybe from eagerness. "Considering how little water came through with last night's rain, I fear the leaks have been plugged by, as Bruce said, crud on the other side. In which case there could be maybe a foot of water waiting for us. If we start at shoulder height, I can't imagine a flood coming through."

"Makes sense to me." Greg gestured back out of the little room, and they parted to let him step out to where he had left his larger tools.

Eden nearly laughed when she saw him come back with a sledgehammer on a handle at least two feet long. Would there be enough room to swing it? In his other hand, though, he had a chisel and an ordinary hammer. That made sense. He would start small and only bring in the larger force if necessary.

Four strikes with the hammer on the chisel, and the same effect began, the spider web of cracks radiating downward. Greg started a rhythm of two strokes, then stepping back and watching the cracks grow. Two strokes and step back.

"Does the sound help you identify the materials?" Bruce asked during the fourth pause.

"Might. I don't have any experience with tearing down composites that reacted this way." Greg bared his teeth. "Always learning something new in this business."

After the sixth hit-and-pause, the crackling got louder and a chunk larger than Greg's fist fell away, revealing a hole in the wall. They all grinned at each other.

"Light?" He put down hammer and chisel and reached back blindly. Bruce snatched up the high beam work light with the square battery pack and handed it to him. Greg put it up to the hole on the right and tried to angle himself around to see, Eden supposed, without being blinded.

"What do you see?" Amos demanded. He turned to Eden and grinned. "Wonderful things? Do you feel like Howard Carter when he opened Tut's tomb?"

"I don't know," Greg said. "Looks like things kind of curve around … I'm gonna have to widen the hole. Eden, you got maybe night vision or something on that camera?"

She shook her head. He shrugged, then stepped back and picked up the sledgehammer. Three hard blows and the hole widened and extended down to his waist. He picked up the flashlight again and shined it in.

"Oh, heck …" He held still for what felt like an unnaturally long time. Then he exhaled, stepped back, and beckoned to Eden to bring the camera forward. "Amos … you want to call the police?"

"Why?" Eden got that shiver, and she was afraid she knew.

"Looks like another body."

"You're kidding." She knew he wasn't, but she could always hope. "Okay, I don't think I have to tell any of you, but…" She gestured at the hole Greg had made in the wall. "This is as close as we can get. Leave it up to the police. Doesn't mean I can't get pictures, though," she added, lowering her voice.

Amos chuckled, and when she turned to him, he winked at her. He tapped his cell phone. She noticed he didn't have to look up or even dial the number. Maybe after last week, he figured he should put the Cadburn police department on speed dial?

~~~~~

Saundra felt her phone buzz in her pocket near the end of the kindergarten storytime. Daphne had been leaning against her, and the little girl flinched and then looked up at her and giggled. Clearly, she had felt it. Saundra tried not to feel guilty, or glance over to where Ashley Cadburn sat with the mothers.

At least the other mothers were being supportive. It had taken a few weeks after Roger got hauled off to jail for threatening her life. It didn't
~~~~~

matter that he used a squirt gun, he had threatened her life to force her to hand over books she had never taken from the library in the first place. And once he started his fall from grace, suddenly all sorts of complaints that had been circulating about him for years took on weight and substance and created an avalanche that was still tumbling down on him. On the advice of his lawyer, he had stepped down from his position as trustee and was practically never seen in public. Ashley and Daphne had to put up with the questions and the whispers that started up whenever they appeared in public. It just showed how much Ashley loved her stepdaughter, and might just be a nicer person than first impressions indicated, that she fought to give Daphne as normal a life and routine as possible. Which meant taking her to kindergarten activities and letting her socialize. Saundra was proud of the women who were being supportive and kind, and quite frankly, forgiving of all the airs and authority Ashley had taken on herself, as wife of the head trustee, and a Cadburn.

She couldn't check her phone for another half hour. The children asked their questions and made their requests for next storytime and put away the puppets they had been using to act out the story. She responded to the questions and comments from the mothers and hoped her face didn't reveal the inner chant of, "Just go, please go." Gut instinct told her this phone call was important. Her friends knew her schedule and would wait until storytime was over to call. So either Aunt Cleo was calling, or something had happened when Greg got back to work in Bee Wilkinson's cellar. Eden had promised to call if anything interesting showed up.

Her second theory proved true when she checked. Eden left a voicemail.

"Can you access those pictures you got? All the pictures you got in research. Sorry for being so mysterious, but … Sunderson will institute a lock-down as soon as she gets here. So I'm giving as few details as possible, to avoid trouble. I know I can trust you to be discrete." A strained chuckle escaped Eden. "Send all the photos you can find? I'll head over to the Mug to update Olivia in a while, and we're making a conference call to Bee. If you get this before you go to lunch, join us? You've got a right to know. At least, I think Sunderson will agree."

"Come join us!" a man called. Saundra thought that was Amos's voice.

She checked her calendar, to make sure she was indeed free after lunch. Then she went to Mrs. Tinderbeck's office. Maybe she should bring her superior, since she had been there at that interesting dinner party.

~~~~~

"Why do I have the feeling Cadburn was right, and you and your cousins are troublemakers?" Captain Sunderson said, as she stepped through the door that opened out of the basement, under the deck. Ted
~~~~~

Shrieve and two members of the crime scene team followed her.

"This has nothing to do with us," Eden said, raising her hands in mock surrender. "We might have some answers, but a whole lot more questions. At least, if I'm right. I'm waiting for some photos Saundra had ..." She gestured through the basement and led the four around the corner, to where Greg had set up something of a command post, with a folding table and half a dozen chairs.

Eden had gone out to her car to get her travel computer while Greg set up the furniture and added lights. The few light bulbs in the ceiling just didn't provide strong enough lighting. She set up her computer to play the memory chips, while Greg led Sunderson to the new hole in the wall. The silence as the captain studied the scene was telling.

"I hope you understand," Amos said, pitching his voice to be soft, "if I say that I hope you are terribly wrong."

"Me, too." Eden turned her computer so it was at the best angle for the four newcomers to see the screen. She settled at the end of the table where she could reach the controls. Quite a lot would be fast forwarded.

She had started the video sweep of the revealed chamber on the righthand side, stepping as far to the left of the opening as she could get without crossing the line established by the yellow crime scene tape over Steve Edison's last resting place. Greg was one of those intelligent people who knew instinctively how to work with others. It also helped that he was nearly a head taller than her, so he could hold the maga flashlight over her head to illuminate everything the camera caught.

"Nobody stepped inside?" Captain Sunderson asked, as she and Greg joined them at the table. She gave a flat smile and shook her head. "Stupid question. I trust Eden to know how to avoid problems and preserve evidence. And I trust you, Amos, to have the sense to listen when someone says no. Thank goodness none of the history radicals were here."

Amos chuckled evilly. "By this time, Myron would be calling every TV station and the History Channel and taunting Western Reserve how they missed all the clues. Never mind that he's missed all the clues that poor girl ..." His merriment died like a fire doused with an iceberg. "Be assured, Captain, I have great respect for the hard work your people put in to keep us safe. Eden only had to stop me once. Yes, I almost threw myself through that hole, but common sense did prevail."

"Besides, you've still got lots of crowing rights over the other gang," Eden murmured. Amos winked, and the other officers exchanged grim smiles. "I've downloaded all the video files and emailed them to you already."

"Thank you. For not making me argue. I'm assuming you already notified the homeowner, and Fletcher and the lawyers involved?" the captain said. She visibly relaxed when Eden nodded. "I probably won't remember to say it often enough, but I'm grateful for how much easier you make my job." Sunderson gestured at the image on the computer screen, which was paused at the point where Eden had turned the camera to look into the new chamber beyond the hole.

Eden clicked the control as the officers settled into the chairs. Greg provided narration, condensing what they had done, his theories about the materials used, why it had fallen apart so easily, suggestions for identifying the manufacturer, and when it might have been sold locally. Then the camera and the overhead light illuminated the far right wall of the new chamber.

The stone glistened with moisture. Scaly, pale material that Eden guessed was lichen or mold of some kind marked the rough stone in splotches. She relived that moment when she realized she was looking at clear chisel marks, and a ledge that had been dug into the stone.

Underneath the ledge, obscured in places by that lichen or mold, maybe by water that had gotten in and dripped down over the decades, images and words and numbers had been cut into the stone. Stick figures of people. Names. Dates. Flowers.

Eden glanced up, at Amos who stood behind the three officers, visibly bouncing on his toes and grinning with delight. He had crowed, ecstatic when she paused the recording to rewind the camera and show him on the tiny side screen what she had seen.

The camera image flicked away, then came back to the spot. Eden explained what had happened. That got an understanding smile from Captain Sunderson. The image on the screen resumed the slow, careful pan down the right wall, with periodic close-ups to catch details, then moving on. It got to the visible end of the chamber, where the room narrowed. The beginning of a tunnel turned to the left. What looked like boards, maybe more of the two-bys that had held the plastic to the wall of the cellar blocked the tunnel opening. Greg pointed out the similarities.

"I sure hope we're wrong, but it looks like that entrance was blocked by the same people who sealed up the cellar and put up that plywood panel and disguised it as part of the stone wall," he said.

"The same person or people who killed Steve Edison and sealed up his body?" Joe muttered. "Makes sense to me."

"Hold off your speculations until we see everything," Sunderson said. She glanced up and met Eden's gaze. The other officers hadn't seen into the chamber like she had.

From that point, the camera angle shifted. Eden had slowly sidestepped to the right, with Greg behind her, holding up the light to reveal as much as possible. She had panned up the left side of the chamber. More scratched figures on the walls. More signs of water getting in over the years. Eden braced for the first reaction when the camera showed what had caught her attention before everything else.

Niches, dug into the stone and dirt of the chamber. Large enough for people to lie down in. Two levels. She thought of the images she had seen of the catacombs in Rome, where generations of victims of persecution had buried their dead.

Her phone chimed in her pocket, making her jump. She pulled it out quickly, blindly, and pressed the button on the side to quiet the ringer. Not for anything did she want to miss the reactions of Joe and Ted when the camera moved over to—

Ted swore. Joe flinched, starting to stand up and push his chair back, but caught himself in time and settled down again. They both leaned forward, to get a closer look.

Eden glanced at her phone screen. Good, Saundra had responded. Hopefully she had sent those photos. Then she leaned in and stopped the replay and tapped the keyboard until the image expanded.

A skeleton. In what was clearly a blue Union uniform. It lay curled up on its side, knees drawn up, revealing those niches in the wall weren't quite long enough for someone to lie down comfortably.

"Another murder victim," Amos said unnecessarily.

"Are you sure?" Joe said. "I mean, look at …." He gestured at the body, tracing the lines of the uniform without touching the screen.

"The first body was naked, other than the tanned leather of his boots. He was only there three years. If that was a genuine uniform from the era, the all-natural fibers would have decayed with the flesh and left just the skeleton." Amos sighed. "That uniform is synthetic and resisted decay. That is not only not a genuine Civil War uniform, but that is not the body of a genuine reenactor."

"Hold on a second," Eden said. She tapped the keyboard and adjusted the focus of the image, to show a handful of small globes, partially hidden by dust and probably dried bits of corpse, sitting in the remains of a long, dried braid. Still brightly colored under it all. She opened her phone and tapped into Saundra's response. A text, with "more coming," followed by a long string of photos. Eden held her breath as she scrolled slowly down, until she got to the ones she remembered. She held the phone out to Captain Sunderson to look at.

The captain murmured under her breath, her expression going grim.

"Lyndsy Auretta," Captain Sunderson said.

Eden had been mentally reviewing all the steps she had taken so far to track down the college student's path, her family, her records. All without success. As if the girl had never existed. Maybe, as much as she hated the idea, it was time to ask another favor from Nick West.

~~~~~

Kai's phone rang, making Olivia jump. Common sense said the
~~~~~

longer she had to wait to hear something from Greg and Eden and Amos, the better. It meant they hadn't found anything problematic that she had to report to Bee. So why was she so edgy?

She glanced over at him, at the far end of the front counter, just in time for him to turn around and lock gazes with her. He said only a few words more, watching her, nodded, and put the phone back in his pocket.

"Something wrong?" she said as he walked over to where she prepped for the lunchtime rush.

"Eden is heading back here. You need to take the rest of the day off."

"What did they find?" She congratulated herself that she hadn't shouted the question. A handful of people were walking in the door, with more visible in the big windows across the front of the coffee shop.

One of those people was Carson Fletcher. Kai raised a hand, gesturing for her to wait. Olivia didn't know if she was grateful or irritated right now that he was such a good boss who got involved in his employees' problems.

Truman and Kelli stepped up as the influx of people approached the counter. They got to work with Olivia and Kai, taking orders, cutting slices of deli sandwich, scooping up pasta salad and potato salad and pulling bowls of assembled salads from the cooler. When Olivia had handed off the order to her last customer, she looked around and found Carson leaning against the end of the counter, by the drawbridge, watching her, looking relaxed, yet a little too somber.

"Take him up to the office," Kai said. "The rest are coming."

He gestured with his chin at the front door. Olivia looked around as she headed for the drawbridge and saw Saundra just coming in. She beckoned for Saundra to follow as she led Carson to the elevator.

"Do you know what's up?" she asked Saundra, once the three of them were in the elevator and the door had squealed shut.

"Eden asked for all my research photos. They've called the police, so I'm guessing they found something."

Carson gave them a wintry smile. "Eden passed on a request from the captain to investigate the previous homeowner, Fendergast."

"They won't get any answers from him," Olivia said, as the doors clanked and squealed open. "Bee bought the house from his family. He has dementia. They dumped him in a nursing home about a month before the house went on the market." She stepped out of the elevator, into the office the three cousins shared.

"So maybe Fendergast wasn't exactly in command of all his faculties when he acted." He nodded, gaze seeming to turn inward.

They settled at one end of the long conference table.

"Fendergast is a murderer?" Olivia shook her head almost as soon as the words left her lips. "I mean, he could get scary, especially when he was wailing for the ghost to come back, but … no."

"How did the body get in his house, then?" Carson said, his voice gentle. "It's a good guess we'll be discussing that. Your memories of him from three years ago could provide clues to help us figure out what exactly happened."

"Right." Olivia took a couple deep breaths to settle her fluttery feelings. "Coffee? Something cold?" She felt a little odd playing hostess, but she knew the cousins would want her to make everyone comfortable. Especially if this was going to take a while.

She gestured for them to help themselves from the small refrigerator tucked under the table set up with supplies: cups, bowls, mugs, hot water pot, hot chocolate mix, utensils, and other items for hospitality. Olivia decided she needed chocolate more than coffee right now. Interestingly, Carson chose apple juice rather than coffee or cola.

Eden arrived next, with Amos and Greg in tow. She was setting up the wide-screen TV that folded out from the wall and connecting her computer when Captain Sunderson arrived, accompanied by Bill Worter.

"I've already talked with Deborah Wilkinson," Captain Sunderson said. "We have her verbal permission, and she's sending over a document with written authorization. We're borrowing some ground penetrating radar equipment from the archeology department at Case, and I have a team searching for the other end of the tunnel.

"We're also in the process of obtaining permission to use the equipment on the property where the tunnel crosses property lines. Nobody is exploring that tunnel, however, until all evidence has been properly examined and documented and removed."

"What kind of evidence?" Saundra asked. Olivia was grateful. She just didn't want to put it into words.

Eden turned on the TV and took them through the recording she had made. Amos made comments about the archeological and historical significance of the carvings they saw. Then Greg discussed the materials that had blocked the tunnel, and if those two-bys hidden in the shadows and around the bend in the tunnel were of the same era as the ones he had removed from the wall in the cellar.

Bill Worter made notes from time to time, so Olivia felt a little better. She wasn't the only one catching up on all the details. The room fell silent as the camera moved up the left wall of the tunnel, revealing the niches.

Saundra gasped and pressed one hand over her mouth when the skeleton came into view. Eden manipulated the image, to stop the frame and then slowly move over the details of the body. Olivia recognized the stringy remains of a braid. She shivered when she saw the hair bobbles, still bright despite the dust and other material that coated them.

Olivia shook her head and held back the need to shout, "No," at the top of her lungs.

As if refusing to accept what she saw would change anything?

"She didn't go home to her family, did she?" Saundra said. She bent down and picked up her purse from the floor next to her chair and pulled out a tablet. A few taps, while Eden took them through the end of the recording, and then Saundra called up photos from her research. A few more taps, and then Lyndsy Auretta smirked mischievously at them, in her illegal, synthetic Civil War uniform, with her long braid studded with multi-colored hair bobbles.

"Does anybody need anything to drink?" Olivia said. "We're going to be here for a while, aren't we?"

"There's a lot to discuss, and a plan of action to assemble," Eden said. "It's a pretty good guess that whoever killed Steve killed her and went to a lot of trouble to hide their bodies. And probably hide a valuable historic site at the same time."

"Considering the things I heard about the two of them, their passions, their arguments," Captain Sunderson said, "it's a little ironic that their deaths might have necessitated the coverup, instead of revealing what they were both trying to find."

Eden opened the refrigerator and brought out a selection of cold drinks, and asked Olivia to get a pot going in the coffeemaker. Everyone took advantage of the break to use the facilities. Then they went through the sequence of events.

Greg had just finished explaining why the materials used to block the tunnel failed when Olivia's phone rang. It was Kelli, saying a call had come in on the coffee shop's line. Myron Ellsworth wanted her.

"I want to hear what he has to say," Captain Sunderson said. "The timing is suspicious."

Eden took over, transferring the call to the conference line in the office, and put it on speaker. She set it up to record, for good measure.

"Now you've done it!" Ellsworth growled, before Olivia could finish saying hello. "The gall of you, destroying a historic site. Did you really think you could scare me off by pretending to have the police involved? When we get through with you—"

"How exactly do you know there's a historic site involved?" Captain Sunderson said.

"Oh, don't be a complete idiot! Of course it's a historic site. You and your moron friend are in big trouble now."

"No, Myron Ellsworth. You are the one in trouble, for threatening an innocent civilian who is cooperating with a police investigation."

Ellsworth spewed a stream of profanity, expressing his doubts about Olivia's innocence and the competence of the police.

"This conversation is being recorded. And you are speaking directly to Captain Amber Sunderson. Is there anything else you want to add, while you're on the record?"

Ellsworth didn't believe that, either. His voice tightened to the point his curses were incoherent. Then the connection died, in mid-cuss.

"Wow," Saundra said. "Can I have a copy? Mrs. Tinderbeck could use it to ban him from the library. Someone with a mouth like that shouldn't be around children."

"A mouth like that shouldn't be around civilized human beings," Bill said.

"I'd be very interested in how exactly he knew a historic site was involved," Carson said.

"Like maybe he knew about the tunnel and those carvings all along?" Eden said. She shared a chilly smile with him.

Captain Sunderson called the station to send out a request for Myron Ellsworth to come to the station to answer some questions. With a strong threat of using legal means if he didn't cooperate. Before she finished, Bill got on his cell phone and placed a call to Judge Gruber to issue a search warrant for Ellsworth's home and office and any storage facilities he had access to. Just in case it became necessary.

"Considering he's the nasty face and voice of a historical group that has a record of harassment," Carson said, "maybe it would be wise to have a warrant to search his phone records and emails, and credit card records, going back to the time of the deaths. For instance, any uncharacteristic purchases of building materials."

"You need to know something," Saundra said, just as Amos opened his mouth to speak. From his grim expression, he probably had more evidence of Ellsworth's activities. "Mrs. Tinderbeck asked me to ask for help from Nick. Nick West," she added, nodding to Captain Sunderson. The police captain nodded back. "She wanted some help for Josiah Crandall. He's been blackmailed and hasn't asked for help because the blackmailer is able to hurt people who matter to him." She glanced around the table. "There are hundreds of emails and electronic records to go through. Pastor Roy is helping in the investigation. But from what Nick was able to determine, both men have been blackmailed by someone since about the time Lyndsy and Steve vanished."

"I don't suppose he's identified the blackmailer yet?" Captain Sunderson asked. Her voice had that softness that was either weariness, a headache brewing, or the calm before the storm, in Olivia's experience.

"No, there are all sorts of boobytraps and alarms along the electronic trail. Whoever is doing this is very good. Nick doesn't want to warn them he's coming after them."

"I need to talk to him."

"So do I," Carson said. He shook his head, his grim smile going crooked, and let out a long sigh. "Is anyone else getting the awful feeling that maybe the blackmailer has evidence that those two men are the murderers?"

"Why would they hide the bodies in Bee's house? They weren't getting along with Fendergast at the time," Olivia protested. She had to say something. Nice Mr. Crandall could not possibly be a murderer. No matter how nasty he was back at the time Lyndsy and Steve vanished, he couldn't be guilty. He was Uncle Josiah. The children loved him. They couldn't love a murderer, could they?

"That's true," Captain Sunderson said. "Clearly, there are quite a few pieces missing from this puzzle. We need to work quickly, quietly, and with extreme caution, so the guilty parties don't get spooked and either destroy the evidence or flee beyond our reach."

By the time their group split up, just over an hour later, they had a plan of action.

Bill Worter got to work tunneling his way through the bureaucracy at Case Western Reserve, to get Lyndsy's student records opened. Captain Sunderson took Steve Edison as the focus of her search.

Olivia called Bee to update her, and asked permission to use her house as the headquarters for the new team to assemble and confer and share their information. Bee agreed.

"It kind of makes sense why Ellsworth is so vicious about no changes to the houses along the river. If someone digs far enough, they could open up that tunnel, and that would lead them back to the skeletons. What's weird was his surprise when he came to the house after I moved in and saw the deck. Like he didn't know it was there. If he was involved in hiding the bodies, wouldn't he know about it?"

Olivia was still upstairs in Eden's office, and the conversation was on speakerphone.

"We'd have to find out when the deck was built," Eden said.

"That summer," Olivia said. "I remember looking across the creek and seeing the delivery of all those building materials, and thinking the creep would have a hissy fit when he saw what Fendergast planned to do without his permission."

Eden nodded slowly. "So you're thinking Fendergast acted alone in hiding the bodies? And a check of Ellsworth's purchases wouldn't reveal anything. It'd be hard to do all that cosmetic work inside the cellar without the owner knowing. At the same time, he was mentally deteriorating, so it's possible the murderer decided it was a convenient time and place to hide the bodies." She snorted. "If Ellsworth was involved, it must have made him sick, losing access to those carvings and proof of Underground Railroad activity. You can't hide dead bodies in the same place where archeologists will be working."

~~~~~

Olivia insisted on going back to work. She needed some sense of normalcy. That evening, as she prepared to clock out, Eden called her up to the office. Captain Sunderson had called and emailed over the official autopsy report on Steve and the preliminary report on Lyndsy. The addition of a new victim had ramped up the importance of this case and the coroner had sped up the process.

Steve had been shot. Two bullet holes in the chest. Both bullets had been among the debris scooped up with the skeleton when it was discovered.

Lyndsy had suffered a cracked skull. The coroner was unsure if it had killed her instantly. There were no other signs of injury, and no telling how long she had lingered before dying. Perhaps she had even been brought to the tunnel and left to die.
~~~~~

Chapter Sixteen

Saturday, November 5

When the team convened at 9:30 Saturday morning in Bee's house, Eden had a few answers. Bill had gotten through to several people at Case Western Reserve University who had bits of information on Lyndsy. Not that anyone on the team expected that information to be much help, since they already knew she was using a fake identity. Phoebe had called several members of the Spirits of '62 to track down someone who still had Mike's contact information, and through him locate Macy. Lyndsy had never said what her last name was.

Saundra was thoroughly impressed. Despite all the resources available to librarians, and all the contacts she had made in her years of doing research for Aunt Cleo, Eden had better strings to pull to ask for help and get answers.

"Clandestine Costumers," Eden said, once everyone had settled in the TV room with coffee, hot chocolate, or tea. "Sunderson gave me a screen shot of the tag in Lyndsy's costume."

Olivia, Amos, Saundra, Mrs. Tinderbeck, and Troy. Captain Sunderson hoped to join them that afternoon. Bill couldn't make it, being busy preparing for a big case that would open up court proceedings on Monday, but had promised that if anything came in while he was working over the weekend, he would copy Saundra and Eden on the information.

Eden put down on the table a blow-up of the label taken off Lyndsy's costume. "A professional costume design shop. They provide most of the costuming for the local universities and colleges when they need something special their in-house costume shops can't handle. Greta, the owner, remembered Lyndsy and the costume, mostly because she was surprised Steve sent Lyndsy to her. He was so infuriated a year before over a costume she made with synthetics she had on hand and not historically accurate material, he vowed he would tell everyone to take their business anywhere else."

"How come I don't feel sorry for the guy?" Olivia muttered.

"Oh, but that's not the important part of the story. Lyndsy paid for the costume with her credit card," Eden said, looking around the room and meeting everyone's gaze. Her voice softened as she spoke, snagging everyone's attention. "And the name on the card wasn't Auretta. Or

Linda-Sue O'Hara."

Troy leaned back and shook his head, grinning. "Was that what had you up tapping and texting and stomping around in the office until three this morning?"

"Part of it." She pulled a folder out of her stack of materials and handed it to Saundra, to pass around the circle. "Lyndsy Thomas, age twenty-eight, not twenty-two. Turns out, according to what Bill could get, Lyndsy had a note on her student records asking that they be sealed. She claimed she was living under a borrowed identity. She implied she was in Witness Protection."

"The plot thickens," Amos said.

"Hmm, maybe not. There was a note in her file from a US Marshall— alleged Marshall—to back up her story, but so far he doesn't seem to be real. Plus, I've heard from her previous three universities—" She paused while the others reacted to that bit of information. "Well, basically she's got a reputation for having a very loose grasp on reality, or at least the concept of honesty. She'd say whatever she needed, to get what she wanted. Once I had this name, it wasn't hard to track her backward to previous schools and employers. She's done a lot of student assistant work, all in history departments, all specializing in the years and societal changes leading up to the Civil War. She left her last university a year before showing up at Case. In between, she worked for a historical writer, L.K. Tanner. It looked like she was straightening out her life and breaking the lie habit."

"Until?" Olivia said, putting the folder Saundra had just handed her on her lap, instead of looking at it.

"According to Dr. Tanner, they had a falling-out over some research Lyndsy wanted to follow up on. Dr. Tanner had her doubts as to the authenticity of the source. Lyndsy quit in a huff and vowed she would come back with proof."

"Let me guess," Amos said. "Underground Railroad station houses in northeast Ohio?"

"Pretty much. What's sad is that Dr. Tanner regretted the argument they had and was trying to repair their relationship. When she tracked down Lyndsy's family, she learned they hadn't heard from her in years."

"Sounds like Lyndsy has a habit of cutting people off and just starting over," Saundra offered.

"But that last phone call, she said she was going home," Olivia said.

"Did she make that call?" Eden said.

That silenced everyone in the room for several moments.

"There's a pattern, don't you see?" she continued. "Steve didn't talk face-to-face with anyone before he just took off. No one questioned it, because he had a habit of giving people the silent treatment, keeping them at arm's length. Lyndsy was supposedly the only one who knew he had that internship lined up, until all of a sudden, a couple phone calls and emails, and he's gone. Then she does the same thing. Phoebe was the last one to talk to her, and she might have caught up with her if Caruthers hadn't gotten in the way."

That got some snorts and muttered comments from the others. It seemed everyone had had an unpleasant or even ridiculous encounter with Caruthers before he finally slit his throat, career-wise.

"Then Lyndsy is just gone, one phone call. We need to get hold of Mike, and even better, this Macy, and see what their stories are. And if they stay consistent. They were the last ones to see Lyndsy alive."

"Or maybe they weren't, is that what you're saying?" Amos asked.

"The problem is that this Macy is a trouble magnet, just like Lyndsy indicated," Eden continued. "Hard to find. I think she was living under a false identity, too. So far, it looks like she was never a student at Case. Her number is unlisted, and according to the landlord of the place she and Lyndsy shared, she moved out less than a week after Lyndsy left town. No warning, just a note in an empty apartment. Her credit card and bank account were canceled the same day. I need to wait on some contacts who can backtrack that activity and find out where she went, what new accounts she opened."

"I've got some information on the roommate that just makes things worse, so be careful if you do track her down," Saundra said. "I asked Nick for some help, because I wondered what happened to Lyndsy's car." She shrugged. "Fortunately, some of those photos I got included her car, and a really good shot of her license plate. Nick got the VIN, and it turns out Lyndsy's car was sold, right here in Cuyahoga County, four days after Mike picked up all her stuff." She opened her accordion file and brought out a slim sheaf of papers held together with a small bulldog clip. "Nick did some more digging, because the details seemed a little suspicious and he found—" she tugged several papers out from the bottom of the stack and held them up, "—Lyndsy's signature from registering for classes at Case doesn't match the one on the title transfer of the car."

"Lots of questions to ask," Eden murmured. "We need to find out what happened to Steve's car and his belongings. Maybe that same handwriting is on that title transfer too." She rubbed her eyes, looking tired, and Saundra remembered Troy saying how late Eden had stayed up, working on this puzzle. "I know I'm going to regret asking ... anything else West found?"

"He's been busy with a few other things, but he was planning to dig into Lyndsy's financials next." Saundra shrugged. "I guess that wouldn't have done much good, since she was using a fake name. He tracked down the person who bought the car, to see if he could follow the money trail. It turns out the guy is not only a reckless driver who totaled the car eight months after he bought it, but he paid cash for it."

"We should talk to him, get a description of who sold him the car. Maybe this Macy was involved."

Saundra grinned. "You don't sound too happy to have that information. Because it might be a dead end, or because Nick got it?"

"The spook knows too much, has too many sneaky connections," Troy said. "And yeah, he likes knowing all the secrets just a little too much for my taste."

"You and me both!" Eden said.

"I'd like to meet him," Amos said, giving them a patently fake smile of innocence. "He sounds like a very useful friend to have."

"He's Saundra's friend," Eden said. She frowned into the open space on the floor between them all for several moments. Then she sighed and pulled out her tablet and tapped on the screen. "Even if we don't exactly trust him, we trust you to keep him in line."

"Or beat some good manners into him?" Saundra asked.

"Sounds good. I'm sending you all the info I have on the roommate, even if most of it is dead ends. She has a talent for ghosting. I'd be interested in whether she or Mike got a nice boost to their bank accounts after Lyndsy allegedly went home. Did they sell her other possessions?"

"I'd be interested in how fast they did that. The right kind of wrong connections," Troy offered. "Can the spook find that out, too?" He fluttered his eyelashes at Saundra, earning a few snorts of laughter from her and Eden.

Troy and Eden had brought an assortment of cables and connectors and worked the right magic to enable them to put the tunnel video on Bee's fifty-two-inch flat-screen. They rewound portions several times, looking for more details. The coroner hadn't reported yet on any items that were found with Lyndsy's body.

Twenty minutes into getting to work on the video, Saundra's phone chattered, announcing an incoming text. Nick. She caught her breath at the announcement of what he had found. She pulled out her tablet and opened it up, so she could more easily read the attached documents. This was a breakthrough, definitely. She forwarded everything to Eden. When she looked up, Troy and Eden were both watching her.

"What?" Troy demanded.

"I forwarded you the email Nick sent me. Lots of documents. He's working on something else, so he tagged some friends who got into financial records for him and followed the money trail," Saundra said. "Like attracts like. Lyndsy worked under a false identity and records, and so did her roommate. Nick speculates that's how they met up. Whoever helped Lyndsy create her new name and record hooked her up with a girl going by Macy Sutton three years ago, who became Kayla Pierce a few days before Lyndsy vanished. So she was preparing to take off, maybe those problems Lyndsy told Olivia about, maybe other reasons. Nick and his friend both find it suspicious that she has no trouble sliding from one identity to another, with bank accounts and credit cards and insurance all ready, and no blips or glitches to make anyone suspicious. Maybe indicating she does this sort of thing for a living, making new identities. Or needing them.

"Anyway," Saundra glanced down at her tablet, reading the report, "Kayla made several large deposits that same month. The exact amount of money paid in cash for Lyndsy's car was deposited in her primary account the day after the sale."

"Now that's not incriminating, is it?" Amos said.

"Primary account?" Olivia said.

"She has had over a dozen bank accounts in the last three years, all either transferring money to the Kayla account or receiving money from it, all under different names. She has a history of closing down accounts and opening up new ones on a regular basis. Almost a rhythm, he said." Saundra again checked her tablet, editing what she would say next. She hadn't sent all the documents Nick sent, because he had marked several as "your eyes only — for now." She fought down resentment that he made her keep secrets. She was going to tell the team as much as she could, and if Nick got irritated, that was his problem.

"He highlighted some information for me that he's still investigating and doesn't want to discuss. But he says it might be helpful. There is a particular succession of accounts that caught his attention, because the only activity in all of them comes from regular deposits, the same amount of money, from the same two sources, every month. He suspects she has at least one accomplice, because when those deposits come in, she splits them in half and sends half to another account that isn't hers. When he knows more, he'll tell us."

"Why?" Eden said. "Does this have anything to do with the murders?"

Saundra shrugged and focused on her notes. She hated keeping secrets, but she had worked with Nick too long to disobey him when he asked her not to share information just yet. That didn't mean she had to like it, though, and she would let him know.

"Does he know who's paying that money, and when did it start?" Troy said.

Saundra offered a thin smile. She had a brief bad taste in her mouth. This secret, on top of the secrets she had to keep from her new friends when it came to the Venetian glass heart lockets, made her head ache. "I can't tell you that. He asked me not to," she added, when Troy opened his mouth. "But yes, I'm afraid this might have something to do with the deaths. The payments started two weeks after Lyndsy and Steve vanished."

"Are you thinking blackmail?" he said, turning to Eden.

She shrugged. "Let's keep digging to find out who, then we'll figure out why. If Kayla or Macy or whoever she really is didn't kill Lyndsy, she knew enough to extort the ones who did."

"That doesn't make sense," Olivia said. "Macy was terrified of somebody, and they were threatening Lyndsy because of her. If she's afraid for her life, where did she get the guts to blackmail someone?"

"The easy answer," Troy said, "is that someone is lying. Either Macy was pulling a fast one on Lyndsy, or Lyndsy lied to you."

"She did seem to make a habit of that," Amos offered, his tone apologetic.

Saundra found great satisfaction in reading the report Eden put together at the end of their meeting to send to Captain Sunderson, Carson Fletcher, and Bill Worter. What each of them would do with the information would vary, but it would bring results, and hopefully an end to the mystery.

~~~~~

Saundra came back to Book & Mug with Eden after their meeting at Bee Wilkinson's house. Kai saw her walk in and it occurred to him that he hadn't been able to spend as much time with Saundra as he wanted lately. They were both busy, and she had gotten involved in the mystery of the skeletons. He supposed the only solution was to find something for them to do together.

Troy came out of the back stairwell with a double handful of mail from the box facing Apple Street. He stood at the corner of the counter, sorting through the envelopes and throwing most of them in the trash while Kai made drinks for Eden and Saundra. He slid a thick business envelope down the counter to Kai. Eden slapped her hand down on the envelope just before it collided with her glass.

"Haven't you answered them yet?" She picked up the envelope to show the return address to Kai.

He groaned. The winter street festival committee. Yes, he had meant to answer more than a week ago, but he was still scrambling for ideas of what Book & Mug could sponsor this year. Then his gaze landed on Saundra, and he knew he had his solution. For several conundrums.

"Hey, Saundra, would you like to help me with a Christmas fundraiser? It's for kids." Another detail attached itself to his sudden brainstorm. "Ties into your department at the library. A book fair." He flipped the envelope over between his fingers, his gaze focused on her face, willing her to say yes.
~~~~~

"A children's book fair?" She glanced over her shoulder, probably checking to make sure no customers were coming in, then moved down the counter to face him. "That sounds like fun. What would it involve?"

"A bunch of different things." He would have to figure out what those were. "But a friend was telling me about a fun thing he did at a conference a few weeks ago. A blind date with a book. Wrap books in wrapping paper and write a description of what happens in the book, and people put in raffle tickets to try to win it. We could ask people to donate kids' books. But what would be more fun," he hurried to add, "is go to estate sales and used bookstores and find kids' books. The ones they don't print anymore. Want to help me? I don't really specialize in kids' books here, but ..." He spread his hands. "You're the expert."

She smiled, and that smile erased signs of what must have been a rough couple of hours, working on the mystery of the skeletons in Bee Wilkinson's cellar.

"Yeah, that sounds like fun. When do we start?"

Sunday, November 6

Sunday afternoon, Captain Sunderson called Olivia and Bee on a conference call, to let them know that the searchers had found what they theorized was the end of the tunnel. It opened out onto the former Gibbons property next door. Under the pile of large stones that came from the flood wall, dismantled a month or so before the deaths, the tunnel had been blocked with boards that seemed to match the two-by-fours from the cellar. Three-quarters of the ridge of land on the east side of Bee's property, buried under all that stone, was on the property next door.

The preliminary testing done on the site confirmed the walls inside the tunnel were put up the same time Fendergast had his deck built.

"You don't say?" Amos said, when Olivia called him with the news. "That's interesting. And wouldn't there be a whole 4th of July of fireworks, if those two idiots were still living here? Fendergast and Gibbons, those two couldn't stand the sight of each other. I was playing with a theory that Gibbons found the tunnel opening, and he sealed it up just to spite Fendergast. Or Fendergast found it, and he sealed it up because he couldn't stand the thought of Gibbons having a secret entrance to his place.

"He finally gave up his grumping and retired to Arizona about a year after Fendergast's family hauled him away. I suppose it wasn't fun anymore, having nobody to snipe at or argue with. I had way too much fun being agreeable and denying him any excuse to turn on me." He chuckled. It was a thoroughly mischievous chuckle.

"What if ..." Olivia almost wished she hadn't started speaking.

"What if what?"

"Were either of them the kind to get really nasty, I mean, like dangerous, if they caught someone trespassing on their property? Or was it only the two of them fighting all the time?"

"You're thinking Gibbons found the boy's dead body and put him in Fendergast's cellar, to try to frame him? And then killed Lyndsy when she was looking for the boy? Hmmm ... honestly? I'd be more likely to believe Fendergast would do that to frame Gibbons."

Chapter Seventeen

Monday, November 7

Carson Fletcher was waiting when the doors opened at Book & Mug Monday morning. He asked for a private meeting with Olivia and Eden.

"I've sent my report to Captain Sunderson and Bill Worter and Deborah Wilkinson as the most interested parties. Not counting you two," he said, settling down at the conference table in the second-floor office. "The simple version of what you'll be getting is that Lyndsy's family was estranged from her since she was in high school. There was a lot of family bickering, and she just washed her hands of them all and got emancipated. They were very surprised to learn that she was supposed to be heading home, because they had all split up and moved away. There was no home for her to go to, and they didn't think she had anyone's phone or address."

"Just more proof that phone call wasn't from Lyndsy," Eden murmured. "From the information West dug up, it looks like Macy had the tech skills to synthesize Lyndsy's voice to make that call."

"Makes sense. I got hold of the landlord's records and compared the signature on the title for Lyndsy's car to Lyndsy's signature on other paperwork and Macy Sutton's signature on her lease agreement. A handwriting expert is willing to testify she sold Lyndsy's car."

"How are you doing on tracking down her physical location?"

"That's going to take time. Mike Kioto claims he broke up with her, but he'd be our first lead to find her. The thing is, he seems to have taken a last-minute vacation right after Captain Sunderson called him in to ask about Steve Edison's disappearance."

"Innocent people don't run," Olivia murmured.

Carson chuckled, but it wasn't an amused or pleasant sound.

"I've been thinking a lot about the videos she made of the reenactors," Eden said. "A lot of angles, meaning many cameras. Olivia saw her installing several cameras. What we found in Mrs. T's attic indicates she had quite a sophisticated setup with remote cameras feeding into her computer. Rufus and I finally cleared up some priority work that kept us busy, and we're going to focus on Lyndsy's files now. My gut tells me something there will explain what made her leave her hiding place and go looking for Steve."

"You think she found the original video of his death?" Olivia said.

"She probably knew where it happened and thought she could find evidence." Carson shrugged. "Maybe she even thought he wasn't dead, just in trouble. Why didn't she go..." He snorted. "Forget I was about to say that. We're talking about Cadburn three years ago."

"Why didn't she go to the police for help?" Eden said, nodding. "Yeah, that's part of the problem."

"And maybe if she died where she spent so much time, and those cameras were in the right place, at the right time, and were running, they caught her killer?"

"We won't know until we go looking."

Olivia stayed while Eden and Carson discussed different issues that sounded like business concerns all investigators had. When he had left, Eden turned to her.

"You want to help, don't you?"

"Just tell me what to do."

~~~~~

Rufus, Eden and Olivia started off by organizing the video files and deciphering the tags. Each camera's uploads went into a separate file, to hopefully cut down on the searching time by avoiding duplication, looking at the same scene multiple times. Part of the puzzle was understanding the code for the time stamp. The original hackers who had encrypted Lyndsy's computers had done something to mess with that.

Rufus theorized that Lyndsy had ten cameras feeding into the computer found in the attic. Once they caught something interesting on one camera's feed, they could try to coordinate what was recorded at that same point in time on the other cameras.

When that was done, Eden assigned Lyndsy's email account to Olivia, while she and Rufus worked on the videos. Rufus had cobbled together a program to do preliminary scans of the videos to avoid looking at hours and hours of tree branches and birds and squirrels. To avoid causing changes to the original files, and at Captain Sunderson's request, everything they worked on was copied over from Lyndsy's computer to auxiliary computers Eden had on hand to keep suspicious programs and files contained in case they were contaminated with viruses and boobytraps.

The first thing Olivia discovered was that this wasn't Lyndsy's student email account. That had been closed down and wiped out when she withdrew from the university. According to Carson, Kayla/Macy had forged Lyndsy's signature on the withdrawal papers, too.

Lyndsy had opened this email account when she arrived at Case Western Reserve and started classes under her false identity. This was a free account that didn't monitor activity or shut down accounts that hadn't had activity in months. Or in this case, years. When Olivia
~~~~~

remarked on it, Eden said this was a case where the users were the product, meaning the email host site earned their money from advertisers, and the emails were loaded with advertisements. So it was in their best interest to keep email accounts going, even if there was no activity on them. They got paid by the advertisers depending on how many email accounts were open.

Eden already had permission to read anything found on Lyndsy's computer, since it could be considered evidence. She sent a report on what Olivia had discovered and checked if Sunderson's people had been able to get to work on the files sent to them, to avoid duplicating effort.

While they waited, Saundra called with news from Nick West. Someone had used Lyndsy's credit cards for two months after she vanished. All the purchases took place in the Cleveland area. A large number of them were for groceries and gas, and what struck Olivia as strange, at the Case Western bookstore. They knew Macy/Kayla wasn't a student at Case, so who used Lyndsy's cards at the university? The first suspect was Mike.

When the bills became overdue, and the credit card companies couldn't reach her, they canceled the cards.

When word came that none of Sunderson's people had been able to get to the computer files yet, Olivia got back to work.

Lyndsy emailed Steve several times a day immediately after his estimated death. In several emails, she accused him of playing a nasty joke, faking his death in the blackmail video. She refused to give him the location of the tunnel she had found, if that was what he was going to demand, and challenged him to be a "real man" and face the music.

Olivia moved backward to the start date of Lyndsy's account and gathered all the emails between her and Steve into one folder. She wasn't surprised that the first few emails were from Lyndsy to Steve only. No response from him for nearly three weeks. She apparently had irritated him. Then she offered a piece of information that caught his interest. Olivia caught her breath when she opened a JPG and saw what looked like the same quilt square she had found under the table at the Book & Mug after Lyndsy had met with Josiah Crandall.

The emails that followed were all academic in nature. Lyndsy didn't try to flirt or catch Steve's interest outside of historical research. He didn't seem interested either. They bickered in public and collaborated in email. Both of them apparently didn't see anything wrong with wearing different faces in public and in private. Olivia found that kind of sad. She commented on it to Eden.

"This is about the warmest, most personal communication they had. 'Hey,'" she read aloud, "'just want to make sure you understand. Don't take it personally. I've got this reputation as a—'" Olivia chose not to use the words Steve put in his email. As an apology, she didn't think much of it. "'—to keep up. You're having fun yanking my chain, and everybody else's, but it's not personal when I ride you. Okay? We're still on for Saturday? I'll pick you up at 5, we'll get breakfast at Der Dutchman on the way and hit the museum before it opens. My guy is opening, so we'll get a chance to see all the stuff they can't fit in the display.' Then he listed some war journals and artifacts from the Underground Railroad."

"That's what he considered a date?" Eden snorted.

"Lyndsy didn't seem to care. Unless she thought a research field trip was the height of romance."

Olivia felt somewhat disappointed when she finished skimming through the correspondence in less than an hour. Neither Lyndsy nor Steve were chatty, even when they were excited about something.

In one email, Steve proposed meeting at 2am so Lyndsy could show him what she had found and "that crazy old coot" wouldn't come racing out, shrieking at the top of his lungs.

"Which crazy old coot?" Olivia said, after reading the email aloud to Eden and Rufus. "According to Amos, there were several along the creek. Fendergast and his neighbor were feuding. We certainly heard enough shouting, living on the other side of the creek from them."

Rufus wheeled over to read over her shoulder. He laughed and traced the last line of the email, where Steve signed off with a jaunty, "This is it, babe!"

"Oh, now that makes it really interesting," Eden said a moment later, after they had both read:

You did a great job. Besides scaring the old farts into leaving us alone, you got a lot of people talking and remembering, when they're usually too good to talk to us "youngsters who don't know nothing about history." I should have thought of this Cadburn ghost scam years ago.

"I wonder how long after he wrote that, Steve became part of the legend?" Eden murmured.

That gave Olivia the shivers.

The last four emails from Steve were more of the same, laughing at the homeowners they had freaked out, daring Lyndsy to stand on the sweetheart bridge across the creek in the moonlight, and finally send Fendergast over the edge. Olivia found it hard to feel sorry for him. No one deserved to be killed for being an arrogant jerk, but she suspected Steve had brought his demise on himself. He wasn't innocent by any measure.

After putting all the Lyndsy/Steve emails into one file, she skimmed through the rest of the account, clustering emails to and from the same people in their own files, to make them easier to go back and read later. She had to laugh a little when she was able to delete at least a quarter of the emails as advertisements and spam. What was wrong with Lyndsy that she didn't rid out her files?

"Well, if she did delete, we wouldn't find anything useful," Rufus commented when she voiced that thought.

"Have we yet?" Olivia got up to use the bathroom and get a fresh bottle of peach iced tea. Then she got back to work color-coding the emails.

The office was quiet for another ten minutes, until Troy came in, his coat tucked into the crook of his elbow while he unbuttoned his matching vest. He nodded to Olivia when she looked up at his entrance, but didn't say anything. He dumped his briefcase at his workstation and hung vest and jacket on the back of his swivel chair, then wandered over to where Eden was tapping her way through the images on her screen.

Olivia found a name she recognized. For a moment, she was surprised, then she remembered that Lyndsy had been trying to build a relationship with the man: Josiah Crandall.

She must have made a sound. Eden turned around and Troy crossed over to stand by Olivia's chair. He bent down and read the email. Their gazes met. He grinned.

"Guess who's suddenly buddy-buddy with your dead body?"

Eden gave him a withering look. Troy chuckled and gestured for Olivia to take over.

"Mr. Crandall is all polite and interested. And ..." Olivia turned the computer screen to make it easier for Eden to read as she moved over to join them. "He's very interested in the artifact she found."

"'Our mutual interest,'" Troy read aloud. "Kind of gives you the creepy-crawlies, doesn't it?"

"Well, since he was boasting for a while that he was going to make a historic breakthrough, yeah," Eden said. She bent down to read through the email.

There wasn't much to it, just a polite, business-like email responding to a request she had made when they met at the last trustee meeting, to get his opinion on an artifact.

Then, Olivia found that the last ten emails in the account were all from Josiah, and Lyndsy didn't respond to any of them. She found the explanation for that when she looked at the dates on the emails.

The first of the ten emails came the day after Lyndsy had come back to Mrs. Tinderbeck's house, intent on finding Steve, and then vanished. Olivia shivered, suspecting that timing was important.

I must warn you to proceed with caution. Yes, some might say we were arguing. You were rather distraught and I admit I was impatient. I had nothing to do with that moron, Ellsworth, following me or what he chose to do. I did not set you up. Surely you remember enough to know that. I came alone as you requested. Ellsworth surprised us both. He struck you from behind.

You must remember that I helped you get to the bank and then chased Ellsworth away. He turned on me, struck me with the same tire iron he used on you. That's why I didn't return to check on you. I was stunned, and then someone was pulling him off me, and I ended up at the hospital. I know you were awake and sitting up when I drove him away. I apologize from the bottom of my heart that I wasn't able to return.

You do believe me, don't you?

Olivia shivered and looked up at Eden, who turned from studying the screen, her face creased with concern.

"Keep reading," she said after a moment. "I'm calling Sunderson."

"Smoking gun?" Troy murmured. He pulled up a chair next to her, and Olivia was grateful for his presence as she flipped through the emails. When a pattern emerged, she felt even colder.

Lyndsy didn't respond to Crandall's emails. He wrote to her once the next day. Then twice the following day. Then the day after that. Each email was shorter than the one before, hammering home what he considered the most important detail. Ellsworth had attacked her, Crandall had intended to come back to help her, and he was increasingly concerned for her welfare.

"We need to find the videos dated from that night at the creek," she said.

"Not that easy," Rufus called from his computer station. "Yeah, we can put them in order by all that crazy coding Lyndsy used, and separate what files came from what camera, but ... we need a starting place. It's gonna take time. What's up?" he said, as Eden put down her phone.

She had spent most of her phone conversation with Captain Sunderson murmuring responses such as, "Uh huh," or "Really?"

"Sunderson's been kind of busy." Eden's face twisted into the most wickedly satisfied, mischievous expression Olivia had ever seen her wear. It emphasized the resemblance between her, Kai and Troy more than ever.

"What happened?" Troy drawled and leaned back in his chair. "Is it good?"

"Depends if you think that Ellsworth having a screaming conniption in the library parking lot and then going pro wrestler on Crandall proves he's guilty of something."

"Oh, please, please, tell me there's a security camera close by that recorded all that. I would pay big money to see that."

Eden left to meet up with Captain Sunderson and deal with the fallout from the fight in the parking lot. Olivia finished reading through the rest of Lyndsy's emails, but nothing else stood out after the frantic emails from Josiah Crandall.

~~~~~

Eden and Bill Worter were allowed to be on the other side of the glass, once Ellsworth had been processed. Witnesses said Crandall hadn't offered any resistance, hadn't responded to Ellsworth's accusations, other than trying to walk away. When he went down under the other man's attack, he hit the edge of the sidewalk right on his temple and had been taken to the hospital. Captain Sunderson was holding Ellsworth on every charge she could find, while waiting for Crandall to press charges.

Ellsworth had apparently blown his last circuit. He trembled with righteous fury, and every time someone asked him a question, his response was always that he was the victim. No matter what question anyone asked him, even if it had nothing to do with the attack. He refused the offer of a court-appointed lawyer for his questioning. Sunderson handed the questioning chore over to Dara Greg, who had negotiation training and a degree in counseling. She had to do little more than look sympathetic and make comforting noises that encouraged Ellsworth to babble all the ugly details.

The trigger for the attack was an email that Ellsworth received within an hour of the official announcement that a second body had been found in the tunnel and identified as Lyndsy Auretta. The email claimed the sender had proof that he had killed Lyndsy and demanded four times what Ellsworth had been paying in blackmail for the last three years.

"Blackmail?" Eden said. She immediately thought of that last email Olivia had found. All the pieces came together.

She glanced over at Bill and Sunderson, who were in the small room with her, watching the interrogation. Bill nodded, his lips twitching in brief amusement. She guessed that Nick West knew all along that Crandall and Ellsworth were blackmail victims. He probably knew or at least had a good idea who the blackmailer was. And if so, why didn't he want Saundra revealing that information?

Was the blackmailer the true murderer? Had he or she been down at the creek, saw the attack, and finished up what Ellsworth started once Crandall drove him away?

Ellsworth was incensed by the realization that Lyndsy had to have been dead all this time. He believed he had been paying the blackmail money to her. He jumped to the conclusion that Crandall had been pretending to be Lyndsy to perpetrate blackmail.

When Dara expressed more sympathy, he eagerly spilled a story where Lyndsy had harassed him, demanding he meet her down in the creek behind Fendergast's house. He claimed Crandall had snuck up
~~~~~

behind her and clubbed her with a crowbar. Ellsworth insisted he had chased Crandall away. He had been paying the blackmail because the blackmailer sent him a video of the attack.

"Clearly, it's edited, it's played with, they do that sort of trickery in the movies all the time. They switched me for that skunk, Josiah. He killed her, not me!" Ellsworth insisted multiple times.

The blackmail letters started just two days later. He claimed his nerves were so shattered by the shock of that night, he hadn't known what to do except pay. Then he detoured for several moments, vilifying former police captain Beakman, who had promised to support him and abandoned him in his "hour of need." Apparently, Ellsworth had forgotten that Beakman was facing his own overdue justice at that time.

Ellsworth's face turned red and he shook more and gripped the edge of the table as he vilified Crandall. The questioning deteriorated after that point. Eden couldn't make out half the words the shaking, sweating, spitting little man said.

"Searching those video files is now top priority," Captain Sunderson said. "Who really attacked Lyndsy? If she died from that blow, who put the body in Old Man Fendergast's house?"

The pieces were coming together to form a whole picture. The timeline crystalized in Eden's mind as she only paid partial attention to Bill Worter and the police captain discussing the legal aspects and who to notify and what steps to take. Eden imagined that Macy/Kayla gained access to Lyndsy's computers when Mike cleared out her rooms. If Lyndsy's cameras recorded to more than just the computer found in Mrs. Tinderbeck's attic, then Macy could have found the video showing her murder. She had read Crandall's emails and realized quickly the opportunity for blackmail.

How long had Nick known the blackmail victims' and blackmailer's identities?

"I can answer that question," Sunderson said, when Eden voiced that question. "Pastor Roy came to me, to keep things above board. West was working with him to identify who was blackmailing Josiah. They had an appointment to come see me today. Josiah stopped at the library to meet Lydia Tinderbeck, so she could come with him, and that's when Ellsworth attacked."

"I find it hard to believe Josiah would hide a murder. Or even commit a murder. No matter what a dictator he was back then," Bill said.

"According to the emails we found in Lyndsy's account, he thought she was still alive," Eden said.

"And with the political situation three years ago, the mess when Beakman finally got ousted …" Sunderson shook her head. "No wonder he was afraid to go to the local authorities to help him."

"Why didn't anybody hear anything?" Bill mused.

"They did." She scrubbed her face with her palms and for a few seconds seemed to wilt a little with weariness. "Fendergast was having his fits practically every night. There was a lot of mist that summer, and the mist always stirred him up, hallucinating that the ghost of Annabelle Cadburn was coming to him. Whatever people heard, they thought it was him, and they had learned to ignore him."

"If it happened that night Lyndsy came back to the house and Phoebe got arrested by Caruthers, I'm guessing Lyndsy was asking Crandall for help. She had an idea where Steve was. Maybe she knew Steve was in Fendergast's house. Crandall was one of the few people who could get through to him when he was having his fits," Eden said. "She never got a chance to tell him what she needed. Ellsworth snuck up behind her through the mist and clubbed her."

Chapter Eighteen

Tuesday, November 8

When Eden went to bed just before midnight on Monday, her head full of tangled ideas that needed straightening out in her subconscious, Rufus was still hard at work, tapping and muttering at the videos, begging them to play nice. She left her apartment door open, just in case he needed to call her with questions or problems.

She woke at 2:19am, hearing him chuckling softly and chanting what sounded like the victory jeer for the Cadburn High School Bulldogs. A good sign. She checked her clothes. The weather had turned chilly, so she had opted for lounging pants and a long-sleeve thermal underwear shirt. She was decent enough for cousins and co-workers, so she headed out into the office.

Rufus was at the refrigerator, pulling out another bottle of that energy drink he liked, in a nuclear shade of blue. He grinned at her, popped a wheelie, and headed back to his station.

"What did you find?" she demanded, her voice cracking.

"Gobs. Did you know 'gobs' is a theological term?"

He snatched up the universal remote that controlled quite a bit of equipment in the office. The semi-jumbo-tron, as Kai referred to the large flat-screen TV hanging from the ceiling, used for holiday parties and sports-all-day weekends, flared into life.

"Theological?" Eden rubbed the sleep from her eyes and headed for the refrigerator. If she was going to fully wake up for this, then she needed some liquid caffeine. She mostly kept the bottled lattes to irritate Kai, but sometimes when she was working late into the night, or early into the morning, she needed the high caloric content as much as the caffeine. The first one she snatched was vanilla. She shook it up and settled down on the padded bench facing the TV while Rufus cued up the video. A yawn cracked her jaw and she hurried to pop the bottle open and chug.

"According to my Sunday school teacher, anyway," Rufus added, and pivoted to watch the screen as static flowed across it. "A gigundus number, as in 'gobs of angels,' supposedly the number for how many can dance on the head of a pin."

"You need some sleep." She chuckled.

"Yeah, I'll sleep when I'm …" His grin fell off his face. "Nope, not the right place for that. Anyway … I found a few good things, and they gave me an anchor date, for figuring out what happened to Steve and then Lyndsy. Some patience will pay off in the end." He pointed at the screen.

"I'm putting this together as insurance," an alto voice announced as the video showed a pile of what looked like rocks, partially covered with vines and brambles and underbrush. The lens moved out again, showing a sliver of creek on the bottom of the image, and trees and thick foliage.

"This is the lot line between 4368 Creekbend Court, and 4384 Creekbend Court. Properties owned by Fendergast and Gibbons. On the north side of Cadburn Creek. Two nights ago was a full moon, with no clouds in the sky. Cancelled out my night-vision lens. All the moonlight would have just burned out everything, so you have to put up with the shadows and big portions of the picture the moonlight didn't touch."

Rufus rolled his wheelchair over next to Eden's bench. "She spliced in a lot of images, got some really good stuff from different angles. If it was me, I'd have sued her for trespassing and invasion of privacy, with all those cameras. How did she get them hung without the psycho old men going batso-wacko on her?"

The image flickered, darkening to a scene mostly of blacks and dark greens and silver, shifting from daylight to nighttime and moonlight. Movement on the right resolved into two figures splashing through the creek. They stepped into moonlight. Lyndsy and Steve. Both in costume. Eden thought of the skeletons found in Bee's cellar and something tightened in her gut. She thought of that email, crowing about frightening the property owners and stirring up legends of the Cadburn Ghost.

"It's right here," Lyndsy said, and bent down at the water line to pull back a thick layer of what could have been long grass or maybe even vines and brambles falling down the bank. "It's the symbol for shelter."

Steve moved in, blocking the image, and bent down. "That's kind of frustrating, considering all the time me and Crandall and others spent down here, looking for signs like this."

"The flood wall hid it. Who knows what else has been finally uncovered?" Lyndsy said.

"Sshh!" He half-way stood up, looking around.

Likely reacting to some sound. They had good reason to fear Fendergast and his rifle showing up.

They talked in softer voices for several minutes. The microphone didn't pick up anything understandable. Eden estimated the camera was on the other side of the creek, a good twenty feet away.

Steve stepped back, fists on his hips, studied the stone carving, then raised his head and looked at the pile of rocks at the foot of the ridge.

"What do you think?" Lyndsy splashed to a low spot on the bank of the creek and stepped up onto dry ground.

Eden had stood on that spot in the rain and studied Bee's backyard just days ago. Had Lyndsy discovered the tunnel opening on the other side of that ridge? Eden kept watching the video as she stepped over to her desk and picked up a notepad and pen. She made a note to ask Amos if his group had an expert on the Underground Railroad markers to help fugitives find station houses.

"You're in a lot of trouble." Steve pointed at the ridge. It meandered back and forth, coming down the slope from the higher ground where all the houses had been built.

The ridge of rocks and stones and brambles was a distinctive feature. Part of it had probably been created by flooding moving stones and other debris until they hit a higher bit of land here. Back in pre-Civil War times, it would have looked entirely natural, and not a construction hiding a tunnel.

"Why?" Lyndsy said. She mimicked his pose, her fists at her hips.

"The tunnel might be in there, but do you know where it comes out? The ridge goes across the lot line. Neither one of those old farts is going to give permission to go digging. They're going to either say no because you start out on Gibbons' property, or they're going to say no because if the ridge marks the tunnel, you'll go onto Fendergast's property."

"Well ... who says we have to ask permission? I bet all we need are a couple machetes and crowbars. Dig through all that junk and uncover the door, then pry it open. But be careful to disturb as little as possible, so we can sneak in and out. Get all the documentation done at night, prove our theories, then reveal it to the world in such a way they have to cooperate or just prove what a bunch of stupid old, selfish farts they really are." She took a few steps toward the ridge.

"Stop right there," Steve said. "Want to go to the hospital to have them pick bird shot out of your backside? Or worse?"

"That old fart wouldn't really shoot us, would he?"

"He won't shoot me. I'm still safe in the creek. You signed your death warrant the minute you stepped up out of the water."

A rumble in the distance felt like ominous punctuation to his words.

"And now it's going to rain," he added.

"Then let's hurry. Find the opening and get out of here." Lyndsy looked up as clouds cast shadows through the moonlight, sending first Steve, then her, into darkness.

The wind kicked up, fluttering the leaves of the trees surrounding them. More rumbling spilled through the night quiet.

Lyndsy stomped forward, gesturing at the spot on the creek bank where she had pulled up the grass and vines. "How many of them have been down here, have dug around here, but did any of them find it? No, it took me, the outsider, to put the clues together."

"Preaching to the choir, babe. Now, we're gonna be soaked in another minute." Lightning flashed above the tops of the trees and houses framed in the video. "Can we please go somewhere comfortable and come up with a plan? If we have to trade a little glory to grease the wheels, that's the price we gotta pay."

"You can pay it. I'm tired of paying and getting nothing but a pat on the head," she snarled.

Light speared across the yard behind her. A cracking tenor voice cut through the rising rumbling of thunder and wind in the leaves.

"Duck!" Steve leaped forward and grabbed hold of Lyndsy's hand, yanking her down into the creek with him. She went to her knees. He wrapped an arm around her waist and half-carried her until they left the camera frame.

"Lyndsy spliced a bunch of stuff together. Like she said, this video was her insurance policy if anything happened." Rufus slouched a little in his wheelchair and gestured a salute at the screen with his can before tipping back and taking a big gulp.

Static streaked the image, then switched to show what Eden recognized as the other side of the ridge. A chill touched her when she realized Lyndsy had indeed found the tunnel opening.

"I am in big trouble," Lyndsy said, in a voice-over, as the video showed her sliding between rocks, vanishing among them.

The image changed to what Eden assumed was a hand-held camera. It followed the curve of the tunnel, lit by a strong light that either came from the video camera itself, or was maybe one of those headband lights popular for spelunkers, to leave their hands free. The walls were covered in semi-familiar carvings in the stone.

"I found these carvings four days ago," the voice-over continued. "I came back two days ago, to do some rubbings. Someone has been digging since I got in." Her voice cracked. "They've changed. Someone has been adding to them."

The video flicked back and forth between several groups of carvings, with Lyndsy indicating pictures she took four days before, then the most recent ones. Eden could see the changes, small gouges, lines and circles. She was trained in noticing small details, but she thought an untrained eye could catch them too. She supposed geologists and experts in such carvings would have to be called in to determine what had been done, but someone had worked to alter the initial carvings. Why?

"I don't know who to go to. Everybody thinks I'm a troublemaker. I wish I hadn't been so snippy with Dr. Tanner when I took off. How do I ask for her help? Would she even believe me? I have to keep the few original, genuine carvings from being destroyed or lost among all the fakes. This is too important to history to let some cheat not just destroy the real stuff but take credit for my discovery!"

"That girl had her priorities way messed up," Rufus said. He tapped the control, pausing the video. "You want to wait until morning, call Sunderson, before you see what's next?"

"I'm guessing Lyndsy put this together just before she vanished … and she found the originals showing who really killed Steve?" She managed a smile. "Technically, it's already morning, but … yeah. The fewer times any of us have to see this, the better."

~~~~~

Apparently, Captain Sunderson was having just as much trouble sleeping as Eden and Rufus. Eden left a message at 5:30, and by 7:15 the police chief was on her way up in the elevator. She had texted Bill Worter, and he was on his way. He needed to see this new evidence Rufus and Eden had found, as he was now officially representing the township and Bee Wilkinson, as owner of the property that was the crime scene.

Much of the video was familiar to Eden, as she and Rufus had teased it apart three years ago, trying to prove Lyndsy had been framed. No one was surprised to see Mike Kioto's face and body instead of Lyndsy's in the struggle, then shaking the bridge until Steve fell off and landed on his head in the creek. Several cameras had microphones, so everyone reacted to the distinctive crack of his skull hitting a stone in the shallow water.

In the original video, Mike waded out and turned Steve over and searched him. He took what looked like a notebook and a camera and car keys. When Steve feebly fought him, he kicked him hard enough to roll him over on his face again. As Steve struggled to get his arms under himself and get his face out of the water, Mike stomped down the creek, heading for the bank.

A gunshot cracked through the air. Mike ran, vanishing from the camera pickup.

The picture shifted. Lyndsy had spliced in another camera, a different angle. Steve struggled to his feet, facing the camera. He staggered toward the bank, holding one hand against his forehead. Eden imagined the pain that made him stumble. He took four steps toward the bank and went to his knees.

"There." Rufus pointed to the top of the TV screen.

A dark man-shape emerged from the shadows of Fendergast's yard, into the moonlight. Eden couldn't pick out any details other than long gray hair streaming out from under a battered, Western-style hat sitting low on his head, a dark, long coat, like a duster, and a rifle. Eden had seen enough images of Andrew Fendergast through this investigation, she knew it was him. The man had lived in another era, to match the deterioration of his mind.

Fendergast stepped into the creek and tucked his rifle under his
~~~~~

armpit. Then he bent down and grabbed Steve by his upper arm and yanked, hauling him upright. Steve batted at the man's hand, visibly in pain. Then he gave up, gave in, and clutched at the man's arm as he struggled to his feet. Fendergast dragged him to the bank. Steve stumbled, and the man caught him by his collar and yanked hard, so he fell forward onto his face.

Seconds ticked by until Fendergast prodded Steve with the barrel of his rifle. Steve struggled to his feet. They moved forward.

The image flipped to another camera angle, showing the two walking toward the dark shape of the house, hidden among trees and shadows. There were no lights on in the house, and that made everything more ominous. Eden braced herself for the final gunshot, remembering the coroner's report of the two bullet holes in Steve's chest, but it never came. She flinched when the video went black.

"If Steve isn't dead, he's being held prisoner," Lyndsy said, the voiceover tight with either fury or fear. "I don't dare go to the police. Whoever made that video framing me, they've probably already sent it to the cops. Beakman hates me. He'll accuse me of making a fake video to defend myself, throw me in jail, instead of going into that crazy old fart's house to rescue Steve. He's already threatened me a dozen times for invading privacy. I can't go to any outside cops, because they'll just send me back to Beakman.

"I'm meeting Mr. Crandall in an hour. He can talk to Fendergast and get Steve out. If he's still alive. Whoever is seeing this, no matter what happened tonight, I'm posting this on the web to get the truth out. Maybe someone will see this and do something. I can't. I'm in too much trouble as it is. I'm out of here. Wish I had somewhere to go."

"So she was planning to take off," Bill murmured. "She never got a chance to come back and post the video."

"So what happened after Crandall chased away Ellsworth? Did she go to Fendergast's house to look for Steve? She wasn't shot," Sunderson said. "For all we know, she got in through that tunnel, found the way blocked, and lost consciousness and died from her injury." She sighed and rubbed her eyes and turned to Rufus and Eden. "I'm sorry. I'll assign my own people to finish this. You've both gone above and beyond."

"No," Rufus said. "We couldn't finish the job three years ago when Lyndsy asked for our help. I'm in until the end."

"What he said," Eden said.

~~~~~

The team gathered in the second-floor office to have a call over speakerphone with Bee that afternoon. Saundra showed up late, accompanied by Nick West. Eden supposed he had a right to be there, since he had provided a few pieces to fill out the puzzle. They discussed
~~~~~

what had been discovered so far and saved the video for later when Bee disconnected. She would have to watch it on her own computer later.

"Well, Lyndsy was right, wasn't she?" Bee said. Her voice crackled slightly over the speaker. "I feel so bad for her, trying to get help, and nobody she could trust."

"Until we find what the cameras caught that night, if the cameras were still working, we can't really be sure what happened that night she met Crandall," Eden admitted, speaking slowly. "We have two different stories, and both he and Ellsworth were self-righteous creeps back then, so whose story do you believe? Mrs. T says he changed drastically after that summer, so … who knows? Something scared him, but what if he committed murder and was so traumatized by it, he changed his entire life? He didn't fight back when he was blackmailed. That kind of implies a guilty conscience."

"I've got a lot more questions than I did when we sat down," Saundra said. She glanced at Mrs. Tinderbeck, who had been silent once everyone had made their greetings and settled with their beverages of choice around the table.

"Indeed, so do I," the head librarian said, nodding. "I don't particularly want to see that video of Lyndsy's encounter with Josiah and Myron, but I think I need to. Just to settle my questions, and my doubts about Josiah. Did Lyndsy get a chance to tell him what happened to Steve? If she did, he should have at the very least confronted Andrew Fendergast. I am sick at the thought that Steve could have still been alive at that point, and he was left to suffer and die, locked up in that cellar."

"It's a good thing I don't believe in ghosts," Bee commented.

No one smiled, and Eden supposed she wasn't trying to make a joke or lighten the mood.

Amos was interested in how soon the crime scene would be cleared to allow historians access to the tunnels, to study the markings on the walls. He had contacted Lyndsy's Dr. Tanner, to notify her about the discoveries Lyndsy had made. The woman had been concerned about her former assistant, despite the dark cloud tainting their parting. She wanted to be among the experts when they got into the tunnel.

Bee thanked them, acknowledged receipt of the video, and left the conversation. Then it was time to finally watch the insurance video, as Lyndsy had called it.

"Oh what a tangled web we weave," Mrs. Tinderbeck murmured when the screen cleared.

"Who exactly would profit from altering and falsifying historic carvings?" Nick said, breaking the silence while those gathered in the office digested those words and the implications.

"Could I make a suggestion?" Bill Worter said. He leaned down and pulled a folder from his always overstuffed briefcase. "I've got a large handful of testimonies that Fendergast was rabid about protecting his property. What if he caught Lyndsy digging around, saw her discover the tunnel opening on Gibbons' side of the ridge, and *didn't* chase her off because he knew the trespassing would hack off his neighbor?" The lawyer glanced around the room with a grim smile. "What if he went into the tunnel, and when he realized that it ended up on his property, under his house, decided to alter the carvings, to embarrass the history experts who would come in on Gibbons' invitation?"

"Somebody needs to talk to Fendergast," Nick said. "Visiting hours at his memory care facility are over for the day, but they open at 10:30."

"He would know that," Troy muttered. "Anybody else wonder why he has to know everything?"

"I've complained for years," Saundra said, and wrinkled up her nose at Nick, who gave her a wide-eyed, patently false look of innocence. "It doesn't do any good."

"Do we have any volunteers?" Eden said.

"If I recall ..." Amos shrugged, giving them his own, more believable smile of innocence. "Lydia, he was rather sweet on you once."

"Only because he wanted to, as William has so eloquently stated, hack off Josiah," Mrs. Tinderbeck said.

"Got to keep in mind, folks," Nick said, "the guy is living in the past, and he slips from one year to the next without warning. On the plus side, he's turned into a sweet old idiot, according to the nurses. He tells stupid jokes and spends his days watching Loony Tunes and the Three Stooges."

"Doesn't sound like he would have much to offer us," Bill said.

"You might be surprised what a face from his past might trigger. He doesn't have any visitors, except ..." He glanced around the room, inviting the question. When no one asked, he didn't look disappointed, but smiled a little wider. "Josiah Crandall."

"Why?" Olivia said.

"Somebody needs to ask, don't they?"

Chapter Nineteen

Thursday, November 10

Bill Worter finally heard from Fendergast's nearest living relative. Eden felt a little sorry for the old man because the nearest relative, Jason Malone, was the grandson of a cousin. He worked for a reality TV production company currently following the antics of a group of people trying to survive with 17th century technology in Alaska.

Malone gave permission to talk to Fendergast and wished them luck getting anything coherent out of him. The old man had been raving about finally settling the ghost when Malone and his elderly father took care of all the legalities to settle him in the nursing home. Malone's only contact with him lately was composed of reports from the family trust on how the investments that paid for Fendergast's care were holding up, and reports from the doctors on his physical and mental deterioration.

"Settling the ghost?" Eden said, when Bill related that part of the short, static-filled phone conversation. She glanced at Mrs. Tinderbeck, who looked troubled. That worried Eden, because the woman was one of the most calm, un-flappable people she had ever met.

"Yeah, that caught my attention, too," Bill said.

On the drive out to the facility in Medina, a very nice one that ran commercials portraying it as a country club sort of place, they agreed on their tactics. They would keep the meeting simple. Bill was there to cover legal concerns. Eden was there as lead investigator, and to write a report for Captain Sunderson's records. Only Mrs. Tinderbeck would speak to Fendergast. The other two would stay in the background.

"Did you say Lydia?" the young woman at the reception desk asked, when they signed in, and Bill presented the document sent by Fendergast's family's lawyer, giving permission to question him.

"Yes. Why?" Mrs. Tinderbeck asked.

"Every once in a while, he talks about his Lydia. Sometimes he's quite concerned for her, afraid she'll come under bad influence. Then he cheers up when he remembers that he saved her from that scoundrel, Josiah, and she's safe." She tipped her head to one side, her sweet smile turning mischievous. "Would that happen to be you?"

"Well, I admit, there was a tiny bit of rivalry between Andrew and Josiah, but ..." She shook her head, but that didn't hide the spots of blush touching her cheeks. "That was a long time ago, and I never encouraged him. Too erratic for me."

"Mrs. T, when you've got it, you've got it," Eden said.

That got giggles from the receptionist, and a soft chuckle from Mrs. Tinderbeck.

"He really is the sweetest old man," the receptionist said as she led the way down a long, carpeted hallway. "My predecessor was worried when his grandchildren stopped visiting, but he didn't seem to notice, so everybody just assumed they moved or life got in the way or ... well, families do drift apart, don't they?"

"Grandchildren?" Eden traded concerned glances with Bill. "About how long ago did they stop visiting?"

"I'll have to check the records. Why?"

"Andrew doesn't have any grandchildren," Mrs. Tinderbeck said. "He never married."

"Oh, that's a problem, isn't it?" The receptionist slowed and gave them all a concerned look.

"There's no need to worry," Bill said, and reached into his coat pocket. "We're here on legal matters. This is my business card. This card is for Captain Sunderson of the Cadburn Township police. She can verify we're here legitimately. If you could find those records of Mr. Fendergast's admission and his visitors, we'd appreciate all the help you can provide."

"Of course," she said, her voice going soft and thin. She took the two cards gingerly, as if she thought they might bite her. Then she continued leading them down the hall.

Two turns took them to an interior courtyard, open to the sky. A concrete fountain sat in the center of the octagonal space, shut down for the season, with leaves floating in the water that had likely collected over the long days of rain. A few fallen leaves littered the pavement between small clusters of wooden park benches sitting under gazebos tangled with bare vines.

"He likes to come out here to sit, no matter what the weather is like," she whispered as she stepped aside and held the door open for them.

A gangly figure slumped on a park bench, the sole occupant of the courtyard. His head tilted back to face the sky, eyes closed. Everything about the elderly man spoke of a strong, long-boned body that had wasted away with the years. Where skin didn't cling to his bones, it sagged in loose folds.

The receptionist hurried away once they stepped into the courtyard. Mrs. Tinderbeck took slow, careful steps approaching the man. He sat so still, Eden stared at his chest to make sure it moved to breathe. She and Bill stayed back by the closed door, although Eden suspected they could have stood in front of Fendergast, and he wouldn't have noticed them when he opened his eyes.

"Andrew," Mrs. Tinderbeck said.

Fendergast snorted and his limbs jerked. Another snort and he opened his eyes and looked around. A delighted, sweet smile lit his face when his gaze landed on Mrs. Tinderbeck.

"Well, hello there! Haven't seen you for the longest time. Where have you been? Off gallivanting?" He shook his finger at her. "I warned you there'd be a steep price to pay if you ran off and had fun without me."

"Oh, really?" Mrs. Tinderbeck settled on the bench facing him. As far as Eden was concerned, the four or five feet between the benches wasn't far enough. "And what price is that?"

"You owe me a kiss, ladybug."

"Ah, no, I don't." She smiled gently, even sadly, and shook her head. "You have me confused with someone else."

"Now what makes you say something so cruel as that?" He chuckled and pulled himself up straighter. "You think I don't know my ladybug when I see her?"

"Andrew, I'm Lydia."

His smile slid off his face and his eyes widened and he leaned forward, bony elbows on equally bony knees as he stared at her. Eden counted to twenty before he took a deep, rattling breath and nodded.

"Lydia, of course. How are you, darling? Please don't tell me that scoundrel Josiah stole the march on me."

"No, he didn't. Neither one of you stood a chance against my Augustus."

"Hah, that's right!" He sat up and slapped his knee. "How is the old bulldog?"

"I see what they meant, about him sliding between times," Bill whispered. "Augustus Tinderbeck died sixteen years ago. From what I heard, they were grade school sweethearts."

"So we really can't trust what he tells us, because he's got a pretty slippery grasp on reality?" Eden whispered back. He just shrugged.

"Andrew, I'm curious. The lovely young woman who bought your house," Mrs. Tinderbeck began.

"Bought my house? Why would anyone buy my house?" A flush touched his high cheekbones. "How could anybody buy my house? I'm still living there."

"Don't you remember? You got sick, and you needed someone to take care of you. Jason, your cousin's grandson, brought you here." She gestured around the courtyard.

"Here?" Fendergast turned his head right and left and tipped it back and looked around again. His eyes widened, and he shook a little, so Eden thought he might start crying. "That's right. I'm sick. They're taking care of me. How could I forget? What's wrong with me, that I forget?"

"It's all right, Andrew. That's why you're here. To make you well. They're taking very good care of you." Mrs. Tinderbeck got up and moved over to sit next to him on the bench.

She patted his knee. Eden thought she was the bravest person she had seen in a long time. And also rather foolhardy. There was no telling what that old man could do to hurt her, if he got upset enough. Already, it was clear his emotions could change on a dime.

"And when you're completely well, you can go home. That lovely young lady is taking very good care of your home for you. Remember?"

"She's good," Bill whispered. "If we had her for a trustee, we'd get a lot more done in a lot less time."

Eden repressed a chuckle.

"Yeah. I remember. She's a good girl." Fendergast chuckled, a raspy sound like he had something caught in his throat. "Can't remember her name. Craziest thing."

Eden shivered, sensing Mrs. Tinderbeck was going in for the attack. She brought out her cell phone and prepared her camera for video recording.

"Deborah. She had some questions about those silly boys who were playing at being Civil War soldiers and acting out battles in the creek. Remember?"

"Yep." The humor left his face. The bones under his saggy skin suddenly looked as sharp as his voice. "Nasty, disrespectful brats, every one of them. Came up on my land. Poking around. Looking for things that weren't none of their nevermind." He made a coughing sort of sound. Eden wondered if he used to chew tobacco, and he was about to spit.

"What were they looking for, do you remember?"

"Slaves." His voice took on a growl. "Told them and told them, me and my folks, we ain't never held with slavery. Downright barbaric, if you ask me. Don't matter the color of somebody's skin or what language he speaks, if he's poor or rich or can't read nor nothing like that. Nobody's got no right to treat other people like property. My granddaddy held that, and them slave hunters, they ambushed him and dang near lynched him because they said he was a stupid Northerner, and he needed to be taught a lesson. Great-granddaddy and all his sons and their sons, they stood up for the runaway Blacks. Was only right." He turned his head and hawked and spat.

Eden flinched, chilled by the subtle changes in Fendergast's posture and voice. He really had slipped back into the past.

"Are you sure they were looking for slaves? Maybe they were looking for people who helped the slaves escape," Mrs. Tinderbeck said. She rested one hand on Fendergast's arm.

"Ain't none of their nevermind. I made a promise, just like my daddy and all his kin. You never know when those soul-sucking bullies and their ilk will come back. Gotta protect the secrets, protect the hiding places, if we ever need them again. Look what happened with Hitler and them Nazis and those idjits in Italy, them facers." He paused, his expression twisting almost comically as he visibly sought for the word.

"Fascists?" she offered.

"Yeah. Them. Gotta keep the secrets. Ain't never gonna tell nobody. Can't risk them finding out and knowing where to find the folks that get hunted next. Blacks and Jews and Gypsies and the Injuns and who knows who else? Everybody gets hunted, one time or another. People just ain't no good, so you gotta be ready to help whoever gets a target painted on them next. You know?"

He turned a pleading expression on Mrs. Tinderbeck. She murmured assurances and patted his shoulder. Fendergast breathed shallowly, rapidly for a few moments, struggling against the fear that made his pale skin even paler. Then in a few more breaths, his shoulders hunched again and his breath got tight and angry.

"And then that goldarn idjit, Gibbons, starts talking stupid and joining them history wreckers and wanting to dig around and bring what needs to stay hidden out into the daylight. It ain't right, I tell you!" Tears glistened in Fendergast's eyes.

"So what did you do?"

"Protected my land, like I promised. Them history folks, they got high-and-mighty, started telling me what I couldn't do with my own land. My family's owned that land longer than all of them and their grandparents been alive." A cracked chuckle escaped him. Anger turned to mischief. "Got them good. They said don't change anything, so I did. Went and got me an architect guy to add onto the cellar and built me a fancy deck, and when I get back home, gonna build me one of them conversa—conserves—dagnabbit, what's the word? That fancy place all full of glass where you grow fancy plants in the winter?"

"Conservatory? Arboretum?" She patted his knee again. "That's a lovely idea, Andrew. Did you build your deck?"

"Yep." His smile faded. "Leastways, what I can remember, I got started. Then that idjit, Butterworth, he knuckles under to that Barnes harpy, and suddenly, no sir, can't make no changes to your place without permission from the history folks."

"What did you do?"

"Pulled out my shotgun and told him to git and not never come back. He started yammering, and that idiot Beakman showed up and threatened to haul me off to jail if I kept the idjit's tools and such. But I paid for the concrete and the wood, so I kept it. Hired me a man from Akron to build the deck. Turned out nicer than Butterworth would have done, too." He nodded for punctuation. "He was cheating me. New guy told me he only needed half the concrete and whatnot to do the job. Butterworth would have taken all the leftovers home with him."

"What did you do with the extra supplies?"

"Eh?" Fendergast's expression turned sharp again.

"What else are you going to build with the concrete the contractor didn't use?"

"Ain't none of your nevermind." He slouched forward, resting his elbows on his knees and his head in his hands. "Why you gotta keep asking me things? Makes my head hurt."

Mrs. Tinderbeck pressed her lips flat, studying him. She glanced over at Eden and Bill.

"Andrew, there was a girl who was following the boys around. The boys playing at being soldiers. Do you remember her?"

"Eh?" His head snapped up and he blinked several times. "Why for would a girl hang around with a bunch of troublemakers?"

"She wasn't hanging around with them. She was watching them, following them. Trying to keep them from causing trouble for good people like you. Do you remember her?"

"Girl them boys were yelling at? Especially that blondie snot." He nodded, the mischievous expression back. Something about it made Eden shiver. What was going through that old man's mind? "Yep. I remember. He got what he deserved, didn't he?"

"What happened to him? What did he deserve?"

He shrugged and looked away, bobbing forward now, bouncing a little on the bench seat like a little boy who needed the bathroom.

"Do you remember what happened to her? Did you yell at her?"

"Why would I do that?" He paused for a few heartbeats, his eyes wide, looking stricken.

"Well, she was dressed up like a Civil War soldier, just like the boys. Maybe you didn't realize she was a girl, and you chased her away, too, like you did the boys."

"Nah. Didn't want her to go. Didn't want my ghost to go away again. She came back home, just like she promised, don't you know? Yeah, gotta help her rest. Ain't no need to wander no more. The ghost." He nodded, smiling at a spot in the air, bobbing his head. A chill ran up Eden's spine.

"Did you talk to her?"

"Her who?" His smile flicked into a frown, just for a moment. Then his gaze turned distant again and he kept bobbing.

"The girl dressed up like a Civil War soldier."

"No girl. Just the ghost." He hunched forward, bobbing more.

Mrs. Tinderbeck tried more questions, different angles, but

Fendergast said nothing more. He didn't seem to hear her. Common sense said to give up. They left him in the courtyard.

They found a nurse at the duty station just down the hall from the courtyard entrance. Bill reported that Fendergast seemed somewhat agitated, maybe someone should check on him. The nurse thanked them with a searching, disapproving look.

"I feel like I'm being blamed for picking on the teacher's pet," Eden whispered, when they had turned a corner and left the nurse behind.

"They like the old guy," Bill said.

"He's certainly changed from the combative old curmudgeon I used to know," Mrs. Tinderbeck said, punctuated with a sigh. "He's almost sweet. I feel sorry for him."

"He's given us some clues. We just need to untangle them," Eden said. "Am I imagining it, or did we get confirmation he was at least involved in hiding the bodies?"

"Let's leave that for the professionals to decide," Bill said. He sighed. "Yes, you are a professional. You know what I mean."

"No harm, no foul."

This was turning into one of those situations where she would be very glad to turn over everything to the authorities and let them sort through all the evidence.

A text came as they were getting into Bill's car.

Rufus.

Found it.

~~~~~

"I need your help," Lyndsy said, coming out of the shadows cast by the ridge of rocks and brambles. Mist from the water swirled around her, giving the feeling of an old-style horror movie.

All this video needed was ominous music to signal when the monster would appear. Rufus had had enough time to find all the bits of videos from the other cameras and set up the computer to let him switch back and forth to better angles. Eden looked around at the members of the team who had joined to watch and wondered if that was a good idea. If everything happened as her imagination had woven the scene together, some images would be rather disturbing.

A man stepped into the moonlight, the top of his head entering the frame of the video lens. After watching all the videos and the different angles that Lyndsy had spliced together, Eden thought this particular camera had been anchored on a tree on the far side of the creek from Bee Wilkinson's house. She wondered what had happened to this camera. Did Mike take it, or had Fendergast found it and destroyed it, or had hikers taken it? They would never really know, she supposed.

"What is it you think I can do for you? And why this meeting in the
~~~~~

middle of the night?" he asked.

"We'll trade. I found the tunnel you've been looking for. Help me, and I'll show you and let you keep all the credit." Lyndsy stepped closer to the bank of the creek.

"What tunnel?" The man staggered forward several steps. Now he was visible from the middle of his back, upward. Through the shreds of mist, his short, glistening white hair and a dark sport coat were clearly visible. Eden thought she recognized that coat. "Where?"

"That crazy old Fendergast. I think he killed someone."

"Don't be ridiculous. That rifle of his is filled with rock salt. He couldn't hit the inside of a barn at five feet away."

"Then go talk to him, if he's not dangerous."

Movement from the far left of the frame caught Eden's attention. At the same time, the speaker turned, revealing his face. Josiah Crandall.

"You have to help me." Lyndsy jumped down into the creek. Mist off the water churned around her, as if it wanted to tangle her feet. The water splashed, just ankle deep, getting deeper with each step she took. On her third step, she apparently stepped into a hole in the creek bed, past her knee, and stumbled.

She struggled to catch herself and get back on her feet. Ellsworth leaped out of the shadows. He raced off the bank, splashing into the creek, raising one arm as he lunged at her.

Olivia gasped, and Eden didn't blame her.

Ellsworth held a short, thin object in his hand. Rufus, with the computer on his lap, tapped several keys. The angle changed, a closer shot from the left of Ellsworth. This was close enough to show the bulbous end of the black bar, and the angled tip at the other end. A tire iron. He lunged out of the camera view. Crandall cried out, demanding to know what he was doing, then shouted for Lyndsy to look out.

The view changed to another camera, on the far right, showing Ellsworth's backside as he swung down, just as Lyndsy turned. She raised a hand to block the blow and Ellsworth grabbed it, yanked and spun her around, and clubbed the back of her head.

Lyndsy went face-first into the water. She caught herself with her bent arms and struggled to keep her face out of the water.

"What are you doing?" Crandall staggered off the bank of the creek, splashing into the water, and threw himself at Ellsworth. He ducked the first swing of the tire iron and rammed the other man in the stomach with his head. Ellsworth went down.

"Good one," Nick muttered. Eden glanced at him, and he winked. "Not bad for an old guy."

Crandall stumbled to Lyndsy and hauled her to her feet. She choked and coughed and whimpered. She pressed her hand to the back of her head and cried out louder. It came away bloody.

Ellsworth staggered to his feet and stumbled after them as Crandall settled Lyndsy on the bank, her feet in the water. She let out a cry and pointed. Crandall turned. Ellsworth swung and missed, knocking himself off his feet with the force of his blow. Crandall lunged at him. Ellsworth staggered away.

"Are you all right?" Crandall called, gasping for breath. He bent over and braced himself on his bent knees. Ellsworth stumbled up onto the bank and vanished into the shadows.

Lyndsy waved him away. She wrapped her arms around herself, shuddering. Crandall looked back at her once, then stumbled after Ellsworth.

"Please," she whimpered, and reached into her pocket. A wail escaped her, cut off a moment later. Eden imagined the sound made her head hurt more. Lyndsy staggered to her feet and searched her pockets. What was she looking for?

She went out into the creek, to the place she had fallen, and went to her knees in the water, searching. Whimpering. More mist swirled around her. Eden hated horror movies. Not the blood and gore and screams, but moments like this, when everything was quiet, poised and waiting, and about to go terribly, horribly, painfully wrong.

Eden wanted to shout for her to get up, to get out of there.

Sounds of traffic came from far away, and Eden imagined people coming home from late night shifts, crossing one of the bridges nearby, maybe coming to one of the houses that sat with their backs to the creek. And no one in those houses knew that Lyndsy fumbled around in the water, her head aching from that crack in her skull. The injury hadn't killed her. Yet. Maybe she lost consciousness and fell into the creek and drowned?

A familiar, tall, lean figure dressed in a long, dark coat stepped out into the moonlight where it touched the bank of the creek. Andrew Fendergast. He stopped and leaned on his rifle like it was a cane. Then he smiled. A sad kind of smile. He put the rifle down and stepped out into the creek.

Lyndsy must have heard him, though the camera didn't pick up the sounds of splashing footsteps. She turned around, still on her knees. With her back to the camera, her reaction wasn't visible. The image flipped through several different camera angles, but none of them showed her face, lost in shadows and mist.

Her expression wasn't necessary. She struggled to get to her feet, crab-walking for a few steps, scrambling away from Fendergast. He just smiled at her as he caught up with her, in no hurry.

Lyndsy overbalanced, trying to get upright, and went down on her back, submerging. Fendergast caught up with her then. He caught her by her shoulders and lifted her head up out of the water. Lyndsy coughed and spat and whimpered what sounded like, "No."

"Don't you worry none. You're home now, my ghost," Fendergast said.

His tone turned into a croon, and Eden shivered.

Then one hand shifted to grab hold of Lyndsy's braid. His other hand around her throat, he pushed her down into the water. He held her there as her body bucked and arms flailed. No sounds escaped the weak splashing, but Eden imagined her begging for her life, with no one but the crazy old man to hear her.

"You're home now," he crooned.

Just a few more bubbles. The struggling ended in moments.

"Gonna let you rest now. Ain't gonna be alone no more." He lifted her up and slung her over his shoulder in one smooth move that indicated what strength he still possessed. "Gonna take good care of you. Gonna protect you. Gonna send them all away, and ain't nobody gonna ever scare you ever again."

Everybody in the room held still as they watched Fendergast carry Lyndsy's body out of the creek and up onto the bank and vanish into the darkness under the trees. The night grew quiet, as if even the insects and the wind and the night creatures were afraid to move after what had just happened.

"Just a few more seconds," Rufus murmured. He shifted the camera angle. "Lower right corner."

Eden wasn't surprised when Mike stepped out of the shadows and mist to splash into the creek where Lyndsy had knelt and searched. He scraped the creek bed with his foot, all the while watching the other bank. Eden had grown familiar with the camera angles by now and was sure he watched Fendergast's house.

Mike bent down and picked up something. He wiped it on his sleeve. A stray streak of moonlight glinted off a black, rectangular surface.

"Her phone," Olivia whispered. "Lyndsy was trying to call for help, but she dropped her phone."

"How many people can we charge as accessories to murder from that night?" Bill said, as they watched Mike cross back the way he came, from where he had probably watched everything, and did nothing to help.

The screen blanked, and for a few moments the only sounds came from Rufus shutting down the computer. He pulled a flashdrive out and held it up, offering it to Sunderson. The police captain nodded and stepped over to take it from him.

"You know what I find truly sad in this whole mess?" Sunderson said. "Josiah is a good member of my church. He turned himself around, got right with God, even tried to reconcile both history groups." She scrubbed her face, as if trying to wipe away her weariness. "Too bad he's got some nasty stuff resting on his conscience. I can see how something like that—" she nodded at the blank TV screen, "—could knock a man flat and make him straighten out. But the fact is, even though he knew it was too late, he didn't tell anyone what happened. Nobody looked for that poor girl down in the creek because nobody but him and Ellsworth knew where she had been. I would have conducted house-to-house searches along the creek. We might have found both those bodies before they were sealed up."

"But Beakman was still in charge back then," Olivia said.

"True, but we had enough good men on the force back then who would have risked their jobs to do what was right. We just didn't have the right information to make a difference."

"You're going to arrest Ellsworth for attempted murder, at least?" Eden said.

"Oh, yeah. And that will be the highlight of my week."

Chapter Twenty

Friday, November 11

After so many blissful days of not seeing or hearing from Ellsworth, Olivia's Friday started off on a sour note. His equally sour face glared at her as she went to open the front door of Book & Mug. She knew she was in fact three minutes ahead of schedule, and for about five seconds she considered showing him her watch and just standing there, arms crossed, waiting until the minute hand hit the twelve before opening the doors. There were five other customers standing behind Ellsworth, all people she liked, and she couldn't justify inflicting his whining on them.

Why had he been released from jail after attacking Josiah Crandall? Why not keep him until they could make the case against him for attacking Lyndsy? The statute of limitations for attempted murder had to be longer than three years, didn't it?

Plastering a pleasant smile on her face, she refused to look at Ellsworth. She unlocked the door he was standing directly in front of and pushed it open. He had to move back to keep from being hit. She kept pushing it and held it open so the other customers got inside first. Still ignoring him, she let go of the door and hurried to take her position behind the counter before the first customers reached it.

By the time Ellsworth's turn came and he stomped up to the counter, Olivia had an epiphany. If she treated him just like everyone else, smiling and acting like she didn't despise him, that would drive him crazy. He visibly got some perverted pleasure out of people showing their disgust toward him.

Ted Shrieve spoiled her big acting moment. He walked in the door just as she handed a triple shot double-pump caramel frozen whip to Ellie Jacobs, the customer before Ellsworth. Olivia took a deep breath and pulled her shoulders back and made sure her isn't-this-a-wonderful-day smile was in place. Ellsworth stepped up to the counter, his mouth opening for the first nasty salvo.

"Myron Ellsworth." Ted smoothly slid around to block him from taking another step closer.

"What do you want now?" Ellsworth snapped.

"You're under arrest." Ted gestured at the door, which was opening to allow another dozen customers in.

Olivia knew she should feel guilty for finding delight in a growing audience for Ellsworth's humiliation, but he so deserved it.

"For what?" Ellsworth's voice cracked.

"The attempted murder of Lyndsy Auretta on the night of—"

"You can't prove it!" Ellsworth sidestepped, right into Gabe Peterson and four other men from Chandler Construction, stocking up for their morning of tearing up pavement. "Besides, the statute of limitations has run out."

"You really need to talk to your lawyer. There's no statute of limitations on murder."

"She's alive! She's been blackmailing me for years!" Ellsworth twisted aside as his voice rose through two octaves.

"You attacked Josiah Crandall and accused him of blackmailing you," Olivia said. "Can't you keep your stories straight?"

Ellsworth's eyes got big, so she thought they might pop out of his head. Then, screaming profanity, he launched himself across the counter, his hands flexing wide, reaching for her throat.

Olivia froze.

Ellsworth was in no shape to leap over a counter. He hit the edge right below his ribs, knocking a gust of rancid breath out of him with a yelp that went even higher than his scream had been. Ted caught hold of him by his collar and the belt of his trench coat and hauled him down.

"You okay?" Ted asked her.

Olivia nodded. Everyone moved back as Ted half-dragged, half-led Ellsworth out of the coffee shop. Then the tide moved in, and a dozen voices asked what was going on. The events and discussions of the last few days sped through her mind. She surprised herself by laughing.

"Sorry, everybody, but the police investigation is still ongoing, and if I tell you anything, I'll have to kill you. And believe me, Kai will be seriously pissed if I kill off his favorite customers. Especially before they've bought anything."

That got laughter, and she liked to think that several people bought much more expensive drinks than usual that morning. From the looks in their eyes, and comments they made, she knew they would push her for an explanation. Maybe not today. Maybe not tomorrow. But eventually everybody would demand to know what had happened.

Well, it would bring them in every day, hoping to hear the story before everybody else. That had to be good for business.

~~~~~

Just before Eden was to leave to join Captain Sunderson and Bill Worter in going to Josiah Crandall's house to confront him with his part in the events leading up to Lyndsy's death, she got a text from Nick West. He had found Macy and Mike, in Chicago.
~~~~~

In jail. New names. Same tricks and schemes. No one to help them. Sending info to Sunderson to extradite. Tell Olivia. She earned it.

That was nice of him, and more than she had expected. Eden wasn't sure if that irritated her, because she wanted reasons to dislike him. There was just something about Nick that made her think he knew far too much about her and her cousins, things they needed to know, and he was keeping secrets for the fun of it.

If Nick knew things … what were the chances Saundra knew?

Eden pushed that thought away. She liked Saundra too much to believe she would keep secrets from them. Especially if she knew how much that information meant to them.

Half an hour later, Eden, Bill, and Captain Sunderson went to Josiah Crandall's home. He was under doctor's orders to take things slowly and quietly and avoid stress. Eden's admiration for the chief of police doubled, when the woman approached Crandall as a member of his church, and not as the chief of police. She offered to show him the video Rufus had put together, showing the confrontation at the creek, the attack, and the drowning. Crandall refused. He spoke quietly and simply, relating a story that matched what had appeared in the video. He went pale and his voice shook a little, when he asked if they knew what Lyndsy had wanted him to help her do. He shuddered when he learned that she wanted his help in rescuing Steve from Fendergast.

He refused again to charge Ellsworth with assault. He seemed to be amused, in a weary sort of way, when they revealed who had been blackmailing him and Ellsworth.

"Can I assume that I'm under arrest?" he said, after several moments of thoughtful silence. "Contributing to the death of that poor girl? Helping the real murderers get away with it all these years?"

"I think we'll leave that up to the county officials," Sunderson said. "You did try to protect her, and the records from that night prove you were injured and unable to go back. You tried to help, you just gave up too soon. And I think we've got enough proof that you reformed. That's a lot of community service you've put in over the years."

He sighed. "There's still an awful lot to make up for."

~~~~~

"So, I heard you had an interesting morning," Eden said, when Olivia stopped into the office at the end of the day.

"Proof I've still got a vindictive streak in me." She raked her fingers through her hair and obeyed when Eden gestured for her to take a seat at the conference table opposite her work station. "What's up?"

"Another piece of the puzzle." Eden's eyes held a weariness that made Olivia ache for her. "Turns out Macy was part of an identity theft
~~~~~

ring. That's how she and Lyndsy became roommates, and those are the people she hacked off and she was scared of for a while. That part of the story was true. The guy who made Lyndsy's new identity sent her to Macy. She was supposed to keep an eye on her, because the higher-ups in the identity ring suspected her of cheating them. Macy got into Lyndsy's computer, stole a lot of her research and gave it to Mike. When Lyndsy confronted them, things started spiraling down. They turned on her. Turns out Mike's got a nasty past, vandalism, theft, assault, and blackmail. That video framing Lyndsy was his idea."

"Will they ever pay for what they did?" Olivia found it slightly amusing to realize she actually felt sorry for Lyndsy again.

"It'll take time," Eden promised her, "but it's all coming together."

Saturday, November 19

A short woman with tangled, white-streaked black curls and bottle-bottom glasses stood on the front step when Olivia answered the door at 9:35am. In one arm, she clutched a battered leatherbound journal with multi-colored flag stickers marking different pages, and held a smartphone up with the other hand, probably taking video of the street.

"Can I help you?" Olivia shivered when a gust of icy air swirled through the open door and seemed to slam into her bare feet. This was her one Saturday off, meaning she had planned to sleep until at least noon, and she wasn't in any mood to deal with people who ignored the NOPEC Do Not Knock sticker on the front door. Nobody had the right to yank her out of her nice warm bed, even if the sun was up and shining brightly despite the freezing wind.

"Are you Deborah Wilkinson?" The woman flashed a bright, eager smile at her.

"No. Bee is out of town for a few days." Nothing would convince Olivia to admit that Bee wouldn't be back for at least two more weeks. Her grandmother had made such a remarkable recovery, she had insisted on taking her relatives on a scenic train ride through the Rockies and up into Canada to celebrate.

"Then you must be Olivia. My dear, I am delighted to have a chance to meet you. I am Lauren Knight Tanner. I don't know if you heard anything about—"

"Lyndsy's Dr. Tanner?" She gaped for a few seconds, while the woman grinned even wider and nodded. Olivia knew she should do something, say something. She had just rolled out of bed, after all, and until now, her few awake brain cells had been focused on grumbling and doing mental damage to whoever had pulled her out of bed.

Then her manners kicked in.

"Come in. Please. You must be freezing." She pulled the door wider and danced backward on the frigid tiles that numbed her bare toes. "Sorry, it's Saturday." She gestured at her thermal underwear, which served as her pajamas from November through March. At least these were her newest pair, hot pink and yellow camouflage pattern. No food stains or thin spots yet. "Would you like some coffee or something else to drink while I get some clothes on?"

"No, thank you. I filled up at a Cracker Barrel in Akron. If I could use the bathroom, I would be forever in your debt." She had a chuckle that reminded Olivia of a troublemaker cartoon character, though she couldn't recall the name or even the face immediately.

Olivia showed Dr. Tanner to the bathroom and made a mad dash into her bedroom. She settled for pulling on a clean pair of sweats and a Cleveland Guardians sweatshirt over her thermal underwear, dragged a brush through her hair, and tossed three breath mints into her mouth by the time the woman emerged from the bathroom. They settled in the kitchen, at the table in front of the bay window.

Dr. Tanner had refused coffee or tea, but she did accept the apricot Danish Olivia had bought from Sugarbush Bakery yesterday. She didn't have to admit they were on the day-old rack.

"You didn't know Lyndsy, did you?" the woman began, after they had both made appreciative noises over the bakery.

"We rented rooms in the same house for a while. There wasn't much time to get to know her, but I liked her. I felt sorry for her. I feel like I got to know her better through all the digging we did to find out what happened."

"She was ... complicated. Let's be kind and leave it at that." Dr. Tanner studied the swirl of icing on the edge of her Danish for a moment. She sighed. "She did good work, but she was just a little too selfish. Some selfishness and a touch of paranoia is necessary in our line of work. Especially for women in our line of work. We have to fight twice as hard as the men to protect our discoveries, our theories, our careers. Well, Lyndsy had more than she needed and that ... well, it poisoned her relationships, and her outlook. And yes, some things I've learned about her family life make what she did and said more understandable. She was wrong, you understand, but it's a little easier to forgive her. To feel sorry for her. She was betrayed on so many levels. I feel like I betrayed her, and that is inexcusable. I want to ensure she gets the credit she deserves."

"How?"

Olivia glanced out the bay window, and for a moment she saw a ghost, an image of Lyndsy prodding and poking at the ridge, following clues, using the Underground Railroad markers as signposts to find the hidden entrance. The brambles had been torn out, making the ridge look shrunken, denuded. Much of the rocks and bricks had been cleared away by the investigators. Bee's backyard would never look the same. At least the nasty, griping Mr. Gibbons wasn't there, and the people who had bought his house were much more understanding.

Dr. Tanner took several dainty nibbles, and her gaze went distant as she chewed. She licked her lips, swallowed, and shook her head.

"I need to make connections, first. It's useless to start digging around without getting permission and cooperation from the local people. I don't suppose you could make some introductions?"

"I know just the man," Olivia said, and got up to get her phone.

Dr. Tanner asked Olivia to help her bring some things in from her car, while they waited for Amos to join them. They had just reached the front door, each of them carrying a milk crate full of journals and ring binders. Olivia hoped she didn't imagine it, but she thought she saw a spark of interest the moment Amos bowed and nearly snatched the milk crate from Dr. Tanner's hands, insisting on carrying it for her.

"A nice young man named Nick West sent these to me," she explained, when they had settled at the kitchen table. "He said that one of Lyndsy's rivals had stolen them, and he felt I was the right person to make the best use of them."

Now they all had fresh English toffee tea, and the chocolate croissants Olivia had also found on the day-old rack. She considered it a miracle when something that good lasted long enough to show up on that rack.

"These are all her journals, all her research. Scads of photos she took of the terrain and historical documents, hand-drawn maps, rubbings, what have you."

She reached into one milk crate and withdrew several journals and accordion folders to display the items she mentioned. Olivia shivered, seeing the photos of the carvings that Lyndsy had lamented over.

"I knew she was ambitious, and a hard worker, when she was motivated, but the amount of work she produced after she left me ..." Dr. Tanner sniffed and blinked. "Despite all her flaws, she most certainly deserves credit for all the work she did. I want to continue her work. Out in the open, total honesty and cooperation with the local experts. None of the sneaking and hiding and lying that Lyndsy relied on to protect her work. Mr. Green, will you guide me?"

"Amos, please," he said. He held out his hand across the table, then chuckled and withdrew his hand, to wipe a smear of chocolate off one finger. "Sorry about that. Madam, I would be honored to work with you. However ..." He nodded to the photos of the carvings. "I'm not the local expert when it comes to the Underground Railroad signs and codes. You need to work with Josiah Crandall. He was working on a book and put away his research after Lyndsy was killed. I dare to hope that he didn't destroy that work. For all his flaws, he was a good researcher, an inspiration to the rest of us. Let's hope that you are the one to ignite the spark in his heart and mind once again."

THE END

BOOK DISCUSSION GUIDE

Here's a lively set of discussion questions for your book club's *Skeletons in the Cellar* chat!

Themes & Plot
1. History vs. progress: The HIGs (History Is God group) clash with Kai over renovations. Do you side more with preserving history or embracing change? Why?
2. Small-town secrets: Cadburn seems full of rumors (Underground Railroad tunnels, hidden rooms). How does the author use gossip and local lore to build tension?
3. Modern meets historical: The skeleton turns out to be a recent murder victim, not an ancient relic. How does this twist reframe the story's stakes?

Characters & Relationships
1. Teamwork makes the dream work: Olivia, Kai, Charli, and others collaborate to solve the mystery. Who stood out as the most resourceful—or the most frustrating?
2. Lyndsy's role: She's framed in Steve's video and tied to the Fendergast house. Do you trust her? Why or why not?

Reader Reactions & Speculation
1. Best red herring: Were there any clues or characters you *totally* thought would matter… but didn't?
2. Unanswered questions: The manuscript leaves some threads open (e.g., Steve's full backstory, the introduction of Rufus's college buddy, a fireman bookworm). What do you hope gets explored in future books? (In previous stories, scenes and characters were inserted to prepare for future stories. Mention was made of the Cadburn Ghost, rumored Underground Railroad Tunnels, and the reenactors group.)
3. Casting call: If this were a TV show, who would you cast as Kai, Olivia, Eden, Fendergast, or Lyndsy?

Fun & Creative
1. Book & Mug's vibe: The café sounds like a cozy hub. What's your

dream bookshop/coffee combo (e.g., themed drinks, quirky decor)?
2. Title wordplay: *Skeletons in the Cellar* works literally and metaphorically. What other punny titles could fit this series?
3. DIY mystery: If you found a skeleton in *your* basement, what's the first thing you'd do? (Call the cops? Grab a shovel?)

Bonus Round
1. Series potential: This is Book 4 in the *Book & Mug Mysteries*. Would you read more? What kind of case should the gang tackle next?
2. Book club snack pairing: What drink or treat from Book & Mug would you want to sip/munch while discussing this? (Bonus points for recipes!)

These questions keep things light but deep—perfect for sparking debates, laughs, and maybe even a conspiracy theory or two! Happy discussing!

If you would like book discussion guides for the other books in the Book & Mug Mysteries, contact Michelle for your free guide to the series: MichelleLevigne@gmail.com. Please check out her website, Mlevigne.com, or her blog, MichelleLevigne.blogspot.com, and sign up for her newsletter, to stay on top of the latest releases!

THANK YOU!

Thank you for reading this book from Mt. Zion Ridge Press.

If you enjoyed the experience, learned something, gained a new perspective, or made new friends through story, could you do us a favor and write a review on Goodreads or wherever you bought the book?

Thanks! We and our authors appreciate it.

We invite you to visit our website, MtZionRidgePress.com, and explore other titles in fiction and non-fiction. We always have something coming up that's new and off the beaten path.

And please check out our podcast, Books on the Ridge, where we chat with our authors and give them a chance to share what was in their hearts while they wrote their book, as well as fun anecdotes and glimpses into their lives and experiences and the writing process. And we always discuss a very important topic: *Tea!*

You can listen to the podcast on our website or find it at most of the usual places where podcasts are available online. Please subscribe so you don't miss a single episode!

Thanks for reading. We hope you come back soon!

About the Author

On the road to publication, Michelle fell into fandom in college and has 40+ stories in various SF and fantasy universes. She has a bunch of useless degrees in theater, English, film/communication, and writing. Even worse, she has published over 100 books and novellas with multiple small presses, in science fiction and fantasy, YA, suspense, women's fiction, and sub-genres of romance.

Her official launch into publishing came with winning first place in the Writers of the Future contest in 1990. She was a finalist in the EPIC Awards competition multiple times, winning with *Lorien* in 2006 and *The Meruk Episodes, I-V,* in 2010, and was a finalist in the Realm Awards competition, in conjunction with the Realm Makers convention.

Her training includes the Institute for Children's Literature; proofreading at an advertising agency; and working at a community newspaper. She is a tea snob and freelance edits for a living (MichelleLevigne@gmail.com for info/rates), but only enough to give her time to write. Her newest crime against the literary world is to be co-managing editor at Mt. Zion Ridge Press and launching the publishing co-op, Ye Olde Dragon Books. Be afraid … be very afraid.

And please check out her newest venture: Ye Olde Dragon's Library, the storytelling podcast. Listen to the podcast on your favorite podcast app or listen on the website: YeOldeDragonBooks.com, and click on the Ye Olde Dragon's Library link.

www.Mlevigne.com
www.MichelleLevigne.blogspot.com
www.YeOldeDragonBooks.com
www.MtZionRidgePress.com

NEWSLETTER:
Want to learn about upcoming books, book launch parties, inside information, and cover reveals?
Go to Michelle's website or blog to sign up.

Thanks for reading! If you enjoyed this book, would you help Michelle by posting a review on Goodreads?
Are you a member of Book Bub? If so, please follow Michelle on

Book Bub, and you'll get alerts when new books are coming out.

As a way of saying thanks, Michelle invites you to the Goodies page on her website. It will change regularly, offering you a free short story, a sample audiobook chapter, sneak peeks at new cover art, inside information on discounts and new release dates, etc.

Please go to: *Mlevigne.com/good-stuff.html*

Also by Michelle L. Levigne

Guardians of the Time Stream: 4-book Steampunk series
The Match Girls: Humorous inspirational romance series starting with A Match (Not) Made in Heaven
Sarai's Journey: A 2-book biblical fiction series
Tabor Heights: 18-book inspirational small town romance series.
Quarry Hall: 11-book women's fiction/suspense series
For Sale: Wedding Dress. Never Used: inspirational romance
Crooked Creek: Fun Fables About Critters and Kids: Children's short stories.
Do Yourself a Favor: Tips and Quips on the Writing Life. A book of writing advice.
To Eternity (and beyond): Writing Spec Fic Good for Your Soul. A book defending speculative fiction.
Killing His Alter-Ego: contemporary romance/suspense, taking place in fandom.
The Commonwealth Universe: SF series, 25 books and growing
The Hunt: 5-book YA fantasy series
Faxinor: Fantasy series, 4 books and growing
Wildvine: Fantasy series, 14 books when all released
Neighborlee: Humorous fantasy series
Zygradon: 5-book Arthurian fantasy series
AFV Defender: SF adventure series
Young Defenders: Middle Grade SF series, spin-off of *AFV Defender*
Magic to Spare: Fantasy series
Book & Mug Mysteries: cozy mystery series
Quest for the Crescent Moon: fantasy series
Steward's World: fantasy series reboot and expansion
The Enchanted Castle Archives: fantasy series